A PLACE IN THE WIND

"The top-notch storytelling, appealing characters, and timely controversy here guarantee energetic book-group discussions."
—*Booklist*

"Nail-biting . . . [Jimmy] doesn't rest until he uncovers the truth in this tense page-turner."
—*Publishers Weekly*

"This is a perfect choice for any mystery-lover looking for a new series."
—*Huffington Post*

"Detective Jimmy Vega returns to Chazin's exceptionally powerful series that examines the racial tensions in small-town America. The characters are moving and like portraits of real people. The novel is one of her best."
—*RT Book Reviews*, 4.5 Stars Top Pick

"Another excellent mystery in the Jimmy Vega series . . . Chazin continues proving she's a marvelous writer . . . Best of all, Chazin reminds us that sometimes family is made of the most unlikely people."
—*Sunday Star Ledger* (Newark, NJ)

NO WITNESS BUT THE MOON

"Suzanne Chazin writes the kind of book that makes mystery readers rave and mystery writers jealous. Chazin delivers a complex, suspenseful story with the grace of a ballerina and the impact of a boxer's fist.
—**William Kent Krueger**

"Jimmy Vega and his girlfriend, Adele Figueroa, are the kind of fictional heroes every reader roots for: noble and flawed, united in spirit, split by their loyalties. Don't miss this series."
—**Robert Dugoni**

"Chazin's novel is one of the most genuinely phenomenal examples of storytelling. Full of twists and turns, the narrative leaves readers guessing, but it also does a brilliant job getting them invested in the characters. It's a powerful read."
—*RT Book Reviews*, **4.5 Stars Top Pick**

"The intricate plot and the important social issues combine in this strong debut of a promising series."
—*Booklist*

"Riveting, suspenseful, tragic, hopeful, with realistic settings, authentic voices, continuous action and enough twists and turns to keep readers up all night. The Latina Book Club looks forward to the series and seeing Detective Jimmy Vega in action again."
—*The Latina Book Club*

"It's been a while since I stopped on sentences, allowing the beauty of the words and the wisdom of the writer to envelop me. Suzanne Chazin is that rare writer. But the best part of this book is that Chazin has brought to life, in very rich hues, people who so often go unnoticed. You will be rooting for them and the prose from this uncommonly talented writer."
—*Jersey.com*

"Chazin's respect for the courage and quiet determination of the immigrant community comes through in a nuanced story about race, class, and belonging. A good choice for mystery book clubs."
—*Library Journal*

Also by Suzanne Chazin

The Jimmy Vega Mystery Series
Land of Careful Shadows
A Blossom of Bright Light
No Witness But the Moon

The Georgia Skeehan Mystery Series
The Fourth Angel
Flashover
Fireplay

A Place in the Wind

SUZANNE CHAZIN

KENSINGTON BOOKS

http://www.kensingtonbooks.com

KENSINGTON BOOKS are published by

Kensington Publishing Corp.
119 West 40th Street
New York, NY 10018

All Kensington titles, imprints, and distributed lines are available at special quantity discounts for bulk purchases for sales promotion, premiums, fund-raising, educational, or institutional use. Special book excerpts or customized printings can also be created to fit specific needs. For details, write or phone the office of the Kensington Special Sales Manager: Attn. Special Sales Department. Kensington Publishing Corp, 119 West 40th Street, New York, NY 10018. Phone: 1-800-221-2647.

Kensington and the K logo Reg. U.S. Pat. & TM Off.

ISBN-13: 978-1-4967-0523-5
ISBN-10: 1-4967-0523-8
First Kensington Hardcover Edition: October 2017
First Kensington Mass Market Edition: October 2018

eISBN-13: 978-1-4967-0522-8
eISBN-10: 1-4967-0522-X
Kensington Electronic Edition: October 2017

10 9 8 7 6 5 4 3 2 1

Printed in the United States of America

To Gene West, for his good heart, great mind
and the best stories in the world.

I have drawn the route
towards my place in the wind.
Those who come cannot find me.
Those I await do not exist.

"Fiesta" by Alejandra Pizarnik

Chapter 1

Teenagers don't run away in January. Not in upstate New York.

In summer, they'll go out drinking with friends, pass out in a field somewhere, wake up hungover and covered in mosquito bites. In the spring and fall, they'll hop a train down to New York City after a fight with a parent or a problem at school. The Port Authority cops will pick them up, usually after a day or two when they discover that there really *is* no place to sleep in the city that never sleeps—and worse, no place to shower.

But a January disappearance was different. Jimmy Vega had only to look out at the early-morning ice sparkling on his windshield to understand that no teenager would choose to walk off into the blue-black heart of such a night as last night.

Especially not a girl like Catherine Archer.

He cranked up the heater in his pickup and palmed the sleep from his eyes. The teenager had been gone since ten p.m. yesterday. It was going on eight a.m. now. The sun held the sharp edge of promise through the bare trees as Vega drove into Lake Holly. But he knew it was just a tease. Sunny-side up for now. Over easy by midmorning. Hard-boiled by this afternoon. There was snow in the forecast. There was *always* snow in the forecast this time of year. Vega should be used to it by now. He was a native New Yorker. Bronx born. But the Puerto Rico of his parents' youth still ran like a Gulf current through his veins. He wasn't built for upstate New York winters.

He'd turned in early last night. His girlfriend, Adele Figueroa, had gone to see her nine-year-old's choral concert at the elementary school. Vega also had parent duty last night. He took his eighteen-year-old out to the new Ethiopian restaurant. Paid forty bucks for what looked like two unrolled burritos. Joy loved it. Vega ended up raiding his refrigerator for a frozen pizza afterward. Joy suggested they take in the new Norwegian film at the art cinema, but Vega didn't want to pay to see snow on film. He had enough of the real thing. So they called it an early night. He went back home and fell asleep on his couch with his mutt, Diablo, snoring beside him, then repeated the same routine on his bed. He'd planned to get up early this morning, lift weights and run at least five miles around the lake. He didn't want anything to stand in the way of him going back to full duty.

That was before he got the seven a.m. call from Adele.

"Jimmy, I need your help. Something terrible has happened at La Casa."

Vega was barely conscious, but the cop in him ran

through all the possible scenarios in his head. A fist-fight at the community center. A fire. A roof collapse. *(Lord knows, the landlord was overdue fixing it.)* An immigration raid. Adele always referred to the immigrants at La Casa as her "clients," a holdover from her days as a criminal defense attorney. But everyone in and around Lake Holly knew that a large portion of the people she served were undocumented. Vega sometimes wondered why Adele ever mothballed her Harvard Law degree to found and run this struggling outreach center. Something was always going wrong.

"One of my volunteers is missing," said Adele. "The police won't tell me anything."

Vega pictured the volunteers he normally saw at La Casa on weekdays when Adele was working—earnest, gray-haired men and women who sat patiently with circles of day laborers or young mothers and played English-language games or taught them useful phrases for their work. He couldn't imagine any of those people venturing out on a Friday night in January, much less disappearing. The roads in and around Lake Holly were winding, narrow, and poorly lit. The ice just made things worse, especially for older people.

"You think they got into an accident?" asked Vega.

"No. Her car's still here. In the parking lot. She never drove home. Jimmy, I'm not talking about one of my seniors. I'm talking about a seventeen-year-old girl. A student at Lake Holly High. Her family owns the Magnolia Inn."

The 150-year-old mansion was a venerable land-mark in Lake Holly. All the important people in the county ate there: Wall Street CEOs. U.S. presidents and senators. Broadway actors. Hollywood directors.

The Archers, who had owned the place for generations, were like old-line royalty in Lake Holly.

"So this girl? She's an Archer?" asked Vega.

"She's John Archer's daughter, Catherine."

Vega got dressed and drove over to La Casa as quickly as he could. Not because he thought he could do anything. More for moral support. In all likelihood, the Lake Holly cops were doing all they could already to track Catherine down. And whether they were or they weren't, there was no way they'd let a detective from the county police tell them how to do their jobs. Especially not some desk jockey who spent his days giving ink manicures to the steel-bracelet set.

Every cop in the county knew Vega's story. And every one of them was glad it wasn't his own.

The community center was housed in a former seafood wholesaler's building that still smelled like low tide on damp days. It sat on a dead-end street across from an auto salvage yard, a propane company, and a janitorial cleaning service. A dozen or so people were gathered behind a blue police sawhorse at the entrance to the street, their breath clouded white in the early-morning air. Everything felt hushed and expectant—as if the ground beneath them could shatter at any moment. Beyond, Vega saw three police cruisers, a couple of unmarked detectives' sedans, and the county crime-scene van.

Things were going from bad to worse if crime scene was here.

A uniformed cop Vega didn't recognize stood behind the sawhorse, stamping his feet to keep warm while he spoke to the onlookers. *Family members? Rubberneckers?* They were bundled in hooded jackets, scarves, and hats, but Vega could still see their eyes—

that jumpy, hyperalert, almost feral quality that Vega recognized as fear. Catherine's parents were no doubt someplace warm, being cared for by loved ones. But these people—friends, family or neighbors—clearly had a stake in this girl's disappearance.

Vega nosed his truck up to the sawhorse and powered down his window. He flashed his gold detective's shield and ID at the officer. "Who's catching?" he asked. He spoke like he belonged here. Not that he belonged anywhere much these days.

"Detectives Jankowski and Sanchez," the cop answered. He frowned at Vega's ID. "Did Lake Holly call in the county on this?"

Vega gestured to his department's crime scene van, parked in front of La Casa. "Hey, not for nothing, the county's already here." Nothing like a little creative misdirection. Then, for good measure, he name-dropped. "Is Detective Greco working?"

"Everybody's working this one." The officer wiped his runny nose. He looked miserable standing point. Vega opened his center console and pulled out a package of chemical hand warmers. He always kept a few in the car in winter. He held them out to the cop.

"Here. You need these more than I do."

"Thanks." The officer pulled back the sawhorse. "No sense both of us freezing out here."

Vega waved to the man and drove through. He parked his pickup next to the propane company. Across the street, La Casa's parking lot was roped off with yellow crime-scene tape. A single car sat in the lot. A silver Subaru Forester. A sign across the front doors read: CERRADO HASTA NUEVO AVISO—CLOSED UNTIL FURTHER NOTICE.

Vega frowned at the security cameras mounted on the corners of the former warehouse. One was pointed at the front doors. Another was pointed at the parking lot. Their footage must have told the Lake Holly cops something about what time Catherine left the building and whom she'd left with. The temperatures last night were in the midthirties—reasonably balmy for upstate New York in January. But not the sort of weather that people hang around in. The teenager couldn't have gone far on foot. Which meant she was either nearby—or she'd been picked up by another vehicle. The license plate readers in the area would be able to give the Lake Holly Police a readout of all makes, models, and car plates in the area last night at that time.

And yet, they hadn't found her.

Surely by now, Catherine's family and the police had canvassed her friends, the other students who were tutoring English last night at La Casa, and the immigrants who were being tutored. That should have provided another layer of knowledge. The more subtle kind. Not just movement but motive.

And yet, they hadn't found her.

Vega stepped out of his truck and walked across to La Casa's lot, where the silver Subaru Forester was parked. It appeared to be a recent model. No obvious dents. A sticker on the bumper read: PROUD PARENT OF A LAKE HOLLY HIGH SCHOOL HONORS STUDENT. Catherine didn't put that on her car. Which meant the vehicle probably belonged to her parents. The car doors were open and two county crime-scene techs—a man and a woman—were combing the inside for clues. The woman crawled out as soon as she caught sight of Vega. She pulled down the hood of her white Tyvek coveralls and lifted her face mask. Jenn Fitzpatrick was the spitting image of her old man: round, freckled face, like a Cabbage Patch doll. Curly hair the color of spun maple syrup.

"You know, Jimmy, most people try to sneak *out* of a crime scene, not into one."

"I'm not sneaking in."

"*Riiight.* You just wanted to give the Lake Holly PD an early valentine."

"C'mon, Jenn. I'm just trying to get some answers. Is Adele inside?"

Jenn nodded. "With two local detectives. Who aren't going to be thrilled to see you. My father used to say that crossing jurisdictions is like dating somebody else's girl."

Vega grinned. "Knowing Captain Billy, I'd say the analogy was a bit coarser than that."

Jenn laughed. "Yes. It probably was."

"Have you found anything so far?"

"The car was pretty clean. Not even the usual candy bars and junk." She tilted her head toward the building. "Not for nothing, Jimmy, you have enough troubles with the department right now. You don't need to buy more."

"I'll keep a low profile, I promise. But can you let me know if you find anything?"

"I'll do my best."

"Thanks." He turned to walk inside.

"I almost forgot," said Jenn. "Break a leg tonight."

Vega stopped in his tracks. "Tonight?"

"Your gig? At the Oyster Club?" Jenn gestured to her white coveralls. "I'm bummed I have to work, so I'm going to miss it."

"The . . . Oyster Club. Sure." Vega had been so caught up in Adele's dilemma, he'd completely forgotten that his band had a gig tonight. At a sleek new waterfront bar south of here in Port Carroll. Jenn's boyfriend, Richie Solero, was the band's drummer. *Armado,* they called themselves. Spanish for "armed." All the band members were in law enforcement. Which meant half their gigs expected them to double as unpaid security and the other half worried they were undercover narcs. Being a cop never elicited a neutral response.

"You *are* going, aren't you?" Jenn must have read the uncertainty in Vega's eyes. "Christ, Jimmy, you can't back out. You're Armado's lead vocalist. Their lead guitarist. It took Richie and Danny, like, six months to get the band booked there. You go AWOL, you'll let everybody down."

"I know, I just . . ." *I can't leave Adele like this to go play guitar with a bunch of cops.* "Maybe Catherine will show up before then."

"She's been gone ten hours," said Jenn. "I think you need a Plan B."

La Casa was usually bustling on a Saturday morning. In the front room, there were typically English and computer classes for adults and tutoring for their school-age children. In the back, people shot pool, drank coffee, met in self-help groups, or just relaxed and chatted in the one place that welcomed them in their own tongue and never asked why they were here.

There was none of that today. The computers sat idle. The chalkboards were bare. The pool tables stood empty and silent. Vega could hear Adele's voice coming from the tiny conference room down the hall. He started to head in that direction when he caught sight of two men in off-the-rack sports coats and identical bad buzz cuts. The Lake Holly detectives, Jankowski and Sanchez. Both men were square in every direction: the face, the shoulders, the torso. The taller one was white with dark brown hair, silver at the tips like a hedgehog. All his features were scrunched up in the middle of his big square face: tiny pale eyes, a slash of lips, a nose that zigzagged unevenly between them. When Vega was a boy, he used to press Silly Putty to the newspaper, then stretch and compress the photos he peeled off. Jankowski's face looked like the compressed version.

The shorter one was Sanchez. Same square build, though with a broad nose and thick black eyebrows. The Silly Putty when you pulled it sideways. Both men wore hip holsters under their dark suit jackets. Jankowski must be a lefty, judging by which side his jacket bulged out. They gave Vega that cop stare as he approached. Like junkyard dogs just itching to take a bite out of him. Vega pulled out his badge and ID and thrust it in front of him like it was some force field that could shield him from their wrath.

"We didn't send county an invite," growled Jankowski. "And if we did, it wouldn't be you."

Everywhere Vega went, his reputation preceded him. He wondered if he'd ever live down that incident last December. He spread his palms in a gesture of surrender.

"C'mon, guys. I'm just looking for a little information. Cop-to-cop." Vega decided to hold off mentioning Adele for as long as possible. As the head of a community outreach center that serviced both legal and undocumented immigrants, she was not a favorite of the local police.

Jankowski braced an arm against one of the cinderblock walls. He looked as if he could knock down the whole wall if he had a mind to. All of Vega's running and weight lifting would never take him up to the size and build of a monster like Jankowski. Sanchez, the compact model of the same vintage, closed in on Vega from the other direction. They were like bookends—physically and mentally.

"What's the matter?" asked Sanchez. "You don't trust we can do the job?"

"You kidding me?" asked Vega. "The Lake Holly PD is first class." An ego stroke. No county cop thought any of the townie patrols could catch a cold without them. "I worked a couple of cases with one of your guys. Good friend of mine, Louie Greco?"

"*Greco* invited you here?" asked Jankowski.

"Not . . . exactly." Vega regretted pulling his friend into the mix. He didn't want to create the impression that Greco was meddling. "Adele Figueroa gave me a call. She's my, uh . . . ." Vega hated the word as much as Adele did. It made them sound like two teenagers. ". . . girlfriend."

Vega directed his words to Sanchez. A fellow Latino. A Mexican American, according to Adele, though she had no particular love for him. She felt that most cops were the same once they put on the uniform. Maybe she was right. Sanchez didn't appear moved by Vega's dilemma.

"The best way you can help right now," Sanchez

told Vega, "is to get Adele to assemble better records on the clients who pass through her doors."

"This place has more fake IDs than a college bar," Jankowski grunted.

"She has intake sheets," said Vega. "I know she asks every client who comes into La Casa to fill one out."

"We looked at those sheets already," said Jankowski. "I could train my dog on them, that's how worthless they are. There were twenty-eight men being tutored at La Casa last night. Do you know how many checked out cleanly through our criminal and immigration databases? *Five.* Twenty-eight people, and only five were who they said they were."

Vega wasn't surprised. He'd heard the same from cops down in Port Carroll and Warburton and other towns in the county with large immigrant populations.

"How about their addresses?" asked Vega. "Were they also bogus?"

"We found five more guys at the addresses they listed, but they couldn't provide us with any verification of their legal names," said Sanchez. "The remaining eighteen are ghosts. All we've got to go on are the head shots in Adele's computer and word of mouth on the street."

Vega cursed under his breath. He understood the detectives' frustration. It was a never-ending struggle to get a full legal name from an undocumented immigrant. There was a host of reasons why. Some were relatively benign. The person lived under a fake ID or a relative's ID to secure work or open a bank account. Others were not—like hiding a criminal conviction or a prior deportation. Not that Adele could have done anything about it. Even Vega, as a police officer, had to have probable cause to verify someone's ID.

"Maybe you can track down their identities through family connections," Vega suggested. "A lot of these people are probably local, even if their names and addresses don't check out."

"Yeah, but we're racing against time here," said Jankowski. "None of Catherine's family or friends have seen her since ten last night. We haven't been able to locate a signal from her cell phone. And now, on top of everything, we don't even know who these people are that she was tutoring." Jankowski's features scrunched up so tight, he looked like the before shot on an ex-lax ad. "I mean, no offense to the Hispanic community. But Mike Carp is right. This whole illegal thing has gotten way out of hand."

Mike Carp. The billionaire developer who won election to county executive in November by promising to reduce the number of undocumented immigrants in the region. Adele openly campaigned against him— as did everyone in the Latino community. Vega felt queasy thinking about how Carp might use this girl's disappearance to drum up supporters. He had plenty already. There were rumors he was just keeping the county exec seat warm as a dress rehearsal until his run for governor in two years.

"You seem a little sure that one of La Casa's clients is behind this," said Vega. "You got some evidence besides the fact that this was the last place Catherine was seen?"

"Not yet," said Jankowski. "Still, a beautiful girl like that disappears from a place like this without a trace, what would *you* think?"

"I haven't seen a picture of her," said Vega. "Do you have one?"

Sanchez pulled out his cell phone and scrolled to a picture on the screen. He handed his phone to Vega. "This is her last yearbook photo."

Vega stared at the screen. Catherine Archer was the girl that teenage boys everywhere conjure up in their wet dreams and first flushes of hormonal glory. It wasn't just the way her straight blond hair spilled like water down her back. Or the pale, bleached-denim hue of her eyes. Or the slight slouch to her narrow shoulders that suggested more child than woman about her. It was her smile. A small press of the lips that felt shy and hesitant yet welcoming. Vega could recall himself as a teenager—pimply and lacking confidence. A dark-skinned Puerto Rican kid in a high school full of sharp-edged Nordic beauties who treated him, like the janitor, or at best, like an exotic pet. It was the smile he would have fixated on and lusted over. The forgiveness in it for the anxieties of a clueless boy who didn't feel he could ever fit in.

Vega handed Sanchez's phone back to him. "And her friends?" Vega asked the two detectives. "Are they the jocks? The school druggies? The popular crowd?"

"All. None," said Jankowski.

"Huh?" Vega wasn't following.

"Everybody liked her," he explained. "But we can't find a best friend or close circle of friends."

"Really?" That surprised Vega. From his experience with his own daughter, girls dropped boyfriends like banana peels. But they always had at least one or two besties on their speed dial.

"She was an honors student. A varsity tennis player.

A volunteer English tutor." Sanchez ticked off her accomplishments on his stubby fingers like he was putting together a college admissions packet for her. "But she didn't socialize after school with any of the kids we spoke to, not even the other students who volunteered at La Casa."

"She was shy? Socially awkward?"

"On the contrary," said Jankowski. "Everyone describes her as very friendly. But she kept to herself, mostly helping out at her parents' restaurant and hanging with her family."

"No boyfriend?"

"None that anybody was aware of."

"So you're back to the twenty-eight men in this center last night," said Vega.

"Yep."

It was after eight a.m. Catherine Archer had been missing ten hours. They all knew that if someone was likely to be found alive, it usually happened in the first twenty-four hours. The golden twenty-four. Every second counted.

One of the uniforms appeared at Jankowski's elbow to speak to him. Jankowski turned to Vega. "Tell Adele nobody's on a witch hunt, much as she'd like to believe otherwise. But we've got a girl to find. La Casa is ground zero—and we're running out of time."

Chapter 2

Wil Martinez awoke with his cheek pressed against his textbook, the pages smooth and cool on his skin, the subheading, *Measurement of Helical Pitch in DNA,* swimming around in his brain. Swimming right beside orders to clear table twelve and clean up the shards of broken glass at table seven. By day, he was one person. By night, another.

He wasn't sure who the real Wil was anymore.

He squinted at his watch still strapped to his wrist. Seven a.m. A pale, milky light drifted in through the dark blue bedsheet covering the window. Slowly the attic room the nineteen-year-old shared with his brother came into focus. The bunk bed that sagged and creaked with every shift of their weight. The soft hum of the mini fridge with its hot plate and coffeemaker on top. The scrape of bare branches against the roof's uninsulated rafters. The steady drip of a leaky showerhead down the hall—the one bathroom shared by all the upstairs tenants.

It was cold in the room. Wil felt the bite of the air on the tip of his nose. He forced his feet off the top bunk to the bare plank floor and dressed in as many layers as he could throw on. Socks. Sweatpants. Thermal shirt. Hoodie. He poked at the lump on the bottom bunk beneath a tangle of blankets.

"Get up, Rolando."

"No me jódas!" Rolando cursed at Wil. He pulled the blankets over his head and turned his body to the wall. His bedsprings squeaked in response.

"Come on, Rolando," Wil pleaded in Spanish. "You've got to get up for work."

"Do you have to be so loud?"

"Do you have to be so hungover?"

Rolando sat up, hit his head on the upper bunk, cursed in English and Spanish, and flopped back down on his pillow. He stared up at the sharp coils that had just assaulted him and massaged his black wavy hair that was standing up at every angle. There was dirt under his fingernails and dark smears across his unshaven face and army-green T-shirt. "Never again," he rasped in Spanish.

"You say that every time."

"No. I mean it this time, *chaparro.*" Slang for "shorty" or "squirt." Rolando's nickname for Wil, ever since their days in Guatemala. Rolando was Wil's protector back then, his mother's firstborn, before Wil's father ever stepped into the picture. Rolando was nine years older than Wil, a rangy, good-looking boy with the speed and grace of a Jaguar. He was twenty-eight now, though at this minute, he looked more like a man pushing forty.

Wil sat down on the edge of his half brother's bunk.

The thin mattress dipped into the frame. Rolando winced—from the screech or the movement, Wil couldn't be sure.

"You were supposed to come straight home from La Casa last night," Wil said to him.

"I know."

"Where did you go? You didn't answer your phone."

"I didn't hear it."

More likely ignored it, thought Wil. He should have read the signs before Rolando went out Friday evening. The way he paced the floor and checked his messages nineteen times. The way he grunted out replies to Wil's questions. It was how he always got when the pressure built. Antsy. Distracted. As a boy, he'd been gentle and shy and infinitely patient. But that was before that day in the freight yard. Before those six weeks when no one knew where he was. All these years later, and Rolando still never spoke about that time. It came out in other ways. When the shy and gentle boy Wil once loved gave way to the other Rolando.

The dangerous one.

"So what happened?" asked Wil. "Did you even *go* to English class?"

"I . . . went." Rolando answered like he was dredging up the memory from ten years ago instead of last night.

"And then you got drunk."

"I . . . had a few beers."

"A few beers? You woke up everybody in the house when you came home. The other tenants are mad. The landlord threatened to throw us out if this keeps up. Lando, it's January. I'm stressed-out enough."

"About what? School?" Rolando's dark, hooded

eyes turned sober and focused. He grabbed Wil's hand. He was obsessed with his little brother staying in school. Wil was the first person in their family to finish high school. And now, Rolando bragged to everyone he knew that Wil was a freshman at the community college studying to become a doctor. In Rolando's mind, Wil's here-and-there college credits that he gathered while holding down a full-time job were going to magically make him an MD. Rolando had no concept what a long and uncertain journey that was likely to be. Especially with Wil's status.

"School's going okay," Wil assured him. "I've just got a lot on my mind."

"*Mami?* Money?" Those were the usual concerns. "Last night was the last time, I promise," said Rolando. "I'll work double shifts. Skip meals. Whatever you need, *chaparro.* Don't worry. I'll take care of everything. You just concentrate on school. That's all that matters."

Not anymore.

Rolando swung his legs out of bed and cradled his head in his hands. He probably had a monster of a headache. He felt around his neck and cursed. "I think I lost *Mami*'s religious medal."

"*What?*" Wil pushed himself off his brother's bed. "Where did you leave it?"

"I don't know."

"Think, Lando. *Think.*" That necklace was the one part of their mother the men in jackboots and flak vests hadn't taken away when they came for her three years ago.

Wil knelt down on the bare plank floor and pawed through the jumble of clothes his brother had worn last night. Rolando's jeans and jacket were covered in sticky pine needles and dead leaves. His sweatshirt reeked of alcohol and the faint odor of sweat and vomit. Wil didn't see the gold chain or medallion. He wanted to cry.

"Lando, how could you?"

Rolando raked a hand through his unwashed hair. His eyes had a glazed look, as if he were trying to hold on to the edges of a dream that was floating away. He'd been babbling like a lunatic last night. His words and thoughts had been like stray sentences chosen at random from a book.

Wil wished he'd asked Lando then about *Mami*'s religious medal. But he wasn't sure he'd have understood anything his brother said anyway. When Lando was like that, he mixed events with hallucinations, actions with desires. Everything he said or did was unpredictable. Even downright scary. Lando had awoken from blackouts next to women he didn't know, with injuries he couldn't recall getting. Last year, he walked home with a deep stab wound on his thigh that had missed his femoral artery by an inch. He told the doctor in the emergency room that it was an accident. Self-inflicted. Wil was sure it wasn't.

"Hurry up and get that medical degree," Rolando had teased Wil when he was feeling better. "I need you to be able to stitch me up."

Wil never mentioned the knife he'd pulled out of his brother's coat pocket afterward. Or the blood smears on the blade that may or may not have been his.

Rolando would need more than a doctor to save him from his messes.

Wil laced his feet into sneakers and shrugged into his jacket. A faded green parka two sizes too big for his frame. The stuffing was coming out of the quilting. He looked like a molting goose. He had to bike to the library this morning and get in several hours of studying before heading over to the Lake Holly Grill to start his shift. But first, he needed to catch the bathroom when it was empty and brush his teeth.

He walked over to the window and drew back the dark blue bedsheet. Daylight flooded in. Rolando threw a heavily-tattooed arm across his eyes.

"*Ay,* the sun is so bright."

"You'll feel better if you move around."

Wil's toothbrush was on a shelf by the window. Through the double-hung panes of glass, Wil could see the square of cement yard in back, halfway covered in snow and rimmed in chain-link fencing. Beyond the fence were rails of track. Every night, the trains chug-chugged through his sleep, pulling his memories back to that freight yard in Mexico where his mother hitched their dreams to the beast that carried him north, forever leaving behind the Guatemala of his childhood.

Rolando scoured the floor for a semiclean shirt. He pulled off the one he was wearing and slipped into the other. His back, chest, and arms were covered in tattoos that extended halfway up his neck. Wil caught him patting the pockets of his jacket on the floor. It was finally dawning on him that their mother's religious medallion was really and truly gone. He sank back on his heels. "I'll find it," he vowed softly. But already, defeat frayed the edges of his words. He'd broken so many promises, he no longer trusted himself.

"Do you remember taking it off?" asked Wil.

There was a long pause. "Maybe. I think maybe I gave it to somebody."

"Who?"

"A girl?" Was he trying to please Wil? Or did he really remember? Rolando used to be a ladies' man in his younger days. Not so much anymore. Booze was his mistress now. Wil leaned on the window ledge and cursed. "*Mami* gave that medal to both of us. *Both of us!* She's dying, Lando. And you gave away the only thing we have of her?"

Rolando dropped his head. He looked ashamed and miserable.

"Who was the girl?"

"I don't remember."

"How can you not remember?"

Rolando didn't answer for a long time. When he spoke, his voice was barely above a whisper. He sounded tired and spent.

"Chaparro?"

"Yeah?"

"How do you . . . ." Rolando's voice drifted off.

"How do I what?"

"How do you know what's real?"

"I'm real. *Mami*'s Virgin Mary medal was real."

"Sometimes I think things. And I don't know if they happened or not."

"What kinds of things?"

"I don't know." He massaged his forehead. "Stuff you tell me. Stuff other people tell me. Like right now? I close my eyes and I see this . . . girl. She's very young and sorta . . . pretty. I shouldn't even be talking to her. I know it's wrong, but I can't help myself."

"*Joder,* Lando!" Wil cursed. "Who are you talking about? The girl with *Mami*'s medal?"

"Maybe. Maybe I imagined it. All I can remember is the feeling. Like I was doing something I shouldn't be doing."

It wouldn't be the first time. Wil swallowed back something bitter-tasting in his throat. He thought of all the possibilities. But no. He wasn't going there. He couldn't go there. He had enough troubles of his own.

"It's the drink talking," Wil assured him. "Just shower and clean yourself up, okay? Maybe the medal will turn up. In the meantime, try to stay out of trouble."

"Okay." Rolando stared up at his little brother with bloodshot eyes. He'd been handsome once. Before the tattoos that covered his body. Before the drink that bloated his once-muscular frame. Before the cuts—seen and unseen—that had carved him up from the inside out. Wil thought about that bloody knife he'd taken from Rolando's pocket all those months ago. And he wondered if it was already too late to warn his brother to stay out of trouble.

The trouble was here. And it wasn't going away.

Chapter 3

"What did the detectives tell you? Did they give you any leads?" Adele Figueroa had been at La Casa all last night. She looked exhausted. Her makeup had gone soft and smudged around her almond-shaped eyes. Her lipstick had blurred and faded. She was shivering in a thin buttoned-down cotton shirt. Jimmy Vega wrapped his coat around her, but she still shivered. The cold seemed to be coming from within.

"Come on, *nena,*" he murmured in her ear. His term of endearment for her. "Babe" in Spanish. "You need to go home. Get some sleep. The police are doing all they can. There's no point in you being here any longer."

"But what did they say?"

What *could* they say? The Lake Holly cops had their suspicions. They were the same as Vega's. Catherine Archer was a beautiful young girl. She was working closely with men who were twice her age and more. Some of them were in this country without their families, sometimes for years. They were lonely. They were horny. Even the most honorable among them would look at her and feel something. How could they not? What's more, a seventeen-year-old girl would not necessarily be off-limits in their own culture the way she would here. But Vega saw no point in telling Adele any of this right now. It would only make her more upset.

"Please, *nena*. Let me get you to your car. Where is it? I'll follow you home."

"It's up the street. Near where the crowd is gathered. I had to move it when they roped off the parking lot."

The crowd had doubled in size since Vega arrived. This wasn't just friends and family anymore. Vega saw the satellite dish of a news van. No way was Adele going to be able to slip into her pale green Toyota Prius and just drive away. Not to mention that it was obviously her car. It had a big La Casa magnet on the trunk with a logo of smiling stick people encircling the planet. It had a small flag from Ecuador— her parents' country of birth—dangling from the rearview mirror.

"Maybe I should drive you," said Vega. "I don't want some reporter sticking a microphone in your face."

"I can't run away, Jimmy. Those people are Catherine's friends and family. She's one of my volunteers. I owe them my time and attention." Adele pushed open the front door and walked toward her car. Vega scanned the crowd. Their heavy coats and hoods couldn't hide the stiffness in their postures, the squint in their eyes. These people weren't looking for Adele's sympathies. They were looking for someone to blame.

"*Nena*," Vega grabbed Adele's elbow. "Go back to my truck. This isn't such a good—"

Before he could say more, a young man pushed his way past the sawhorses and ran up to Adele.

"Where's my sister?" he shouted. "What sort of people are you letting into this place?" His big blue eyes were wild with rage. His upturned nose was red from the cold. A five o'clock shadow of reddish beard made him seem older than he probably was. Vega put him somewhere in his early twenties. Anger sharpened the almost girlish contours of his face.

Vega threw himself between the young man and Adele. A uniformed officer escorted the brother back behind the barricade. He shook off the officer's grasp, but held up his arms, like he was disgusted with all of them, and faded back into the crowd. Several people tried to calm him down.

Adele stood frozen in place—a stray dog in the center of a four-lane highway. Vega locked an arm around her shoulder and ushered her into his truck.

"But my car—"

"I'll fetch it later this afternoon," he promised. "Right now, you're coming with me."

He made a three-point turn. The police officer parted the sawhorses and Vega drove through.

"That was Catherine's brother," Adele murmured as she stared into the rearview mirror.

"So I gathered."

"I wish I could talk to him."

"You can't," said Vega. "Not even to say you're sorry. Do you understand that now?"

Adele hunkered down in her seat as Vega drove along Lake Holly's Main Street. Century-old wood-frame buildings and brick storefronts sat mute and dark, waiting to open. It was still early. At the train station, day laborers huddled in groups, waiting for jobs that might never come, especially this time of year when contractors didn't need help with landscaping or paving. The men probably would have preferred to wait for work in the cozy comfort of La Casa, but it was anybody's guess when the center would open again.

"I feel like all of this is my fault," said Adele. "I'm beginning to understand what you went through."

"You mean, in December?"

"Yeah. After . . . you know."

The shooting. It was going on seven weeks now since Vega fired those four fateful shots that ended a man's life. An *unarmed* man. Not that Vega knew it at the time. Eighteen years of solid police work—some of it in dangerous, undercover situations—and not once had he fired his gun. Two seconds in the woods had changed all that. And although Vega had been cleared of any wrongdoing, the man's face still haunted his dreams. Six weeks of desk duty and half-a-dozen therapy sessions had done little to shake his inner sense of guilt and anguish. He prayed Adele wasn't about to travel the same road.

"You can't think like that," Vega told Adele. "A, we don't know yet what happened to Catherine. And B, even if it's something bad, you aren't responsible."

"I feel like I am," said Adele. "I feel like it's my duty to be there for the family."

"They don't want you there, *nena*—any more than the family of the man I shot wanted me around. You're not on the same side. It's something you may have to accept."

"You're talking like one of my clients is definitely involved in this."

Vega reached across the gearshift and gave Adele's thigh a reassuring squeeze. "Just take this one step at a time, all right? Food. Sleep. We can talk about the rest later."

Adele lived a short drive from La Casa, in a narrow blue Victorian a handshake's width from the houses on either side. Too close for Vega's comfort. He loved looking out the back deck of his cabin and seeing nothing but trees and a crystalline lake. She loved sitting on her open front porch and waving at neighbors as they strolled past. When Vega stayed over—on those occasions Adele's nine-year-old, Sophia, wasn't home—he felt like he was living in a fishbowl. When Adele stayed up at his lake house, she left all the lights on at night, certain that a pack of wild coyotes was going to break in. Never mind that the house was locked and Diablo, Vega's dog, slept on the bed with them. They both agreed that the only thing that mutt was likely to catch was fleas.

As Vega pulled into Adele's driveway, he noticed old Mr. Zimmerman next door in a fluffy bright pink bathrobe, struggling to drag his garbage can to the curb for pickup. He was taking baby steps across his icy front path. He looked like a roll of fiberglass insulation in moccasin slippers.

"He's going to break his neck," said Adele.

"Worse," said Vega. "He's going to ruin the image of Victoria's Secret in young men's minds forever."

"Can you go help him?"

"He's managing okay. It's you I'm worried about."

"All I want to do is soak in the tub and clear my head."

"Great. I'll run your bath—"

"I can do that myself, Jimmy. Really. I need a little time alone. If you want to help me, you can do it by helping him."

"You sure?"

Adele leaned across and kissed him. "I'm sure."

Adele went inside. Vega turned off his engine and got out of his truck.

"Mr. Zimmerman!" he shouted. The old man was hard of hearing, especially over the scrape of the can as he dragged it across his flagstone path. Vega hopped the low white picket fence that separated Adele's house from Zimmerman's and ran over.

"Nice robe." Vega grinned.

"It was my late wife's. What? I should throw it out because it's pink?" Zimmerman's voice carried a trace of accent. Something European.

"Looks good on you. Here, let me do that." Vega grabbed the can from Zimmerman and carried it out to its place on the sidewalk. It was an old-fashioned aluminum can, dented in so many places it was a wonder it could still hold garbage. Vega suspected Zimmerman had used the same can for twenty years. Everyone else had big plastic ones with wheels.

"You know," said Vega, "for, like, a hundred bucks a year, the garbagemen will pick up at your door so you don't have to carry it curbside."

"A hundred dollars? For that price, they should gift wrap it too."

"It would be easier on you."

"You think I can't carry my own garbage?" Zimmerman flexed an arm beneath his Pepto-Bismol–colored robe. Liberace at bedtime. "I could lift you and put you on the driveway if I had to."

"I don't doubt it, sir." For a man in his late eighties, Max Zimmerman still had a surprisingly robust build. Thick, squared-off shoulders. A full head of silver hair slicked down with so much styling cream that Vega could see the tines of the comb he ran through it each morning. Sharp, intelligent eyes behind heavy black-framed glasses. He was so physically competent that you had to know him awhile to realize he was missing part of the middle finger on his left hand.

"Well, thank you anyway, Jimmy. Now go keep the streets safe in Gotham City." Zimmerman chuckled. He seemed to equate Vega—or perhaps cops in general—with Batman. Vega didn't mind. He'd been called worse.

The old man turned to go back inside his house. It was a small white Cape Cod–style home with dormered windows on the second floor. Vega eyed the flagstone path that led to the front door. It was slick with ice that had melted and refrozen several times over. He was surprised Zimmerman hadn't broken his neck just walking out here.

"Mr. Zimmerman, do you have a shovel?"

"What do I need a shovel for?" Zimmerman lifted his flared pink sleeves to the milky sky. "The Big Man who put it here will also take it away."

"Yeah. In April. Let me get you inside. I'll see if Adele has a shovel."

Vega locked an arm under Zimmerman's elbow and guided the old man back to his front door. His movements were tentative. He was getting frailer, Vega noticed. Not that he was the sort of person to discuss such things.

In the nine months Vega had been dating Adele, he'd never heard Zimmerman ask anything of her. He was already widowed by the time Adele moved to the neighborhood twelve years ago. Very occasionally they saw a younger man here. A son, perhaps. Vega thought he lived in California.

There were few other visitors—which was why Adele always tried to look out for him. She sent clients from La Casa to cut his lawn and trim his hedges in summer and vacuum and dust inside every now and then. The old man always gave the people a few bucks—never enough. His wage scale seemed permanently stuck in 1974. Adele made up the difference. She didn't tell him, of course. But she hated seeing him struggle.

Vega helped Zimmerman up the front steps. On the scuffed molding to the right of the front door was a small brass holder the size and shape of a pencil case. It was mounted at an angle. There were words printed in Hebrew. The old man touched it before he opened the door. Vega noticed one of the screws was coming loose.

"You want me to tighten that screw on the mezuzah for you?"

Zimmerman peered at Vega over the tops of his black glasses. "What do you know from a mezuzah?"

"I know it contains prayers from the Torah. My ex-wife is Jewish. So's my teenage daughter."

"Hmmm." Vega couldn't read the old man's expression. Surprise? Discomfort? The first time Vega met him it was because Zimmerman had called the cops on Vega as a prowler. Vega suspected the old man saw a dark-skinned Puerto Rican and automatically assumed the worst. Vega tried not to hold it against him. Max Zimmerman came from a different generation. He'd always been nice to Vega since then. And at the very least, he was looking out for Adele's safety.

Vega helped the old man inside. The house smelled of too much steam heat and too many layers of dust. And something else too—some faint smell of things that had hung around too long. Food. Dead plants. Dirty laundry. Newspapers and books that should have been tossed ages ago. The living room sported heavy carpets and drapes, lots of big, dark Colonial furniture and brass floor lamps. But it was neat at least.

Vega got the old man settled and tightened the screw on his mezuzah. Then he walked back to check on Adele. She was still in the tub. He knocked on the bathroom door.

"You okay, *nena*? You've been in there awhile."

"I wish," she replied. "I got tied up with emails and phone calls. Can you give me maybe fifteen minutes?"

"Take as long as you need. I'm just borrowing your shovel to clear Mr. Zimmerman's walkway."

The front steps to the old man's house were easy. It was the path along the side that was more problematic. Not because of the snow or ice, but because of the piles of dried dog feces and fast-food wrappers. Not Zimmerman's. He didn't even own a dog. The trash came from the Morrisons on the other side of his house. Three thuggish preteens and their surly mother. They were always dumping their garbage on his lawn. Zimmerman never confronted them. After today, Vega was more than ready to.

The old man called to Vega as he was finishing up.

"Come here. I want to give you something."

"I don't need anything, sir. Thanks."

"You don't even know what I'm going to give you."

Vega trudged over. Zimmerman held out a white mug. *I Love You A Latke* was stenciled across the side. Vega laughed.

"Where'd you get this?"

"Just something I had. Maybe your daughter would like it."

Joy was on the fence these days about her culture—both the Jewish and the Puerto Rican sides. But Vega didn't want to disappoint the old man so he took the mug.

"Thanks very much, Mr. Zimmerman."

When Vega returned to Adele's, mug in one hand, shovel in the other, a dark blue Chevy sedan was pulling into the driveway behind his truck. Vega recognized the man behind the wheel before he even hefted himself from the driver's seat. Body like a shell casing. Bald head circled by a fringe of graying hair. A scowl across his chins that sometimes doubled as a smile. He was wearing a puffy jacket. Black goose down. Not his best wardrobe choice. It made Lake Holly detective Louis Greco look like an overinflated tire.

Greco took a red Twizzler out of his pocket and stuck it in his mouth. His addiction. Vega could never see the attraction. He chewed as he frowned at the mug in Vega's hand. "What's that?"

Vega held it up so Greco could read the words.

"I finally get used to all your Puerto Rican crap and you turn Yid on me?" Greco didn't believe in PC. He said if God wanted everybody to love and accept one another, he wouldn't have created Congress. Or Kanye West.

"I shoveled Adele's next-door neighbor's walkway. He gave it to me."

"Well, aren't you the busy Boy Scout. The bosses take you off desk duty yet?"

"Captain Waring keeps talking about reviewing the situation. But I'm starting to feel like that's not going to happen for three more Windows updates."

"Bureaucracies have long memories, Vega. And you have a bad habit of sticking your nose where it doesn't belong."

"Is that why you're here?"

"Part of the reason." Greco polished off the rest of his Twizzler. "Let's get you and your bar mitzvah favors inside. I don't want my guys catching me here. They're pissed enough already."

Vega left the shovel on Adele's front porch. There was snow in the forecast. He had a feeling she was going to need it.

"You want coffee?" asked Vega as Greco shrugged off his puffy black jacket. He wasn't any less puffy beneath.

"What I want," said Greco, "is to be out of here as quickly as possible."

Vega plonked the latke mug on the mission-style

table next to two bright-colored Mexican pottery candlesticks. The house was Victorian in architecture, but the interior was pure Adele: lots of deep, vibrant colors and Latin-American art. Vega heard water draining from the tub upstairs.

"Adele was in the bath, but it sounds like she'll be down any minute."

"Let's leave Adele out of this for the moment," said Greco. Vega didn't need to ask why. The two had been on opposing sides of most issues in Lake Holly for the better part of a decade—far longer than Vega had known either of them. They were like marinara and hot sauce. Some of the same ingredients. Best served apart.

Vega leaned against the wall and folded his arms. "Okay. Shoot."

"First off, Catherine Archer isn't my case. She belongs to Jankowski and Sanchez. I'm just another pair of eyes and legs, cataracted and arthritic as they are." Greco was always talking about retiring, but Vega sensed his heart wasn't in it.

"It's not your case. Got it."

"Not soon enough or I wouldn't be here." Greco wagged a finger at Vega. "In the future, you want something from me, ask. Quietly. On the side. Don't go using my name as leverage, *capiche?*"

"I didn't know it would bite you in the ass."

"It wouldn't have if you were just another local cop with a police interest in the case," said Greco. "But you're connected to Adele. And you're county. Nobody likes you assholes in the first place—and they especially don't like one who's sleeping with the enemy, if you get my drift."

"I just asked a few questions."

"Which I'm here to answer. And then we close down this channel and you let Lake Holly do its job, got it?"

"You haven't found her yet, I take it."

"We haven't even found half those clients—and I use the term loosely—that were in La Casa last night."

"Did you bring in the K-9 unit to do a search?"

"Duh. What would we do without you county hotshots telling us how to do our jobs? K-9 was useless. The dog lost the scent at the end of the block. The ground was frozen last night and warmed up this morning. Hence, moisture—which tends to wash away scent cones, as you know."

"La Casa has two surveillance cameras. They give you anything?"

"They told us Catherine never got in her car. Never even went near her car. Just headed off in the same direction as the clients—most of whom we can't locate now."

"Car trouble?"

"The car started up perfectly when we tried it."

"Any phone or credit card activity?"

"None."

"Have you checked other surveillance cameras in the area?"

"We're checking them now. So far? Nothing."

"How about the twenty-four-hour deli in that little shopping center near La Casa? A lot of immigrants hang there."

Greco shot Vega a smoldering look over the tops of his black glasses.

"Okay, okay. I get the point. You're doing all of this already. So why are you here?"

"To deliver a little word of warning. One to Adele, and one to you," said Greco. "The Archers say Catherine volunteered Wednesday and Friday evenings at La Casa. But Kay, the head volunteer, says Catherine usually came in on Wednesdays. She doesn't remember her being there most Fridays."

"La Casa must have sign-in sheets."

"Yes. But Kay can't find the ones for the last six months."

"Ay, puñeta," Vega cursed. Cops were meticulous record-keepers. They had to be. You could blow a whole case with one erroneous date or sloppy report. La Casa was full of social workers, who tended to view paperwork as government intrusion, a necessary evil at best. "So in other words," said Vega, "you have no idea who's telling the truth. What do you know about this girl?"

"Her family owns the Magnolia Inn," said Greco. "They're old-money Lake Holly."

"So I've heard. But what about the girl?"

"Honors student. Varsity tennis player—"

"Sanchez and Jankowski told me the same things," Vega interrupted. "But I mean, what was she like? Did she do drugs? Did she have a boyfriend? Did she take off periodically where no one could find her?"

"No, no, and no," said Greco. "She worked as a hostess at the Inn. She tutored at La Casa. She got good grades and played a mean backhand. Sounds to me like you want to blame the victim, when we both know Adele should have been checking her clients better."

"And it sounds to me like you want to blame Adele for not doing something even *we* can't do," said Vega.

"I mean, you and I as cops can't ask these guys for their real names without probable cause. How can Adele be held to a higher standard?"

"Say all you want, Vega. But Mike Carp's gonna see it differently. Trust me. Our new county exec's already got his people crawling up our butts demanding hourly updates on what we're doing to find this girl. He's calling for press conferences like he's already running for governor. So if Adele doesn't want to sound as clueless as a nun in a whorehouse, she'd better get her records in order pronto."

"I'll let her know. What's the other thing you wanted to warn me about, Don Corleone?"

Vega was teasing, but Greco's face lost all its playfulness.

"There is one video we did get from last night, not from La Casa. From the Magnolia Inn."

"Of Catherine?"

"No." Something pained flashed in Greco's eyes. "Of your ex-wife."

Chapter 4

"Wendy?" Vega didn't understand why Greco was alarmed. "Her second husband's an investment banker on Wall Street. Mr. Moneybags probably takes her to the Magnolia Inn twice a week to celebrate his latest swindle."

"Down, boy," said Greco. "You might feel sorry for the poor schlub when you hear me out. The video shows your ex-wife leaving the Inn with John Archer. Catherine's father. At midnight. The place shuts down for dinner at ten p.m. All the staff are gone by eleven."

"You're not seriously suggesting Wendy had anything to do with this girl's disappearance?"

"That's just it, you dope," said Greco. "This probably has *nothing* to do with Catherine's disappearance. But it's the stuff of gossip mills. A prominent local girl is missing. And while she goes missing, her married father is having an affair with a married middle-school psychologist. You get my drift?"

Vega did—belatedly. Then again, when Wendy was

fooling around on him, Vega was just as much of a dope. She wasn't his wife anymore. Hadn't been for six years. But she was still Joy's mother. His daughter didn't deserve that kind of humiliation.

"That's why I'm here," said Greco. "To give you a friendly warning."

"Did you ask Wendy about it?"

"Steve Jankowski did. She refused to discuss it. So did Archer. But given the hour and their reticence, it's safe to say they weren't playing pinochle."

"Okay. Thanks for the heads-up."

Vega saw Greco out. Then he went upstairs to check on Adele. He found her standing by her bedroom window, staring out at her driveway through a parted slat in the blinds. Clouds, thick and gray as dryer lint, had begun to gather on the horizon. They mirrored something dark and unsettled in her face. She looked like a feather could knock her over.

"Any word?" There was so much hope in her voice.

"Not yet." Vega came up behind her and put his arms around her. She was wearing a sweater and jeans, but she was still shivering. He brushed her silky black hair to one side and kissed her cheek. It was wet. And salty. He could tell she'd been crying.

"I heard what Greco said about the missing paperwork," said Adele. "He blames me, doesn't he? They all do. The police. Catherine's family. The community."

Vega turned Adele to face him. Her whole body felt like it was being held together by rubber bands. Worry carved small crosshatches into the space between her brows. It compressed the bow of her lips. Weighted down her shoulders. Dimmed the fire in her ale-colored eyes. Each pain came to him as if it were his own. He chucked a hand beneath her chin and brought her gaze up to his.

"Listen to me, *nena,* you didn't do anything wrong."

"Ten years I've been running La Casa. And in all that time, we've had maybe a handful of petty thefts. A couple of fistfights. None of it directed at my volunteers. If one of my clients hurt this girl, I don't think I can live with myself."

"Don't say that." Vega's words came out sharp and panicked. He'd never heard her talk this way. He pulled her closer. "Things happen. Things you can't control. If anyone understands that, it's me. I fired my weapon for all the right reasons. I followed all the rules and laws. And it still went bad. But I'm here. I'm getting through it. And you will too."

"You're stronger than I am, Jimmy. You held up."

"You *held* me up. I wouldn't be here in one piece right now without you. You don't think we can get through this together?" He brushed a thumb across her cheek. "I'll cancel tonight."

"Tonight?" She stepped back, confused. Then she remembered. "You're playing the Oyster Club. With the band."

"I'll get Danny or Richie to find someone to fill in."

"On lead vocals and guitar? It'll never happen. They'll have to cancel. You'll let the whole band down."

"I don't care. You need me."

"There's nothing you're going to be able to do for me tonight. I've got a ton of phone calls to make and memos to write and meetings to schedule."

Was she being selfless? Or just practical? Vega wasn't sure. Adele was hard to read sometimes. Either way, he knew how *he* felt about it. "I don't want to leave you."

"I'll be fine, though I think Sophia's going to have to stay at her father's." Adele's stomach growled.

"You hear that?" Vega frowned. "You need food and rest, *nena*. I saw your refrigerator. There's very little in it."

"I can grocery shop tomorrow," Adele assured him. "What I really need is my car back."

"I'll walk back and fetch it now." A thought occurred to him. "Hank's Deli is around the corner from La Casa. How about I bring you back a sandwich? You like their ham and cheese. I could get you some bagels, too. They're good to munch on."

"All right." There was no enthusiasm in her voice. After the shooting, Vega couldn't imagine eating. Food tasted like damp socks. He had a sense Adele was going through the same thing. He didn't want to leave her like this. Not to fetch her car. Not to play with his band.

"*Nena,* I don't think I should—"

She pushed him back. "Would you go already?"

Three television news vans were parked at the police barricade by the time Vega walked back to La Casa. The story was growing. Two reporters saw Vega unlocking Adele's car and made a beeline for him. He fended them off by flashing his badge and claiming police business.

He got in and drove a short distance to the one-story brick-front shopping center that housed Hank's Deli, along with a pizzeria, a hardware store, a laundromat, and a liquor store. The deli still bore Hank Cipriani's name, even though Hank had retired to Florida six years ago and sold the business to his Guatemalan manager. Now Oscar and his family worked the business twenty-four–seven, even though they kept the name. "My American customers like to think that the señor is still around," Oscar once told Vega. The man was nothing if not smart.

Usually Hank's was busy on a Saturday afternoon. Today, however, the deli was empty, save for Oscar. Even the laundromat next door seemed more subdued than usual. People were sitting on chairs by the washers and dryers. But there wasn't the normal spillover of conversations into the parking lot. A Latina walked out with a stroller and a wheeled cart of folded laundry, but she walked quickly, head down.

"Hola," Vega said to Oscar as he walked into the deli. "Where is everybody? You run out of jalapeños or something?"

Oscar didn't smile at the lame joke. He was normally a cheerful man, his wide face breaking into a grin that compressed his eyes into slits and showed off the gap between his two front teeth. He wiped his hands on his stained white apron.

"You've heard, right? About the missing girl? It's terrible. Just terrible."

Vega nodded. "I just came from Adele. I'm here to get her a sandwich. Ham and Swiss on a roll with hot peppers. Make that two." Vega found it refreshing to be with a woman who ate the same foods he did. His ex and daughter treated anything with meat or gluten like it was radioactive.

Oscar pulled the ham from the deli case. "How is the señora?" Oscar was never a client of La Casa's. He'd clawed his way up before the center existed. But he felt an affinity for those who came after him—and for the woman who tried to help them.

"She's upset," said Vega. "Nobody seems to know anything. Did the police speak to you?"

"This morning," said Oscar. "They took the videos from our store camera and one in the parking lot."

"Were you working last night? Did you see anything suspicious?"

"I wasn't here," said Oscar. "My wife's cousin Adolfo was working." Oscar hefted the ham onto the slicer. He had the broad shoulders and muscular arms of the stonecutter he'd once been, until Hank took him on all those years ago. "The señora likes it thin, right?"

"Yes. Thanks. Did Adolfo see anything?"

"The police showed him pictures of the men at La Casa last night. Adolfo said he sold beer to one of them."

"At what time?"

"Around ten-thirty, judging from the video."

"How much beer did the man buy?"

"A twelve-pack."

Hank's was close to La Casa. It was a Friday night and a grown man buying beer didn't make him guilty of any crime. But it could make him a witness.

Oscar put the ham back in the case and removed the block of cheese next. He seemed grateful to have somewhere to turn his attentions.

"This guy Adolfo saw? Have you ever seen him before?" asked Vega.

"He comes here pretty often."

"Do you know his name?"

"No. But the police said he went by the name 'Darwin' at La Casa. I don't remember the last name they gave." Oscar didn't need to add that the name likely wasn't real.

"Is he Guatemalan? Mexican? Ecuadorian?"

"He's no *Chapin* to me," said Oscar, using the affectionate term Guatemalans give to one another. "He's nothing but a *cholero*." Guatemalan slang for "low-class person," often someone with Indian blood. Vega had to laugh. Here was a man who'd no doubt struggled under the yoke of Anglo prejudice for years. And yet he had no qualms expressing prejudice himself. It reminded Vega of when he was a boy in the Bronx and the Puerto Ricans chafed when Jewish shopkeepers and landlords treated them like slackers and thieves, and yet a lot of the Puerto Ricans did the same to the Dominicans. Wendy told him the story of how her grandmother was ostracized from her German Jewish family after marrying a Romanian Jew. Everybody, it seemed, was at the top of their own pyramid, even if they were at the bottom of someone else's.

Oscar wrapped up the two sandwiches and put them by the register. Vega grabbed two Snapple ice teas from the refrigerated case and put them on the counter. He was still the only customer in the store. Vega wondered if Latinos were afraid to be out—especially near a place the police had grown so interested in. As for the Anglos who usually came—Vega didn't want to think about what was keeping them away.

"I'll take a half-dozen everything bagels and a container of cream cheese too."

"You want them sliced?"

"Sure. Thanks." Vega squinted up at the store camera. "This Darwin—you never said—was he alone?"

Oscar started to slice a bagel. His hand froze halfway

through the motion. Vega noticed the lift in his broad shoulders. The deep inhale in anticipation of something sharp and painful. Oscar had his own suspicions—and they weren't good.

"He came in alone. But the video from the parking lot . . . there was a girl on it."

"A girl?"

"Waiting outside for him." Oscar lowered his voice. "A *canche*." Guatemalan slang for "a blonde."

"Did it look like the missing girl?"

"I can't say for sure. Neither could Adolfo. Her back was to the camera."

"But she was with him? Not just there at the same time?"

"She appeared to be waiting for him to buy the beer, yes. They walked off-camera together."

Vega felt something heavy settle on his chest. What were the odds that this Darwin would be with some blonde and it *not* be the girl who'd just tutored him a block and a half away? Then again, why would a girl like that go anywhere with him?

But Vega knew the answer to that one before he'd even finished the question. Catherine Archer was seventeen. Underage. Whatever else this Darwin was, he was old enough to buy beer. For an underage girl. Who would probably drink too much, too fast, and pass out. The rest was almost a cliché.

"Did the police take any other evidence besides the videos?" asked Vega.

"No." Oscar rang up the order. Vega took out his wallet. Next to the cash register was an ad for the New York State lottery. All the immigrants played. That was the real American dream these days. Most of them had a better shot at winning the Pick Six than they ever did at becoming legal.

"How about lottery tickets?" asked Vega.

"You want to buy some?"

"No. I'm asking about this Darwin guy. Did he buy any lottery tickets?"

"I can check the play slips in back," said Oscar. "They haven't gone out yet."

"Mind if I look too?"

"No problem."

Vega followed Oscar into the stockroom—a narrow space with shelves on one side and a computer on the other. If Darwin bought a lottery ticket, he'd have had to fill out a play slip—a card with little ovals that had to be colored in like a score sheet. His DNA and fingerprints would be all over that card. The DNA could take a while to process, but the fingerprints would be quick. The Lake Holly PD could run them through the FBI's crime database and Homeland Security's immigration database. There was a good chance one of them would produce a hit.

Oscar pulled up an Excel spreadsheet on his ancient computer. He ran his finger down the page. The play slips were all time-stamped. It took no time to match Darwin's purchase with the actual slip.

"If you wait a moment, I'll get it for you."

"No. Uh-uh." Vega stepped back and waved his hands in front of his face. "I can't touch it. It's not my case. I'm going to call it into the Lake Holly PD now." *Not the PD. Greco.* Vega didn't trust Jankowski and Sanchez. If they could miss this, what else could they have missed?

Vega wished, not for the first time, that he was back

working cases. God, how he missed it! Six weeks—six long weeks—he'd spent sitting at a desk answering phones and reviewing arrest reports and time sheets. Every Friday, he asked his boss the same question: *How much longer?* And every Friday, Captain Waring gave the same answer: *It's under review.* Whose review? What more did Vega have to do? He'd posted the second highest score of the past six months at the police shooting range. He ran five miles every other day. He lifted weights. He was in the best shape he'd been in since the academy. And none of it mattered until the bosses decided it did.

Vega pulled his business card out of his wallet and handed it to Oscar. "Don't let these play slips leave your store until the police get here. You run into any problems or the police don't come within two hours, call me. I don't want to see this evidence lost."

"Okay." Oscar shoved the card into his pants pocket beneath his white apron. He looked out at the deli counter again. "Almost nobody's come into the store since that girl disappeared. A few *Chapines*. But no *norteamericanos*. This is bad."

"It's just a slow day," said Vega. "Probably because it's going to snow." Though in truth, Vega had never seen it this slow on a Saturday afternoon.

"It's not the snow," said Oscar. "It's the girl."

"You didn't do anything."

"Doesn't matter," said Oscar. "The police were here. Word has gone around that a Guatemalan immigrant bought beer at my store and then did something bad to that girl. As far as the *norteamericanos* in town are concerned, I'm to blame."

"They don't think that."

"No?" Oscar raised an eyebrow. "You know the gas station in town? The one owned by the two Sikh brothers?"

"Sure." Vega bought gas there regularly when he was in Lake Holly. They had the cheapest prices around.

"After nine-eleven, they almost went out of business," said Oscar. "They were Sikhs! From India! Not Muslims. Not Arabs! But the *norteamericanos*—they couldn't tell the difference. A brown-skinned man with a piece of cloth on his head was a terrorist to them, plain and simple. To them, I'm the same as that *cholero* who bought beer at my store. Now, you tell me what will happen if they find out that he did something to that girl?"

Chapter 5

A heavyset white man stopped Wil Martinez as he rode his beat-up Huffy to the service entrance of the Lake Holly Grill.

"You," said the man. He wore a puffy black jacket and a knit wool hat that stuck up from his head like a used condom. "You speak English?"

"Yes," said Wil.

"Well?"

"Fluently."

He looked surprised. He obviously wasn't used to Central American busboys with New York accents and perfect command of English. Wil turned away and chained up his bicycle. The man stepped closer and lifted his overcoat. Wil wasn't sure if the man wanted to impress him with his gold badge or scare him with the gun in the holster at his hip.

"Detective Greco. Lake Holly Police. Can I talk to you a moment?"

"I'll be late for my shift." It was Wil's job to slice

the tomatoes and dice the onions (the worst job—and he always got it). He didn't want his boss, Pedro, to yell at him if stuff wasn't ready for the dinner crowd. Plus, he liked to grab a bite to eat before things got crazy. If he didn't, it would be midnight before he'd have a chance to eat again.

"The job will wait," said the detective. Wil sensed neither he nor Pedro had much choice in the matter. "You heard about the missing girl?"

"No."

"Really?" The detective raised an eyebrow. "You live under a rock or something, kid?"

"I was at the library studying all day."

"Studying?" The detective said it like he didn't believe him. "Got any ID?"

Wil reached into his back pocket and pulled out a black leather wallet that had gone white at the edges. He opened it and fished out a Valley Community College student ID. He handed it to the detective. The detective squinted at the name: *Wilfredo Martinez.* He was named after his father, a good man who'd died too young in a country where just walking down the wrong street can be lethal.

He'd dropped the other part of his name, Ochoa. From his mother. It was the *norteamericano* way. They had erased her from his name the same way they'd erased her from his life—with the stroke of a pen.

The detective frowned as he held Wil's college ID up to the light.

"Next time, get a fake Social Security card like everyone else in there." He nodded to the kitchen.

"The ID's not fake," said Wil. "That's really my name and I really am a freshman at Valley."

"Studying?"

"Premed."

"Uh-huh. Sure."

Wil felt a slow burn in his gut. All his life, he'd had to cower before men in uniforms. First, to protect his mother, and now, to protect Rolando. But he was alone at the moment—and infuriated by the way the cop was treating him. So he pulled out another ID and handed it to the cop. His legal-residency permit.

The detective barely glanced at it. "You're one of those Obama kids—am I right? A DACA." *Deferred Action for Childhood Arrivals.* Wil could tell by the way the detective said it what he thought of the former president's executive order that granted temporary legal status to young people who came as children without papers to the United States. There was a time when Wil thought DACA was going to be his bridge to a new life. But the world is never a stable place when you don't have permanent papers. These days, the government seemed to be looking for any excuse to snatch it away. Every day on the news, Wil heard about undocumented immigrants being arrested in their homes and deported. Everyone was frightened.

The detective handed both IDs back to Wil and pulled out a notepad. "Address?"

"Of the campus?"

"No, professor. *Your* address. You live in town, right?"

"Yes."

"Where?"

Wil hesitated. Rolando had already been deported once. Wil wasn't about to invite the law in to do it again. That was how his mother got deported three years ago.

The cops ordered Wil to open the door of his mother's basement apartment, and like the dopey sixteen-year-old he was, he obeyed. He only found out later that he could have refused.

He hadn't seen his mother since. He probably never would again, especially since the cancer was taking a piece of her every day, two thousand miles away. In a country he couldn't visit. A country she couldn't leave.

Wil straightened and tried to wring the shakiness from his voice. "Can I ask what this is about?"

"We're looking for anyone with information about this girl's disappearance."

"A little girl?"

"A high-school student," said the detective. "She left La Casa last night after tutoring English. No one's seen her since."

"A . . . high-school girl. At La Casa." The words felt heavy on Wil's tongue. The implications felt even heavier. "You think . . . one of the students did something bad to her?"

"We're just trying to cover all the bases." The detective's tone was casual, but his eyes betrayed a wolfish hunger. Wil had a sense the police were already zeroing in on the men who were at La Casa last night. *Rolando.* Wil's gut felt like someone had thrown it in a trash compactor. He thought of his brother's conversation this morning. He'd mentioned a girl: *"I know it's wrong, but I can't help myself."*

"You know La Casa, right?" asked the detective.

"Yes."

"Know anyone who was there last night?"

"I don't go there."

"That's not what I asked," said the detective. "I asked if you knew anyone who did."

Yes. No. Wil couldn't think. He couldn't breathe. This was his brother. His flesh and blood. The only part of Wil's family left in this country. Wil loved him. But more than that, he *owed* him. Always would. Ever since that day in Monterrey. That was thirteen years ago. A moment in a dusty freight yard that changed everything. For as long as Wil lived, he would never forget that burning Mexican sun. The stench of diesel smoke and soot. People called the freight trains that traveled fifteen hundred miles north from Guatemala to the U.S. border, the "beast." For good reason. Catch a ride, tie yourself on, avoid getting crushed by the wheels or beaten by the Mexican police, and you just might make it. One slip, and it was over.

Wil was six when he made that one slip, losing his grasp and tumbling to the gravel and trash below. He got to his feet, bruised and bleeding and stood frozen by the enormity of his situation. The train he was supposed to catch was lumbering out of the freight yard, carrying his mother and fifteen-year-old brother away forever. He was alone. In a foreign land. Without family or money.

He would have died if not for Rolando.

What happened next, Wil would only ever be able to recall in freeze-frame snatches. Rolando's leap from the train. The way he ran over, grabbed Wil, and then half lifted, half threw him up to the people on top of the boxcar. The angry faces of the Mexican police officers who raced after them with raised batons. His mother's cries. One minute, he was in Rolando's arms.

The next, his brother was losing ground as he ran alongside, growing smaller and smaller as the train gathered speed.

"My son!" his mother cried. She tried to jump from the train. Some people held her down. Others made the sign of the cross.

"You can't help him," they told his mother. "You can only help your younger son now."

Wil barely paid attention to any of the people on the train. He was focused on the freight yard, on the Mexican police as they encircled Rolando, kicking and beating him. In dreams, he saw the gravel where Rolando fell stained with blood. He heard his brother's anguished cries. His mother said he imagined that. But it didn't make it any less true. For six long weeks, the police kept Rolando in a Mexican prison. They beat and tortured him in an effort to extort money from him or a contact in his family who would pay for his release. By the time they gave up and deported him back to Guatemala, the beatings and torture had taken their toll. Rolando looked outwardly normal. But some essential part of him felt missing. It was nine years before Wil saw his brother again. The fifteen-year-old he'd known—gentle and shy—had become a tattooed, scarred man who used alcohol to drown his pain. Wil could never look at his brother and not wonder how different both their lives would have been if Rolando had not jumped from that train.

The big cop tapped his pen on his notebook and stared down at Wil.

"Look, kid, you may be this whiz-bang premed at Valley. But right now, you're brooking an F in straight answers. I have half a mind to haul you down to the station house and make you sit there while I run a check on that precious ID you're so quick to wave about. So you can either start cooperating or you can tell your boss why you won't be working tonight. Which is it gonna be?"

"I don't know anyone who was at La Casa last night," said Wil.

"You're sure about that?"

Wil felt like the big detective with the condom hat could see right through his lies. His chest burned like he'd run a marathon. The back of his throat felt fizzy like he was going to hiccup.

"Yes."

"And where were *you* Friday night?"

"Home. Studying."

"Where is home?"

The cop wasn't going to let up until Wil gave him an address. So he rattled off an old address—the one he and Rolando lived in before Rolando lost his last job and they had to move to something cheaper. Wil figured he could claim he'd misunderstood if the cop ever came back.

"You live by yourself?"

"Yes." He was keeping Rolando out of this.

"Did you attend Lake Holly High?"

"For a short while." He attended every school for a short while. His mother was forever looking for someplace cheaper to rent.

The detective reached inside a pocket of his jacket and pulled out a flyer. He handed it to Wil. "Maybe you know her. She's only a couple of years younger than you."

Wil stared at the flyer. He had the sensation of falling from a great height.

"This is the missing girl?"

"Yes," said the detective. "Catherine Archer. Her family owns the Magnolia Inn."

She was wearing a crisp white shirt beneath a turquoise-colored V-neck sweater. A silver chain glinted from her breastbone. You couldn't see the pendant at the end of it. But it was there. Hidden. Like so many other parts of her. Her eyes locked on Wil's. There was a questioning look to them that mirrored his own.

"Do you know her?" asked the detective.

It took all of Wil's energy not to collapse against the metal railing where he'd just chained his bike.

"No." The word felt like it had a hundred syllables and ninety-nine were still lodged in his chest.

This can't be happening.

But then, so much else that had happened shouldn't have either.

Wil closed his eyes and saw himself and Rolando in that freight yard in Monterrey again with the train slipping away.

Only this time, neither was on it.

Chapter 6

The Oyster Club was packed on a Saturday night. Sweaty bodies swayed to the kinetic beat of rock, blues, and Latin pop. Colored spotlights strafed the gauzy purple silks that hung from the ceiling. Glasses clinked. Laughter and chatter rose over the grind of the bartender's blender and the thumping bass of the music. The whole room vibrated with excitement and energy.

Jimmy Vega drank in every minute. In life, he felt shy and tongue-tied. But behind his Gibson Les Paul or Fender Stratocaster, he could let his fingers do the talking—dancing across the frets as fast as a hummingbird's wings. Or coming in low and slow on a backbeat until the rhythm grabbed and lifted him, breaking like a wave on the dance floor. Even singing came naturally. It didn't matter if it was R & B, salsa, rock, or reggae. The adrenaline rush was the same. As sensual as sex. As comforting as a good woman.

Music was in his genes, Vega supposed. His father had been a part-time bass player before he became a full-time deadbeat dad, splitting from Vega's mother when Jimmy was two. Vega himself had planned a music career—until Joy came along unexpectedly. He'd had to ditch those dreams for his daughter's sake. But it was hard not to wonder, as he did on a night like tonight, with the band in perfect sync, no missed cues, everybody grooving on the dance floor, what life might have been like had he followed his heart instead of his head.

He wouldn't have killed a man, for one.

But no. He wasn't going there. Not tonight. Instead he sang until he was hoarse and played until the sweat poured off his body and the calluses on his fingers felt like well-earned battle scars.

He wished Adele had been here to see Armado play the Oyster Club. He loved when she came to his gigs. She couldn't sing for her life, but she was a great dancer. Vega enjoyed watching her from the stage, the music a shared thread between them—always a prelude to their lovemaking.

"You think Jerry will invite us back?" Vega asked the keyboardist, Danny Molina, when they were taking a break between sets. The club owner, a guy named Jerry, was a childhood friend of Molina's. That's how they got invited to play.

"Sure hope so." Molina was a large, stocky Port Carroll cop with a perennially cheerful disposition. Every Christmas, he played Santa Claus at the local community center. He didn't need much stuffing. Molina toweled the sweat from his face and shaved head as he and Vega stood by the rear door of the club, both of them cooling off in the frigid breeze and eyeing the customers grabbing a smoke in the parking lot. They were musicians, sure. But they were cops too. They always had an eye out for trouble.

Vega and Molina checked their phones for texts. Vega had one from Joy to confirm she was safely at her father's house, dog-sitting Diablo. He had another from Greco, telling him the Lake Holly PD had bagged the lottery play slip from Hank's Deli and was testing it for fingerprints and DNA. He had a third from Adele, wishing him luck at the gig. She didn't say how things were going on her end, only that Sophia was back with her and they were sharing a quiet evening together. He texted back that he missed her and that he was playing her favorite song by Bruno Mars last, in her honor.

A pretty young cocktail waitress in a miniskirt and high heels poked her head out the back entrance where Molina and Vega were standing and pressed two beers into their hands.

"Compliments of Jerry." She blushed when she handed a beer to Vega. Molina grinned as the waitress left. He clinked his bottle against Vega's. "You charm 'em every time."

"I didn't do anything."

"If Adele were here, she might say otherwise. How's she doing with that situation in Lake Holly?"

"So you've heard."

"It's all over the news," said Molina. "The aftershocks are already being felt down here in Port Carroll. The immigrants are afraid. Our day laborer center at St. Augustine's got a death threat this afternoon."

"Aw, man." Vega was afraid this would happen. He just didn't think it would start so soon.

"I hate to say it, Jimmy. But I think one of those guys offed her."

Vega stared out at the parking lot. A light snow blanketed the cars and softened the black waters of the harbor beyond. Everything was silent and white.

"It's not hard to imagine one of them doing this," Molina continued. "She attracted men easily."

"You're talking like you know her."

"I do. A little," said Molina. "She works as a hostess sometimes at the Magnolia Inn. Her family owns it."

Vega gave Molina a once-over. "Port Carroll cops get a discount there or something? I couldn't afford a toothpick in that place."

Molina laughed. "Hey, I wasn't eating. I was working. I fill in for their regular pianist sometimes at their bar. The cash comes in handy. My daughters' Christmas wish lists get longer every year." Molina had two preteens. Vega didn't envy him.

"The hourly rate sucks," Molina continued. "And you have to wear a tux. But the tips are great. People in those circles? They show off. Request a song and then try to impress their friends and associates with how much money they can throw down on little guys like me."

Vega grinned. Molina used to play defense for his high-school football team. "Since when were you a little guy?"

"Since being one got me fifty-dollar tips." Molina rolled his beer bottle between his fleshy palms. "Tell you one thing, Catherine was very much noticed by the kitchen help. There was this one good-looking waiter? He was always flirting with her—until Catherine's brother fired him."

"How long ago was this?"

"A couple weeks ago," said Molina. "Not long after the holidays."

"You remember the waiter's name?"

"Not sure I ever heard it. But the Archers would know. Especially her brother, Todd."

"Any sense this waiter was doing more than flirting?"

"From what I could see? No. But her brother fired the guy, so who knows?"

"I'd have fired him too, if he was hitting on Joy," said Vega. "Why wait until something happens?"

"You got a point." Molina drained the rest of his beer. He looked like he was thinking of his own two girls. "I get the impression Catherine's parents keep her on a tight leash."

"Yeah," Vega agreed. "All anyone can tell me is that she's an honors student and a varsity tennis player. No boyfriend. And more interesting, no close girlfriends. Either she was being raised in a bubble or . . ." Vega's voice trailed off.

"Or what?"

"Nobody the cops talked to so far really knows her."

"She was close to Todd," said Molina. "You could see that. He was very protective of her. I'm sure that's why he fired that waiter. He didn't want someone like that taking advantage of his kid sister."

The wind had picked up, blowing snow across the two men. Vega felt it working its way down the back of his shirt, mixing with the congealed sweat on his skin.

"We should go inside," said Molina. "We're back on in five."

*   *   *

By the time the band finished the rest of their set, it was after midnight. The breakdown took another forty-five minutes. There were duct-taped cables to rip up off the stage floor; amps, instruments, and mics to unplug and put away. The snow was falling harder. They would have to dig out their cars and scrape down their windshields.

"Jerry wants us back," said Molina as he handed Vega his share of the night's take: just under a hundred dollars. The band made more doing weddings and *quinceañeras*—Latina coming-of-age parties. But playing a club was more fun. Here, the music was the main attraction, not just something between the entrée and the dessert.

Vega tucked the bills into his wallet, cranked up the heater in his pickup, and focused on a hot shower and a chance to see his daughter. He was barely a mile from the Port Carroll waterfront when he heard the ding of a text on his phone. He didn't check it. He'd seen the results of too many texting-while-driving accidents to ever take that chance. There was no place to pull over on the narrow road he was traveling. Not with snowplows still out and flurries still coming down. He drove on until he found a gas station. He pulled in front of the station's convenience store and checked his messages. The text was from Adele: **The police found her. Call me ASAP.**

There was no mention if Catherine was alive or dead. But Vega had a sense that if the news had been good, Adele would have said so. It was almost two a.m. Almost twenty-eight hours since Catherine

Archer had walked out of La Casa into a frigid January night. They were past the golden twenty-four—if indeed it had ever been golden. Vega felt the rock-hard certainty that if it took the cops to find her, it was not the way any parents wanted their child to be found.

Chapter 7

"Dave Lindsey called me with the news."
The rest of Adele's words spilled out faster than Vega could process them. Something about the woods and the post office and a volunteer search party. It all ran together. Vega was always a little deaf after a gig—even when he used earplugs. Plus, he was parked at a gas station next to a tractor-trailer that the driver had left idling while he bought something in the convenience store. The rumble of the big truck's diesel engine reverberated through Vega's pickup like someone gargling.

"Wait," said Vega. "Back up a minute. The chairman of the board of La Casa called you? Not the police? How would he know what happened to Catherine?"

"His wife plays tennis with a friend of Robin Archer's. She was the one who found her."

"Lindsey's wife?"

"No." Vega could hear impatience in Adele's voice.

She was always a beat ahead of everyone, including him. "Robin Archer. Catherine's mother! She was in the search party combing the woods behind the post office. She found her own daughter's body."

"Jesus." Vega flicked his wipers, cutting an arc through the snow across the glass. The steady thump felt like a heartbeat. The windshield went from clear, to salt-streaked, to blurry, and back again. A flashing lottery sign in the convenience store window lent everything a sickly greenish glow. It matched the queasiness Vega felt inside.

"Did Dave say anything about how the girl died?"

"I don't think he knows."

"Maybe it was an overdose."

"Jimmy . . . some of her clothes were off."

Vega closed his eyes and cursed under his breath. Every one of his worst fears was coming true.

"I want to go over there," said Adele. "But I can't. Sophia's asleep."

"The cops wouldn't let you within a hundred feet of that crime scene anyway."

"They'd let *you* in."

"No, they would not."

The truck driver lumbered out of the store, hefting a bag of Doritos and a gallon of Gatorade. He climbed into his cab and put the engine in gear. When he drove off, Vega became acutely aware of Adele's silence.

"*Nena,* I can't just waltz into another jurisdiction's crime scene. For cops—especially male cops—that's like flopping down on their living-room sofa and reprogramming their remote. It won't get you the answers you need. It'll only piss them off."

"Like they're not pissed off already."

She had a point. "Look, let me come over and stay with you so you're not alone."

"I'm *not* alone. I'm with Sophia. If you won't go speak to the police, then I will. I'll take Sophia to Peter's and then stand there all night, if I have to, until I get some answers."

"Even if they let you in for some reason, trust me," said Vega, "you *don't* want to see that." There are some things, Vega knew, that you can't unsee. Cruelties and savageries that you can't forget once you've witnessed them. He didn't want those nightmares visited on Adele. That was reason enough to take her place.

"All right," said Vega. "You win. I'll go."

"You will?"

"You have to promise me that you won't wait up. These things tend to take a while." Vega flicked the wipers across his windshield again. The snow wasn't letting up. He looked down at his clothes. He was wearing sneakers, jeans, and a T-shirt—all of it sweaty. Even with a couple of hand warmers and his insulated jacket, he'd be sorely underdressed for a winter romp in the woods. But if it kept Adele away from the crime scene, it was worth it.

"I'll text you the basics and call you tomorrow morning. All right?"

"Thank you, Jimmy."

Snow at a crime scene makes everything harder. Collecting evidence. Keeping personnel on the scene. Determining time of death. Vega could only imagine how this was going to impact the case.

He couldn't get within three hundred feet of the post office parking lot so he parked at a business up the road and hiked back. His dark blue police jacket, black knit hat, and lined leather gloves provided enough protection on top. But his sneakers and jeans were soaked and coated with clumps of snow by the time he made his way to the police checkpoint. The cop on site protection, a rookie who barely looked old enough to carry a gun, knew Vega—and knew he wasn't supposed to be here.

"Can't let you in, Detective," he said. "Jankowski and Sanchez would have my head—and a few other parts besides."

"Is Greco here?"

"*Everyone's* here."

Vega counted four marked cruisers. Several more unmarked SUVs. A fire truck. The medical examiner's van. His own department's crime scene unit—probably Jenn and her partner. This was their case after all.

Emergency lights flashed across the pure white of the landscape—each vehicle at different intervals. An epileptic's nightmare. It gave Vega a headache just looking at them. The wind had died down and the temperature hovered just below freezing so the flakes grew thick and fat on the bare trees. The snow muted almost everything. The slam of car doors. The officers' voices. The static from their walkie-talkies. It could never mute the horror. Twenty feet back in the woods, bright halogen lights lit up the night. There was no mistaking where the body was.

"Can you radio Detective Greco? See if he'll give me an update?"

"I'll try to reach him."

Vega stamped his soggy feet as he watched men and

women with grim expressions traipse like ants back and forth through a narrow path into the woods. He counted the initials of at least six different agencies. Why the hell were their vehicles parked all over the lot? The first cruiser, he could see. Maybe the officers didn't know. But the rest? They were messing up the crime scene.

Now, if this was my crime scene, I'd cordon off the vehicles. Restrict movement along narrow lines of access.

But it's not your crime scene. Those words hit Vega like a wet towel to the face. He was ashamed to admit that beneath the anguish and alarm, he felt something else—something he could only describe as excitement. The adrenaline rush he used to get when he showed up at a homicide. *His* homicide. That he'd run *his* way. He missed it. God, how he missed it! He felt guilty to even admit that. A young girl's life had ended brutally here. How could he feel anything at the minute but sorrow? And yet he did. It was the detective in him. To do the job well, you had to have fire in your heart and ice in your veins.

He'd been like that once. He wondered if he'd ever get the chance to be that again.

The officer turned back to Vega. "Detective Greco said to meet him at the entrance to the woods. He said not to go farther."

"Thanks. Got it."

Vega was careful to pick his way across the snow in tracks already used by others. But already, there were too many trails. Car tracks. Truck tracks. Boot prints all over the parking lot. It was still snowing, so they were filling up fast. It might not matter in the end. But still.

He pulled up the collar of his jacket and did a quick scan of the one-story post office with its veneer of brown bricks. There was a fenced-off area at the far end of the building with mail trucks behind it. There were two surveillance cameras in front, aimed at the entrance, and two on the side, aimed at the fenced-off area. None of them were likely to yield any usable footage.

Greco emerged from the woods like a grizzly bear roused from hibernation. Snow coated the shoulders of his puffy black jacket. His knit cap looked like he'd rolled in coconut.

"This is a courtesy, Vega," he growled as he trudged over. "A little good will from the Lake Holly PD. So make it quick. I have work to do."

"What have you got so far?"

"Volunteer search party found her," said Greco. "A party that unfortunately included her mother."

"I heard," said Vega. "Is there a lot of trauma to the body?"

"Her jeans and underwear were down around her ankles. Her sweater and bra were bunched up around her neck. Was she sexually assaulted? I can't say for sure. I didn't see any bruising in that area. She has no obvious injuries outside of a small bruise to her chin."

"You said her sweater and bra were around her neck," said Vega. "Did you notice any ligature marks?"

"No marks to suggest she was strangled," said Greco. "Not by her clothes or anything else. No gunshot or stab wounds either. At least not that I can see."

"Is it possible she wasn't murdered?" asked Vega. "Maybe she overdosed? That heroin and fentanyl stuff is making the rounds and it's superpotent. Maybe somebody panicked."

"It's possible," said Greco. "Then again, someone pulled down her pants. It has all the appearances of a rape or attempted rape."

"How about lividity?" asked Vega. He was referring to the purplish marks after death that indicate the settling of blood beneath the skin.

"There was some on her back where she was lying," said Greco. Which meant that Catherine died in the spot she was found in—or was brought to it soon after death. "If I had to bet at this point, I'd say she was a victim of opportunity—and we both know where that opportunity probably came from."

La Casa.

Vega and Greco were standing less than a quarter mile from Adele's community center, in a wooded area that extended about a mile along a streambed to the old stone bridge. In summer, the marshy land attracted the heavy drinkers and semi-homeless among the immigrant population, who passed out near the stream or sought shelter under the bridge or in the abandoned cars that riddled the thick brush—remnants of a former mechanic's garage that went bust and was torn down years ago.

Vega didn't have to say what both men were thinking: If Catherine was assaulted, the most likely suspect was an immigrant she'd tutored Friday night.

Mike Carp, the new county executive, was going to have a field day with this.

"Can you walk me back there?" asked Vega.

"No can do, my friend. This is Jankowski and Sanchez's case. And I'm just a pair of eyes and legs—"

"Don't hand me that cataracted crap again, Grec. You could do it if you wanted to."

"What part of 'this isn't your case' don't you understand? You want to play detective? I'll take you down to our local five-and-dime. Buy you a supercool cowboy badge and a shiny set of plastic cuffs."

"*I'm* playing detective? Let's not forget who gift wrapped that lead on the play slips at Hank's Deli." Vega gestured to the tracks running through the snow. "Look at this lot. You've got Grand Central Station walking through here. I'm not gonna mess up Lake Holly's precious crime scene any more than it's already messed up."

Greco stood there, jaw set to one side, snow piling up on his shoulders like pigeon droppings. He unwrapped a Twizzler from a cellophane bag in his pocket and chewed thoughtfully.

"Head down. Don't touch anything. And the next time you come to a crime scene?" Greco frowned at Vega's sneakers. "Do me a favor and dress for it."

Vega followed Greco about twenty feet down a slope to a snow-encrusted canopy. It looked like a lunar-landing module under the glow of halogen spotlights. The glare bleached out any sense of day or night. Radios squawked but voices were muted, visible in the clouds of shimmering breath that rose from the officers' lips and evaporated into the night.

Catherine was lying on her back under the canopy, her blond hair frozen in matted strands at her sides.

The middle of her body, from her breasts to her knees, was bare and blue as an old lady's veins. With the exception of the twilight cast to her skin, she could have been sleeping. There was no blood. No trauma, save for one thin bruise on her lower left jaw. A silver chain still dangled from her neck, weighted to one side by a small charm. An elephant with a raised trunk. Costume jewelry most likely. But still. In most violent encounters Vega had seen, necklaces were the first things to get broken or disappear. Yet this one remained intact.

Jenn Fitzpatrick was kneeling beside Catherine's body, her white Tyvek coveralls perfectly blending in with the landscape. With her freckled face and curly hair, she looked more like a ski instructor than a crime scene tech. She was tucking one of Catherine's hands inside a plastic bag to preserve any trace evidence under her nails. The nails were painted blue with yellow polka dots. None of them appeared to be broken. That surprised Vega even more than the necklace. A girl fighting for her life should have broken a nail or two. Then again, maybe she'd been wearing gloves. Or maybe she'd never seen the assault coming until it was too late to fight off.

He crouched down next to Jenn. "Wish you'd been at the club tonight," he said softly. "Wish neither of us was here."

"Keep this up, Jimmy, and I'm sure your wish will be granted—permanently." She pulled out a zip tie to secure the bag around Catherine's wrist. "You can't possibly have permission to be here."

"I got a hall pass from Detective Greco."

"Ah." Jenn moved over to bag Catherine's other

hand. "How was . . . ?" Her voice trailed off. This was no place to talk music. There was no music here.

"Good. Great, in fact." Vega tried to recall the feeling, but it was gone. Catherine's death had rendered everything else insignificant. He forced himself to run his eyes along the perfect, unblemished contours of the girl's body. She had died faceup, staring straight at her killer.

"Her mother found her like this?" asked Vega.

"Basically," said Jenn. "She had a black jacket covering her face and upper torso. The search party told the police they removed it. They shouldn't have. But really, can you blame them?"

"Makes me think whoever did this knew her." Vega straightened and looked past the tent at the bushes surrounding the clearing. Even with their delicate blossoms of snow on top, he could see that there were no obvious broken branches.

"Some predator lures her out here," said Vega. "He's looking to subdue her and get out. So where's the struggle? There's no evidence there was one."

"Maybe she'd already passed out," Jenn suggested.

"Then why kill her?"

"Maybe it was an accident."

"I'd buy that," said Vega, "if the scene wasn't so obviously staged to look like a rape. Something's not adding up." He stepped back from the body. "Did you find her wallet?"

"Negative."

"Her cell phone? Car keys? Mittens or gloves?"

"We haven't found any of that so far. Detective Jankowski told me she owned an Apple 7S. It was in a case embossed with a photograph of her playing tennis."

"It's probably in some Dumpster by now," said Vega. His feet were numb. His pants and sneakers were soaked. He needed to get back to his truck and warm up. So he thanked Jenn and left the tent.

By the time Vega hiked back across the parking lot, the news vans had set up. Two reporters were interviewing a hefty white man in a dark overcoat, with a mop of silver hair. On either side of him were other white men in dark overcoats, with cell phones to their ears and umbrellas in their hands—not to shield themselves, but to protect the man in the center.

Mike Carp had arrived. This was bad news. Very bad news.

"Vega!"

Greco lumbered toward him, out of breath. Vega held up his hands in a gesture of surrender.

"Keep your shirt on. I'm leaving."

"Good. But before you do, I thought you'd want to know—a fingerprint from those play slips came back."

"You get a hit?"

"Affirmative. To a twenty-eight-year-old Guatemalan national named Rolando Benitez-Ochoa. And get this: Benitez has a record for sexual assault. Convicted seven years ago in Colorado for beating and raping a woman. Did eight months and then got deported."

"*Eight months?* For rape and assault?"

"Some kumbaya liberal judge probably thought it was cheaper to deport him," said Greco. "And now we've got a dead girl on our hands as a result."

Vega shot a glance back at the woods. How did a hardened ex-con with a record for violent sexual assault talk a pretty high-school girl into those woods? Did he loosen her up with alcohol? Feed her some sob story that excited her girlish fantasies? Charm her with bogus tales of danger and heroism? Who knows the mind-set of a sheltered and gullible seventeen-year-old? Either way, by the time he tricked or forced her into the woods, she didn't stand a chance.

"You got an address on this guy?" asked Vega.

"Not yet. But we'll get him." Greco watched Carp giving a statement to reporters. "This story is going national. By the time we're through, Rolando Benitez-Ochoa won't be able to find a sombrero to crawl under. He's finished."

Camera lights bounced off Carp's shellacked hair. His fleshy jowls rose and fell in practiced indignation. He stretched out an arm and gestured in the direction of La Casa—just a quarter mile away. And Vega wondered if Benitez wasn't the only one who was finished here.

Chapter 8

Wil Martinez dialed Rolando's cell phone on a break. But all he got was a robotic voice in carefully modulated English asking the caller to leave a message.

Wil dialed a second time. Maybe Rolando was in the shower. Maybe he'd pulled himself together enough to go to work this evening.

Same number of rings. Same robotic message. *Pick up, Lando. Please!* The Lord's Prayer came to Wil now. He could hear his mother's gentle voice reciting it.

Padre nuestro,
Que estás en el cielo.
Santificado sea tu nombre.

Wil would always be six when he heard that prayer, holding tight to his mother on the top of that soot-choked boxcar, watching his brother grow smaller and smaller in that cauldron of fists and batons. Only now, the fists and batons were whispered accusations too terrible to speak.

Wil finished up his break and walked back into the kitchen of the Lake Holly Grill. It was cold outside, but inside there was steam and commotion. Everybody was speaking Spanish, yelling insults and commands with equal gusto. Cooks and busboys were chopping and slicing and boiling and frying. The dishwasher was scrubbing pots and pans. Waiters were placing orders in Spanish for foods that were anything but: Eggplant parmigiana. Chicken teriyaki. Moussaka with pita bread. Matzo ball soup.

Wil found his boss, Pedro, in the middle of the fray, pulling a tray of something in tomato sauce out of the oven. Beads of sweat settled in the creases on his leathery, lined forehead. No matter the temperature outside, it was always hot in the kitchen.

"I'm sorry, Pedro. I can't work anymore this evening. I think I'm getting sick."

Pedro frowned at Wil like he was a cockroach. "*A la chingada!* You couldn't have figured that out before you started your shift? Now we're short staffed."

"I didn't feel sick until now." Wil's stomach was turning somersaults, a mixture of panic and fear. And beneath that, something else. Anguish. Loss. He closed his eyes and saw the photograph the detective had shown him. Was this who Rolando had been talking about? Wil wished he'd known. Not that it would have changed anything. If Rolando was caught up in this, everything Wil had worked for—his legal status, his college credits, his toehold on the American dream—might vanish anyway.

He blamed Rolando.

But even more, he blamed himself.

One of the other busboys walked up to Pedro as he was setting the platter on a counter. Chicken parmigiana. Wil couldn't stand to look at it, he felt so sick. The busboy told Pedro that they needed a cleanup in the dining room and he couldn't find the mop.

"Do I look like a mop, *teto*?" Pedro called everybody a "bumbling idiot." He could be a tyrant when the kitchen was hopping. "I swear, I could get ten more— faster and cheaper—than you." One of Pedro's favorite expressions. Probably because it had been used on him often enough when he first came here from Mexico.

Pedro turned back to Wil. Wil expected to receive another reprimand before being dismissed. But Pedro's eyes softened. "You don't look so good. You still going to school?"

"Yes."

"Don't give up school. School is the most important thing. You understand?" Pedro had dozens of pictures tacked up all over his locker of his own four children in caps and gowns. He'd put them all through college in Mexico and bragged about them every chance he got. His daughter, the teacher. His son, the engineer. Another was an accountant. A fourth was still in school. Pedro never talked about the fact that he hadn't seen them since they were children; providing for them meant being here, and being here meant never being there. The closest Wil ever got to that conversation was when Pedro learned that Wil's mother had been deported. Pedro put a thick, callused hand on Wil's skinny shoulder and gave it a squeeze.

"Work all the holidays," Pedro advised. "Christmas.

Birthdays. Easter. You don't want to be alone on those days." Pedro never spoke about it again.

The other busboy located the mop and scurried out of the kitchen. Pedro turned back to Wil. "Go. I'll count you as here until the hour. You want me to put you on the schedule for tomorrow?"

"Yes. Thank you."

Wil left the Grill by the kitchen door. Then he un-chained his bicycle and pedaled home as fast as he could. The snow was falling hard now. His sneakers and jeans were soggy by the time he got to his own block, a tired-looking string of row frames huddled to-gether like cereal boxes on a shelf. Wil half expected to see several police cars double-parked at the curb. To see Rolando being yanked out in handcuffs, still in his undershirt and socks. But the street looked the same as it always did on a winter evening. Snow shovels and boots graced the scuffed front porches. Bicycles were chained under awnings. Lights and televisions flick-ered behind bedsheet curtains as people settled in for the night.

Wil nosed his bicycle around back and locked it under the porch. He fished a key out of his pocket and unlocked the main door. The hallway was dark and narrow. It smelled of damp clothes and fried food. A single uncovered lightbulb lit the stairway. Wil raced up the steps. One flight. Then two. All the way to the attic. To the door under the eaves. Wil let himself in. The smell of unwashed clothes was thick in the air. Rolando was sitting up in his bunk, wrapped in his quilt. Not sleeping. Just huddled there, staring off into space. This wasn't just a hangover.

"What's going on?" said Wil. "I called. You didn't answer."

"I didn't feel like talking."

Wil sat on the edge of Rolando's lower bunk. The Sheetrock walls were thin. Wil spoke softly. He didn't want the other tenants to hear. "You have to tell me what happened last night," he said. "A police officer spoke to me when I got to work this evening. He said a girl who teaches English at La Casa is missing. When you came home, you mentioned a girl. Lando—please tell me it's not the same girl. Tell me it's not *this* girl."

Rolando raked his hands through his hair. Wil studied his arms. There were so many tattoos. Mayan gods. A heart with a dagger going through it. Chains of razor blades. Birds and snakes. No gang initials, thankfully. But even so—Wil had no idea what half his brother's tattoos stood for. He wasn't sure he wanted to know.

Wil waited for Rolando to say something, but all he could hear was the clang of pots from the tenants cooking on hot plates down the hall.

"Lando—"

"I heard you the first time," his brother snapped. "What do you want me to say?"

"Do you understand what I'm asking you?"

"I know already." Rolando fell back against his pillow and threw an arm across his eyes. "The police went to the Calderons' door. I overheard them talking. I hid under the bed. They knocked, but I didn't answer."

"If you have nothing to do with this, we can talk to the police—"

"No one just *talks* to the police." Rolando shivered,

whether it was from the cold or from that long-ago memory in Monterrey, Wil wasn't sure.

"They won't beat you up if you just talk to them."

"And tell them what? I know who this girl is. She's the *canche* who tutored me in English at La Casa."

"But . . . you never saw her outside of La Casa, right?"

"It doesn't matter what I tell them. The moment they run my fingerprints, they'll see I've got a record for rape and assault. They'll deport me, *chaparro*. That is, unless they send me to prison for the rest of my life instead."

"Just tell them where you were last night. That you were drinking . . ." Wil's voice trailed off. He saw the blankness in his brother's eyes. "You didn't *do* anything, Lando, did you?"

Rolando pushed the heels of his palms to his eyes. "I don't know. I don't remember. I want to. But I can't."

"You . . . can't remember *anything*?" Was it the alcohol that addled his brother's brain? Or the terrible beatings he suffered all those years ago? Wil couldn't say. For him, it was just the opposite. Wil remembered everything. Useless, worthless stuff. The combinations to locks he no longer had. Addresses he'd left years ago. Phone numbers of people long gone from his life. The information stuck to the synapses of his brain like some television jingle he hated even as he was singing it. There were things he wanted to forget and couldn't. Things that made him burn with pain and shame every time he thought of them.

Maybe Rolando had it right after all.

"I remember going to La Casa," said Rolando. "But then—I don't know. It's just a big blank spot in my head. Like that time in Colorado."

Wil had heard a dozen different versions of the story of Rolando's arrest for rape and assault in Denver when he was twenty. Everything from him being set up by a sexy Latina prostitute, who later got beaten up by her gangbanger boyfriend, to waking up with blood and bruises and no memory of how he'd gotten them. With Rolando, the truth was always elusive.

"Lando, this is worse. Much, much worse. This is a high-school girl. From a prominent local family. Not some gangbanger's girlfriend."

"I know."

"So you remember her?"

"From La Casa, yes," said Rolando. "Not after."

"You remember her tutoring you?"

"That part, yeah. You should have seen her, *chaparro*. I could barely concentrate on the lesson. I swear, she could have been teaching a sewing class, and I'd have volunteered to be the needle—"

"Lando! Don't talk like that!"

"I'm just saying."

"You can't. Not now. If somebody hears you—hears us." Wil's throat constricted. A headache pulsed behind his eyes. "Maybe the thing to do is call that lady who runs La Casa. What's her name?"

"Señora Adele?"

"I could find out her number and call her for you," offered Wil. "We could go see her. Maybe she could be with you when you spoke to the police."

Rolando picked at a hangnail and said nothing.

"You can't just sit in this room," said Wil. "Sooner or later, the police will find you. Or come back to me when they find out I lied."

"About what?"

"I told them I didn't know anyone at La Casa last night. I gave them our old address. And I . . ." Wil's voice trailed off.

"You what?" Rolando propped himself up on one elbow and searched Wil's face. Wil saw a simple hunger in his brother's liquid brown eyes—the same hunger he used to see in his mother. A woman who used to work three jobs to make ends meet. Who used to walk two miles to her closest job so she'd have bus fare to take Wil to the library on Sundays after church. She and Rolando had sacrificed so much for Wil. He was their human corkboard. The one they'd pinned all their hopes and dreams to. He couldn't crumble. Not now.

"I just want everything to be okay."

Rolando put a hand on Wil's knee. He forced a smile. A press-lipped one. He never smiled fully anymore. He'd lost one of his lower teeth to the Mexican Police and another in a drunken brawl. He was self-conscious about it.

"If we go see the señora, do you think the police will leave you alone? Let you go on with your life?" Rolando asked him.

"I think the señora would try to help you. Try to help *us,*" said Wil. "You didn't do anything bad, Lando. You couldn't have. I refuse to believe that."

Rolando chucked a hand under Wil's chin. "So long as you get through this. That's all I care about. That's all I've ever cared about."

"No, Lando. Us. *Us—*"

"Shhh." Rolando put a finger to Wil's lips. In the half-light of the room, it was easy to pretend away the tattoos and scars and missing teeth that had remade his once-beautiful face and body. "No. You, *chaparro*. I'm so proud of you." For a moment, Rolando's dark bloodshot eyes looked clear and bright and devoid of the alcohol and ugliness of his life. "No matter what happens," he said. "Keep making me proud. Keep making *Mami* proud."

That was a heavy burden. Wil wondered if Lando or his mother ever knew just how heavy. "Find somewhere to lay low," Wil advised. "Not here. The police will find you here. Keep your phone turned off so they can't trace you. Just check it now and then. I'll see if I can find Señora Adele or a number where I can reach her to set up a meeting. I'll text you with the details, okay?"

"Whatever you think is best," said Rolando.

Wil let himself out of the room. He heard his brother whisper behind him:

"Vaya con Dios, chaparro." ("Go with God, shorty.")

They had been apart for nine years, then together for a year with his mother before immigration took her away. For the last three, it had been just the two of them. In rooming houses and tents. Whatever they could pull together. Rolando drank. He lost jobs. He disappeared for a night or two sometimes. But he never said farewell because they both knew he'd always be back.

Wil walked down the stairs. With each step, he felt the same queasy weightlessness he'd felt that day his brother had lifted him onto that train. Rolando was supposed to be right behind. But he wasn't. Only one of them could make it.

Only one.

Chapter 9

The snow had stopped by the time Vega pulled into his gravel driveway behind his daughter's hand-me-down white Volvo. Vega was glad Joy had chosen to drive up before the storm started, even if that meant he'd have to shovel her out. In good weather, the trip to his two-bedroom lake house was a hike. In bad weather, it was an odyssey. Twisty, unlit two-lanes. Lots of blind curves and black ice. When Vega bought this former summer cabin and winterized it six years ago after his divorce, friends said he was crazy to bury himself up here, a whole county north of his job. But Vega loved looking out the sliding glass doors of his back deck and seeing the lake through the fingers of bare trees. It calmed him. The crack and groan of ice in winter. The stillness after a snowfall. The rest of his life could be in turmoil. Yet here on this lake, nothing but the seasons ever changed.

Vega grabbed a shovel from the back of his truck and began digging his way into the driveway. Diablo was barking to come out. Vega would have liked to believe the greeting was just for him, but Diablo barked at everything. Squirrels. Deer. Fallen acorns. The television. He had a thing against *Jeopardy!*—or maybe he just thought he knew all the answers.

Vega was almost done creating a path when Joy opened his front door and Diablo bounded into the snow. He jumped on Vega, showering him in slobber, the soft flaps on his upturned ears jiggling like charms on a bracelet as he danced around Vega's legs. Diablo was supposed to be half German shepherd and half golden retriever, but he seemed not to have read the shepherd part of the dog manual. He was an effusive and unselective greeter who would gladly welcome anyone in Vega's house—invited or not—in return for a good belly scratch. The only things he was afraid of were Canadian geese, the vacuum cleaner (not that that was any sort of regular worry in Vega's house), and thunder. The only thing he growled at was his own reflection in the mirror. And yet Vega loved him. He *owed* him. After the shooting in December, Vega sorely needed a companion who would love him unconditionally without asking a single question. None of his two-legged friends even came close.

Diablo raced back and forth between Vega and the front door, where Joy was standing, cocooned in an old plaid quilt. She gave her father a sleepy smile. She looked ten with that thing wrapped around her. Vega had to remind himself that she was going on nineteen, halfway through her freshman year of college.

Vega kissed Joy on the cheek. "Sorry to wake you."

"You're later than I expected." She stifled a yawn. "Must have been a good gig."

"It was." He'd have to tell her the other stuff. But not out here. Not yet. It had killed him to have to text those details to Adele. "Let me get my guitars and gear inside, okay?"

The house was one big open room downstairs anchored by a fieldstone fireplace. Upstairs under the eaves were two small bedrooms and a bathroom. Vega had made up the spare bedroom for Joy. He'd put clean sheets on the bed and everything. But he could see as he dumped his gear inside that she'd been sleeping on the lumpy corduroy couch by the fireplace. A science textbook lay on the rug next to the couch. Every light was on.

"Too cold upstairs?" he asked as he closed the door.

"A little," said Joy. "I don't like being up there by myself when you're not home. And then I got the news. After that, I couldn't sleep. I couldn't even study." She pulled the quilt more tightly around her.

"Come here, *chispita*." Vega's childhood nickname for her. "Little spark," in Spanish. Joy sank into his embrace. He held her tight. "You heard, I guess."

"Mom called. And then after that, I got a bunch of texts from friends. I can't believe she's dead." Joy's voice turned ragged. "Someone at La Casa murdered her, didn't they?"

"Nobody knows that for sure yet," said Vega. Joy shivered beneath his touch. He rubbed his hands down the sides of the quilt. He could feel her arms beneath, small and fragile as hummingbird wings. "How about if I build a fire?"

"Okay."

Vega grabbed some logs and kindling from his woodpile in back and carried them into the house. Diablo trotted back and forth with him, nearly tripping Vega a couple of times, until they were both trailing wood chips, mud, and leaves into the house. He opened the glass doors of the fireplace and tented pieces of dried kindling over a nest of wood chips and crumpled newspaper. Within minutes, he had a crackling blaze going. It warmed the whole room.

Joy made herbal tea for both of them. Vega thought of it as barely-flavored water, but he happily accepted a mug, if only because he could drink it sitting next to his daughter.

"Thanks for taking care of Diablo tonight." He stared at the mug. And then he remembered. He walked over to his backpack.

"Here." He placed Max Zimmerman's gift in Joy's hands. She read the words.

"'I Love You A Latke'? Where did you get this kitsch?"

"Adele's next-door neighbor. He's this old Jewish guy. I shoveled his walk. He gave me the mug."

"Strange payment."

"It wasn't a payment, Joy. I did it to be neighborly. For Adele's sake. Mr. Zimmerman's proud. He doesn't like people doing things for him. He wanted to give me something to say thanks. He found out you were Jewish, so he thought you might like it."

She put the mug down on the table. "It's sort of . . . hokey. Nobody makes a big deal out of being Jewish these days."

"He's in his eighties. From somewhere in Europe. I think back then, it was a very big deal."

Joy stared into the fire. Vega watched the flames dance in her big, dark eyes.

"Not the time for hokey, I guess," he said. "Did you know Catherine well? I gather she was only a year behind you in school."

"Mom and Alan are good friends with the Archers."

Maybe too good, thought Vega. But he hoped to keep Joy ignorant of that for as long as possible. "How about Catherine? I've never heard you mention her."

"She was nice."

"*Nice?* That's all you can say?"

"We didn't travel in the same circles."

"But you must know stuff about her. Who her friends were. What she liked to do on weekends. If she had a boyfriend."

Joy cradled her mug and stared at the steam rising from it. "I'm sure her parents have already answered those questions."

"I'm sure they have," said Vega. "But unless John and Robin Archer have been tracking Catherine by surveillance camera since she reached puberty, I'm betting that half or more of their responses were wishful thinking divorced from reality."

Joy's lips curled in a small, sad smile. Vega had only to think of his own complicated relationship with his daughter—close as it was—to realize the limited influence and even more limited awareness most parents have about their teenager's actions.

"What do you want me to say, Dad? Catherine's dead. I don't want to disparage her memory. Or hurt her parents."

"But if you know something that can help the police figure out what happened—"

"Everyone *knows* what happened," said Joy. "That

creep, Benitez, raped and killed her. His picture's all over the news."

"It's too early to say for sure what happened—"

"Oh, come off it, Dad!" Joy's dark, doe-shaped eyes flashed with anger. She ran a hand through her tangle of long black hair. "I know you and Adele are an item and all. But I hope they close that place down. I hope all those people go away! They're a menace."

Vega reared back. He couldn't believe the words coming out of his own daughter's mouth. *"Joy—your high-school boyfriend was an undocumented Mexican. His whole family was undocumented."*

"They were different." She threw up her hands. "Or maybe I was just naive. You always said you didn't like the idea of anyone breaking the law."

"I don't," said Vega. "It goes against my grain as a police officer. But that said, one person's actions shouldn't define an entire group of people. And besides, nobody knows what happened to Catherine yet. It's going to take time to sort that out."

"You really believe this immigrant had nothing to do with her rape and murder?"

No. No more than Vega believed that Joy's mother and John Archer were doing anything legit together at the Magnolia Inn Friday night. But he kept that thought to himself.

"If you know something about Catherine, please tell me," said Vega. "I won't take it back to Mom, if that's what you're concerned about."

Joy stroked Diablo, who had muscled himself between them and was claiming more of the couch with each passing minute. The dog was a total space hog.

Vega scratched his belly and waited. He'd learned as a cop not to fill in the silences. It took a minute or so, but Joy finally answered.

"The Archers . . . like to keep up appearances. Perfect bodies. Perfect clothes. The right schools. Todd graduated Yale and then went to Kellogg for his MBA."

Vega had no idea what university Kellogg was attached to. All he could picture was Tony the Tiger dancing across a box of sugar-frosted flakes—which said more about Vega's college experiences than it did about Todd's.

"You walk into their house and nothing is ever out of place," Joy added. "It's like a museum."

"Was Catherine like that?"

"She was when we were younger. It used to infuriate me when I'd go over there and she wouldn't let me sit on her bed because she didn't want me to wrinkle the bedspread. Everything had to be perfect."

"She was spoiled, in other words."

Joy got a stricken look to her face. "I can't believe I'm saying these things."

"You're just giving me an idea what she was like."

"But that's just it," said Joy. "She wasn't like that. Not really. That was how she was raised. But then later in high school, she became friends with some girls in my grade who were . . ." Joy's voice trailed off.

"Who were what?"

"Sort of the last girls you'd expect a girl like Catherine to become friends with."

"Druggies? Delinquents?"

"No," said Joy. "Smart girls. But not popular or wealthy. Definitely not connected. I saw her hang mostly with Lydia Mendez and Zoe Beck. Lydia's parents were undocumented from Ecuador, and Zoe's mom is single and works at the Safeway supermarket in town."

"Where are these girls now?"

"Lydia got a scholarship to a college way upstate. Zoe goes to Valley, like me. She works a bunch of jobs to stay there. One of them's this great internship in environmental science, so I'm a little jealous."

"Were both girls still friends with Catherine?"

"I don't know about Lydia, but I'm sure Zoe was still friends with her. That girl hung on Catherine like glue. Not that you'd know it from the Archers. I'm sure neither Lydia nor Zoe ever set foot in their house."

"The Archers didn't like them?"

"The Archers didn't *know* them," said Joy. "They didn't *want* to know them. Lydia's mom cleans houses and her dad mows lawns. Zoe dyes her hair purple and wears a ring through her nose. Catherine's mom was very much into her being with the right sort of people. They wouldn't have qualified."

Vega wondered what Robin Archer would have made of him. He probably wouldn't have gotten past the front door either. "Did Catherine have a boyfriend?"

"She never mentioned one."

"Perhaps . . . she didn't run that way?"

"Are you asking if she was a lesbian, Dad? You can say the word, you know."

"Well? Was she?"

"No. I don't think so."

Vega sat back on the couch and stared at the fire. "Sounds like Catherine had a soft spot for people who were struggling. She volunteered with the immigrants at La Casa. She was friends with the girls that girls like her normally snub. You think this Benitez could have charmed her in some way? Maybe painted himself as some sort of dashing desperado and won her sympathies?"

"I don't know," said Joy. "From the mug shot I saw on the news, he looked pretty scary. Tattoos all over his arms and neck. Dr. Jeff says gangs are rampant in Central America."

"Who's Dr. Jeff?"

"My environmental-science professor," said Joy. "The one Zoe's interning with. He's spent a lot of time in Guatemala and Honduras."

Vega nudged the textbook on the rug at Joy's feet. *Our Changing Earth.* "Is this his class?"

"His class *and* his book. He wrote it."

Vega picked up the heavy tome. "Let me guess. He makes you buy the latest volume."

"He just wants us to be as up-to-date as possible."

"Riiight," said Vega. "It has nothing to do with book sales." Vega thumbed the pages. He found the professor's picture and CV near the front. Jeffrey Langstrom was a lanky, balding, lifelong academic, with John Lennon glasses, a gray beard, and a ponytail Vega assumed was there to compensate for what was missing on top. The two styles Vega hated most on men were bow ties and ponytails, and this man sported both.

"Says here, he's the founder of POW. What's that?" asked Vega.

"You don't remember the petition drive I was involved with back in November?" asked Joy. "To protect Lake Holly's wetlands?"

"Wetlands. Right." Vega was embarrassed to admit that he couldn't remember a thing about it.

"Protect Our Water was behind it. Dr. Jeff's organization is the only one fighting to preserve our water."

Vega pointed to the snow piling up outside the sliding glass door to the deck. "I don't think we lack for water, Joy."

"It's not about quantity, Dad. It's about *quality.* About trying to stop projects like that golf resort Mike Carp wants to build that will destroy the wetlands that filter Lake Holly's drinking water."

"Mmm." Vega's eyelids drooped. He knew this stuff was important. But it had all the sex appeal of a gypsy moth mating study. He yawned.

"It's late, *chispita.* Let's get you upstairs to bed. I'm here now. There's no reason for you to feel unsafe, okay?"

Vega half coaxed and half carried his daughter upstairs to bed. He tucked her in like she was five again. Then he took a shower and fell into a deep sleep, with Diablo at the foot of his bed and the sound of the lake ice pinging in the distance like a stretched rubber band.

Vega's cell phone rang beside his bed early Sunday morning.

"Jimmy?" It was Adele. "I'm so sorry to wake you."

"No, no. It's okay. I'm awake," he lied. The huskiness of his voice betrayed him.

"Is there any way you could maybe cut short your father-daughter time this morning?" Her voice lacked its normal breathy vibrato. She sounded like she was talking through a straw.

"What's going on?"

"I went through all my phone messages from work this morning." By "morning," Adele must have meant four a.m. It was only seven now. "One of them was from a teenage boy. He said his brother is the man the police are looking for."

"His brother is Rolando Benitez?" That snapped Vega awake. He sat up straight in bed. Even Diablo perked up his ears.

"He called to ask if I could arrange his brother's surrender. I called him right back and left my cell number, but so far, he hasn't responded."

"Did you alert the Lake Holly PD?" asked Vega.

"He said his brother wants to surrender to me, and me alone. No police officers."

"Yeah, and I want to win the lottery and retire to Florida—"

"This might be the only way to bring him in peacefully."

"Using you as bait? No goddamn way, Adele. Either you call Lake Holly right now or I do."

"All right. I'll call," said Adele. "But I want to be involved. I owe it to the Hispanic community to try to affect a peaceful surrender."

"Then set up a meeting," said Vega. "We can talk to the PD together and stress your concerns. I'll be your eyes and ears if it makes you happy. But there's no way you're stepping within twenty feet of a guy like Benitez."

"I'm not going to trick this kid into giving his brother up to the police."

"This *kid* could be an accomplice, for all you know," Vega reminded her.

"He sounded like a scared adolescent to me," said Adele.

"Yeah? Well, so was Catherine Archer."

Chapter 10

The brother called back. But the news wasn't good. Rolando Benitez would only surrender if he could do it to Adele alone. At La Casa.

"Yeah, right?" Greco snorted. He played with the cellophane from a half-eaten stick of licorice and shared a look with the other cops gathered around Adele's dining table: Vega, Steve Jankowski, and Omar Sanchez. Vega jiggled his legs. Jankowski rolled his pencil across his notebook. Sanchez doodled. Adele wasn't used to having four large, armed, hyperactive men in her dining room. She felt like she was corralling a herd of wild bulls. The place was too small and orderly to contain them. That's why she sent Sophia to play in her room.

"Benitez wouldn't make it past the gauntlet of protesters," Greco added. "They'll break him open faster than a piñata in a room full of baseball bats."

"Maybe he's counting on the cameras," said Adele. Every major station in the country was broadcasting the story—and La Casa was front and center in it.

"Yeah, he's counting on the cameras, all right," said Greco. "But are you? Are you prepared to have *your* face in the middle of all this?"

Greco had a point.

"Either way, she's not part of this," said Vega.

It irked Adele that Vega was answering for her. She knew he was anxious for her safety. But she had other concerns to think about as well. Like her reputation. She nudged his thigh and shot him an annoyed look. He ignored her.

"How about Our Lady of Sorrows?" Vega suggested to the table, almost like she wasn't there. "A priest is a good intermediary."

"Benitez refused," said Adele. "He said there would be too many fellow Guatemalans there on a Sunday. It would be too embarrassing."

"Then arrange the surrender in the priest's office."

"He said no." Adele found herself gritting her teeth. Vega was supposed to be here to support her wishes, not convert them to his own. "And besides, a church is filled with old people and children on a Sunday. Innocent lives could be placed at risk."

"Your life is innocent too," Vega countered.

"My life is my own," said Adele. "And I would appreciate it if you stopped treating me like a child. I'm capable of making my own decisions."

"Not this time, you're not—"

"Jesus H. Christ!" Greco threw his hands in the air. "You two wanna fight? There's a boxing ring down at the Boys and Girls Club. You can go at it when we're through. In the meantime, we've got a murder suspect to bring in. Do you mind?"

Adele and Vega both hunkered down in their seats.

Jankowski leaned across the table and focused on Adele.

"I think we can all agree that surrendering at La Casa is out," he said. "So where does that leave us?"

"Wil said his brother wanted someplace private. Someplace I knew well and the police didn't." Adele's palms turned sweaty when she thought about what she'd agreed to. "I suggested the preschool."

"The . . . preschool?" asked Sanchez. "*La Casa's* preschool?" His broad shoulders compressed as he absorbed the news. Like he was flinching from a blow.

"Yes," said Adele. "At two o'clock."

The room turned so quiet, Adele could hear the collective breathing of the men. Vega was the one to break the silence.

"No. No way, Adele."

"Has running La Casa rotted your brain?" asked Greco. "You want a convicted rapist to surrender for a murder at a *preschool*?"

"No, Detective Greco," said Adele. "This is *not* what I want. What I want is for this man to surrender peacefully and away from the spotlight. We explored every other avenue—"

"Adele," Vega interrupted. "Your preschool?"

"It's a Sunday. There are no children there. Benitez was unwilling to turn himself in, any other way." Adele pressed her palms on her dining table and fixed the three Lake Holly police detectives in her gaze. "I want to be crystal clear about this, gentlemen. This is a *peaceful* surrender. No SWAT teams. No cops in body armor with stun grenades." She turned her gaze on Vega. "And I want to be the one who meets Benitez and hands him over—"

"No! Absolutely not!" Vega looked across the table at the other three cops. "Tell her no."

Jankowski winced like he'd been asked to preside over a marital dispute. "He's right, Adele. The whole situation's too unpredictable."

"We can't guarantee your safety," Sanchez added.

"Or even that your boy will show," said Greco. He looked the most wary of all. He was not a great optimist when it came to human nature.

"I think he will," said Adele. "His brother seems sincere."

Jankowski shoved Benitez's old Colorado mug shot and arrest records across the table to her.

"Whatever you think about the kid, he's still the brother of this monster."

The photograph was seven years old. Benitez had filled out since then. But Adele still recognized him. He had tattoos all over his arms and neck. The bridge of his nose had a flattened look. And yet, even then, she couldn't call him menacing-looking. He had big soulful eyes that registered something pained and embarrassed beneath their glaze of fear. It was like he'd woken up from a dream and couldn't place his surroundings.

"I already know what Benitez looks like," said Adele. "I remember him as Darwin from La Casa."

"And this *Darwin,*" Jankowski mocked the fake name. "He didn't give you pause?"

"No," Adele said. "He never caused any trouble that I knew about. So he has a lot of tattoos. So what? A lot of law-abiding Americans have tattoos these days. He had nothing with any gang insignia that I could see. Nothing on his face. Like I said, his brother seems like a good kid. He told me he goes to Valley Community College, same as Jimmy's daughter."

"Wilfredo Martinez has taken about a semester's worth of classes over eighteen months," said Greco. "A Nobel Laureate, he's not."

"Which means you checked him out already," said Adele. "Which means you tracked down where he lives and tried arresting him and Benitez at their place of residence before you even came to my house."

Greco smiled his Cheshire smile. "Could have saved a lot of time and trouble."

"Except they'd already split."

"It was worth a shot," said Jankowski. "We're just doing our jobs, Adele."

"Behind my back. With information I'm providing you."

"If it allows us to take Benitez out—"

"Aha!" Adele pointed a finger at Jankowski. "That's the problem. I'm talking about affecting a peaceful surrender. And the three of you"—she scanned the faces across the table—"even you, Jimmy"—she turned to Vega, who gave her a mock surprised look—"keep talking about 'a takedown' and 'taking him out.' Can't you hear yourselves? You want to turn this into a SWAT operation. I don't want cops in riot gear and rifles swooping down on my preschool!"

"You think that's what *we* want?" asked Jankowski, his features compressing even more than usual into the center of his face beneath that hedgehog hair. "We want things to go the same way you do. We're just less convinced they will."

"If you want Benitez, you'll have to do it my way, gentlemen," said Adele. "I'm handling the surrender.

End of discussion. You can all be outside the preschool. Nearby—"

"No way, Adele," Vega jumped in. "If you're inside that building, *I'm* inside that building. I want eyeballs on you at all times."

"He won't surrender if he sees you," she argued.

"You've got surveillance cameras, don't you?"

"Of course," said Adele. "So the director can keep an eye on teachers and children."

"Any outside? I can't recall."

"One in front and one on the playground in back."

"The monitors are in the director's office upstairs, right?"

"And your point is?" she asked.

"What about this?" Vega asked the cops at the table. "Me and Grec can go in the director's office and keep an eye on the monitors. Jankowski and Sanchez—you guys can sit tight in an unmarked nearby and stay in radio contact with Grec. If all goes well? Adele can call you both in to arrest Benitez, and nobody will even know we were there."

"Better put an unmarked at the corner of the two inter-sections north and south of the school too," said Greco. "That way, we'll get a heads-up if he's coming in."

"Yeah. Good idea," said Vega.

The three Lake Holly cops rose from their chairs. It was like an army unit moving out. The noise. The com-motion. The adrenaline. Adele grabbed Vega's arm and pulled him aside.

"Promise me that you'll do this my way, Jimmy. My whole career and reputation are riding on bringing Benitez in peacefully."

"Your safety comes first—"

"*Promise* me."

"Okay, okay." Vega held up his hands. "If Benitez does what he says he's gonna do, I'll make sure it goes down without a hitch. But just in case"—he stuck a hand in his pocket—"you want my pepper spray?" He usually carried a small one in his pocket.

"No. With my luck, I'll end up spraying myself."

"*Nena . . .*"

"Put it away. Really, Jimmy. I'm not comfortable with it."

"What if you need it?"

"Then you'll get to spend the rest of my life saying, 'I told you so.' That should keep you happy for a long time. Here's hoping it's a long time." Adele tried to turn her words into a joke.

Vega wasn't laughing.

Chapter 11

Greco, Jankowski, and Sanchez cleared out. Adele told Sophia she could come out of her room. The girl looked sullen and frustrated by the morning's activities. Vega felt bad for her. He knew that Adele was going to have to talk her ex into watching the girl again later this afternoon while she handled Benitez's surrender and the dozens and dozens of emails, calls, and texts that were coming into her computer and phone since this started. He knew, too, that Peter wouldn't understand. Adele's connection to La Casa had been one of the undoings of their marriage. Vega decided the best thing he could do right now was to keep the child occupied—and keep out of Adele's way. She didn't seem too happy with him at the moment either.

"You want to go in the backyard?" Vega asked the child. "Build a snowman? It's great packing snow."

Sophia brightened right away. Nine-year-old girls were easy. It was when they got into their teens that everything turned difficult.

The snow in Adele's backyard was heavy and wet—perfect for packing. Vega was dressed for the weather today. He had his lug-soled boots, heavy socks, and waterproof gloves that he hadn't needed last night at the gig. Sophia frowned at his holster.

"Why do you need a gun to build a snowman?" she asked as she zipped herself into bright pink snow pants.

"I just carry it, sometimes." Vega wasn't about to tell Sophia the truth—that with Benitez on the loose, he wanted to be sure he could protect the child and her mother on a moment's notice.

Last night's storm had dumped a good six inches on the ground. The backyard was as smooth as a sheet cake and begging for a child's imagination. Sophia flopped down and made angels. Then she and Vega began rolling the snow into balls. In no time, they had a five-foot-tall snowman. They got a carrot from Adele's refrigerator, two rocks for eyes, and some branches for hands.

"We need a hat," said Sophia. She got a thoughtful look on her face that was a perfect imitation of her mother. Those same dark, intelligent eyes, with just a hint of fire. Vega liked the girl. He knew she liked him too. But he was careful—always careful—not to overstep his boundaries. She had a father. Vega didn't want to get in the way.

"Maybe we can find something in the garage," Vega suggested. Adele's garage was two stories high. It sat on the edge of the property adjacent to Max Zimmerman's. Boxes and gardening tools cluttered the shelves, many of them covered in cobwebs.

"Mommy keeps Halloween decorations somewhere in here," said Sophia. "I think we have a witch's hat."

"You want your snowman to be a witch?" asked Vega.

Sophia put her hands on her hips and frowned. "Who says it has to be a snow*man*? It *could* be a snow-woman. Or even a snow-witch."

Vega laughed. Yep, she was her mother's daughter. "Okay. Sounds good."

The Halloween box was on a shelf above a garage window that overlooked Max Zimmerman's kitchen. Vega pulled the carton down for Sophia. While she pawed through it, Vega noticed a chair next to Zimmerman's dining table.

The chair was turned over on its side.

"I found the hat!" said Sophia. Vega cupped his hands to the dusty window and squinted into Zimmerman's kitchen.

"Jimmy?" asked the child. "What's the matter?"

"Mr. Zimmerman's kitchen chair is overturned. Maybe it's nothing, but I should check it out."

"Can I come with you?"

"No." It was probably nothing, but Vega didn't want to go walking into a situation with a little girl in tow. "How about if you put the hat on our snowman— snow-*woman*," he corrected. "And then ask your mom if she has any hot chocolate? I'll be there in a minute."

Vega escorted Sophia out of the garage, then hopped the fence and walked up to Zimmerman's front door. He rang the doorbell. No answer. He pounded, then put his ear to the wood and listened. He could hear a television blaring from within. Zimmerman's light gray

Cadillac Seville was parked in the driveway. He had to be here. Vega walked the perimeter of the property. There were no footprints in the snow, no tracks in the driveway. He was definitely inside. If he wasn't answering his door, something had to be wrong.

Vega peered in through the glass at the back door. He couldn't see anything past a mudroom. He didn't want to break in and cause a lot of damage if the old man was just snoozing or in the bathroom. He hopped back over the fence and opened Adele's back door. He was covered in snow, so he stamped his feet and called to Adele.

"She's on the phone," groaned Sophia. "She said she'll be off in a minute."

"Do you know if she has a key to Mr. Zimmerman's house?"

"I'll ask." Vega heard Sophia's footsteps racing up the stairs. A few seconds later, Adele was in tow.

"What's wrong?"

"Maybe nothing," said Vega. "But I noticed a chair overturned in Mr. Zimmerman's kitchen. He's not answering his door. If you've got a key, I think I should go inside, check things out."

"Hold on. It's somewhere," said Adele. She came back a few minutes later with a brass-colored key and handed it to him. "Want me to go with you?"

"Nah. I'll just check it out. If anything's wrong, I'll call you."

Vega hopped back over the fence and rang the doorbell again. Still, no answer. He stuck the key in the lock and swung it open. He kept out of the door frame. He didn't want to end up as a statistic—another dark-skinned man who got shot for being in the wrong place, at the wrong time.

"Mr. Zimmerman?" he called. "It's me, Jimmy Vega. Your next-door neighbor's boyfriend. I just want to make sure you're okay, sir."

That's when he heard it. Over some commercial on television for life insurance for seniors. Over the clank and hiss of the steam radiators. A faint, hoarse voice. It was coming from the kitchen. Vega left the front door open in case he had to make a quick exit. He felt for his Glock 19 and wrapped his fingers around the grip.

"Mr. Zimmerman?"

The old man was sprawled on his kitchen floor, his strong bony hands gone white from clutching the chrome legs of the overturned kitchen chair.

"Jimmy? I can't get up."

Vega reholstered his weapon and knelt. Zimmerman clutched Vega's hand. His fingers were ice cold. The old man was terrified. He was shaking all over.

"Did you fall, sir?"

"I went to the kitchen for a glass of water. I tripped and I . . . I can't get up. I think I broke my hip." Zimmerman went to try to right himself.

"Don't move, Mr. Zimmerman," said Vega. He didn't want him to risk further injury. "I'm here now. You're gonna be okay." Vega pulled out his cell phone and punched in 911. "This is Detective James Vega, county police," he told the dispatcher. "I need an ambulance at 320 Pine Road in Lake Holly. I have a man in his eighties who took a fall in his home. He thinks he broke his hip."

Vega stayed on the line, fielding questions from the

dispatcher. Zimmerman had trouble hearing the dispatcher's questions so Vega had to repeat everything.

"She asked when you fell."

"I don't remember."

"Was it light out? Dark?" asked Vega.

"Dark." *So he'd been like this for many hours.* Vega felt terrible that he and three other strapping cops were right next door with Adele this whole time and they had no idea. How long would he have lain here if Vega hadn't gone into that garage for Sophia's witch hat?

Vega used Zimmerman's landline to call Adele and give her an update. She and Sophia ran over with pillows and blankets. Vega used the blanket to cover him. But he rejected the pillow.

"We can't move him," Vega explained. "The EMTs need to stabilize his head first."

Zimmerman was a tough old guy. He didn't complain. He just kept asking Adele to make sure she locked up after him. "I don't want someone thinking they can rob my house while I'm gone!"

Adele cooed her assurances. The ambulance came and took Zimmerman to the hospital. Vega straightened up the kitchen, turned off the television and turned down the heat. Adele and Sophia took a quick walk through the rooms to make sure there wasn't some open window or running faucet that could cause a problem. Zimmerman was a big Yankees fan, it seemed. There was a wood-mounted plaque in the hallway. It was a replica of the *Daily News* cover story when the team won their twenty-seventh World Series. He also seemed to love carousels. There were pictures of them all around the house.

"Jimmy?" Adele called to him. "Can you come down to the basement?"

"Is something wrong?"

"No. Just—come down here."

The door to the basement was off the kitchen. Vega descended—and found himself staring at shelves stacked floor-to-ceiling with canned goods. Some of the cans were so old, they'd begun to rust.

"Whoa. It's like the Lake Holly food pantry down here," said Vega. "What was Zimmerman before he retired? A grocer?"

Adele shook her head. "He used to work the carousel at the county amusement park. I think they let him keep doing that until about five years ago." So that's where the carousel fixation came from. "Before that, I believe he owned a men's clothing store until it went bankrupt."

"It's like he was preparing for the end of the world."

"Maybe he thought he was," said Adele. "I noticed on his bedroom dresser upstairs, he had a gun."

"*A gun?* Max Zimmerman?" asked Vega. "This is a guy who won't confront the Morrison boys and tell them to stop throwing their dog's doo over the fence."

"I know. I'm surprised too," said Adele.

"What kind of gun?"

"I don't know guns, Jimmy. And I certainly wasn't about to get close enough to check!"

"Okay," said Vega. "Stay down here with Sophia. Let me check it out."

"It's none of our business."

"It is if it's not licensed. I'm just gonna pull the registration number and run it through the system. If it comes up clean, fine."

Vega padded up the stairs to the bedrooms. Stale, overheated air mixed with the scent of aftershave and hair creams. Still, it was tidy. There were three small bedrooms under the eaves, all with big, heavy, dark furniture that packed the space like commuters in a train car. It looked to Vega as if nothing upstairs had been moved or altered since the 1970s. One bedroom had clearly been a girl's at some point. The walls were pink and there were frilly curtains with smiley faces on them.

In the largest bedroom—Zimmerman's—Vega saw the gun, lying on top of a dresser covered in a lace doily. It was a Smith & Wesson .357 Magnum, a six-chamber revolver that was the handgun of choice maybe forty years ago. Vega was betting Zimmerman bought the gun when he owned his clothing store, especially if the store was in a high-crime neighborhood. Vega picked up the gun. It was fully loaded and appeared to be well cared for and in good working condition. The only cops he knew who owned these anymore were retired guys. Vega's own Glock 19 was lighter, mostly plastic, and used a magazine that held fifteen rounds—a much more efficient weapon, in his opinion.

Vega opened drawers, scrounging around for a piece of scrap paper to copy the serial number under the grip frame. An old photo caught his eye. It was a sepia-toned photograph of a small, chubby-cheeked preschooler in a double-breasted wool peacoat with brass buttons down the front. The picture looked as if it had been snapped in the 1930s. The coat hung to the boy's knobby knees, which were bare. The child was wearing short pants and black shoes, which Vega suspected was the style at that time. On his carefully combed head of dark hair was a newsboy cap. Vega assumed the boy was Max. It looked a little like him in the eyes. It was probably taken in whatever country he'd immigrated from long ago.

Adele appeared in the bedroom doorway. "What are you looking at?"

"Huh?" Vega shrugged. "Just trying to find a piece of paper to copy the gun's serial number. Don't touch it," Vega cautioned. "It's loaded. And keep Sophia away as well."

"She's downstairs," said Adele. "I've got to take her to Peter's soon so we can get ready for Benitez."

Adele opened some drawers until she found an empty torn envelope. "Here," she said, handing it to Vega. "Write the serial number on this."

Vega put the photograph down and copied the number. Adele stared at the picture.

"You think that was Max as a boy?"

"I guess."

"It's strange," said Adele. "Usually in old people's homes, there are a lot of pictures, especially of children and grandchildren. I can't find any. He has a son, I thought. I've seen him."

"He has a daughter too," said Vega. "Judging by one of the rooms." Vega shrugged. "Maybe he doesn't like pictures. I've got all those albums of my mother's and I never display them. I don't like being reminded of people I loved who died."

"Hmmm." Adele returned the old photograph to the drawer. "Still. When you're old, I would think that memories are all you've got."

Vega thought about all those cans in the basement. What would make a man think he needed that much nonperishable food? "Maybe his memories aren't something he wants to be reminded of."

Chapter 12

Vega tried to calm his nerves as he stared at the video monitors in the preschool director's office. Everything was in place for Benitez's surrender. One unmarked at the intersection south of La Casa's preschool. One at the north. Jankowski and Sanchez in another unmarked behind the plumbing building across the street from the preschool. All of them in radio contact with Greco, who was seated in a chair next to Vega, a radio receiver wrapped around one ear, unwrapping the cellophane from a package of Twizzlers. The noise felt like ice picks on Vega's eardrums. He was sure the other cops could hear it over their radios too.

"Do you have to do that now?" snapped Vega.

"What's it matter?" Greco crushed the wrapper in his pocket. "Adele's the only one downstairs. Besides, the heating system's so loud, nobody's gonna hear us anyway."

"You're making me glad we don't work together anymore."

"And you're making me sorry we ever did. You're jumpier than a meth addict in withdrawal."

"Adele's risking her life here."

Greco took a bite of his Twizzler and chewed. "Her choice, Vega. You didn't twist her arm."

"No, but I set this freakin' scenario in motion." He'd even given Adele a signal if she felt in danger or wanted to abort. All she had to do was tug on her earlobe. Vega would be down that staircase and on those mutts before they knew what hit them.

"If all goes well, she'll thank you for it," said Greco.

"And if it doesn't?"

Greco frowned at the monitors without answering. Adele was pacing the playroom downstairs, neatening stacks of picture books and trying to scrape something off an edge of one of the cubbies. The whole preschool building had seen better days. Adele herself admitted that if the Victorian house hadn't been donated to La Casa, they'd never have considered it for purchase. The front porch sagged. The chain-link fence around the playground was buckled and pulling off its supports. Inside, the scuffed wood floors sloped and there were water stains on the upstairs ceilings. Vega had fixed enough things in Adele's Victorian to know what it took to keep a building like this even minimally functioning. The only good thing about it was that it wasn't right near the community center—which meant the press wouldn't have a clue about what was going down here on a Sunday afternoon.

"Requesting radio check," Greco muttered into his receiver. "Alpha check to Bravo, Charlie, and Delta." Cops and military lingo. Vega rolled his eyes. Everyone confirmed. It felt like the rest of them were playing a game that only he and Adele could actually lose at. Vega looked up at a poster in the director's office with a picture of two Hispanic parents reading to their children. He couldn't believe they were about to take down a rapist and murder suspect in a place full of Tickle Me Elmos and Tonka trucks.

Vega and Greco sat in that director's office under the building's eaves with the door closed, the lights off, and the venetian blinds pulled down to the windowsills. Steam hissed from the radiators and turned the room into a sweatbox. Vega and Greco grew hot and ill-tempered waiting for two guys who might never show. It was the same with every stakeout. Hours of boredom and discomfort. Seconds of panic and stress. If you let your attention flag for even an instant, it could be your last. Or your partner's last.

"For chrissakes," Greco growled. "Martinez said he'd be here with Benitez at two. It's almost twenty after. Just once, I'd like to meet a Hispanic who knows how to tell time."

"You're looking at one," said Vega. "I was never late."

"You don't count," said Greco. "You're a cop. Bet you know to the minute how long you've got until you can collect your pension."

He had a point there. "How 'bout Adele?" asked Vega. "She—"

Greco held up a hand for Vega to be silent and leaned into the receiver. "Repeat that, Delta?"

Delta. Officer O'Reilly. Greco turned to Vega.

"O'Reilly just picked up Martinez walking in this direction."

"Only Martinez?"

Greco radioed the question. "Yeah," he grunted. "Only Martinez. Looks like your boy got cold feet."

"Maybe Benitez wanted his brother to make sure it's safe first."

Greco shot Vega a dubious look. He pushed on his earpiece. "O'Reilly says he's carrying a backpack. Can't tell what's inside, but he says he doesn't see anything heavy bouncing around."

A weapon. That's what they were all worried about. If one of the brothers decided to pull out a gun or a knife, even being one floor above and in constant visual contact wouldn't guarantee Adele's safety. But there was no way to get closer without giving their location away.

Vega saw Martinez approaching the building from the outside front video monitor. He was a scrawny teenager in a faded green goose-down coat that looked too big for him. The coat was so old that most of the stuffing had leached from the shoulders so it hung limply on his frame. He had a knit hat over shaggy black hair, which looked in need of a cut. His face was lean and sharp-edged. Vega estimated that he was no more than five foot seven and weighed perhaps 140 pounds. If he wasn't armed, he didn't present much of a physical threat.

If he wasn't armed.

Martinez gave a quick visual sweep of the street before he bounded up the front-porch steps and rang the doorbell. Vega watched Adele on the monitor. She nearly jumped out of her skin when the bell rang.

Adele smoothed her sweater down and finger combed her silky bob of black hair as she walked out of the playroom to the front door. Another monitor showed the view from the hallway. Adele unlocked the front door and Martinez stepped inside. He began speaking as soon as he entered. Vega could hear the general tenor of their voices below. They were calm and measured. He had a feeling Martinez was explaining why his brother wasn't with him. If Benitez wasn't coming at all, Adele could tug her earlobe and they'd abort the mission now.

She didn't.

"Wish we could have wired her for sound," said Vega. "We'd know what the hell was going on."

"She's not a government witness," said Greco. "I don't give a crap if Martinez is reciting his ABCs at the moment. So long as his dirtbag brother shows up."

Vega watched the monitor. Adele was ushering Martinez into the kitchen and snack room in back by the door to the playground. Vega searched the monitors for one that covered that area. *"Coño!"* Vega cursed in Spanish. "Did Martinez tell her Benitez is coming through the back door?"

"Don't know," said Greco. "Guess we'll have to wait and find out. At this point, it doesn't look like he's coming at all." Greco jerked a thumb at the monitor. "Christ. She's making him hot chocolate. What is this? Caillou visits a takedown?"

Vega kept his eyes glued to the kitchen monitor. It was tactically the worst room Adele could have chosen. It emptied into the fenced rear play yard—which made it less accessible to Jankowski, Sanchez, and the other cops on the street. Plus, it was covered in rows of pint-size tables all topped with colorful plastic chairs turned upside down like children doing headstands. Too much clutter. Too difficult to navigate if Vega had to get to her quickly. While he was thinking through the strategic problems, Greco cupped a palm over his earpiece again. He muttered into the receiver, "Delta. Repeat again?"

"What?" asked Vega.

"O'Reilly just got eyeballs on Benitez. He's coming this way."

"That's good."

Greco gave Vega a pained look. "O'Reilly said he's staggering. Probably drunk. Which means he's unstable. There's no telling what he might do."

Chapter 13

Wil Martinez looked even younger than Adele had imagined him. His faded olive-green parka hung from his skinny shoulders like some half-dead molting bird. His big ears stuck out beneath his shaggy black hair like the rest of him was waiting to grow into them. His chin contained only the barest hint of stubble and hope.

"Please forgive me, señora, for putting you in this position." He lifted his gaze before returning it to his wet, snow-caked sneakers. On the phone, Adele had heard a trace of Spanish accent. In person, he sounded totally American.

She opened the door wider and blinked at the street. "Where's your brother?"

"I don't know. I swear. I waited for him where he was supposed to show up. But he didn't come. I didn't want to keep you waiting any longer. He knows where to meet us, so I'm hopeful . . ." Wil's voice trailed off.

Adele had a sense that he'd spent a good deal of his life being hopeful when it came to his brother.

"Come in. Warm up." Adele opened the door wider. "Can you call him?"

"I tried. He's not picking up his phone."

Adele closed the door behind them and locked it. She didn't want the brother running in here unannounced. "Wilfredo? Can I call you 'Wilfredo'?"

"Wil, if that's okay. Only my mother calls me, 'Wilfredo.'"

"Wil. Sure."

He stamped the snow off his feet and peeled off his thin knit gloves. He shoved them in his pockets. His ears had gone bright red. Adele couldn't tell if that was from the cold or nerves.

"There's a kitchen in back. How about if I make you some tea or hot chocolate?"

He smiled. It drew deep lines in his narrow features. Too deep for such a young boy. Adele had the urge to take him home and stuff him full of hot soup and casseroles.

"Hot chocolate would be nice. Thank you."

She walked him back to the kitchen. She noticed that he kept a respectful distance from her. He was calm and measured, which made her feel less skittish too.

"I'm sorry to take up your Sunday like this," he said. "I wouldn't have called you, except my brother—he's had a very hard life. And a very scary time with police. He doesn't trust them."

"The Lake Holly Police are fair," said Adele. She swallowed back all the times she thought they weren't. "I've spoken to the two detectives who will take him in. One of them is Mexican-American and speaks Spanish fluently. His name is Detective Omar Sanchez."

"I'm sure he's a fair man, if you say he is. But my brother's worst experiences were with the Mexican Police."

"Oh. Sorry."

Wil shrugged. "It was a long time ago. And anyway, it has no bearing here. This man is not from the Mexican Police."

"No."

In the kitchen, Adele put a battered kettle on the stove and took down two mismatched cups from a cabinet, along with two packets of hot-chocolate mix. The tables were too low to sit at, so Wil walked around the room. He studied a wall with finger-painted pictures strung across it. He took out his phone, frowned at the screen, then put it back in his pocket.

"No call from your brother, I take it," said Adele.

"No."

She tore open the packets and poured the powder into the cups. "Have you and your brother always lived together?"

"When I was little. In Guatemala. I came here when I was six. And Rolando . . . didn't."

"You have DACA status, I'm assuming?"

"Yes," said Wil. "I just applied for renewal. I hope this situation doesn't change everything. These days, they look for any excuse to take it away."

Adele wished she could say that wasn't true. DACA had been a godsend for so many young people when it started in 2012. It allowed immigrants who were brought here as children to come out of the shadows. They could finally get driver's licenses, hold legal jobs that didn't exploit them, and stop worrying about being deported. It wasn't a panacea. It accorded no permanent legal status. It still barred them from voting, traveling abroad, getting government financial aid, or holding any job that requires a license.

But it was something. A held breath of promise that, like a slowly leaking balloon, kept losing more air with every passing year. Instead of being the hoped-for pathway to citizenship, it was more like a slippery trail along the side of a cliff that led nowhere. Adele had clients who lost DACA on such technicalities as missing a deadline or getting arrested for a misdemeanor they were later acquitted on. Nothing was guaranteed now in Washington—least of all the fates of young immigrants like Wil.

"At least you're taking college classes. That's good." Adele didn't give voice to the fact that very few of her DACA clients graduated four-year institutions. The burdens of paying all the costs and working full-time to help their undocumented families often stretched a four-year degree into an eight-year commitment. Most couldn't do it. "What would you like to do when you graduate?"

"You'll laugh."

"No, I won't."

The kettle boiled. She poured water into the cups.

"I want to go to medical school."

"Really?"

"It's my dream, ridiculous as it is," said Wil. "The way the law stands now, I'll *always* be an illegal immigrant. I could graduate from a top medical school and I couldn't even get a job as a dental technician because I'd need a license."

"I'm so sorry, Wil. I wish I had answers." Adele put the kettle back on the stove. "If my parents had waited eight more months before they left Ecuador, I'd be in the same boat as you." She took a spoon from a drawer and stirred the mixtures. Then she handed him one of the cups.

"Thank you." He cradled the mug in his hands and allowed the steam to wash over his face. Adele studied him more closely now. The long, bony fingers wrapped around the chipped ceramic. The prominent Adam's apple. That little thrust of barely-stubbled chin that suggested intelligence and fire. And something else. Something that jingled like pocket change—obvious and hidden at the same time. She'd had that same combination herself as a girl.

"So," said Wil. "Your parents were undocumented?"

"Yes," said Adele. "My mother was pregnant with me when they came to this country. They pushed me to study hard. But when I told them I wanted to go to law school, they said that was impossible."

"Did you do it?"

"Harvard Law. Summa cum laude," said Adele. "Editor of the *Harvard Review.* I graduated in the top five percent of my class. For a while, I was a pretty hotshot criminal defense attorney. Gave it up to help others like my parents."

"You had a choice at least."

"I know," said Adele. "And for that, I thank their memories every day." She took a sip of hot chocolate. "The world may change by the time you get to medical school. Do you have any idea what sort of doctor you'd want to be?"

"An oncologist," he said without skipping a beat.

"A cancer specialist? Did you have cancer?"

"My mother does."

"I'm so sorry," said Adele. "Did they catch it early?"

"She found out six months ago. It was already stage four."

Incurable. "Oh, Wil." Adele wasn't sure what to say. "Does she have a good doctor?"

"I hope he's good. We're paying him enough. But I really don't know. He's in Guatemala."

"Your mother doesn't live here?"

"She did. For ten years. An old deportation order caught up with her three years ago. She couldn't out-run it—not without yanking me out of school again. She didn't want to do that. Plus, I think she was tired. The running was getting to her. She went back and then this happened." His voice grew thick. "Me and Lando have been paying her medical bills. If he gets locked up, I'm going to have to drop out of college. I have to help her."

"Oh, dear God." Adele understood for the first time the enormity of what this teenager was up against. She'd grown so relaxed in his company that she'd almost forgotten why they were here. It felt like a punch to the gut to remember. "That's a lot on your shoulders."

Wil kept his eyes on the chipped mug as he spoke. "I can't believe Lando would hurt anyone." Adele sensed Wil was talking to himself, weighing the brother he knew against the man he perhaps didn't. "He drinks too much, sure. But he's not a monster."

The teenager's phone rang in his pocket. He pulled it out and stared at the number. "See?" He lifted the phone. "He's calling now." The boy put his mug on the counter and turned to take the call. He spoke in Spanish into the phone. Adele caught snatches of Wil's end of the conversation: "Wait. You haven't been . . . Are you crazy? No. That's not what we agreed on." And a phrase that sent chills down Adele's spine: "Yes. Of course she's alone."

Adele's breathing kicked up a notch. She felt her fingers growing cold around the mug of hot chocolate even as her underarms turned sweaty. She knew Vega and Greco were watching. She knew that all she had to do was tug on her earlobe and Vega would be by her side in seconds.

But Wil was standing before her, so young and hopeful. So determined to snatch some kind of reprieve out of this terrible situation. She had to give him a chance.

He hung up and turned to her.

"My brother." He said the words like he'd long ago resigned himself to the weight of that burden. "I can't believe him."

"What's wrong?"

"He's drunk." Wil shook his head. "He's not dangerous, I swear. He's just—he can't help himself."

"Where is he?"

"Down the street. I told him to come anyway."

"He . . . still wants to turn himself in?"

"Yes. He trusts you, señora. You came by yourself—just like you promised you would. I told him to walk over here and you'd help him surrender. That's still the plan, isn't it?"

Help a drunken, erratic, physically powerful convicted rapist and murder suspect surrender. Adele felt queasy. She'd conferred with plenty of criminals in her time as an attorney. But most were petty thieves, addicts, or white-collar defendants. And even at that, she'd dealt with them primarily in controlled settings, usually with a barrier between her and them or an armed officer right in the same room.

This was different. She was on her own. And sure, Wil Martinez was a nice kid. But it was already clear he had no control over his brother.

Tug on your earlobe. That's all she had to do. Vega and Greco would run downstairs. Jankowski and Sanchez and the other cops stationed outside could pick Benitez up on the street. *Do a takedown,* as they called it. Pin him to the snowy ground. Frisk him. Cuff his hands behind his back. Yank him to his feet. Shove him into the back of a patrol car and process him at the Lake Holly station house. That's what they'd been itching to do all along. She was just bait. She started to bring her hand up to her ear.

No. She couldn't do that. *I gave my word.* If she went against that, nobody in the Lake Holly Latino community would ever trust her again. She might as well turn her back on La Casa. The people at La Casa would certainly turn their backs on her.

And then there was Wil. Standing before her with that peach fuzz face. Those intelligent eyes offset by big goofy ears that only a mother could love. Even if she could betray Benitez, how could she betray this boy?

She dropped her hand to her side and forced a smile. "That's still the plan."

Chapter 14

"He's staggering toward the preschool, Vega," said Greco. "O'Reilly can flank him from the south end. Novak can flank him from the north. Jankowski and Sanchez are locked and loaded across the street. We should abort the mission. Take him down now. Outside. Where we can neutralize the threat. Then pick up the brother after."

"That's not what Adele agreed to."

"Forget what Adele agreed to!" said Greco. "Your boy's forty-five minutes late and three sheets to the wind. Tap a spigot in him and he'd be a keg."

Vega brushed his knuckles across his chapped lips. It was hot in the room. Sweat poured down his body. His T-shirt felt clammy against his skin. He stared at the kitchen video monitor. Martinez had been talking on his cell phone. Now, he was back to having what looked like hot chocolate or instant soup with Adele. She brought her hand up to her hip, then dropped it.

Talk to me, nena. What do I do? Vega turned to

Greco. "Your guys move on him too soon, you could spook him off. End up with a foot chase through a residential neighborhood."

"Possibly," said Greco. "Then again, that dirtbag walks through those doors, there's no telling what could happen."

"Adele said no takedowns," Vega repeated again. "People in the community find out she set this guy up, they'll say her word's no good."

"I don't give a rat's ass what the *community* thinks."

"But *she* does, Grec. Without Adele, we wouldn't have Benitez right now. We agreed to this arrangement."

"Yeah? Well, your boy pissed that agreement away the moment he decided to show up here at a hundred proof."

"Can O'Reilly see a weapon? Even a backpack that might contain a weapon?"

Greco cursed under his breath. "I'll ask." He radioed the question, then delivered the answer. "O'Reilly says it doesn't appear Benitez is carrying anything. He doesn't have a backpack or obvious weapon."

Vega frowned at the monitor. No earlobe tug. Martinez had to know his brother was drunk. But would he tell Adele? Maybe all he told her was that Benitez was coming.

If Adele knew the brother's condition, would she abort the mission? Should Vega abort it for her?

What do I do, nena? Do I chance your safety? Or your reputation?

Vega took a deep breath. "Maintain position."

"You gotta be kidding me, Vega—"

"I *said,* tell your guys to maintain position."

"This is a Lake Holly PD operation," Greco growled. "You don't get to call the shots."

"So in other words, *your* word's no good either—is that it, Grec? You should have a really fine time with the community after this."

Greco gave Vega the finger. But he muttered into his radio: "Bravo, Charlie, Delta—maintain position."

It felt like an eternity after that, the two men sitting there in the dark, sweating and breathing heavily, waiting for Benitez to arrive. His first heavy boot on the porch steps felt like a burst of cannon fire. Like they were hunched in a trench, waiting for the battle to begin, no sense what the outcome might be.

Vega heard staggered steps across the wood planking, followed by a fist on the door. He hunched over the monitors, watching Adele and Martinez put their mugs down and move from camera to camera, like they were on a film set.

Martinez opened the front door—not Adele. That was good, Vega decided. It kept Adele out of arm's reach of Benitez. That's what Vega wanted right now. He wanted Adele as far from Benitez as possible.

Benitez stumbled into the hallway, trailing clumps of snow on his boots. His dark black hair was tousled and greasy. His eyes were glazed. His face was unshaven. He was much bigger than his kid brother. Broad shoulders. A muscular build, if a little bloated from all the drinking. He was tall for a Guatemalan. Plus, he had a menacing appearance—and that didn't even count the tattoos that crawled up one side of his neck. He wore a puffy parka like his brother, only his was black or dark blue—Vega couldn't be sure from the monitors. It had two big patch pockets in the front that could contain anything. Benitez unzipped his parka, but didn't take it off. He was wearing baggy jeans and a loose sweatshirt beneath—also big enough to conceal a weapon. No backpack, at least.

Keep your distance, nena. Just keep your distance and you'll be all right.

Benitez wrapped his kid brother in a bear hug that nearly knocked the smaller, younger man off his feet. He kissed him. Then he started crying. *Coño!* Vega never trusted drunks in the first place—and he especially didn't trust emotional ones.

"I don't like this," said Greco. "Benitez is bawling like a toddler."

Vega didn't answer. He didn't like it either. He was starting to think Greco had been right about aborting the mission. But he couldn't say that now.

Martinez held his brother's face between his hands in a tender gesture that seemed designed to calm him down. Benitez wiped his eyes. He leaned against the wall. Okay, they were going to stay in the hallway— right at the bottom of the stairs. Closer to Vega and Greco. That was good. Adele took out her cell phone. Vega watched her saying something to Benitez—most likely explaining the call she was going to make to Jankowski and Sanchez and how they would proceed from there. Vega felt a tiny bit of air escape his chest. Relief. He hadn't realized that he'd never fully exhaled since Benitez's boots touched the porch.

Adele put a finger to her phone. Martinez said something to her. She paused.

Make the call, nena. Finish up and get out.

Benitez was bawling again. Martinez was hugging his brother, trying to keep him on his feet. Adele dropped the phone to her side. Martinez said something to her.

"What the hell is she waiting for?" growled Greco. "Benitez to sober up?"

Adele turned to Benitez. Her body was loose and soft, with a forward thrust of concern. Vega knew her well enough to read her, even at this distance. It was not in her nature to believe that people were capable of great evil. Adele wanted to help him. She *believed* she could help him. Vega wondered if at some point Catherine Archer had felt the same way. And look where it had gotten her.

Adele took a step toward the crying man.

"Stay back," Vega murmured. "Don't get close to him."

Greco cursed. "What is this? An intervention? We need that asshole to surrender, not get a slot on the Lifetime channel."

Benitez was waving his hands and gesturing to his brother. Vega could hear him over the hiss and clank of the radiators, sobbing uncontrollably. Vega couldn't make out what he was saying, but the tenor was unmistakable. He was panicking. Martinez started crying too. *Ay puñeta!* This was turning into one of those telenovela Mexican soaps on Univision.

Adele put a hand on Martinez's shoulder. She was just steps from Benitez.

"For chrissakes," hissed Vega. "Stay back. Stay back!"

"Benitez puts a hand on her," said Greco, "there's no telling what he'll do after that."

Vega wiped an arm across his sweaty forehead. The

temperature in the room felt like it had risen twenty degrees.

Make the call, nena, thought Vega. *Goddamnit, please! Just make the call!*

Benitez pushed himself off the wall. He teetered as if he was going to fall. Adele stepped forward reflexively. Benitez sank into her embrace.

"Shit!" Greco sprang from his seat. "He's got her. He's got her!"

Before Vega could say a word, Greco was out the door. He was faster on his feet than Vega would have given him credit for. By the time Vega caught up, Greco was halfway down the stairs, with his hand on his holster.

"Police!" Greco pulled out his gun and aimed it at Benitez. Which meant Vega had to do the same. It was part of the code: *You always had your partner's back. Even if your partner overreacted.*

"On the floor!" shouted Greco. "Hands on your head!"

Benitez froze, tears sliding down his cheeks. But his surprise lasted only a millisecond. Then something more primal took up residence in his eyes. It flashed like lightning, changing the landscape of his features. His jaw tightened. His shoulders tensed. His tattoos bulged along the ropy muscles of his neck. The gentle embrace he'd given Adele cinched up into a chokehold. He spun her around like she was a rag doll. In the second it took to do that, he reached into his left front coat pocket and pulled something out. It gleamed in his hand. A knife. Three inches—enough to do serious damage. He waved it at Greco and Vega on the staircase.

"Vaya por delante y máteme!" ("Go ahead and kill me!")

Greco didn't need to understand Benitez's words. He understood his intentions. He pushed the call button on his radio.

"Code Four. Ten-fourteen." *Suspect with a knife holding someone hostage.* Not the kind of thing a cop wants to blurt in plain English over his radio. "All units respond, ASAP."

Benitez kept his right arm tight around Adele's neck and pointed his left hand with the knife at Greco and Vega. Adele's face drained of color. Her whole body tensed. The brother, Martinez, danced around Benitez, waving his arms.

"Put the knife down, Lando," the teenager pleaded. "Let the nice lady go."

"Drop your weapon now!" Greco echoed in much harsher tones.

Puñeta! Vega cursed to himself. *Why couldn't Greco just shut up?* Everything he did made the situation worse. Vega tried speaking to Benitez in calm, even Spanish. Maybe the familiarity would soothe him.

"Escuche a su hermano," said Vega. ("Listen to your brother.") "He wants what's best for you. So does the señora. She's done nothing to hurt you. Come on, man. You can still walk out of this."

"Sólo quiero morirme!" Benitez choked out between sobs. Then he added in English, so that nobody in the room could fail to understand his intentions: "I . . . just . . . want to die!"

He kept a tight grip on Adele and backed up toward the front door. Tears and snot poured down his face.

Vega felt something hard and cold as a river stone settle in his gut. Benitez knew he wouldn't escape. He didn't care. He'd already stated his mission: *I want to die.* He was going to provoke a police encounter. Suicide by cop. Vega knew the statistics. Police bullets hit their target about a third of the time. Which meant there was a two-out-of-three chance they'd hit something other than Benitez.

Adele.

Vega saw all their mistakes in slow motion. Adele's choice of this preschool. Her insistence on handling the surrender herself. The Lake Holly Police's capitulation. Greco's too-quick response upstairs.

All of it paled beside Vega's errors. He was the one who stopped the cops from grabbing Benitez off the street before he ever got in the door. Adele would have been safe if not for him. He made the call. And now she might pay the ultimate price.

"Please, Lando," Martinez continued to plead. "Don't say such things. Think of *Mami*! How will I tell *Mami*? This will kill her!"

Something registered in Benitez's eyes. For a moment, the booze and squalor seemed to wash out of him. A curtain lifted. The black eyes softened and Vega caught a glimpse of the son and brother Rolando Benitez could be—even if he rarely was anymore. *His mother.* No matter what else this hardened ex-con had done, he could not hurt his mother.

Benitez unclenched his arm from around Adele's neck. He lowered his knife. Adele took a step back and tried to breathe. Benitez started to speak. *"No lo hice . . ."* He slurred. A fragment of a sentence. ("I didn't . . .") Benitez spread his palms with the knife still gripped in his left hand. A big, raw hand with a jagged stitch of lightning tattooed on the back.

He never finished his sentence.

Boots raced up the front steps and onto the porch. Someone kicked open the door. It banged back so hard against the inside wall that the beveled glass cracked in its frame.

"Police! Drop your weapon!" screamed voices on the other side. Panicked voices. As scared of their own adrenaline as they were of whatever was on the other side of the door. Detective Omar Sanchez was the first one through. Like a man who'd rehearsed lines for a play that was no longer in production. But he couldn't know that. None of them could—not him or Jankowski or O'Reilly or Novak.

Benitez turned toward the door, swaying like he was ready to pass out. He stood three paces from the opening, still holding his three-inch knife in his outstretched left hand. Still standing close enough to Adele to grab her. His gait was wobbly enough to suggest he just might. So Omar Sanchez did what any cop in that situation would do. What training and instinct told him to do. He fired. Two shots. At close range. He aimed, as he'd been taught, for the center mass. Benitez's chest.

Pop. Pop. The shots exploded like firecrackers. Detective Omar Sanchez had beaten the one-in-three odds. Both bullets hit their target.

For once, Vega wished they hadn't.

Chapter 15

"**Y**ou son of a bitch!" Adele shouted at Omar Sanchez as he knelt next to Rolando Benitez, shoved his trembling fingers into surgical gloves and administered CPR. "You didn't have to shoot him!"

Sanchez kept his head down, kept his hands on Benitez's chest. His pale blue gloves turned red with each compression. Jankowski knelt on the other side, pretending to check for vital signs, but mostly giving moral support to his partner. Vega was pretty sure both of them knew that Benitez was dead. But as cops, they had to keep up the first aid until the ambulance arrived. Only the hospital could declare him dead.

"C'mon, Adele. Give them space." Vega tried to pull her back. Novak and O'Reilly were on the other side of the room with the sobbing teenager between them. Wil Martinez wasn't walking out of here either. Vega had a feeling the boy didn't know that yet. Neither did Adele. With Benitez gone, the police's only potential witness—maybe even accomplice—to Archer's murder was the brother. No way were the police about to release him.

Adele shrugged out of Vega's grip. "Let go of me! You're siding with them!"

"Adele—" Vega patted the air to make her calm down. "Detective Sanchez had no choice. It was a hostage situation."

"He was letting me go. You saw him!"

"He couldn't know that. Nobody could."

Vega heard the wail of an ambulance siren growing nearer. At least Adele and Martinez wouldn't have to keep looking at Benitez's body.

"This was supposed to be a peaceful surrender!" Adele turned her head to where Benitez was lying. His jacket and sweatshirt were soaked with blood. It was dark and glossy, almost like some exotic nail polish. It wasn't flowing anymore. "He's dead, isn't he?" she asked.

Vega wasn't going to answer that. Not with Martinez within earshot. He pulled her close. "*Nena,* you're alive. That's all that matters."

She wiped her eyes. Her mascara came back black in her hands. "I need to talk to Wil." She started to walk over to him. Vega blocked her path.

"You can't. He's a witness. You're a witness."

"And what are you right now? My jailer?"

"C'mon, Adele. You've got to calm down. There are procedures we have to follow—"

"To hell with your procedures!" Vega had never seen her so angry. "Where are the police taking him?" she demanded.

He gave her a pained look. "You're a lawyer, Adele. You know what has to happen here."

She blinked at Vega, then fell against a wall. The adrenaline and anger seemed to drain from her features. But the despair that replaced it cut right through Vega's marrow. "This is all my fault," she said.

Vega wasn't sure what to say or do. He felt the burden of her guilt. He felt the burden of his own.

Two EMTs hustled through the door with a stretcher. There were more sirens outside. More emergency vehicles. This was a police shooting. Every inch of it would be scrutinized.

Greco walked over to Vega. "Can I see you for a minute?" He grunted to Adele. "Glad you're okay."

"I'm not," she shot back.

"You could be a lot worse."

Adele opened her mouth. Vega squeezed her arm. "*Nena,* take a deep breath. We can talk about this later."

"Walk with me," said Greco. Vega followed him down the hall into the kitchen. Adele's and Martinez's mugs were still on the counter, half filled with hot chocolate gone cold and gritty. Greco pushed open the back door and Vega followed him down the steps into the fenced-off playground. It was late afternoon and the sun's shafts were long and amber across the untrammeled snow. Here and there, the bright plastic equipment showed through—the underside of a red slide, the seat of a blue swing balancing a soft cushion of white.

Greco pulled a red licorice Twizzler out of his coat pocket and chewed. "The DA's gonna clear this shooting, you know. Sanchez did the right thing."

"Benitez was letting her go," said Vega.

Greco held his gaze. "You don't know that."

"Are you asking me, Grec? Or telling me?"

"Just . . ." Greco spread his palms. "Stating the obvious. We could've taken Benitez down on the street. One-two-three. He'd have been sitting on a concrete bunk right now with three squares and an attorney on the public dime."

"Are you saying that's my fault?" asked Vega.

"I'm saying, it ain't Sanchez's."

"Well, maybe it's yours, Grec. Ever consider that? Things were going okay until you jumped the gun."

Greco's eyes got as dark as the barrel of a shotgun. "Look, Vega, don't blame me because you don't have the cojones to stand up to your girlfriend." Greco wrapped up the rest of the Twizzlers in his pocket.

"You know as well as I do," Greco continued, "that as soon as Benitez put his hands on Adele, the game was over. We were playing for real after that. Sanchez did the right thing. *I* did the right thing. The only person who didn't do the right thing is *you.*" Greco pointed a thick-knuckled finger at him. "So if you start getting any ideas that you want to play hero with your girlfriend— say, encouraging her to sue the PD for wrongful death or maybe riling up the community for some bogus police protest—just remember who's really to blame."

"I wouldn't do any of those things," said Vega.

"Good," said Greco. "Didn't think you would. Then this conversation never happened."

A uniformed sergeant took Adele's statement and escorted her home. It took Vega another hour to extricate himself from the scene. He had to give a statement to an investigator from the district attorney's office. He had to file an incident report with his own department.

By the time he drove back to Adele's, she was curled up on the couch, in the dark, physically and emotionally spent.

"They arrested Wil." Her voice came out as a hoarse whisper.

"The police have to hold him until they can sort this all out," said Vega.

"His brother's dead. His deported mother's dying in Guatemala—"

"I'm sorry his mother's dying. But you didn't create those circumstances." Vega bent down and put an arm around her. "Come on, *nena.* Let me help you upstairs into bed. You're exhausted. Sleep for a little while. Please?"

"I need to get food in the house. For Sophia."

Sophia was staying at her father's tonight. Everything could wait until tomorrow. But Vega sensed Adele was desperate to make the house feel like home again. If not for her, at least for her daughter.

"I can do that," Vega offered. "Just sleep for me, okay?"

He got her into bed. Then he drove to the grocery store and ran around the aisles like a madman, shoving foods in his cart he wasn't even sure she'd want. Grapes—*did she let Sophia eat grapes?* Cereals—*how much sugar was too much?* Eggs—*did it matter if they were free-range? Organic? Brown?* He was anxious to do something—anything—to help.

By the time he finished up at the grocery store, he was hungry himself—and too tired to cook. He wasn't far from Pizza City, the tiny joint in the same strip shopping center as Hank's Deli. It was dark by the time he drove there. Streetlights flickered to life, washing out the nighttime sky. Yesterday's snow sat in glazed and gritty heaps at the edges of parking lots and drive-ways.

The pizzeria was at the far end of the shopping cen-ter. Vega pulled his truck into a spot by the hardware store, closed on Sundays, and got out. At the entrance to Hank's, someone had placed a votive candle embla-zoned with an image of the Virgin Mary. It flickered in the cold night air. Rolando Benitez had been dead only a few hours and already people in the community were mourning his death. Not at the preschool. It was crawl-ing with cops and no immigrant wanted to chance an encounter. Hank's Deli—the last place anyone had seen Rolando Benitez—was the next-best best. Vega felt bad for Oscar. He didn't need this constant re-minder of a notorious murder suspect connected to his store.

Vega pulled up his collar against the cold and walked over to the pizzeria. It consisted of a counter, two tables with chairs, and a refrigerated soda case. The staff was Latino. The staff at every pizzeria within twenty miles was Latino.

Vega ordered a pizza with pepperoni and took a seat in one of the chairs to wait. A television was mounted in the corner, turned to the local news. Benitez's shoot-ing topped the hour, along with a recap of Catherine's murder. There were head shots of Mike Carp praising the "swift actions" of the Lake Holly Police in "taking down an armed and dangerous suspect." There were shots of officers walking out of a dilapidated Lake Holly row frame.

The reporter, who barely looked older than Vega's daughter, squinted at the teleprompter. "Police have just confirmed that a key chain containing a photograph of Catherine Archer has been identified among the items removed from the SRO Benitez shared with his brother."

Vega tuned out the kitchen noise and leaned in closer. The key chain was significant. No way would Catherine have given something like that to an immigrant she was tutoring. He had to have taken it from her. Maybe as a trophy.

There was a quick establishing shot of La Casa, followed by a head shot of Catherine's brother, Todd, his voice quaking, as he read a statement from the family, thanking the police for their help in finding his sister's killer. Vega wondered whether the family felt relief that Benitez was dead, or frustration that they would never have the chance to confront him.

On the one hand, they wouldn't have to suffer through a trial and watch this guy smirking or fidgeting a few feet ahead of them in a courtroom, while their daughter and sister lay six feet underground. On the other, Vega had the sensation of having caught the ending of a movie before he'd watched the middle. There were so many unanswered questions—at least for him. How did Benitez convince Catherine to walk into the woods with him? Why didn't the crime scene show more of a struggle? If Catherine's key chain was at Benitez's, why not her phone or wallet?

"Your pizza's ready," said one of the men behind the counter. Vega paid, then headed out to his truck. He placed the pizza on the seat beside him. He looked over at the makeshift shrine next to Oscar's front door. There were two Virgin Mary votive candles now. Someone else had heard the news. Someone else had come to pay respects.

Vega didn't think Benitez sounded like the sort of man anyone should feel too broken up over losing. But poor communities could be funny that way. Sometimes the ones most at the fringes of life commanded the most respect in death. Vega had only to think of his own grandmother's endless treks to wakes and funerals—even for people who were a neighborhood nuisance in life or whom she barely knew. Grief for her was cathartic—less a matter of the individual's loss and more for the suffering that the world unleashed on those least able to bear it.

Vega hopped in the cab of his truck and cranked up the heater. His phone rang. He thought it might be Adele. But it was his boss, Frank Waring.

"Captain?" The only good thing about desk duty was that Vega didn't have to work evenings and weekends, the way he did when he was catching cases. His heart quickened at a hopeful thought. It was a Sunday night. Was Waring putting him back to full duty? Giving him a case?

"I received a call this afternoon from an investigator in the DA's office." Waring's tone was measured. "He told me that you were involved in this police shooting incident today in Lake Holly."

"I wasn't *involved* exactly. I was there. But I had nothing to do with the arrest or shooting." Vega began to sweat. He felt like Captain Waring had tugged at a small thread that had seemed so inconsequential this morning when he and the Lake Holly Police were sitting around Adele's dining-room table. And now, all of a sudden, it was starting to unravel. "I just . . . helped facilitate a meeting."

"A meeting that you were present at."

"But not involved—"

"A meeting that resulted in a hostage standoff and a suspect's fatal shooting."

"I didn't know it would . . ." Vega saw the futility of his explanation. He took a deep breath. "Yes."

"So in other words," said Waring, "you were party to another police department's tactical operations without clearance or authorization."

Waring never raised his voice, never exhibited anything that would qualify as a temper. And yet Vega would have preferred a stream of invectives to the steely assuredness of Waring's accusations. The events today had slipped by in such small increments that Vega hadn't realized the magnitude of his mistakes until Waring put them together. His presence at the meeting with the Lake Holly PD. His decision to involve himself in Benitez's surrender. His concerns over Adele that just bogged him down further—drained him of objectivity and twisted his judgment. He'd done it all because Adele was so vulnerable right now. She needed him the way he'd needed her after that shooting in December. He just wanted to help. To ensure that she was safe. And now, it had all come crashing down on him.

Vega tried to backpedal. "This whole situation went down in a couple of hours, Captain. On a Sunday! I didn't have time to ask for permission. The suspect could have skipped by then."

"That's the Lake Holly PD's concern—not yours, Detective," said Waring. "This wasn't a bank robbery in progress. You are a county police officer—on modified duty, I might add. It never occurred to you to seek clearance?"

Vega stopped himself from arguing. If there was one thing Captain Waring couldn't forgive, it was an officer who couldn't own up to his mistakes. "I apologize, Captain. I should have informed you. Things snowballed quickly. I regret my actions."

"So do I, Detective. I want to see you in my office at oh-nine-hundred tomorrow morning. In full-dress uniform."

"In . . . uniform?" Vega had a uniform, of course. Dark blue pants. Double-breasted jacket with brass buttons down each side. Epaulettes on the shoulders. An eight-point cap with a shiny black brim. He wore it to formal police ceremonies and funerals, then stuffed it back in its garment bag and hung it in the rear of his closet, behind his old rock concert T-shirts and threadbare flannel shirts that Adele said were long overdue for the Goodwill bin. He didn't normally wear his uniform to work. "Am I . . . facing charges?"

"We'll talk about that tomorrow," said Waring. "I'll see you then." He hung up.

Vega stared at the pizza, growing cold on the passenger seat of his truck. Another votive candle had been placed at the entrance to Hank's Deli. Benitez's death at the hands of police had not gone unnoticed in the Latino community. Vega had a sick feeling that for all their good intentions, Adele was going to have to pay for this.

And so, it seemed, was he.

Chapter 16

Adele's phone rang Monday morning while she was fixing Sophia's breakfast and getting her ready for the school bus. It was Dave Lindsey, La Casa's chairman of the board.

"We're meeting at Frank Espinoza's law office at nine," said Lindsey. He sounded testy. He'd been kind when Adele called him about the shooting last night. He was cooler this morning. Maybe the weight of the situation was sinking in. Everywhere Adele went in town, there were reminders of Catherine. At the high school, a posterboard-size enlargement of her varsity tennis team photo was mounted outside. In front of it sat a huge impromptu memorial with candles and flowers and stuffed elephants, apparently her favorite animal. All the lampposts in town were adorned with turquoise ribbons, her favorite color. There were banners strung across Main Street calling the community together for a candlelight vigil this evening in her honor.

But beneath the call to remember Catherine, Adele sensed a seething resentment. She saw it in emails and texts from clients and her Latino friends. The police shooting of Rolando Benitez had been applauded by Anglos as swift retribution for a heinous crime. For Adele's friends and clients, the shooting wasn't so simple. Not that they didn't feel terrible that this girl had been murdered. But for them, there was another part of this tragedy. A man from their community had been tried by public opinion and executed without so much as a hearing. His kid brother, the one who'd turned him in—a teenager with no criminal record—languished in jail. Nobody seemed to be voicing any outrage over that.

"You've heard the news, right?" said Lindsey.

"Which news, Dave? We've had so much lately."

"Carp is holding a press conference this morning to announce some new county law he wants passed to clamp down on immigrants. He's naming it after Catherine."

"He's not wasting a minute, is he? I'll get over to Espinoza's as soon as I can."

Adele hung up the phone and tried to concentrate on getting Sophia ready for school. She packed her lunch and braided her hair. She tried to pay attention to a long story about Sophia's best friends, Emma and Madison, and some argument that put Sophia in the middle. But inside, Adele felt like a swarm of bees was buzzing through her brain. She couldn't concentrate on anything.

Catherine's murder had rippled across the country, spurred on by the relentless press coverage Mike Carp was giving it—and himself. Now that Benitez was dead, Anglos and Latinos alike wanted to hold someone accountable. And that someone seemed to be Adele and La Casa. To the anti-immigrant faction, she and her community center were the careless radicals who'd cavalierly turned an undocumented rapist and ex-con loose on the community. To immigrants and their advocates, she and La Casa were in collusion with the police, offering up Benitez's head and "arranging" his execution to appease a lynch-mob mentality.

She couldn't win.

Adele dropped Sophia off at the elementary school— where more turquoise-colored ribbons fluttered from the flagpole—and then headed over to Frank Espinoza's one-man law office. It was the third firm La Casa had employed in its ten years of operations. Not that this was surprising. Adele basically arm-twisted the firms to do most of La Casa's work pro bono. Their first law firm was big and impressive. White men in Brooks Brothers suits and thousand-dollar watches. They took lots of photos of La Casa for their walls—then dodged the work or palmed it off on their most junior associates. Their second law firm was headed by a man who eventually got disbarred.

Frank Espinoza—Venezuelan-born, Lake Holly-raised—was the best of the lot. A reedy man with collar-length hair and wire-rimmed glasses, he looked more like a sociology professor than an attorney. Adele's best friend, Paola, also a criminal defense attorney, recommended Espinoza for the job after he and Paola worked together on a case to free two immigrants wrongfully accused of setting a fire. Paola had all the resources of her big-bucks law firm in Broad Plains. But it was Espinoza, a one-man operation, who uncovered the witness whose testimony freed the men. He'd been representing La Casa ever since.

Espinoza's office was three boxy rooms on a second-floor walk-up above a beauty salon. At regular intervals, the rotten-egg stench of hair dyes wafted up through the floorboards. On Fridays, when the salon had its mani-cure-pedicure specials, the whole place reeked of nail polish remover. Espinoza's secretary was a cousin named Alecia.

Adele was ten minutes late to the meeting because Sophia couldn't find her homework. Adele ran across the parking lot and raced up the stairs so fast that by the time she was standing in front of Alecia's desk, she was sweating.

"They're waiting for you," said Alecia.

"I figured." Adele opened the door. Espinoza and five others stared back at her—the five people who made up the volunteer board of directors of La Casa. Two women. Three men. All of them white. Adele hadn't planned it that way. She'd sought out people in the com-munity who had the know-how and contacts to bring in resources and talent to build the organization. Her ide-alistic side wanted them to be a blend of ethnic groups. But her practical side understood that money and con-nections were needed to keep the place afloat. So her board consisted of a well-known philanthropist, the head of Lake Holly Hospital's emergency medicine department, a tax partner in a blue-chip accounting firm, the owner of a local car dealership, and Lindsey, the chairman, who owned the largest real-estate firm in the area.

The room went silent as Adele pushed open the door. She felt the way she used to during her freshman year at Harvard, like she was this little brown-skinned Latina walking around with a big "fraud" sign on her head. The memory still haunted her. Flushed her cheeks, dampened her armpits, and twisted her tongue so tight that even saying "good morning" sounded hesitant.

"Sorry I'm late." She took a seat that had been squeezed in at the table. No one but Espinoza looked at her—not even Dave Lindsey. They all looked at their notepads before them.

"We were just going over our options with Frank," said Lindsey. He folded his long, bony fingers until they formed an imaginary wall in front of him. He was a tall, gaunt man, with a massive jaw and long legs he never seemed to know where to stow. Right now, they were taking up most of the room under the table, folded on top of each other like a set of hedge clippers. Although Adele was the founder of La Casa and ran its day-to-day operations, the real power resided in Lindsey and the board. They held the purse strings and could hire and fire at will. Adele was in effect a straw boss—something her ex liked to remind her often.

Espinoza shuffled some papers in front of him. The steam radiator clanked and hissed, turning the room even hotter and stuffier than it already was.

"As everyone in this room already knows," he began, "La Casa is facing its greatest crisis in over a decade of operations. Our entire budget comes from grants, fund-raisers, and donations, which will be severely impacted by the negative publicity and reduction of goodwill that Catherine Archer's murder has created in the community."

"That's why we need to impress upon our donors and the community at large that now more than ever,

Lake Holly needs La Casa," said Adele. "We need a safe harbor, a place where people can come together to air their concerns." Adele pressed her palms to the table. "As soon as possible, we have to get everybody in the same room. Community and business leaders. Clergy. Concerned citizens. Folks at the high school." Adele took a deep breath. She was in her element now. Navigating her way out of a crisis. "I've also put a call in to the Archer family to express our condolences and see if they'll meet with us."

"You contacted the Archers without consulting the board?" asked Lindsey.

"If the family expressed any interest in a meeting, I would, of course, have notified you. Dave, Catherine was one of us. A member of our family of volunteers. We need to let the family know that we're grieving her death too. Just as we're grieving the police decision to open fire on Benitez. There's no reason for this situation to degenerate into an us-versus-them sort of thing. Mike Carp would love that. He's banking that all our funding dries up and we fold. We have to show him that Lake Holly and La Casa are stronger than that."

The only sound in the room was the knocking of the steam radiator. Espinoza and Lindsey exchanged glances.

"Adele," Lindsey shifted his legs like they were pieces of barn siding he couldn't find a way to store. The room—the chairs—everything was too small for him. "It seems, once again, you are taking too many matters into your own hands."

"I'm just trying to be proactive."

"The board and I have some serious problems with your behavior yesterday. You arranged Benitez's surrender on La Casa property without consulting a single member here."

"There wasn't time," said Adele. "The brother called Saturday night, but I didn't discover the message until Sunday morning. He was down to fifteen percent power on his cell phone. What was I supposed to do? Tell him to find a power source and sit tight while I get *permission*?"

"But . . . our preschool?" asked the emergency room doctor, a woman with short iron-gray hair and no-nonsense hands. She was usually Adele's biggest ally. "You let this man surrender in our *preschool*?"

"No children were there," said Adele. "Benitez wasn't willing to surrender anyplace else. The school offered the best opportunity for what I thought would be a peaceful resolution. I wanted La Casa to be part of that."

"No," said Lindsey. "*You* wanted to be part of that. Because you think of yourself as synonymous with La Casa. You take everything personally here, Adele. The good and the bad. But it wasn't your decision to make. And it put this organization in an even more untenable position. Now, not only are we having to justify our existence to the larger community, we're also having to convince the Hispanic community that you didn't cave to the Lake Holly Police and deprive a suspect of his right to due process."

"I was a hostage, Dave!" Adele shot back. She couldn't believe what she was hearing—from her board chairman, no less, a man twice her size who sold real estate behind a desk all day. "Do you think I was on some ego trip? I've had nightmares all night about what happened. I'm a mother, for chrissakes! I did what I did for La Casa. For Catherine's memory. For the people of Lake Holly, both Anglo and Latino. Because I wanted this situation to end peacefully and fairly. Do I think the police overreacted? Yes. Did Benitez need to die? No. But never once was I in collusion with them to be this man's judge and jury. I'm a lawyer. I respect the law too much to circumvent it."

"Well, now it has been," said Lindsey. "And immigrant communities from Fall River, Massachusetts, to Pasco, Washington, are feeling the backlash, from bomb threats to graffiti to picket lines outside their centers. They see Catherine's pretty yearbook photo on the nightly news. They see Benitez's tattooed mug shot right next to it. They can't take their anger out on Benitez anymore. His kid brother—who may or may not be involved—is locked up. So guess who they're blaming? Not the Colorado judge who gave him eight months for rape and assault. Not the border patrol that let him slip back into the country. Not the federal laws that prohibit us from asking for proof of identity. They're blaming *us,* Adele. Our little community center and all the people who've peacefully been part of it for years." Lindsey looked around the table. "And even more specifically, they're blaming *you.* Adele Figueroa. The face of La Casa."

"What would you have me do?"

Espinoza rubbed a finger along the top of his lip and looked at Dave Lindsey. Lindsey folded his wall of fingers in front of him and shifted in his too-small chair. He looked at Adele. Everyone else looked away.

"We've got two choices basically," said Lindsey. "The first is to close La Casa permanently—"

"No!" Adele nearly sprang from her seat. "You can't be serious—"

"Between all the negative publicity and the likely drop in donor money, we can't hope to survive."

"We can and we will," said Adele. "This is a temporary setback. A big one, yes. But there must be another option. There *has* to be."

"There is," said Lindsey. He leaned forward. "You can resign from La Casa."

"What?"

"You can accept responsibility for the Benitez shooting on La Casa property and the improper oversight of client background checks."

Adele looked around the room at all the uncomfortable faces. She understood for the first time what she was up against. This had all been talked over and decided before she stepped in the room. She felt like they'd slipped a noose around her neck when she wasn't looking and all that was left to do was pull the lever.

"You all know as well as I do," said Adele, "that we can't do the sorts of background checks that would screen out a man like Benitez. A, because it's illegal. And B, because we don't have the manpower to do something like that."

"Adele," said Espinoza, his sad eyes somehow larger and sadder behind his wire-rimmed glasses, "the board and I have looked at this from every angle. If La Casa is to survive, then someone has to fall on her sword. You are the face of this organization. You've said so many times yourself. You bear ultimate responsibility for its records. Plus, you arranged the surrender of Benitez at the preschool. If La Casa is to survive, you have to let go." Espinoza slid a piece of paper across the table to her. "Dave and I took the liberty of drafting your letter of resignation."

"You're forcing me to sign this *now*?"

"Every second of inaction could hurt us," said Lindsey.

"Could hurt *you,*" Espinoza added. "This morning, someone left a voice mail message at La Casa, threatening to bomb the center."

"And you're only telling me this *now*?"

"We've already turned it over to the police," said Lindsey. "There are no plans to reopen the center until we can be sure it's safe to do so. But the thing is"—he shifted in his seat—"it wasn't just La Casa they talked about hurting. It was you, Adele. The message specifically said that you should watch your back. If you resign, we can make that public. I think it will take some of the heat off you."

"Or make me *more* of a target. Make my fourth grader *more* of a target."

"Dave and I and the board have talked about this," said Espinoza. "We feel you're safer—La Casa's safer—if you resign."

"No one is going to blame you for stepping down," said Lindsey. His voice had an unctuous sweetness to it, like he was closing the sale on a piece of real estate he'd been dying to dump. "This happens all the time in the business community. You'll bounce back at some other nonprofit, where your talents and skills will go far. Or maybe you'll return to the law. I have enormous respect for you as a lawyer. We all do." He looked around the room at the rest of the board. Everyone nodded. They were judge and jury, and Adele's verdict had already been decided.

Adele grabbed a pen and signed the paper. "And

what if this makes me more of a target? Puts me at more risk?"

"The police are aware of the situation," said Lindsey.

Adele tossed off a laugh. "That makes me feel really secure, given the cozy relationship I've always had with the Lake Holly Police."

"Just keep a low profile," said Espinoza.

"Check your locks," said Lindsey. "And maybe think about installing an alarm system."

Chapter 17

Cops never do anything except in pairs. Even the higher-ups. They always take a date. Someone to watch their backs and cover their asses. Someone to remind everyone else that there are two of them and one of you.

So Vega knew there was a good chance Captain Frank Waring wouldn't call him into his office for a reprimand on Monday morning without someone else in tow. Who that person was would tell Vega a lot about how much trouble he was in. If Waring wanted to keep things collegial—maybe punish Vega with some sort of parade duty for a day or two—he'd call in Vega's pal, Detective Teddy Dolan, who would pretend to take notes and then buy Vega a coffee when it was over.

Waring didn't bring Dolan. He brought another captain. And not just any captain. Captain Lorenzo. Head of the county police's special investigations unit—better known as internal affairs.

In police jargon, "special" is never something you want to be.

The rank and file called Lorenzo, "Captain Doom." The name fit. Vega could already feel the guy measuring his coffin.

"Captains." Vega offered a salute. He never did normally, but he sensed he'd better here, especially since his boss was ex-military. Waring's entire office socked you over the head with it. There were flags and eagles and enough reminders that Waring had been a Navy SEAL to make it feel like a museum. Vega didn't know if Lorenzo was ex-military, but he looked the part. Both men had the hollowed, flinty appearance of soldiers too long on point.

"At ease, Vega," said Waring. "Have a seat."

Vega sat stiffly on a cheap padded chair with chrome armrests. It was perfect for Waring's office because it guaranteed you never got too comfortable in his presence.

"Am I facing disciplinary action?" Best to get straight to the point.

"That's what we're here to talk about," said Waring.

Vega felt his breath ball up in his chest. He hadn't done anything illegal or underhanded. He didn't have alcohol or drug issues. He hadn't taken a bribe or covered up a friend's DUI. He hadn't sexually harassed a female cop or tweeted racist stuff across the Internet. There were a thousand ways to get into trouble on this job. He'd dodged them all. All but the most important one, the only one any bureaucracy ever seemed to care about:

He hadn't gone through the chain of command.

"You're an officer on modified duty, Detective,"

said Waring. ("Modified"—another word like "special.") "What on God's green earth made you think you had the authority to engage in the planned takedown of a violent suspect in another department's jurisdiction?"

"It was supposed to be a peaceful surrender."

"Well, it wasn't," said Waring. "At best, you broke about ten department regs by not seeking clearance. At worst—"

"You exposed this department to potential legal action," Lorenzo jumped in. "If Benitez's family or that La Casa community center or God-knows-who-else wants to sue, we're going to end up a party to that lawsuit because of you."

Shit. Vega bounced a look from Lorenzo to Waring. Lorenzo was right. Where was Vega's head in all this? He'd been blind and deaf to everything—everything except Adele. He should have stepped back. Taken a cooler and more measured approach to this whole situation. Don't surgeons get other surgeons to operate on their loves ones?

"I have no defense, Captain, except to say that the situation in Lake Holly involved someone close to me. I lost my objectivity and got more deeply involved than I should have."

"If this department could bring you up on charges, it would, Detective," said Waring. "But if we make an example out of you, then the Lake Holly PD is going to have to go after Detective Greco for allowing you to be there without seeking authorization on his end. We don't want to make another department look bad, especially in a police shooting. We'll never get cooperation from them again."

Vega felt a small kink in his shoulder relax. They were not going to hand him charges.

"On the other hand," Waring continued, "we cannot simply let you go back to the squad as if nothing happened. In order to minimize our legal culpability in the shooting, we need to maintain that you were never authorized to be there and were punished accordingly."

"Punished," Vega repeated, feeling a new dread creep in.

"You're going to write up a statement of what you witnessed during the shooting encounter between Detective Sanchez and Rolando Benitez. I want facts only," said Waring. "No opinions. Nothing that offers even a whiff of blame against the Lake Holly PD. And don't you *dare* allude to the personal nature of why you were there. We're going to file your paperwork and hope this is the end of the matter. I don't want to ever hear about this situation again."

"Yes, sir."

"Now, to address the matter of your new assignment."

Vega was hoping his punishment would entail a few days of lost pay. "Assignment" sounded far more permanent.

Vega began to sweat. Everything he'd done in this job came down to this moment. Eleven years in uniform. Thousands of traffic stops. Accident reconstructions in ninety-degree heat, blinding rain, or two feet of snow. All the civilians who cursed and spit at him, took a swing at him, or reminded him that they paid his salary. The ones who wanted his badge number for no other reason than because he'd caught them texting while driving or doing seventy in a school zone. The five years working undercover in narcotics—always worrying about getting shot—if not by the dirtbags he was setting up, then by the cops who might not realize they were on the same side. It all came down to this.

"Our new county executive has requested that this department supply an officer to drive a couple of police consultants around for a project they're working on," said Waring. "Normally, we'd pull a rookie off patrol for this. But we don't have a spare at the moment. We just have you."

"Tag," said Lorenzo. "You're it." Lorenzo smiled. He never smiled. That's how bad things were. Vega hated that rat bastard. He was behind this move. Vega was sure of it.

"You mean," said Vega, "you're transferring me out of the detectives squad? Out of the building? To be a taxi service for a couple of suits?" *Suits who work for Mike Carp. Adele's nemesis.* Not that that would make one iota of difference to the men in this room.

"You're still a county cop," said Lorenzo. "No one took you off the payroll." He sounded disappointed about it.

"Captain." Vega aimed his plea at Waring. "With all due respect, I feel like the department's throwing me off a cliff. I do this, I'll never get back to investigative work. *Ever.*"

There was an uncomfortable silence. That's when Vega understood: As far as the department was concerned, his investigative career was already over. He was damaged goods. A liability to everyone. The moment Vega stepped into that preschool, he'd sealed his fate.

"Look, Vega," said Waring. "The department already had a sit-down about this. It will not be revisited. You've got your orders." Waring and Lorenzo rose. Vega remained seated.

"For how long?"

"For as long as Mike Carp says," Waring answered.

"And then what?"

Lorenzo answered. Vega could see the hint of a smile in Captain Doom's thin slash of lips. "Carp will be in office for at least four years. Let's just say, you'd better bring a change of underwear."

Chapter 18

The offices of the county government were housed in a beige high-rise in Broad Plains, a nexus of highways that tried hard to look like a city. Shopping malls and office buildings were flopped down with no particular aesthetic. Big-box stores sat next to pocket parks with statues of historical figures no one knew.

Captain Waring had issued Vega one of the county's marked police cars for his new assignment. A six-year-old Ford Crown Victoria. The floor mats were cracked and faded. The interior smelled like Vega had sprayed Febreze on Diablo. The department's mechanic warned Vega that the car had a tendency to overheat in park with the AC on, but not to worry—he had six months before that became a problem.

Six months! Vega couldn't imagine himself lasting six weeks. His police dress uniform felt scratchy and hot. He'd gotten it fitted when he first made detective seven years ago. He'd broadened since then—partly from age and partly because of all the weights he'd been lifting. The shirt collar was too tight. The seams of the jacket constricted his arm movements. He'd noticed these things before, but he didn't wear the uniform often enough for it to matter. And now, unfortunately, it did.

He parked the Crown Vic in the building's underground garage and found a set of concrete stairs that took him to the lobby. A bronze-cast eagle stared down at him over the elevator's doors. The county seal— which looked like Lady Justice smelling her armpits— was embossed on a plaque next to the desk of a bored security guard. Everything felt tired and functional and taxpayer-funded.

Mike Carp's office was on the twelfth floor, at the end of a narrow hallway full of doors with the names of district legislators on nameplates that could easily be removed for the next occupant. The fluorescent lights did little to hide the worn beige carpeting or the stuffy, slightly dank smell. Vega suspected the legislators didn't spend all that much time here anyway. Only their flunkies and assistants did. And now, he was one of them.

Vega pushed open a door that read: OFFICE OF MICHAEL C. CARP, COUNTY EXECUTIVE. Inside, half-a-dozen cameramen and reporters were packing up cables and video cams. Phones were ringing. People were talking. A secretary with big blond hair looked up in the center of the chaos.

"Can I help you?"

"Detective Jimmy Vega." Vega touched the brim of his police cap. "Mr. Carp requested an officer from the county, I believe?"

"He did?" She gave him a blank look. "He just finished a press conference."

Vega didn't have to ask what it was about. Catherine's murder and the Benitez shooting topped the news when he woke up. More distressing, it had unleashed an anti-immigrant backlash all over the country, with protests and fistfights at community centers and hiring sites. One had been firebombed. Several had received death threats. And Mike Carp was likely eating up every minute of it. Before this, he'd had his eye on the governor's seat. Vega wondered if this new round of press had made him think about reaching even higher.

The secretary glanced at her phone. "He's not on a call at the moment. Why don't you just go in?"

"Thanks." Vega knocked on the hollow-core door.

"Yeah?"

Vega opened the door and stood at the threshold. Mike Carp was seated at his desk, a set of gold-rimmed spectacles perched on his nose as he read over some papers. His name perfectly suited his looks. He was a doughy, pasty-faced man in his midfifties, with thick silver hair that glistened like fish scales, blue eyes that bulged slightly from his eye sockets, and small, pale lips. His portrait would have fit in nicely in one of those decrepit European castles. Anyplace with too much interbreeding and too little vitamin D.

Carp flicked his eyes down Vega's uniform. "We get a bomb threat or something?"

"No, sir. You requested the county police send you an officer to drive some consultants."

Carp leaned his knuckles on his desk and rose. His suit jacket was off. His neck sagged over the collar of his shirt. Vega wasn't the only one with collar problems, it seemed.

"I ask for a rookie and they send me you? You're no rookie."

"No, sir. My name is Jimmy Vega. I'm a detective with the county police."

"You're a detective? What's with the uniform?"

"My bosses asked me to wear it."

"Huh." Carp walked around to the front of his desk and perched himself on the edge. He moved like a man who expected things to get out of his way. "Come in. Close the door. My press conference is over. I don't want those assholes in the media getting free scoops."

Vega stood before Carp. He felt the man scrutinizing him. Like a slave up for auction. Carp did not extend a hand.

"Have a seat."

Vega sat in one of two tufted leather chairs facing Carp's desk. Carp folded his arms across his chest.

"What did you do?"

"I was a patrol officer for eleven years," said Vega. "And then I spent five in narcotics, mostly undercover, and then—"

"I mean," Carp interrupted, "what did you do to get sent here? You're not driving me. This is peon work, Detective. So what happened? You take a bribe? Pinch some drugs from the evidence locker? Get in a fistfight with your boss?"

"None of those things," said Vega. "I was involved in another police department's operations without authorization."

"Illegal operations?"

"No, sir. Perfectly legal. I just failed to get clearance through the chain of command."

"Sounds like petty shit to me," said Carp. "You shoot anyone?"

"Negative," said Vega. "But in the interests of full disclosure, I was involved in a separate incident in December that was a line-of-duty shooting. It was ruled justifiable."

"Aha!" Carp pointed a finger at Vega. "I thought I recognized you. You're here because you're damaged goods. Worth less to them than a rookie."

Vega said nothing. He hated to admit Carp was probably right.

"Hey"—Carp shrugged—"it's no skin off my back. So long as you don't go cuckoo on me, you'll do just fine." He checked his watch. "I have my own driver, but he's on another errand this morning. You can drive me over to the Valley Community College campus, meet up with my consultants there. I'm scheduled to inaugurate Valley's new turf field in about an hour."

"I have a Crown Victoria in the lot downstairs, sir."

"I'm not riding in that piece of shit. I've got a Lincoln Navigator downstairs." Carp opened a drawer and threw Vega the keys. "You'll drive that."

"Yes, sir."

The shiny black Navigator was equipped with police lights, radios, and an onboard computer console. It had all the bells and whistles of a patrol car, but without all the odd smells and broken parts no one ever bothered to fix. Vega opened the door for Carp. He slid in back.

"You know the Valley campus, John?"

"Jimmy, sir. And yes, I do." Vega didn't bother to tell Carp that his daughter went there. This man couldn't remember Vega's name. Vega doubted he'd care about his family.

"When we get there, I'll introduce you to Doug Prescott and Hugh Vanderlinden. You'll be driving them."

"Yes, sir."

In the car, Carp looked over some paperwork and handled several calls, talking in bursts of shorthand about quorums and motions and bill sponsorship. At one point, he caught Vega's eye in the visor mirror.

"I'm curious, Jim—"

"Jimmy," Vega corrected.

"What's your, um . . . ethnic background?"

"I'm Puerto Rican, sir."

"You immigrated? Or were you born here?"

"I was born in the Bronx." Vega decided not to point out that everyone born in Puerto Rico was an American citizen and therefore didn't *immigrate* when they came to the mainland. Still, the cultures and languages were different enough that both his parents *felt* like immigrants.

"You speak Spanish?"

"Yes, sir."

"Fluently?"

"I would say so," said Vega. "It was the only language spoken in my home as a child."

"So, as a Spanish-speaking Latino, what do you think of that situation up in Lake Holly?"

Vega felt like he was treading on a minefield. "You mean, the girl who was murdered?"

"Yes. And that illegal who raped and killed her."

"I . . ." *I am the boyfriend of a woman whose life's work you despise.* Vega could see no benefit in laying all his cards on the table here. It wouldn't get him out of this assignment. And besides, he wasn't going to be working directly for Carp anyway. He was going to be working for his associates. So he settled on the part of the tragedy he could speak truthfully about. "I feel terrible for the girl's family. They must be devastated, as any family would be. It doesn't seem fair that one man's actions could do so much damage to so many."

"Precisely! My point precisely!" Carp slapped the papers on his lap for emphasis. "That's the problem with all these illegals. You open the door. You let them in. We inspect our fruit from abroad so we don't bring pests and diseases into our country. Why aren't we as careful with people?"

"I'm not sure I'd equate people with pests—"

"Call them whatever you like," said Carp. "But as a cop, surely you've had to deal with illegals who give you fake names and fake IDs. You have no idea if you're talking to a garden-variety border hopper or a serial killer. You ticket them for driving without a license, and the next day, they're driving again. You arrest them for beating up their girlfriend and nobody puts an immigration detainer on them—or the locals ignore the detainer so they're back on the streets. And even when they commit a serious offense and get deported, they come right back. Tell me as a cop that that doesn't frustrate you."

"It does," Vega admitted. "But I try not to lump every situation under the same umbrella."

"But it *is* under the same umbrella. That's what people don't want to see," said Carp. "A guy like me comes along and speaks the truth? Everybody wants to shoot the messenger. Or stick their fingers in their ears and sing 'Kumbaya.' Doesn't change the fact that it's still the truth. Am I right?"

"I guess it depends on where you're standing."

Carp laughed like Vega had told a good joke. "Trust me, Jim. The only standing that counts is at the ballot box."

Vega didn't try to argue with him. He kept quiet and pulled into the long drive that wound around the Valley Community College campus. Even in good weather, the campus felt like a cross between a truck depot and a small commuter airport. The buildings were low, gray, and block-shaped, with sharp angles and wide-open plazas that funneled and intensified every gust of wind. The trees were lean and planted in rows like sentries. In the dead of winter, the landscape took on a sinister edge. Snow settled along the flat roofs, giving the place the look and feel of a Soviet bunker.

The cold normally drove students inside. But not today. On the main quad, above posters advertising an upcoming concert by the hip-hop group 5'N'10, Vega saw a banner that read: CARP IS CRAP—JUST REARRANGE THE LETTERS. Probably some smart-ass English majors put that up.

By the time Vega pulled alongside the new turf field, a crowd of students had gathered. Many were waving signs that attested to a wide variety of issues they had with the new county executive. There was his immigration stance: NO HUMAN IS ILLEGAL! His building of that golf course: CRYSTAL SPRINGS=POISON WATER. And, this being a college, his refusal to support a freeze on tuition: FUND OUR FUTURE, NOT YOUR PAYCHECK.

Vega had a sense the new field dedication was going to be anything but a straightforward affair.

"Pull around by the gym," Carp instructed Vega.

The county had obviously budgeted some bucks for the turf, but they could have done with an update for the building. Vega saw that as soon as he walked Carp inside. The whole place smelled of damp wood and sweaty gym socks. Water stains bloomed on the ceiling and chunks of plaster were missing from several walls. A group of white men in suits, wool overcoats, and fencepost smiles stood huddled and waiting for Carp by a large trophy case. There were handshakes all around. But not for Vega. He was hired security. Blue-collar muscle and nothing more.

Vega eyed the trophies in the case. This being a very small college, they were all from third-rate leagues, many of them at least a decade old. Down the hall, Vega heard the clink of barbells being set down in the weight room and the thump of basketballs on the court. The athletes either didn't know or didn't care that their newly elected county executive was dedicating their field.

Outside, however, was another story. Through the glass windows on the front doors, Vega noticed that the crowd of students was growing.

"So. You're our new driver."

Vega turned to see two men standing before him. One was tall and spindly, with a long nose like an anteater. The other had an ex-wrestler's build and breathed through his mouth. Both wore aviator sunglasses, even though they were indoors. Vega introduced himself and extended a hand.

"Hugh Vanderlinden," the anteater replied. He shook

Vega's hand like he was doing him a favor. Vanderlinden gestured to the mouth breather. "This is Doug Prescott." Prescott didn't even bother with a handshake. He just grunted.

A photographer arrived. A young Asian man. Student or staff, Vega couldn't say. He ushered the men outside and lined them up in front of the new turf field. It was cold enough for Carp to have just done a photo op and left. But a lectern and microphone had been set up on a small riser, and sure enough, Carp moved to it like an addict to meth. A chorus of boos washed over the field. Carp seemed unfazed. Vega stood close by on the riser scanning the crowd. Whatever Carp's politics, he was still an elected official and Vega had a duty to protect him.

"This field is being dedicated today with taxpayer money," Carp began. "Money from voters. The very same people who elected me to this office."

"I didn't elect you!" one student shouted. Laughter rippled through the crowd. Carp didn't seem to notice he was being heckled. Or maybe he didn't care.

"This morning, I sent a bill to the county legislature called 'Catherine's Law,'" Carp continued. "A girl only a year younger than many of you was brutally raped and murdered by an illegal."

"Who was gunned down by police!" another student shouted. There were hoots and applause.

"The police were doing their job. This *officer*"— Carp gestured to Vega—"will tell you that the police were doing their job."

Ay, puñeta! Vega had spent the last seven weeks trying to live down that civilian shooting and get his life back to normal. And here was Carp, turning him into a poster boy for officers who used lethal force. He could feel all the hateful eyes on him—not for what he'd done. He doubted most of the students in the crowd even knew. Just being a cop was enough these days. People scratched your car. Slashed your tires. Drive-thrus refused you service—or worse, messed with your food. If you fought back in any way, someone always had a video camera. And you were automatically the bad guy. It didn't matter what color your skin was, people saw the uniform and they judged. You were a redneck. You were a racist. You could have delivered five babies in the backseat of your patrol car, saved a toddler from a burning building, and caught the local pedophile lurking near the elementary school. You were still an ignorant bully and a brute.

Vega had heard retired guys on his job who'd served in Vietnam talk about how they used to have to ditch their fatigues as soon as they got Stateside. People thanked soldiers now. Nobody thanked cops.

Vega kept his gaze neutral as he searched the crowd for signs of trouble. Most of the protesters were young. They wore outlandish knit hats and bulky North Face jackets. They hefted backpacks and skateboards and checked their phones so much, Vega wondered how they could possibly pay attention to anything Carp was saying. Here and there, Vega saw older faces as well. Professors, most likely.

And then he saw her. She was wearing a poofy hat with pom-poms on tassels and a tan suede jacket, which was probably on loan from her mother's closet. The hat brought out the kid in her. The jacket, the woman. *Joy.* She had to have seen him. She didn't let on. She was eleven the last time Vega was in uniform. As a small girl, she loved trying on her father's eight-point cap. Back then, it sank halfway down her forehead. Now, Vega sensed, the whole getup embarrassed her. She turned her head and chatted with a girl next to her, like Vega was just one more official on that riser.

"Catherine Archer's death is a wake-up call to every American," said Carp over the feedback on his microphone. "No longer can we allow lawless illegals to make a mockery of our way of life."

Carp went on to explain how his new "Catherine's Law" would provide money for municipalities to fine and jail people for such misdemeanors as unlawful assembly, loitering, littering, public intoxication, and trespassing. It would beef up zoning codes to eliminate illegal rental units, strengthen penalties for minor traffic violations, and empower local police to work with federal immigration authorities to round up undocumented lawbreakers.

Students booed. What did Carp expect? This was not going to be his kind of audience. But even so, Vega thought the crowd was getting worked up over nothing. "Catherine's Law" was a proposal at this point. It would never pass.

The districts with heavy immigrant populations, like Lake Holly, Port Carroll, and Warburton, would consider this new legislation a monumental headache that would only alienate their residents—documented and undocumented—and reduce civilian cooperation with the police.

Rights groups would challenge the proposal's legality, especially if it was only enforced in Hispanic com-

munities. Local landlords—voters, all of them—would
not take kindly to an overzealous application of their
town's occupancy laws.

Even the police unions that backed Carp in the election might balk at having their members take on addi-
tional immigration duties without any commensurate
rise in pay. Which meant that Carp's proposal was
nothing more than political grandstanding. Vega saw
it. Why couldn't the students? Eighteen-year-olds take
everything too seriously, he decided. Especially themselves.

"It's a right-wing conspiracy!" one of the students
shouted. Others cheered in agreement. A chant rose up
from the crowd: "Keep your hate off our campus."
People raised their fists in the air. Things were heating
up fast.

Vega searched the crowd for Joy. He spotted her
walking away. *Good.* He didn't want her in the middle
of this. She was joined by an older man in a battered
felt hat and slouchy canvas coat. A long gray ponytail
snaked down his back. Her professor. *Also good.* He
probably had the common sense to steer them away
from this growing agitation. Every time Carp spoke,
the chanting grew louder and more belligerent.

Vega kept his eyes on his daughter. She leaned into
her professor. "Mr. Ponytail" snaked an arm around
Joy's waist and pulled her close. Uncomfortably close.
Not good. Not good at all.

An orange—soft, ripe, and round—came out of nowhere. Vega saw it a second before it banged against
the side of the lectern. The campus cops hustled in the
direction of where the orange had been thrown. But the

idea had settled in the crowd's head. Soon more things sailed toward the microphone. Soda cans. Crumpled flyers. Paper coffee cups. Plastic water bottles.

Vega stepped in front of Carp and tried to lead him away from the microphone, but Carp shook Vega off. He was clearly a man who liked having the last word.

"The people elected me to bring law and order to this county," Carp shouted. "And that's exactly what I'm going to do!"

Vega's peripheral vision caught something green and heavy whizzing toward him. A beer bottle. Headed straight for Mike Carp's head. Vega jumped in front of the county executive, pushing him down and covering his body with his own. The bottle smashed against the lectern. It sounded like crushed ice in a glass.

Vega helped Carp to his feet as the campus police pushed through the crowd. Students scattered in every direction. No way was the bottle thrower going to give himself up that easy. *Coward.*

"Are you okay, sir?" asked Vega.

"Yeah." Carp brushed himself off. He looked pale and shaky. "Animals. That's what they're educating here."

"I think it was just a few troublemakers," said Vega. Something warm and wet slid down the side of his face. He brought a hand up to wipe it away. It came back bright red.

"I think you need medical attention, Jimmy."

Jimmy. Finally. Vega pressed his uniform sleeve to a spot near his hairline. It didn't hurt that much, but he could feel the gash. Two inches, by his estimate. He was bleeding heavily. The crowd had dispersed. Joy was gone. Vega was glad. She didn't need to see something like this. It would upset her too much. He closed his eyes and replayed that image of the professor snaking a hand around his daughter's waist.

He didn't need to see that either.

Chapter 19

"Get EMS on the scene," Carp barked to campus security. "And the county police. I want a full investigation. I want the animals who committed this assault on a uniformed officer found, charged, and expelled from campus."

Vega sat in a waiting area of the gym just outside the locker room; he had an ice pack and towel pressed to his head. Fortunately, the gash wasn't deep. A couple of stitches done in the emergency room would close it up at the hairline.

"Dad?"

Vega removed the ice pack. He could see Joy's face pale at the streaks of dried blood that marked his face and the sleeve of his uniform jacket. A fat dry-cleaning bill was coming his way. Just what he needed.

"*Chispita!* Why aren't you in class?"

"I got to class and somebody told me that a cop had been hit by a bottle. You were the only one in uniform, besides the campus police." She sat on a bench facing him. "Are you okay? Is there something I can do?"

"It looks worse than it is," Vega assured her. "Head wounds always bleed a lot. I'll be fine." He adjusted his ice pack and held her gaze. "It's you I'm worried about."

"Me?"

"I saw you in the crowd. With Mr. Ponytail."

"That was Dr. Jeff, my environmental-science professor."

"He put his arm around you."

"So?"

"He does that with every coed?"

"Things were getting crazy out there. He was trying to protect me."

"Yeah, he was protecting you all right," said Vega. "That's my job—not his."

She stiffened. "You were a little busy playing muscle for our new Hitler—"

"Joy!" Vega gave her a disapproving look. "Whether you agree with Mike Carp or not, he was elected by a majority of the voters of this county. That doesn't give anyone the right to assault him. Assault *me.*"

"I know that, Dad. I feel terrible for what happened. That's why I cut class to come see you. Hopefully, you'll get a few days off after this, and"—she wrinkled her nose at his uniform—"you can go back to your regular work."

Vega felt an acid drip in the pit of his stomach. He never thought he could be homesick for a job. "I'm afraid this *is* my regular work now—"

"What?"

"I was reassigned." He could see a protest forming on her lips. "This wasn't my choice, okay?"

"Does Adele know?"

Vega shook his head. "I was going to tell her. But then she texted me that La Casa forced her to resign this morning."

"That's terrible. For her, I mean," said Joy. "In some ways, maybe it's for the best."

"I doubt she feels that way," said Vega. "In either case, I didn't want to hit her with my news until I could speak to her in person."

Two EMS technicians appeared by the front doors of the gym. They didn't have to guess who they were here for. Vega's face made it pretty obvious.

"You want me to ride to the emergency room with you?" asked Joy.

"I want you to go to class, *chispita*. I'll be fine. I'll text you later."

Vega expected to get dumped in an ambulance and left to his own devices. But when he arrived at the emergency room for treatment, Mike Carp was there, barking orders for Vega to be seen at once. Vega was ushered into a private room, where both an emergency room doctor and a plastic surgeon were on hand to look at his wound. Nurses and technicians hovered, asking if he was hungry or thirsty and how he was feeling. Everyone called him either "Detective" or "sir."

"Whatever you need, Jimmy," said Carp. "You just say the word. Don't worry about a thing."

"Thank you, sir. I'll be fine."

Outside Vega's room, he heard Carp talking to one of the head doctors in the ER.

"I want the best plastic surgeon you got. The *best,*" said Carp. "This officer's not having some intern do embroidery practice on him. You got that?"

Everyone hopped to Carp's attention. Vega had a sense that even before Mike Carp was county executive, he was used to this kind of treatment. Vega wasn't. He felt embarrassed that Carp talked to the doctors like they worked for him. But he could tell, too, the man's heart was in the right place. He was upset that Vega had gotten injured protecting him. He wanted to set things right.

While Vega was reclined, waiting for the surgeon to stitch him up, Carp walked into his room and closed the door. Vega felt surprisingly naked, even though he was fully clothed.

"You've got guts, Jimmy. I like that."

"Thank you, sir, but I was only doing—"

"I'd like you to be my driver."

"Your . . . driver?" Vega sat up on the examining-room table. "I thought you had—"

"Staff change. My driver will go to Prescott and Vanderlinden. From now on, you're working for me."

Vega stared at Carp, openmouthed.

"Is there a problem, Jimmy? You look like I just asked you to dress in drag and dance the hula."

"Uh, no, sir. It's just . . ." *Not what I want.* On the other hand, what Vega wanted wasn't coming back. Not now. Maybe not ever.

"I guess I wasn't thinking about this whole . . . ," Vega stumbled. "This driving thing . . . being permanent."

"Who says it has to be?"

Captain Waring, thought Vega. *Captain Lorenzo.* Then again, Carp didn't answer to Waring and Lorenzo.

"Let's first see what you can do, shall we?" asked Carp. "Then we can figure out where your talents lie. So . . . do we have a deal?" Was there really a choice here? Vega wondered. Either way, he was working for Mike Carp. Why not work for him directly? The man took care of his people. Vega could see that.

"I would be happy to be your driver."

"Good." Carp checked his cell phone. He looked anxious to leave. "I'm saying a few words at Catherine Archer's vigil in Lake Holly this evening. If you're up to driving me, I would appreciate it. Of course you can take the rest of the day off until then. Go home. Rest up."

"Thank you. I'll do that."

Carp waved a dismissive hand at the uniform. "And come back in a suit, Jimmy. I don't need the uniform. You look like you're about to arrest somebody."

Chapter 20

For the first time in Adele's adult life, she was out of work. She couldn't shake the sense of failure. The fear of the unknown. Could she find a job? Could she support herself? Her daughter? Growing up with undocumented parents, Adele learned that a lost job could spell financial ruin. All the small handholds that were available to poor Americans—food stamps, welfare, housing subsidies—did not exist for them. Homelessness and food scarcity were real possibilities. And okay, it wasn't like that for Adele now. She was American-born. She had savings. An ex-husband who would help with child support. She knew that. Logically, she knew that.

And yet she couldn't shake the panic.

She sat down with her checkbook and savings statement to try to figure out how long she could last without work. She didn't want to take a job far from home. It would be too hard on Sophia. So—a nearby job. But what kind of job? At another nonprofit?

Adele didn't have a master's in social work. Aside from La Casa, she had no background in the field at all. There weren't many high-level positions in non-profits in the county to begin with, and anything lower wouldn't pay enough. The only likely position Adele could take and still support herself and Sophia would be to return to law. She'd kept her attorney registration up-to-date, filing every two years. But that only meant she had the right to practice. It didn't mean she still had the skill set. Criminal law and immigration issues were her areas of expertise, but the rulings were forever changing. Not to mention that it had been years since she'd been in a courtroom.

She could do other sorts of law, of course. She could sit behind a desk all day and review insurance documents and real-estate transactions. *(Shoot me now.)* She could handle divorces. *(Peter was enough, thank you.)* She could take on civil cases, contract breaches. *(Helping rich people get richer.)* With any of those, she would have to start at the bottom and learn the codes and practices all over again.

I have to do whatever I can. For Sophia. No way did Adele want her daughter to feel the insecurity she'd known growing up. She could still remember those nights after her parents were cheated out of their business by a neighbor with legal papers. Her father would make a big show of "getting in shape and losing some weight." What he was really doing was walking three miles a day to his janitor's job to avoid the cost of the bus. Sometimes he would come home after work with a vague scent of rotting food on his clothes and a rattling bag of aluminum cans that he toted like Santa Claus. A hundred cans. Two hundred cans. Only later did Adele understand what pride her father must have had to swallow to paw through people's trash so she and her sister wouldn't go without.

She called Vega to tell him about her resignation. He didn't pick up his phone, so she left him a text message. Then she called her best friend, Paola Rosado. Paola was an attorney for a big firm in Broad Plains. Adele asked if the firm had any freelance legal work—contracts, research—that Paola could send her way.

"I can dig up some things," Paola assured her. "But is that what you want?"

"I want to put food on the table."

"We're not back in our childhoods, okay?" said Paola. "You have savings. A house. Severance. Not to mention a gainfully-employed ex who is regular with child support. You won't starve."

From anyone else, Adele might have bristled at such a statement. But Paola was Adele's longest and best friend. They'd grown up in Port Carroll together, back when the bakery plant was still the prime employer in town and every cupboard and crevice smelled like warm bread. The Latino community was small in Port Carroll back then. And though Paola's undocumented parents were from Colombia, not Ecuador, both Paola and Adele carried the scars of their childhoods like broken bones that never quite healed.

"There's no need to panic about paying your bills," Paola assured her. "I can get you all the freelance you want while you look for something permanent. Just calm down, *chica*. It's going to be okay."

Adele hung up from Paola's pep talk and worked her way through ads for lawyers online, answering anything that was within a thirty-mile radius. The whole idea depressed her. After an hour, she needed a change of scenery so she drove to the supermarket. Max Zimmerman was out of the hospital. She figured she'd drop off some basics for him. She dashed around the aisles to avoid running into people she knew. She exchanged some of the things Vega bought yesterday (she didn't have the heart to tell him) and bought some staples for Zimmerman: milk, bread, eggs, cheese, and bananas. She returned home, put her own food away, and then took the bag of groceries next door.

"They released you so soon?" she asked when she saw him standing in his late wife's pink bathrobe, leaning on a three-pronged cane.

"What? I should stay? Let them make me sicker? They call it 'medical practice' for a reason, you know."

Adele laughed, pleased to learn that his hip was only bruised, not fractured. He could get around on a three-pronged cane, so long as he didn't use the stairs. Fortunately, he had a small den on the first floor. A hospital supply company had installed a bed. There was a bathroom right off the kitchen. But still—he was too old and too frail to live alone.

"You need someone to live with you and take care of you," Adele told him. "I'm sure I could find someone from one of the social service agencies to help you out."

"I'm senior, not senile, Adele. I can take care of myself."

"I know that. But maybe having someone here . . . just for company."

"How do I know she won't rob me blind?"

"Have I ever sent someone to your house who you haven't liked?"

"That's different," he grumbled. "Those were men. Working outside. I'm not comfortable with some young female running around my house. Me, always worrying about covering up."

"I'll find someone older."

"Then she'll be on the phone all day with all her relatives!"

"Mr. Zimmerman—you were just lucky Jimmy happened to notice that overturned chair. You could have been in your house for days like that. You shouldn't live alone. If you won't consider an aide, then how about assisted living? There are some lovely facili—"

"A *home*? Where they tell me what to eat and what to wear? Absolutely not!" He pounded his three-pronged cane on the floor like a judge banging a gavel. Adele smiled because, of course, he was saying this in his dead wife's fluffy pink bathrobe. "I can still take care of myself."

Adele remembered the gun that Zimmerman had upstairs and wondered if he had a different idea about what "taking care of himself" meant.

She put a hand over his and squeezed it. "If you change your mind, you'll let me know, okay?" She turned to leave.

"Adele?"

"Yes?"

"Do you know what a 'mensch' is?"

"No."

"It's Yiddish for a person of integrity and honor. That's what you are."

"Thank you. And don't forget to lock the door."

* * *

Adele let herself out and walked back to her house. A small gray BMW sedan was idling in her driveway. As Adele stepped closer, the driver cut the engine and got out of the vehicle. Adele froze in her tracks.

"Miss Figueroa?"

Todd Archer looked different from the last time Adele had seen him. His broad shoulders were hunched. His blond hair was greasy and uncombed. The sky-blue eyes—so much like Catherine's—looked bloodshot and faded, no longer backlit from within. The anger had left him. But in its place was something spent and weary.

"You called my family? To ask for a meeting?"

"Um. Yes. Of course." Dave Lindsey and the board practically handed Adele her head this morning for contacting the Archers without their permission. What would they make of this? Not to mention that the last time Adele had laid eyes on Todd, he was shouting at her. And now he was standing in her driveway.

"I didn't expect a face-to-face like this. At my house." She scanned the street. There wasn't even a dog walker about.

"I guess I should have called first."

The sun broke through the clouds like a spotlight, somehow stronger for its absence. Archer brought a hand up to his brow to blot out the glare. The first time Adele met him, he seemed like a man, with those broad shoulders and close-cropped reddish beard. But up close like this, he gave off the aura of someone much younger and far more insecure.

"See, the thing is," Archer continued, "my folks don't know I'm here."

"Why didn't you tell them?"

"They wouldn't have wanted me to come. I guess they blame La Casa for what happened."

"I see." Adele was still enough of an attorney to know that the word "blame" preceded the word "lawsuit" every time. Which meant every word she said from this point forward could end up being repeated back to her on a witness stand. It was one thing to have a sit-down with the family in front of La Casa's lawyer. It was another to go freelancing. She chose her words carefully.

"I'm so very sorry about what happened to your sister," said Adele. "Catherine was loved by everyone at La Casa. We are all devastated by her loss. And yes, I called to ask your family to a meeting to talk about the situation. But things have changed on my end, I'm afraid. This morning, I resigned from La Casa. I'm no longer affiliated with the organization."

"For real?" asked Archer. "You quit? Just like that?"

"I was asked to resign. But either way, it puts me in a difficult situation, Mr. Archer—"

"Todd," he offered.

"Adele." She touched her zippered jacket and smiled. "Given the circumstances, I can't comment on anything to do with your sister's murder except to offer my deepest condolences to you and your family."

"Huh." He leaned against his car. A gust of wind fanned the hair on his scalp. His eyes turned teary. From the cold or grief, she couldn't tell.

"I don't want to dump my problems on your doorstep like this," he said. "But I don't know where else to turn. You cared about Catherine. You tried to get her killer to surrender. You're the only person who's been on both sides of this."

"I don't know what I can tell you," said Adele. "The police can probably tell you more."

"The police just seem to be covering their asses at the moment."

Adele laughed. She would have thought that Todd Archer and the cops would be kissing cousins at the moment. He could be objective—which surprised her. She liked him immediately.

The bare branches danced overhead in the stiff breeze, sending clumps of snow raining down on them. Adele felt the flakes, like needles, against her skin. She'd dressed to dash over to Zimmerman's, not to have a long conversation outdoors. Todd's nose and ears looked sunburned, they were so red.

"Would you like to come inside and have a cup of coffee?"

The young man stuffed his hands into the pockets of his leather bomber jacket and stood there, as hesitant as a prom date. "Are you sure?"

"So long as it doesn't go beyond us."

"It won't. I promise."

In the kitchen, Todd settled himself at Adele's Formica-topped table as she busied herself scooping coffee into her machine. It gave her somewhere to focus her attention.

"I owe you an apology," he said. "I had no right to yell at you the other day."

"You are going through a lot," said Adele. "It's understandable."

He fiddled with a white plastic saltshaker, batting it back and forth between his long fingers like a hockey puck. Adele fished a package of Oreos from a shelf and put them in front of him. The only sound between them was the steady perk of the brewing coffee and the maracas-like shake of the salt as the shaker swayed in his hands.

"Everyone is using my sister's murder for their own ends," he said finally. "It's destroying our family. Our business. Our reputation in the community."

"What do you mean?" asked Adele.

"Our waitstaff is afraid to come to work. My mother's cleaning lady got a death threat in her mailbox. People we don't know from across the country are sending us long, angry letters about how much they hate immigrants. They don't even bother to differentiate between legal and undocumented. If they're Latino and have an accent, they're suspect."

He put the saltshaker down and turned to her. He had so much of Catherine in him. Those pale eyelashes, soft and innocent as a newborn calf's. That slight flip of the nose.

"The media is making it look like it's us against them, and that's just not true," said Todd. "Catherine loved the immigrant community. She had immigrant friends. My family's restaurant, the Magnolia Inn, has been employing immigrants for years. They're good, hardworking people and we treat them well. We rely on them to run the Inn. Without them, we'd have to shut down."

Adele had no doubt that was true. All the restaurants in the area were staffed primarily by Latinos, no matter what the cuisine.

"I don't know if that's so much the media's fault," said Adele. "I think it's more the work of Mike Carp. He's using your sister's death to further his political career."

"I'm worried my sister's wake and vigil tonight are going to turn ugly," said Todd. "That that's all people are going to remember. Not Catherine. Not our family's good reputation. Just . . . this hate."

Adele poured the coffee into two big mugs. She put one in front of Todd and sat down at the table with him.

"I understand your concerns," she said. "And I can assure you that no one in the immigrant community is angry at your family. Everyone I talk to feels terrible about what you're going through. There is no hate. Mostly, there is fear. We live in scary times for immigrants already. Your sister's murder upped that exponentially."

"I wish I could do something to make things better," said Todd, "so people remember Catherine, not the way she died."

"You could say publicly what you're saying to me now," Adele suggested. "Tell the world that Mike Carp and this 'Catherine's Law' he's yammering on about aren't the way to go. You're her brother. People would put a lot of stock in your words."

Todd stared at the coffee mug cradled between his long fingers. "I'd like to, Adele. Really I would. But you see, my family is involved in that Crystal Springs Golf Resort deal with Carp's company. If all the permits go through, it would tie the Magnolia Inn to the new resort. My family's pinned their financial hopes on that project. They can't take a public position against him. We could lose everything. You don't cross Mike Carp."

"Yes," said Adele. "I've heard he likes to nurse a grudge."

"I want to do something to help. But given our connection to Mike Carp, donating to La Casa is out."

"There are other organizations in the county that help immigrants—"

"Yeah, but I'd like to help in a way that makes me feel like I've done something real. Something just for Catherine, you know?" He stared at his hands. "Something that won't get back to my folks. Maybe there's an individual I can help. Someone being hurt by all this."

"There is—and you can't," said Adele.

"Yeah? Who?"

"The kid brother of the man who allegedly murdered your sister."

Todd put down his mug and pushed back from the table. "I don't want to help the brother of that scum."

"I totally understand why you would feel that way," said Adele. "But Wil Martinez really is an innocent in all of this. He's a college student who wants to be a doctor. He's the one who turned his brother in. Arranged for his surrender. And then watched him die. And now he's sitting in jail and about to lose everything."

"If he's innocent, why don't the police release him?"

"Short answer? They charged him for initially lying to the police about his brother's whereabouts," said Adele. "If he was an American citizen, at worst, they'd release him on a low bail until they sorted out the evidence. But because he has only temporary legal status, I believe the judge is going to set the bail very high."

"Is it . . . something I can contribute to?" asked Todd. "If he's really as innocent as you say he is, I don't think my sister would want him sitting in jail on account of her."

Adele was touched that this young man, in the depths of his sorrow, would have so much concern for someone else—especially someone he should hate. "That's a very generous offer, Todd. But I suspect it will be in the hundreds of thousands."

"Why so high if he's innocent?"

"To keep him there," said Adele. "Unfortunately, the longer he stays inside, the more he loses on the outside. His college classes. His job. His rented room. All his possessions."

"Can't his family help him?"

"His mother was deported three years ago. She's dying of cancer in Guatemala. Apparently, he has no one else."

"We've had a few busboys like that," said Todd. "They've gotten caught up with immigration and we've given some of our other staff time off to help pack up their things so it doesn't all get plundered."

"That's very generous of your family," said Adele. It pained her to think that the Archers had been so decent to their immigrant employees, only to have their daughter victimized this way.

"I've got an idea," said Todd. "How about I pay this young man's rent for the next month? That would give him a chance to make some arrangements to move his things."

"You'd . . . do that?" asked Adele. "Pay the rent of the brother of the man who murdered your sister?"

"He lost his only sibling, just like I lost mine," said Todd. "You said he was innocent. And we're both hurt-

ing. His rent can't be more than about five hundred. I
can swing it."

"Oh, Todd." Adele felt something warm and fizzy in
her chest. For the first time since Catherine walked out
of La Casa, the world didn't feel like a dark and threatening place. There was goodness. Maybe it just took a
little while to find. "I can't thank you enough."

"Write down his address," he told her. "I'll make
sure I visit his landlord in the next couple of days." He
rose. "This stays between us—you understand? You
can't tell anybody. My folks would have a fit if they
knew."

When they'd finished their coffee, Adele walked
Todd out to his car. She gave him a hug.

"Thank you," she said. "You've restored my faith in
humanity."

"Mine too," he said. "Let's keep in touch. I think we
both need moral support right now."

Adele's mailbox was at the foot of the driveway. She
opened it while Todd walked around to the driver's side
of his car. She found the usual stack of bills, along with
a postcard from her sister, Grace, who was on vacation
with her latest boyfriend. The postcard showed a tropical beach at a Caribbean resort. Adele suspected it cost
more than her monthly mortgage. Grace earned the big
bucks. An MBA. A high-tech banking career. That was
how she kept the demons of their childhood at bay.
That hadn't worked for Adele. Which was too bad, because she really could have used the big bucks right
now.

Adele noticed something else stuffed at the back of

her mailbox. A plain white sheet of typing paper folded in two. Along the top was an offensive caricature of a Mexican in a sombrero, with a red circle and slash mark through it. Beneath, someone had typed: *Keep your people out of our vigil. They've done enough damage!*

Adele's hands shook. She scanned the street. Her sweet little neighborhood where whites, blacks, Latinos, and Pakistanis lived peacefully together. Somebody had walked up to her house, with hate in their heart, and had put this poisoned letter in her mailbox.

Todd must have read something in Adele's face. He leaned across the roof of his BMW.

"Everything okay?"

Adele walked over and showed him the letter. He read it and then pushed it away like it had the power to bite him.

"This is disgusting. This is exactly what I *don't* want at the vigil tonight. I hope you call the police about this." His voice held all the confidence of a young man who was used to viewing the police as an extension of his own will. Adele wished she could feel that same sense of assurance. As soon as Todd Archer pulled out of her driveway, Adele went inside and dialed the Lake Holly PD. She asked to speak to Detective Greco.

"How much police presence are you planning to have at Catherine's vigil tonight?" she asked him.

"Sanchez is on restricted duty," said Greco. "Two guys are on vacation. Everybody else is on, a lot of 'em collecting overtime. Why?"

Adele told Greco about the threatening note. "Someone is showing up at my house—*my house*—with this garbage. I resigned and I'm still a target."

"I'll swing by and check it out when I get a chance," said Greco. "Believe me, we're not any happier about this situation than you are. You see that riot at the college earlier today? It's all over the local news."

Adele was trying to avoid the news as much as possible. All the top stories seemed to be about Catherine and Benitez and that damned anti-immigrant legislation that Carp was trying to ram down everyone's throats.

"Our new county executive gave a speech," said Greco. "Vega got hit in the head with a bottle."

"Is he okay?"

"He's probably got one hell of a headache. But then his new boss is giving us all one."

"Who's his new boss?"

"He didn't tell you?" Adele heard the glee in Greco's voice. "I'll take a front-row seat when he does. Hell, HBO's got nothing compared to the two of you."

"Wait a minute. You're not saying . . . Jimmy's not working for Mike Carp, is he?"

"Round one." Greco chuckled. He sounded like a car that just lost its muffler. "Let me know who's standing when it's over."

Chapter 21

As soon as Adele hung up from Greco, she dialed Vega's cell. He didn't pick up. She left a message, telling him she'd heard about the bottle incident and asking him to stop by her house as soon as he got off work. She couldn't hide the frostiness in her tone. It matched the winter chill in her heart.

I stood by you when you shot an unarmed immigrant. I put my whole career on the line for you. And on the day I'm forced to resign, you take a job with the man who wants to destroy everything I've worked to build?

Adele pushed her frustration to the side when Sophia got off the school bus. She concentrated on emptying her daughter's backpack and washing her lunchbox. She praised the A that Sophia got on a spelling test. Then she assembled a plate of apples and Oreos for the child while she listened to a long story about a fight between Madison and Emma that Sophia had refereed with marginal success.

Inside, Adele felt a slow, simmering fury. By the time Vega's pickup appeared in the driveway, she could barely contain her sense of betrayal. Even his large bouquet of wilted peach roses, which he'd probably bought on special at the gas station, didn't change anything. Or the black thread of stitches at his hairline. She took the roses from his hand with a muffled thanks and kissed him stiffly.

"Look, I'm really sorry about what happened today at La Casa. I know you're upset."

"You think *that's* what I'm upset about?"

"Isn't it?"

Sophia poked her head around the doorway of the kitchen where she was doing homework. Vega quickly changed the subject.

"Hey there, sport. How's it going?"

"Our snow-woman's still in the backyard," said the child. "She's looking a little melty."

"We'll build another the next time it snows," Vega promised. He shot his best wide-eyed, former–altar-boy look at Adele. "If that's okay with your mom."

Adele didn't answer. She kept her eyes on the cabinet, where she fetched a vase for the roses. He was doing just what Peter used to do—playing good cop to Adele's bad. And why was that? Why did she always come off as the unreasonable one?

"We need to talk," she said as evenly as she could. Then she turned and smiled at Sophia. *"Lucero,"*—her nickname of "bright star" for Sophia—"why don't you go print out your science homework on my computer upstairs?"

"Okay." Sophia bounced a knowing look from her

mother to Vega. If Vega's eyes were any wider with innocence, he'd be a golden retriever. As soon as the child went upstairs, Adele lit into him.

"I put my whole career on the line for you when you needed me after that shooting," she hissed. "And you do this? Take a job—a *promotion*—to work with a man who stands for everything I despise?"

"Promotion?" Vega touched his chest like he'd been shot. "You think being a freakin' taxi service is a *promotion*? This is a punishment detail, Adele. I got it because I tried to help you. I tried to do what you asked of me. I should've let the Lake Holly PD take Benitez down, like they wanted. We'd have both been better off."

"You're blaming *me*? For the fact that the Lake Holly Police shot a man in the throes of surrendering?"

"He wasn't surrendering—"

"Well, I say he was. The Latino community says he was. Only people like Mike Carp think that the police can gun down people with impunity!"

"Aw, for chrissakes!" Vega threw up his hands. "That's what this is about, isn't it? You blame me for Benitez's death. For the fact that you had to resign from La Casa over it."

"I blame you for agreeing to work for such a despicable man—"

"A, I was *ordered* to work for him. B, he was duly elected by a majority of the voters of this county. And C, he was a lot more concerned about my getting hit in the head by a bottle than you seem to be!"

"That's not true or fair."

"Well, it sure seems like that to me!"

The doorbell rang. Adele walked into the foyer to open it. Vega hung back in the kitchen, trying to get his temper under control.

Louis Greco stood on the porch, rocking on the balls of his feet. Adele was sure he'd heard their raised voices. Old Victorians aren't exactly soundproof.

"Want me to come back? Or should I remove all the sharp objects from the house first?"

Adele flushed. Vega walked into the foyer. He didn't seem to know where to put his hands. They were both embarrassed.

"What are you doing here?" asked Vega.

Greco stepped inside. "Adele didn't tell you? She got a letter in her mailbox this afternoon, telling her to keep Latinos away from tonight's vigil."

"Where's the letter?" Vega bounced a look between Greco and Adele.

"Upstairs. I'll get it," said Adele. "And both of you, please keep your voices down. I don't want Sophia spooked."

Greco raised an eyebrow at Vega after Adele went upstairs. "Is this over you working for Carp? Or us shooting Benitez?"

"Both," said Vega. "She blames me for everything."

"Well, I blame you for Benitez too, so we're in agreement there. Got paperwork up the yin-yang since the shooting. Sanchez is a basket case—I don't have to tell you how he's taking it. I'm his replacement on the investigation. Everybody's working round-the-clock. Not to mention that it created a lot more bad blood that we didn't need in town."

"Any hate-crime incidents?" asked Vega.

Greco ticked them off on his sausagelike fingers. "Besides the phone threats to La Casa? The letter in your girlfriend's mailbox? The graffiti sprayed on a Dumpster at the food pantry? The fistfights at the high school—"

"Okay, okay. I get your point," said Vega. "Everybody's at each other's throats."

Greco tilted his head in the direction of Adele as she walked back down the stairs. "Even you two can't come together. How do you expect the town to?"

Adele showed Vega and Greco the letter. Vega was relieved to see it didn't threaten harm, only warned her to keep the Latino community away from tonight's vigil. Greco snapped a picture of it on his cell phone, then put the sheet into a clean manila envelope to take back to the station. Vega was sure that Adele thought Greco was going to send it on to the crime lab and run every kind of DNA and forensic test known to man on it. Vega knew the truth. Hate letters are rarely more than that. Greco would keep it as evidence if something escalated. Otherwise, it would just sit in a file, gathering dust.

"Sophia has gymnastics in half an hour," Adele said to both men. Vega got the hint. If they were going to resolve their problems, it wasn't going to be this evening. Besides, he had to be at the vigil later. He hadn't even told her. Why make matters worse?

Vega kissed Adele on the cheek and walked out with Greco. Greco's unmarked was parked behind Vega's truck. Vega beeped open the doors of his pickup and went to climb in. Greco just stood there rattling the big envelope with the threatening letter inside. Vega looked at him.

"What?"

"You can't share this," said Greco. "Not with any-one." He looked across Adele's tiny front lawn, still mostly covered with snow, although the snow was beginning to melt and turn gritty in places. On the other side of the white picket fence was Max Zimmerman's house. And beyond that, the Morrisons. Greco squinted as if he half expected Adele's neighbors to jump out of the bushes at any moment.

"Got the autopsy back on Catherine about an hour ago."

"And?"

"She died from a blow to the back of her head. Dr. Gupta said the blow was consistent with hitting something with an edge on it. Like a tree stump or a rock. It caused a skull injury and bleeding on the brain. Our guys are trying to find the exact stump now, but between the snow and the heavy brush, it's not easy."

"Sounds like her killing might have been accidental," said Vega. "Maybe someone shoved her backward or she tripped and fell when she was trying to escape the rape."

"Except even the rape is questionable," said Greco. "There was no presence of Rolando Benitez's hair, skin, or semen on her. No bruising either. At this point, the most we can call it is attempted rape. There's nothing to indicate any sexual activity—never mind assault—in the last twenty-four hours before her death."

"Was she a virgin?"

"Not likely. That stuff hasn't happened for two thousand years."

"Huh?"

"She was pregnant."

"What?"

"About eight weeks along, according to Dr. Gupta. Could be, Catherine didn't know. Seems like nobody else did."

Vega tried to recalibrate this new Catherine with the image he was carrying around in his head. "And the baby. Was it—?"

"Rolando Benitez's? No. We ran the DNA. I'd have taken odds that Benitez wasn't the daddy. Not that I can tell you who is," said Greco. "Nobody ever saw Catherine with a boy."

"I know someone who did," said Vega. "The keyboardist in my band. A cop in Port Carroll by the name of Danny Molina. He subs for the piano player at the Magnolia Inn sometimes. He saw the brother fire a waiter for flirting with her."

"When was this?" asked Greco.

"You can call Molina and ask him the details. He told me it was a couple of weeks ago. After the holidays. The guy disappeared after that. I don't think Molina knew his name, but Todd Archer, the brother, would."

Vega massaged his forehead. "Pregnant! Jesus! I can't believe it." The girl seemed innocent and sheltered. Then again, maybe you had to be innocent and sheltered to get pregnant in this day and age. The experienced girls knew better.

"Did her parents know she was pregnant?" Vega touched his stitches. They were beginning to itch. Probably a good sign.

"They do now," said Greco. "We just broke the

news. It wasn't pretty. Robin, the mom, seemed very worried that people would find out. That seemed to be her biggest concern."

"This changes everything," said Vega.

"It changes nothing," said Greco. "Because nobody's going to know."

"You're not going to make this public?" asked Vega.

"What do you think's gonna happen if we go out there and tell the *entire country*—because that's what we'd be doing—that our virgin princess got herself knocked up eight weeks before Benitez dragged her into those woods? It opens up all sorts of thorny questions I have no desire to answer right now."

"Are you saying you're not going to investigate it?"

"We're gonna investigate it. Of course we are," said Greco. "But until we know a hell of a lot more, I'm not going out there and telling the whole world that Snow White just became Sleeping Around Beauty. Or that the Lake Holly PD might have—underlined 'might have'—crapped on the wrong guy. The community's in turmoil. Everyone needs some time to heal."

"On a fable, Grec?" Vega couldn't believe what he was hearing. "Catherine Archer was a pregnant teenager. Which definitely ups the odds that she was killed by the father of her unborn child. Doesn't that alternate story need to be put out there? People's lives are at stake here. Benitez's brother is sitting in jail over what happened. Adele just resigned because she's being blamed for a situation she may have had nothing to do with."

"She resigned because La Casa had grown lax and out of touch with the way many people in this county feel about illegals right now," said Greco. "Look at that whole surrender. She was so damned concerned about Benitez, she forgot about all the other lives she was putting at risk. My men. You. And, most of all, her own."

"*You* put her life at risk," said Vega, "when you overreacted."

"Now who's telling himself a fable?"

Chapter 22

Vega had under two and a half hours before he had to pick up Carp and drive him to Catherine's wake and vigil. He didn't want to be late. He drove home, showered, fed Diablo, changed into a suit and tie, then drove back to the county garage and signed out a black Chevy Suburban, which the guard assured him was Carp's choice of vehicle.

He checked his cell phone messages before he set the GPS to navigate to Carp's estate. He was hoping Adele would text him. Maybe tell him about Sophia's gymnastics class or what she was making for dinner. Anything to break the ice between them.

She didn't.

He could text her. He wanted to. He ached to think he'd done something that hurt her. If he could go back to his old job in homicide right now, he'd gladly do it. This whole assignment was an embarrassment. Guys in his squad had started noticing that his desk was empty. That when his name came up, Waring just said he'd been "reassigned."

At first, everyone thought he'd been moved to pistol permits because someone saw him there making sure Max Zimmerman's gun was registered. (It was.) When that rumor turned out to be false, his old pals pressed for details. Vega knew that anything he said would only make matters worse, so he said very little. He felt just like one of those purged officials in the old Soviet Union. Nobody sends postcards from Siberia.

He opened up his screen to text Adele.

Nena, he began.

He couldn't think of a single thing to write after that. Words for him—words with meaning—were like something at the bottom of a deep, dark well. They had to be pulled up, syllable by syllable, in a very small bucket.

He started three different texts and deleted them all. Every one of them sounded too whiny. Or too angry. Or, worst of all, too needy.

Mike Carp lived in Wickford, a town to the east of Lake Holly. The two towns shared about as much in common with each other as canned tuna and ahi. Lake Holly was cops and plumbers, fifth-generation residents and immigrants. Wickford was trust-fund babies, entertainers, and Wall Street CEOs. Lake Holly was nestled in a valley and loaded with small Victorians, sidewalks, and mom-and-pop stores. Wickford was rolling hills full of estates and horse farms nestled around a village that looked like something out of the Revolutionary War. Tiny storefronts in brick veneer. Steepled churches built of white clapboard. Cobblestoned sidewalks. It was beautiful until you discovered that much of the town housed nothing but real-estate firms and dry cleaners.

The fastest way to Wickford was to drive to Lake Holly, then head east out of the valley, past the reservoir that gave the town its name. Vega passed it now on his right. The last pale brushes of daylight skimmed its surface. A flock of Canadian Geese flew low across its southern edge, past the same steep granite cliffs Vega once jumped off as a teenager on a dare from a girlfriend. It was a reckless move that still filled him with embarrassment at how cavalierly he might have thrown his life away.

He was headstrong, he supposed. Joy was like that now. Vega closed his eyes and replayed the moment that professor threaded his arm around his daughter's waist. He hoped she wasn't about to pull the equivalent of a cliff dive with this guy.

In the Suburban's rearview mirror, Vega watched the village of Lake Holly recede by inches into the valley until all he could see were the twin granite spires of Our Lady of Sorrows Catholic Church. And then that, too, was gone.

Vega followed the GPS directions to two enormous black wrought-iron gates. He rang the buzzer and identified himself. The gates slowly opened like some plow horse was pulling them. He drove through, initially mistaking the caretaker's house and barn for Mike Carp's residence. The actual residence was another three hundred feet down the driveway. It was three stories tall and looked like a European boarding school. There was a cobblestoned courtyard with a fountain of peeing cherubs in the middle. The fountain was turned off this time of year—which made the cherubs seem a little less innocent touching themselves with those big smiles on their faces. Maybe he just didn't have the European aesthetic down.

A uniformed butler—the last white servant in America—greeted Vega at the front door. Vega stepped into a grand hallway with black-and-white marble tile, a chandelier, and a sweeping central staircase that fanned out at the bottom. The whole place looked like the set of *The Sound of Music.*

"In future," said the butler, "you should come around back and announce yourself. Then wait outside."

"Nonsense!" boomed Carp as he thudded down the stairs, smoothing the collar of his shirt over his jacket. "Jimmy wants to come in the front doors, let him." Carp turned to Vega. "We'll be meeting a few of my staff at the McCarthy Funeral Home in Lake Holly. You know it?"

"Yes, sir."

"You'll let me off in front and join us after you park. How's the head?"

"Fine, sir." The bruising wasn't too obvious on Vega's caramel-colored skin, but there was no hiding the black surgical thread.

"Good. Glad to hear it."

Carp buried himself in paperwork and texts on the drive over. By the time they arrived in Lake Holly, it was dark. Already, the town was mobbed. The police had cordoned off the funeral home to keep spectators and the media out. The vigil, however, was another matter. People with video cameras were setting up along Main Street to catch the parade of mourners slated to gather after the wake.

"It's going to be a big crowd tonight," said Carp. He looked excited. Vega felt something closer to dread. A lot of these people—almost all of them white—weren't from Lake Holly. Vega could tell that by the clueless way they wandered around, pointing to the ribbons on the lampposts and posters of Catherine in store windows.

A police officer parted the barricade by the funeral home. On the steps of the stately white Colonial, teenagers with soft baby cheeks gathered in small groups, their noses red with the cold, clutching stuffed elephants and turquoise ribbons, their eyes as shell-shocked as their parents'. Vega dropped Carp off in front, where Prescott and Vanderlinden were waiting. He parked the Suburban and walked back.

The McCarthy Funeral Home was styled like a Federalist mansion. Lots of raised wood paneling in shades of pale blues and calming greens. Vega greeted a few people he knew. Volunteers from La Casa. Parents of Joy's friends from high school. They all looked so fresh-faced and homogenous. It was like he'd just walked into a Mormon assembly. Vega looked for evidence of the other Catherine whom Joy had told him about. The one who tutored immigrants at La Casa. Who had friends with purple hair and nose rings. Friends with undocumented parents. That was the girl Vega would have liked to have known. The one who sought out the ignored and the downtrodden. She wasn't in evidence in this room.

Vega tucked himself into a line filing down the center aisle into the main receiving room. He waited while it moved toward the casket and braced himself as always. For all the death he'd seen as a cop—including

Catherine's—he could never get used to viewing it all cleaned up and sanitized like this.

He'd been raised a Catholic, of course. Christened at St. Raymond's in the Bronx. Confirmed at Our Lady of Sorrows, right here in Lake Holly. His mother had been a lifelong believer. And yet the rituals never offered Vega the comfort they did his mother. People spoke about "God's plan." But as far as Vega could see, God seemed to be holding the world together with rubber bands and Elmer's glue. Not much of a plan, to Vega's way of thinking.

The Archers were at the end of the receiving line. Vega had never seen the family up close. Robin was the spitting image of her daughter. She had the same blue eyes and upturned nose, the same shade of blond hair, though hers was likely chemically enhanced. There was a stoicism to her that Vega found both admirable and unimaginable. She was holding it together, offering mourners a pressed-lip smile and accepting hugs and handshakes with a coolness that suggested she never lost her composure, no matter how dire the circumstances. From looking at her, no one would know she'd just been informed by the police that her daughter was eight weeks pregnant. But then again, maybe that was what was keeping her together.

No one knew.

Todd, too, seemed to be modeling his mother, albeit with more difficulty. His face looked gaunt beneath his reddish beard. His eyes were shadowed from lack of sleep. He wrapped an arm around his father.

In pictures Vega had seen, Todd's father, John, was a handsome man. He had the look of an aging European ski instructor, with his salt-and-pepper hair and carefully trimmed beard. But not this evening. His balance was unsteady. His face was flushed and he was sweating, even though it was cool in the room. When he shook Vega's hand, his grasp was so weak, it felt like a four-year-old's. Vega wondered if the man had been drinking. Or doped up on antidepressants and anxiety medication. Not that Vega could blame him. If Joy had been the one lying in that casket, someone would have to sedate Vega too. He could never survive something like this.

Vega offered his condolences, signed the guestbook, and walked into the foyer. Mike Carp was chatting to a couple of mourners, while Prescott and Vanderlinden checked their cell phones and pretended not to. Vega stood close by, in case Carp needed him. That's when he saw her. She was dressed in a tasteful black wool coat, nipped in at her tiny waist. Her dark brown hair was wound up primly in a bun. She was on her own. No Alan. No twins. No Joy. She gave John Archer a hug that lasted a beat too long.

Vega's heart wobbled in his chest. It would always wobble where Wendy was concerned. She took a big chunk of his youth. She gave him his only child. After she left, there were days he wanted to crawl into a hole and die. They'd been divorced six years now. He was in a healthier place than he'd ever been with Wendy. And yet, he could never see her and not feel a certain homesickness for the girl she'd been and the boy he used to be.

She caught sight of him before he could duck out of her line of vision. She was staring at the stitches on his hairline as she walked over.

"Joy told me about what happened on campus. Are you okay?"

Vega shrugged. "I'll live." He turned back toward the receiving line. John Archer looked as if he could barely stand any longer. "Looks like it's taking a lot of meds to get that poor guy through this. Not that I blame him."

"Or know him."

"You do," he shot back. She stiffened. They both seemed to know what he was referring to.

"Discretion was never your strong suit, Jimmy."

"Nor yours."

They were back to their perennial fighting stances. Vega decided to change the subject. "Did Joy happen to mention that little incident with 'Dr. Huggy' today?"

"Who?"

"At the protest, this old guy with a beard put his arm around Joy's waist. I think he teaches some kind of science or something."

"Jeffrey Langstrom," said Wendy. "I think Joy has a crush on him."

"I'm more worried about what he has on her."

Wendy frowned. Or rather, tried to. She had work done on herself these days. She didn't need it. She was five years older than Vega, but she would always be young and beautiful, at least to him.

"You can't read all that from a hand around her waist," she insisted.

"I'm a guy," said Vega. "I know how guys think. First the waist. Then the breasts."

"This isn't the hokey pokey."

"What's she told you about him?"

"She talks about him a lot," said Wendy. "But I'm sure it's just a teacher crush. Girls have so much hidden drama."

Vega held her gaze. "Women too."

"Vega!" shouted a voice from the corner. Doug Prescott. The mouth breather. "We're heading out. Now."

"I gotta go," said Vega. "Let me know if you find out anything from Joy."

Vega followed Carp's entourage out of the funeral home and onto Main Street, now blocked to traffic. Hundreds of people had already gathered along a stretch flanked with turquoise ribbons. Most of the faces were white; however, Vega was pleased to see that there were some blacks and Latinos, too, clustered together primarily with their religious congregations.

At the intersections, volunteers held out baskets of long white tapered candles in plastic cup holders. They looked like Popsicles. Vega took one and touched it to someone else's lit wick. A flame shivered to life, joining all the others that flickered around him. Vega felt encapsulated by a shimmering river of light. It was beautiful. And hushed. Even Carp and his entourage said nothing as they made their way to the front of the crowd, where they were joined by Lake Holly's mayor, the town board, a state assemblyman, and various local religious and civic leaders. Everyone except the Archers.

"Where are the parents and brother?" Vega asked Hugh Vanderlinden, who happened to be standing closest to him.

"It was too much for the father," said Vanderlinden, cupping a hand for warmth over his curved anteater of a nose. "They're being escorted by the police to the

town hall plaza." The vigil was set to end at the war
memorial there. That's where the news affiliates had
parked their vans and satellite dishes.

The procession wound its way past the century-old
railroad station and then turned east toward the plaza.
Some of the mourners peeled off and took a shortcut
through the parking lot and over a footbridge, which
spanned the creek behind the town hall. The glow of
their candles threw shadows across the grizzled trunks
of the weeping willows that dotted the banks of the
creek. By day, in good weather, employees from the
town hall often ate their lunches at picnic benches beneath their graceful tendrils. By night, some of the immigrants gathered there to talk and drink. The Lake
Holly Police Department was forever chasing them
off. That's what drove many of the more hard-core
drinkers into the woods.

Vega followed Carp, the local politicians, and the
clergy into the town hall plaza. In the center of the
plaza was a granite obelisk engraved with the names of
local dead soldiers from all the wars. Next to it was a
pop-up tent. Vega pushed aside the memory of the last
time he saw such a tent. It covered the body of Catherine Archer in the woods. Vega wondered if every cop
in the crowd was making the same connection.

Beneath the tent was a lectern with a microphone
and a row of folding chairs. The Archers were seated
on the chairs. John Archer was sweating. There was
something rigid and masklike to his features. A priest
from Our Lady of Sorrows bent down to speak to the
family as mourners filled the plaza. The light from
their candles danced across the four Greek columns
that anchored the front of the town hall building.

"John Archer doesn't look well," Vega said to Vanderlinden.

"Nobody looks well at something like this." Vanderlinden turned his gaze to Carp, conferring now with the priest, his cheeks pliant with concern, his brow flexed in Old Testament wrath. "Except maybe Mike Carp."

The crowd was still pouring into the plaza. The politicians and clergy were figuring out the speaking lineup. Vega saw a teenage girl pushing her way toward the tent. Vega might not have noticed her except for her bright purple hair, the color of irises. It was shaved into a buzz cut on one side and worn in a high flip on the other. She looked like the girl Joy had told him about: Zoe Beck.

Despite the look-at-me hair, the girl gave off an aura of being used to people not looking at her at all. Her doughy body had a natural question-mark curve to it. Beneath her dark, shapeless trench coat, she wore tan khakis and a red collared shirt. Vega got the sense this wasn't a sartorial preference. He saw the same outfit on all the employees at one of the cut-rate department stores north of town.

She slipped past Carp and his entourage and walked over to the Archers seated beneath the canopy. She bent down and said something into Robin Archer's ear. Vega expected Catherine's mother to do one of her stiff embraces and pressed-lip smiles. But Vega saw something else cross Robin Archer's features. Something more genuine, but also more curious. Embarrassment. Robin Archer's faced flushed. Her big white teeth clenched as if to withstand a blow. She waved her hands in front of her as if she were shooing away a homeless person. Archer's son put a hand on the girl's shoulder—not meanly or forcefully. More like the way you might convince an old pal that they'd had too much to drink. He leaned over and said something into her ear. Then the girl with the purple hair pulled her trench coat tighter around her middle and shrank back into the crowd.

"What do you suppose that was all about?" Vega asked Vanderlinden.

"Beats me. Maybe the girl asked to say a few words and the mother refused. She doesn't look like anyone the Archers would associate with."

The priest finished his blessing. Then the high-school tennis coach talked about Catherine's spirit and determination. The news cameras, set back from the crowd, got their quick video clips. A bagpiper played "Amazing Grace." Everyone stood quietly, some with tears in their eyes.

Their stillness made it easier for Vega to spot the commotion going on just beyond the plaza, by one of the willow trees near the creek. Three big men. One small one. The big men looked white and probably in their teens or early twenties. The small man looked Hispanic and older—maybe in his thirties. His face could have come straight from a Mayan rendering. Those smooth, high cheekbones. Those Asian-looking eyes. He might have been quite striking if not for a general shabbiness. He wore a frayed hunting cap. His black-and-red plaid jacket and baggy jeans looked rumpled and lived in. He seemed angry about some-thing. He waved his hands and gestured to the three white youths. One of them pushed him. He pushed back. Fists flew. Even in the glow of little more than candles and streetlight, Vega caught the hard, fast jabs that could break jaws and fracture ribs.

Vega searched the crowd for a uniformed officer. He saw one he recognized and gestured to the four men by the willow tree. The officer and his partner hustled over as the bagpiper finished his song. Carp stepped up to the microphone to speak. Vega wasn't listening. He had his eyes on the two cops and the four men. The cops had pulled the white youths off the Hispanic man. But as soon as they did, the man ran into the crowd. Vega could see him clearly now. His left eye was beginning to swell shut. His left cheek was swollen and bruised. He was running toward the lectern. Straight for Mike Carp. Vega threw himself in front of the man and blocked his path.

"Slow down," Vega said to the man. "What's going on? *Qué pasa?*" He said it in both English and Spanish, hoping to get as much traction out of the question as possible. The three men who'd beaten him were still on his tail, pushing through the crowd toward him.

Mike Carp stopped speaking and frowned down at the man. "You are interrupting a solemn occasion." He fixed his eyes on Vega. "Get this troublemaker out of here. He has no business being here."

Vega grabbed the man by the collar of his red-and-black plaid jacket. Vega could smell alcohol on his breath. "Take it elsewhere," he said to him in Spanish.

The man tried to shove Vega away, but Vega held tight and ushered him toward the two uniformed police officers. They could take it from here. The man pointed to the three youths less than ten feet away. One wore a Rangers jersey. Another had a Yankees cap on backward. The third had the beginnings of a double chin beneath the dark brown stubble on his face.

"They kick the candles. By the tree. They break everything." He huffed the words out in heavily accented English. It was clear he wanted everyone in the crowd to know what the three young white men had done.

"Rapists and murderers can burn in hell!" shouted the double-chinned one. "Take your candles back to Mexico. We don't want you dirtbags here."

Vega faced the three young men. Now it was his turn to be angry. "This man put down religious candles. And you knocked them over and broke them? Dudes, that's like busting up a church."

"Benitez was scum," Rangers jersey shot back. "He doesn't deserve to be mourned."

"He was innocent!" the man in the plaid jacket shouted. "The police shot an innocent man!"

Two different sets of cops pushed through the crowd. One set grabbed Vega's guy and dragged him away. When they had him over by a police cruiser, they cuffed him and shoved him inside. The original two cops caught up with the three white youths. Vega noticed that they only got a verbal warning to leave.

Everyone was so focused on the fight that it took a moment for the scrape of metal folding chairs by the lectern to catch people's attention. Someone had collapsed on the ground. Carp and his entourage pulled chairs aside. Police officers hustled forward, clearing bystanders out of the way. A sergeant got on his radio. The priest tapped the microphone.

"Is there a doctor in the house?"

A tight circle of grim-faced men in wool coats

crowded around the victim. Vega saw Todd and Robin Archer kneeling on the ground. Carp, Prescott, and Vanderlinden towered over them. The priest edged himself next to the mother and son and bent down. By simple process of elimination, Vega knew.

The victim was John Archer.

Chapter 23

It was all over the Lake Holly Moms Facebook page the next morning. A drunken illegal had interrupted Catherine's vigil. John Archer had had a heart attack—maybe as a result—and was rushed to the Lake Holly Hospital. He died at three a.m.

The news devastated Adele. She grieved for the Archer family. She grieved for Todd, whom she felt she'd come to know and like after his visit yesterday. But that's not what made her throw an extra blanket around her shoulders, even though the heat was turned up and the radiators were hissing. It was the comments from community members that followed the Facebook post:

These people are ruining our town . . .

John Archer would be alive right now if that illegal hadn't killed Catherine . . .

I'm sick of how nobody does anything about them. Why can't they all be deported???

They want to come to America? Let them do it the way my great-grandparents did!

These people weren't Internet trolls. They were her neighbors, the mothers of her daughter's friends, people she saw at PTA events and firehouse fund-raisers. They went to religious services in town and helped out at community events. Some had even supported La Casa before this.

But no more. Catherine's murder seemed to open an artery of hate in the town and nobody could staunch the bleeding.

Adele put in a call to Todd Archer to offer her condolences. His cell phone didn't pick up. His mailbox was full. She sent him a text and promised to sit down and write him an actual card later. While she fixed Sophia's breakfast, she called Greco. He cursed when he heard her voice on the line.

"I've got enough problems right now. Go bother Vega."

Hearing his name brought a thud to her heart. Vega hadn't emailed or texted her since their fight yesterday. He was probably waiting for her to make the first move. Like always. But this time wasn't "like always."

"I saw the news about John Archer on the Lake Holly Moms Facebook page," Adele said as she buttered Sophia a slice of toast and cut up some banana. "I saw, too, that people are saying a drunken and undocumented Hispanic caused the fracas that precipitated his heart attack. Is that true?"

"More or less."

"Which part is the 'more' and which is the 'less,' Detective?"

"There was a fistfight over some knocked-over candles. So we let the guy cool his heels for the night at our five-star bed-and-breakfast." Greco could never tell a story without a little editorial embellishment. "He's going before the town judge this morning, right before Benitez's brother's bail hearing."

"The bail hearing's today? I thought it was tomorrow." Adele wanted to be there. She was hoping to talk to his public defender and see if there was any way he could get Wil released on his own recognizance.

"It's been moved up. To ten-thirty," said Greco. "Our bed-and-breakfast guest—Teódulo Gomez—is going first."

"You said 'knocked-over candles.'" The image was beginning to coalesce in Adele's brain. "You don't mean just candles, do you? You mean religious candles."

"Okay, religious." Greco blew a long breath of air, like he already knew where this was headed.

"And by fistfight—are we talking one-on-one?"

"There were three other gentlemen."

"And these *gentlemen*—were they also arrested and charged?"

"No."

"Let me guess," said Adele. "They're white. They're local. And they're connected."

"Adele—"

"And you wonder why the Lake Holly Latino community is upset about Benitez. This is why I have to be in that courtroom this morning."

"C'mon, Adele, you're not head of La Casa any longer. Just let it go. Gomez will get a fine, at most, and it will be over. You don't have to come."

"See, when you say 'don't,' that kind of makes me want to do it."

"No wonder you and Vega were going at it yesterday," said Greco. "I don't know how you two manage to stay together."

Adele looked at her cell on the counter next to her. Still, no call or text from Vega. She was wondering the same thing herself.

Adele got Sophia on the school bus, then picked up Max Zimmerman's newspaper near the curb. She walked it to his front door and waited while he answered the bell. She had a moment to spy the area on his side of the fence that separated his lawn from the Morrisons on the other side. There was a new steaming pile of dog manure resting on the gritty remnants of snow. She couldn't believe how that family took advantage of an old man.

Zimmerman opened the front door and smiled when he saw Adele standing there.

"The news in the world is so good this morning, you have to hand deliver it to me?"

She laughed. "I was putting Sophia on the bus. I thought I'd walk it over." Adele gestured to the dog manure by the fence. "Would you like me to talk to the Morrisons about this for you?"

Zimmerman shook his head. "Why create problems? The world has enough already."

"But it's not fair," said Adele. "You need to stand up for yourself. If you won't, I will."

"I'm sure you would," said Zimmerman. "And well

too. But let me pick my own battles. Every fight isn't worth the cost."

"If you change your mind, you'll let me know?"

"I can stand up for myself, Adele. Not fighting isn't the same as not being able to."

Adele sent out a few more résumés to legal firms. Then she drove down to the Lake Holly police station, an eighty-year-old brick building that was forever being updated in piecemeal increments. The courtroom was up a flight of worn granite stairs from the station house. It was an unassuming space—more like an elementary-school stage. There was a judge's bench, two tables, a few spectator seats, and a bunch of flags.

Adele took a seat in one of the folding chairs in back. She was the only spectator and a well-known face in Lake Holly. She did not go unnoticed. Judge Keppel looked up from his notes.

"Ms. Figueroa—what brings you here?"

"I have an interest in both your cases this morning, Your Honor."

"A legal interest?"

"Mr. Gomez has no attorney, but I would be happy to help translate for him if it pleases Your Honor. As for Mr. Martinez, I'm just a concerned community member."

"You are doing this as . . . a representative of La Casa?"

"No. I resigned from La Casa earlier this week."

"I see," said Keppel. He shot a quizzical look at the town prosecutor, McMillan, a white man who wore three-piece suits and too much aftershave.

An officer brought Teódulo Gomez up from his

holding cell. He looked like he'd just gone through an MS-13 gang initiation. His left eye was swollen shut. His left cheek sported a large bruise. Adele was betting the other "gentlemen" didn't look half as bad.

The officer put a firm grip on Gomez's shoulder and shuffled him before the judge.

"Mr. Gomez, do you understand the charges against you?"

"I . . . ," Gomez mumbled. He probably spoke a little English, but not enough to call upon in such a stressful situation. Adele got to her feet.

"Your Honor—may I help translate for Mr. Gomez?"

"Come forward, Ms. Figueroa. Be my guest. Please explain to Mr. Gomez that he is being charged with assault in the fourth degree, public intoxication, and disturbing the peace. I would like to hear what he has to say about the charges before I pass sentence."

Adele put the judge's statements and questions to Gomez in Spanish, then translated his answers back to the judge.

"Your Honor, Mr. Gomez says he came to pay his respects to Catherine Archer, like everyone else. But he also put a candle down for Rolando Benitez under a willow tree near town hall, where several other candles were gathered in his memory. When Mr. Gomez put his candle down, three white men demanded he take the whole shrine away. He refused, so the men kicked over the candles and smashed the votive holders. When Mr. Gomez tried to stop them, they beat him up. Mr. Gomez's injuries are consistent with his story."

"Thank you, Ms. Figueroa," said the judge. "And may I remind you that you are not functioning as Mr. Gomez's attorney here. Only as his translator."

"I am functioning as a witness for the Hispanic people of this community, Your Honor—most of whom
are devout Catholics or Evangelical Protestants. For
them, all life is sacred. They would pray for the soul of
Catherine, of course. But they would also pray for the
soul of Benitez. What those men who kicked over the
candles did was a desecration of faith. Were they
charged?"

"We're not here to discuss any other case today, Ms.
Figueroa. Only Mr. Gomez's actions."

"Which were taken to protect his faith. And for this,
he was beaten and thrown in jail while those other
men—*local white men*—went free."

Keppel opened his mouth to argue, then shut it and
banged his gavel. "Defendant is fined one hundred
dollars, payable to the town."

Adele translated the judge's words to Gomez.

"But I don't have a hundred dollars," said Gomez.
"I told the truth last night, señora. I was with Darwin—
Rolando—Friday night. We were drinking together in
the woods. There was no girl."

"Did you tell the Lake Holly Police this?"

"I didn't know they were looking for him until after
he was killed. Then I was afraid."

Keppel banged his gavel. "Ms. Figueroa—this isn't
the place for a personal conversation."

"I'm sorry, Judge. But the defendant is telling me he
has information—information that could exonerate Mr.
Benitez in the murder of Catherine Archer. Which, in
turn, could impact the proceedings against his brother,
who is due in this court."

Keppel motioned to the officer who'd brought Gomez
in. "Take Mr. Gomez downstairs. Get one of the detec-

tives to take his statement. Then hand him the paperwork for his fine."

Adele translated the judge's words. Gomez looked
frightened. "Don't worry," Adele told him. "Nothing
bad will happen to you. You get any problems, you tell
them Adele Figueroa is upstairs and to fetch me. I'll
come down and help."

"Thank you."

"A word of advice?" said Keppel as Gomez was
about to be led out of the courtroom. He fixed Adele in
his gaze. "Tell Mr. Gomez that while I appreciate and
endorse his right to mourn anyone he wishes and worship any *way* he wishes, in the interests of the current
sensitivities in this community, I would suggest that
Latinos limit such celebrations to their houses of worship. The public nature of these shrines . . . I'm sure
you understand, Ms. Figueroa."

"In other words, Your Honor, when people are upset,
the Constitution of this country goes out the window—
in particular, our rights under the First Amendment."

"Ms. Figueroa, I'm not the Supreme Court, okay?
We're talking practicalities here. Mr. Gomez and all
the Latinos in this community are free to worship any
way they choose. I'm just offering up some common-
sense advice. If they start taking the First Amendment
literally, we're going to have someone in this town
who decides to take the Second Amendment even
more literally. I don't want a bloodbath. And neither do
you."

Chapter 24

The call woke Vega at seven a.m. He fished his cell off the bedroom floor, where it had fallen in the night. He answered, hoping it was Adele.

It was Doug Prescott, mouth breathing into the receiver.

"John Archer died at three this morning."

"Aw, man." Vega couldn't believe the family would be burying Catherine and John in the same week.

"Mr. Carp's got a lot on his plate today. He wants you to meet him for a racquetball game at eight at his fitness club in Clairmont."

"He wants me to drive him from the game?"

"He wants you to *play* it, Vega. Don't be late."

Coño! There was no way Vega could get down to the county office building, exchange his pickup for Carp's Suburban, and drive to his club in an hour. Vega explained the physical impossibilities to Prescott.

Not to mention that he didn't play racquetball.

"Mr. Carp says it's okay if you come in your personal vehicle and pick up the Suburban later. But he wants you at the club at eight."

Vega let Diablo outside while he took the quickest shave and shower in history. Then he whistled for the dog to come in and left him fresh water and dry food. He ate a half-frozen bagel in his truck on the drive down, driving ten miles over the speed limit the whole way. He pulled into the circular drive of the Carp Athletic Center at seven fifty-five. The club was a huge adobe-colored collection of cubes that had a vaguely Southwestern feel—all except for the inflatable bubble of tennis courts in back. Out front, two Latinos waited in a heated shed to park cars. *A health club with valet parking.* Vega shook his head. If you couldn't manage a walk from the parking lot to the club, what were you doing working out in the first place?

The front lobby had a black granite counter and a wall of rippling water that created a pleasing sound. The air smelled of lavender and vanilla—a far cry from the county police basement gym where the scent of mildewed towels mixed with sweaty jockstraps.

Vega gave his name to a blond receptionist in neon-pink spandex. Her eyes skimmed the length of his body. He was wearing a faded blue T-shirt, with his county police emblem in the corner, old nylon track shorts, and the same weather-beaten sneakers he used to jog around the lake at home. He had his suit in a garment bag over his shoulder. He straightened under her scrutiny. Male pride and all that.

"You brought some better sneakers, I hope?"

He deflated, feeling every one of his forty-two years. But he tried to suck it back. "I run in these at home."

She shrugged, then passed him a guest key. "The men's locker room is on your left. Use this key to store your stuff in a locker. Mr. Carp is upstairs, first racquetball court on the right. Andre can get you fitted with a loaner racquet and eye protection upstairs."

"Thanks."

The Carp Athletic Center was like a five-star resort. Two swimming pools the color of the Caribbean Sea. Three weight rooms befitting an NFL training camp. Big fluffy towels in a locker room with enough blond wood to deforest half of Sweden. Vega had no idea how much property Mike Carp owned, but this was definitely a first-class place.

Vega climbed the stairs toward the sound of rubber balls bouncing off walls. He found himself in a walkway overlooking an indoor track. On the right were six white rooms, with a wall of glass in front of each. One-way glass. Just like an interrogation room.

A young man with gelled hair and a body like braided rope outfitted Vega with a racquet and eye goggles and directed him to the first court. Mike Carp was standing at a blue line, practicing his serve. For a doughy man, Carp was surprisingly fast on his feet. His thick silver hair puffed up beneath his sweatband. His goggles made his blue eyes bulge even more than usual. He had strong legs beneath his tennis whites and thick shoulders and arms, which suggested he kept in shape despite the heft of gut beneath his shirt.

At a break between serves, Vega knocked on the door. Carp waved him in.

"Ah! Right on time. That's what I like to see." Carp wiped a bare arm across his forehead and studied Vega's. The swelling had gone down around the stitches. Mostly, it just itched. "You heard about John Archer, I suppose?"

"Doug Prescott told me," said Vega. "Tragic. I guess he had a heart attack."

"Yeah, well. His heart stopped. That's for certain." Vega had a sense Carp knew more than he was letting on. He flicked a gaze down Vega's faded police T-shirt, athletic shorts, and running shoes. "What do you say we play while we talk?"

"Happy to," said Vega. "But I don't know racquetball."

"You play any sports? You look like you're in good shape."

"Played a lot of baseball when I was younger. I play some pickup basketball and softball now."

"You can swing a bat, you can play this game."

Carp reeled off the basics. One match. Three games. First two go to fifteen points. The last goes to eleven. Players only score when they have the serve. Carp won the volley for serve—a wicked fastball that went sailing past Vega's face. Carp chuckled.

"Gotta keep on your toes, Jimmy."

"I'll try."

"So . . ." Carp served. "Four commendations, huh?"

"Pardon?" Vega was trying to concentrate on the game.

"Your personnel record," said Carp. "You got four commendations for your undercover work."

"Uh, yes. That's right." Vega came in for a shot close to the wall.

"Scored very high on the shooting range recently too, I hear."

Yesterday, Mike Carp couldn't remember Vega's

name. Today, he knew his shooting score. Vega felt a bit unhinged by this change. He kept his mouth shut and focused on the little blue ball.

"I'm sure you're wondering why I called you here today."

Vega missed a shot. "Clearly, it's not for my backhand." He retrieved the ball and threw it to Carp, who bounced it at the serve line.

"When I asked for a driver, I figured your department was going to send me some dumb-as-a-brick rookie. But the way you took that hit at the campus yesterday—well, it got me thinking that maybe you had a little more going for you than that."

Vega said nothing. Nothing he could say would be the words Carp wanted to hear. There were guys on Vega's job who would sell their kids to have a staff post with the most powerful man in the county. Not Vega. The one job he coveted right now was the one he couldn't seem to get back. And besides, the more he rose here, the more distance he put between himself and Adele.

He was so preoccupied with his thoughts that he completely missed a ball.

"Point for me," crowed Carp. He turned to Vega. "So what does all this mean, right? 'Get to the point, Mr. Carp.'" Carp laughed. He took a lot of pleasure being every voice in the room. Vega sensed he always was.

"I'm going to be making a big push for 'Catherine's Law,'" Carp continued. "As you can see, in the Latino community, this is not a popular law. I need someone like you at my side to help get the word out."

Vega knew what "someone like you" meant here. Carp needed a token.

"I'm a cop, sir. Not a politician. I can protect you and enforce the laws. But I can't advocate for your policies."

"Because you're afraid you'll catch flak from other Puerto Ricans—other Hispanics—about my positions on immigration?"

Carp's blue eyes held a challenge to them behind his goggles. Vega didn't back down. "Because it's not what I'm paid to do. It's not something I'm comfortable with either."

"Let's finish up the match and then we'll talk more," said Carp. Vega tossed Carp the ball. He got behind the serve line, ready to serve again. Vega concentrated on the rhythm of the game, the release he felt smacking the ball, the pleasure he got scoring a point. When his body was in motion, he felt in command and sure of his every move. It was only in thought that he grew tense and uncertain.

Carp won the first game, 15–8. But Vega caught on after that. He won the second 15–13 and the third, 11–6. He knew he probably should have let Carp win the last game, but it wasn't in him to hold back.

Carp removed his goggles and ran a towel across his face as they left the court. "Nice game for a man who's never played racquetball."

"Thanks. I try to catch on to things quickly."

"I'd say you play to win. Just like me. So here's the deal, Jimmy. I need someone like you to watch my back. That's all. Loyalty—plain and simple. You take care of me? I take care of you."

"'Take care'—as in drive you?"

"Drive me. Handle my security. Take care of whatever incidentals I ask you to do. Keep me up-to-date on police matters. I've got a lot of enemies out there. People looking to destroy me at every turn. I see a guy I can trust? Who knows?" Carp shrugged. "There's a good chance I might be sitting in the Governor's Mansion in two years. And believe me, Jimmy, the people who've been in my corner all the way are going to be right there too."

Carp didn't ask if Vega was on board. Really, did he have a choice? It was what he kept trying to explain to Adele, if only she would listen. This was his job, for better or worse. He could do it badly or he could do it well. But either way, he had to do it. It wasn't in him not to give something his best shot. Surely, she could understand that. She was exactly the same.

"Go take a shower and then drive your personal vehicle to the county garage," said Carp. "Exchange it for my Suburban and meet me back up here after that, okay? I've got some paperwork I can handle in my office upstairs in the meantime."

Vega left for the locker-room showers. Carp walked past the racquetball courts and up a flight of stairs to an office he kept at the club. He waited until he was inside to dial the number on his cell phone. The shower could wait. The other appointments could wait.

"Well?" Carp asked.

"He'll do." Two words. Lots of mouth breathing in between. "He's smart. Hardworking. No political connections. Plus, he's coming off that civilian shooting. That's a big black mark that's going to keep him in your corner."

"But, uh—just in case—are we all set?"

"Yep. Hugh got his keys off the valet rack. We were finished in under three minutes."

"And he won't know?" asked Carp.

"Believe me, he could sell that truck three times over and no one's gonna find it."

"So he's ours now?"

"Let me put it this way, we'll have everything we need on him if he ever *stops* being ours."

Chapter 25

It had been less than forty-eight hours since Adele first laid eyes on Wil Martinez. In that time, the teenager seemed to have shrunk. Or maybe it was just the bright, baggy orange Department of Corrections jumpsuit that overwhelmed him in that small courtroom. His legs were shackled beneath the defense table. His eyes sported deep purple valleys, probably from lack of sleep. He had a bruise on one arm, which Adele suspected wasn't accidental. His black hair looked wild and uncombed.

"Mr. Martinez." Judge Keppel said Wil's name like it was an unpronounceable dish he was reluctant to order off the menu. "Do you understand what this hearing is about? That it's to set an appropriate level of bail for the charges against you until such time as those charges are dropped or the case goes to trial?"

"Yes, sir," said Wil.

"You are charged with obstruction of justice for lying to Detective Louis Greco about your brother's whereabouts on the night of Catherine Archer's murder and also for providing a false address."

"Your Honor," said David Stern, Wil's public defender, "my client has cooperated fully—"

"Mr. Stern." The judge peered over the tops of his gold-rimmed glasses. "I will let you know when it's your turn to speak. Mr. Martinez is not on trial for the obstruction today. There is no need to defend his actions." Keppel turned back to Wil. "However, Mr. Martinez, you should understand that the charges currently against you aren't necessarily the only charges you may face. The police are still investigating your brother's connection to Ms. Archer's murder. More charges may be forthcoming. Do you understand that?"

"Yes, Your Honor." Wil's voice was barely above a whisper. The teenager had to be quaking in his shoes at the enormity of what he was up against.

"Mr. McMillan?" The judge turned to the prosecutor. "What is the town's bail request?"

"The town requests bail of a half-million dollars, Your Honor."

Adele gasped. Stern, to his credit, was out of his seat.

"Your Honor—for an obstruction charge? That's obscene."

McMillan, the prosecutor, answered him. "Mr. Martinez is being held in part because he's a potential accomplice in the murder of Catherine Archer—"

"A murder that the Lake Holly Police have yet to prove Mr. Benitez even perpetrated," Stern pointed out.

"The facts speak for themselves, Counselor," said McMillan. "A key chain belonging to Ms. Archer was found in a room shared by Mr. Benitez and your client."

"A key chain that Ms. Archer could have given Mr. Benitez. As a gift. She *was* his English tutor."

"We both know that's highly unlikely."

"And we both know that the only two people who can do anything but speculate on that are dead—one of them at the hands of the Lake Holly Police," said Stern. "Which gives the state a mighty big incentive to hold my client—since he would be a prime witness in any lawsuit against the officers involved in the shooting."

Silence in the courtroom. Adele had always considered David Stern young and green. She'd underestimated him.

Keppel frowned at the prosecutor. "Is that true? Is the state trying to discourage Mr. Martinez from exercising his civil rights?"

"The defendant is a flight risk, plain and simple, Your Honor," said McMillan. "That's the state's only interest in detaining him."

"But . . . half-a-million dollars?" asked Stern. "Don't you think that's a little excessive?"

McMillan shrugged like they were negotiating the price of a used car. "If evidence surfaces at a later date to suggest that Mr. Martinez is either a witness or co-conspirator to this crime, what guarantee does Lake Holly have that he'll stick around to cooperate? He's a foreign national with no firm address or fixed ties to this area."

Keppel peered over the bench at Wil. "Mr. Martinez, do you have any relatives in the area? An uncle? Cousins? Anyone?"

"No, sir," Wil mumbled.

"How about your parents—where are they?"

"My father died in Guatemala when I was small. My mother was deported back there three years ago."

Adele closed her eyes and replayed her conversation with Wil on Sunday at the preschool. She saw in him the girl she had been at his age. Full of hopes and dreams and a determination to rise above her circumstances. Her family made that possible. But Wil had no one in his corner. All that potential was about to wither and die. If only he had someone to speak for him.

"So the people ask again," said McMillan. "How can we be sure Mr. Martinez won't disappear once he's released? There's no one with any standing in the community to vouch for him."

Adele jumped up from her seat. "Your Honor."

Keppel frowned. "Ms. Figueroa—*again?* We don't need a translator here."

"I apologize for the interruption, Your Honor. But you've known me in the community for years. What if *I* vouch for him?"

"Vouch for him how?" asked the judge.

"Well . . ." Adele wasn't sure. "Check up on him. Make sure he's working and going to school."

Keppel tented his fingers to his lips and frowned. Adele could hear the ambient sounds of the small courtroom. The purr of a watercooler in back turning on and off. The buzz of the overhead fluorescent lights. Two secretaries conversing down the hall.

"It would almost be worth it to keep you out of my courtroom." The judge laughed at his own joke. "I'll tell you what I'm willing to do. I'm willing to release Mr. Martinez on his own recognizance."

McMillan was on his feet. "But, Your Honor—"

Keppel put up a hand to silence him. "I will grant this on one condition."

"What's that?" asked Stern.

"That Mr. Martinez is under Ms. Figueroa's guardianship."

"You mean, that I check up on him?" asked Adele.

"No, Ms. Figueroa. I mean that he lives with you or lives in a similar arrangement that this court would agree to—say, with a board member of La Casa or another respected member of the community."

"Your Honor, as I told you earlier, I'm no longer with La Casa. The organization is looking to distance itself from the shooting. Taking on the brother of the shooter, however innocent he may be—"

"So in other words," said Keppel, "you're asking this court to trust him to walk free. But you, yourself, are not willing to vouch for him on the same terms."

"No, Your Honor. That's not it at all. But I have a nine-year-old daughter and my ex-husband . . ." Now it was Adele's turn to feel uncomfortable. "He would *never* consent to a stranger living under the same roof as our daughter."

"I understand your dilemma, Ms. Figueroa. And I'm not insisting the defendant live with you. Only that you make suitable arrangements to allow him to remain under your supervision."

"But, Your Honor—"

"That's my offer. Take it or leave it. You, Mr. Martinez, and Mr. Stern have twenty-four hours to think about it while Mr. Martinez cools his heels back in jail. That should give you enough time to find someone this court considers suitable."

"And if I can't?"

"Then Mr. Martinez stays in jail until he can either secure a half million in bail, the charges are dropped, or the case is adjudicated. At this point, I don't see the Lake Holly Police dropping the charges or Mr. Martinez securing the bail. Which means he would remain in jail at least until his next court hearing."

"And when would that be?"

Judge Keppel flipped the pages of a ledger in front of him. "Judging by my calendar, that would be at least three months from now."

"But his DACA status will expire in the meantime," said Adele. "He won't be able to renew it if he's in jail. He'll fall out of legal status. Who knows what could happen then?"

"You have my offer, Ms. Figueroa. The rest is up to you."

Stern took Adele aside the moment the hearing was over. She'd had only a minute or two to exchange words and promises with Wil before the guards led him away.

"That's a mighty big carrot you just negotiated back there," Stern told her. "I'd like to help you, but I've got a big caseload and I don't know a soul who'd take this kid in."

"Me neither," Adele admitted. "Maybe I can get Lake Holly to drop the charges."

"Don't hold your breath."

Adele walked downstairs and into the Lake Holly station house. As soon as the desk sergeant saw her, he got busy with some paperwork.

"I need to speak to Detective Greco."

"Concerning?"

"A matter for Detective Greco."

"I'll see if he's available."

Greco kept her waiting a good ten minutes. When he did appear, it was with a set of car keys that he flipped around his fat fingers. "I'm beginning to think you have a crush on me," he grunted. "Did somebody slip another valentine in your mailbox?"

"No. And that's not funny," said Adele. "Especially given what happened last night at the vigil."

"You want to talk?" asked Greco. "It'll have to be on the way to my car."

A gust of wind tugged at the door as they opened it, slamming it back on its hinges. An American flag snapped like folded sheets on the pole above. Not a day Adele wanted to have a conversation outdoors.

"Did you speak to Teódulo Gomez?" she asked as they headed to the parking lot. "He told me in court this morning that Benitez was with him when Catherine was murdered."

"We interviewed him." Greco beeped open the doors of an unmarked Toyota Camry.

"And?"

"And nothing," said Greco. "Gomez said he and Benitez were drinking together under the bridge Friday night. He couldn't tell us what time that was, how long they were there, what Benitez was wearing, or whether anyone else saw them. Only thing he seemed sure of was that they were drinking Bowman's Vodka mixed with lemon-lime seltzer. He's as much of a witness as my neighbor's cat."

"Maybe you can find the containers under the bridge," said Adele. "See if there's any validity to what he's saying."

"Finding those containers proves nothing," said Greco. "Not when they were there or who they were with. And that's my final word on the matter. This has nothing to do with you."

"It has everything to do with Wil Martinez," said Adele. "He's in jail because of his connection to his brother. If there's a chance Benitez is innocent, Lake Holly could drop the obstruction charges—"

Greco held up his hands. "Nothing doing."

"Why? Because you're afraid he'll sue the police over his brother's shooting?"

"His brother's shooting was justified," said Greco. "The DA's not gonna see it any differently. Your boy's not coming out because there are too many loose ends." Greco ticked them off on his fingers. "We haven't found Catherine's phone. We don't yet have her phone records—"

"You're telling me why the case against Benitez isn't wrapped up," said Adele. "You're not telling me why you're so sure he's your guy."

Greco jingled his keys. "Call it cop's intuition."

"Well, your 'cop's intuition' seems to have no problem with charging a man who ended up on the wrong side of an unfair fight and socking him with a fine he can't hope to pay."

"Fine's been paid. In full," Greco growled. "Wanna know who paid it?"

"Who?"

"Todd Archer." Greco's eyes screwed up tight as bullets. "This poor kid—his sister's been murdered by an illegal. His father just died of a heart attack hastened by another illegal. And yet he has the charity of spirit to tell one of our officers at the hospital last night that he doesn't want any more hate and suffering. We would have let Gomez go on that alone, but he'd already been charged. So this morning, Todd paid the fine."

"Wow. He's a great young man." She meant it. She wished she'd gotten to know him under better circumstances.

"Yeah. He is." Greco opened his car door. "So let's drop the high-and-mighty crap about all your other *victims*. The only real victims here are Catherine and the Archer family. They're priority one. Everyone else can take a number."

Chapter 26

Vega quickly discovered that it didn't make much difference whether he was working for Mike Carp, his two consultants, Prescott and Vanderlinden, or the ambassador to Zimbabwe. The job was pretty much the same. Drive the Suburban. Park the Suburban. Stay quiet while Carp texted and made phone calls. Vega drove to meetings, civic events, and press conferences all over the county, then sat bored and cold in the car while Carp made speeches or dedicated some new school, post office, senior center—take your pick. At some locales—VFW halls, churches, and, *go figure,* bowling alleys—people cheered him. At libraries, student gathering centers, and any towns with people of color, he was booed.

Never had ten hours felt longer in Vega's life. Never had he ached more to talk to Adele. But she hadn't called or texted. The more time passed, the harder it became for him to make the first move. He had long arguments in his head. Arguments where he pointed out every logical reason why she had no business being angry with him. But each time he tried to commit his words to text, they fell flat. Calling would have been even harder. And so he sat and brooded and checked his screen as often as he could in the hopes that she'd be the one to find a way through their divide.

"I need you to deliver something for me on your way home," said Carp. He handed Vega a big manila envelope wrapped in plastic. The address was for a law firm in an industrial part of Lake Holly not far from La Casa: Kenner & Kenner. Vega had never heard of the firm.

"You can count the delivery time toward your weekly hours," said Carp. "I won't be needing you tomorrow until about noon."

"Thank you, sir," said Vega. "I'll drop it off."

It was dark by the time Vega nosed his pickup off the highway and into Lake Holly. A knot tightened in his stomach as he drove past La Casa and saw large DO NOT TRESPASS signs and police sawhorses out front.

The address for the drop-off was a two-story stucco building that must have been built by contractors with whatever was left over from various jobs. One side of the building was brick face. Another was tile. The plate-glass entrance doors were trimmed in a brass color. The double-hung windows had low-rent aluminum frames. The front doors were open, but the only people in the building at this hour seemed to be the Hispanic cleaning crew. Vega looked on a Velcro board in the lobby to see which office belonged to Kenner & Kenner. Maybe he could just leave it on a secretary's desk.

He took the stairs to the second floor and counted off doors until he found the right one. The roar of an industrial-strength vacuum cleaner down the hall drowned out all ambient noise. Vega tried the door to Kenner & Kenner. It was locked. He followed the vacuum sound to a plumbing contractor's office that was still being cleaned. A chubby Hispanic man was moving a suction wand over the carpet. Vega knew the man would never hear Vega's movements over the noise, so he stepped in front of him and held up the manila envelope. The man turned off the vacuum cleaner.

"Excuse me, señor?" said Vega in Spanish. "I need to deliver a package to a law firm down the hall. Can you let me in?"

The man rifled through a set of keys in the pocket of his jeans until he found the right one. Vega trailed him down the hallway and thanked him for unlocking the door. He stepped inside and turned on the light. The man's cell phone rang. He turned away to take the call, leaving Vega to try to figure out where to put the package.

The address was *Attn: Sarah Kenner*. Vega assumed Sarah Kenner was one of the partners. Both partners had the same last name. Siblings? Parent and child? Husband and wife? Vega searched the wall of degrees and certifications for answers. Mark Kenner's JD degree from Cornell was prominently displayed. He'd graduated ten years ago. Sarah Kenner's JD degree from Cornell was from the same period. Odds were, the Kenners were husband and wife. Tax attorneys, according to their certifications. They'd probably met in law school, just like Adele and her ex. *Adele.* Vega felt the pain of her name like an ulcer.

Vega noticed something else on the Kenners' wall of degrees. Sarah's undergraduate degree. From Oberlin. The name on it wasn't "Kenner." It was "Langstrom."

Sarah Langstrom.

The only Langstrom that Vega had ever heard of was Joy's professor. Was this a relative?

If so, his boss would be furious. From what Vega had gathered from Joy, Jeffrey Langstrom was a vocal opponent of Carp's Crystal Springs Golf Resort. No way would Carp want to do business with anyone connected to an enemy. Carp divided the world into friends and foes. Or as he called it, "the loyal ones" and the "backstabbers." "Backstabbers" got punished, no matter how small the disloyalty or how long ago it was inflicted. The other day, Vega overheard Carp tell the maitre d' at one of his restaurants to remove a reservation for a party of ten because the man who'd booked it had once publicly insulted him.

Vega had no idea what the insult was. But Carp's fury over it chilled him. If he didn't tell Carp about Sarah Kenner's possible connection to Langstrom, and Carp found out, would he blame Vega?

I'm only delivering a package, Vega told himself. But he knew there were no "onlys" to Mike Carp. Maybe the safest thing to do was figure out if there was a connection and then decide.

Three doors led off the waiting area. One of them had Sarah Kenner's nameplate on front. Vega tried the handle. It was unlocked. He stepped inside. The bookshelves were crammed with legal volumes. The shiny wood desk was scrupulously neat. What was he looking for? He couldn't say.

He walked around to her chair and placed the package on the center of her desk. Next to her phone, he noticed a collection of photos. They were the usual assemblage of family snapshots. A pale, frizzy-haired, young white woman appeared in several. Sarah, Vega supposed. In one, she was holding a baby in her lap and posing with a balding man, who was probably her husband, Mark. In another, there were two children. Both girls. In still another, there was some sort of large gathering with babies and children and a very old and hunched woman in a wheelchair. An older man was leaning into the shot on her right.

A man with a gray beard, glasses, and a long ponytail. *Jeffrey Langstrom.* Which meant Sarah Langstrom Kenner was Jeffrey Langstrom's daughter. Or perhaps his niece? Either way, she was family.

Did Mike Carp know? Should Vega tell him?

A woman's scream echoed through the hall, followed by panicked Spanish chatter. Vega threw the package down on Sarah Kenner's desk, slammed the office doors, and raced down the corridor. The voices were coming from below. From the lobby. Vega dashed down the stairs. The cleaning crew—two men, two women, all Hispanic, and probably all or mostly related to one another—were standing by the glass front doors, staring at a young white man who had staggered into the vestibule. He had two black eyes and was bleeding from the nose.

Vega took out his phone and dialed 911. He reeled off

the address of the building, identified himself as a cop, and asked for police and an ambulance. The cleaning crew started to back away. The last thing they wanted was to be involved in a situation with a beat-up white man.

Vega took out his shield. "Police!" he told them in Spanish. "Nothing bad's gonna happen to you. I promise. But you can't leave until the police arrive to take your statements." Then he turned his attention to the white man. He bent down. That's when he recognized the wide, fleshy face and beginnings of a double chin beneath the young man's stubble.

"You're one of the guys I saw at the vigil the other night," said Vega. "Kicking over those candles. What happened?"

The young man wiped his sleeve across his bloody nose. It looked broken. Whatever he'd done to that drunk at the vigil, it looked as if it had come back in spades to him.

"Goddamn beaners!" snarled the man. "Three of them ganged up on me! They'll pay for this. They'll *all* pay for this."

"The police and an ambulance are on their way," Vega assured him. "Do you know the three men who did this to you?"

"Bunch of cockroach spics. They should all go back to Mexico!"

"But do you know their names?"

"No." His voice came out choked. He was probably swallowing blood.

"What's your name?"

"Brad."

"Brad what?"

The young man hesitated.

"Look, Brad, the cops are going to ask you the same question as soon as they arrive."

"They won't have to," he said. "They know me."

"They've arrested you before?"

"No. My dad's Steve Jankowski. He's a detective in town."

Chapter 27

Two uniforms arrived, followed by the EMTs. One officer took Brad Jankowski's statement, while the EMTs loaded him onto a gurney and started a saline drip. The other cornered the panicky cleaning crew—probably all undocumented—and, with Vega's help translating, got their sketchy interviews and even sketchier contact information. Vega's own witness statement could wait. The cops knew that unlike the cleaning crew, he'd stick around.

Vega was finishing up with the other officer and the cleaning crew in the lobby when he felt a gust of cold air at his back. He turned to see the glass doors open and Louis Greco shuffle in. Greco frowned at the finger smears of Brad Jankowski's blood on the panes. Vega caught something he rarely saw on Greco's face. Some rent in that perfect mask of Zen indifference that Greco feigned at most crime scenes. He couldn't be neutral here. Brad Jankowski was the son of a colleague. This was personal.

Vega walked over. "If you're wondering," he said to Greco, "I called this in."

"So I heard." Greco managed to stuff down whatever he was feeling before. The lake went still again, with no evidence of the disturbance beneath. "You seem to be single-handedly responsible for ninety-nine percent of the mayhem in this town, Vega. And you don't even live here."

"I was delivering a package for Carp."

"Yeah? Next time play errand boy someplace else." Greco thrust his chin at the front-entrance doors. "Take a walk with me."

Outside, the moon had a sharp, stainless-steel edge to it. The snow looked like discarded pieces of Styrofoam along the curbs, shaved down to little more than a dandruff dusting on the rooftops and awnings. Everything in this part of Lake Holly was closed at this hour. The propane company. The auto salvage yard. The wholesale carpet warehouse.

"I don't like this. I don't like this at all," said Greco. "This whole town's a powder keg about to explode. Fistfights at the high school. Graffiti in the parking lots. And your boss there, Carp, ain't helping things by mouthing off with that 'Catherine's Law' every chance he gets. All that thing will do is give us paperwork headaches and set the clock back twenty years on race relations in Lake Holly," said Greco. "Hate to say it, but I'm actually beginning to wish La Casa was back in business and your girlfriend was running the show. At least things were smoother."

"For the town and for me," said Vega.

"She still sore at you for working for Carp?"

"I don't know," said Vega. "We can't seem to talk to each other without yelling right now."

"You need to find something you both agree on."

"Like what?"

"I don't know. What do you think I am? Dear Abby? What do I know about anybody's love life?"

"Speaking of love lives, have you found that waiter yet?" asked Vega. "The one Todd Archer fired from the Magnolia Inn?"

"Affirmative," said Greco. "Todd didn't have any information, but one of his waiters had a cell phone contact. We located him down in Port Carroll. He goes by the name 'Alex Romero.'" They both knew "Alex Romero" probably wasn't the waiter's real name or all of his real name, in any case.

"I'm guessing there's a 'but' in there somewhere," said Vega.

"We ran Romero's DNA. He's not the baby's father. Claims he never had sex with Catherine. According to him, Catherine was a look-don't-touch kind of girl."

"Somebody touched," said Vega.

"Yeah, but not him. Plus, he has an alibi for the night of her murder."

"Huh." Vega fingered the raised stitches on his forehead. He couldn't wait to get the thread out in a few days. "You find her phone yet?"

"Negative. We got the printout of her calls. But it looks like she's one of those girls who uses instant messaging, so the records aren't quite as useful as we'd hoped."

"No calls on the night she disappeared?"

"Nothing after she went to La Casa," said Greco. "Before that, she made one call to the Magnolia Inn, apparently to check her work schedule, and one to that friend of hers with the purple hair—"

"Zoe?"

"That's the one. We interviewed her and she said she and Catherine made plans to see each other Saturday for lunch."

"You think Zoe knew Catherine was pregnant?"

"She never mentioned it when we interviewed her. In truth? I'm not even sure Catherine knew. Or if she did, she was keeping it to herself. That Archer family's nothing if not secretive. I'm not convinced John Archer even died of a heart attack."

"He looked pretty out of it at the vigil," said Vega. "I was wondering if he suffered an overdose of pills mixed with booze."

"The ME's office is still running the tox screen," said Greco. "I can't tell you if he was under the influence of any drugs—legal or otherwise. But I can tell you they didn't find any alcohol in his system."

"Really? He looked drunk to me."

"Dr. Gupta found some liver damage, which would be consistent with someone who abused alcohol long-term. Maybe he was on the twelve-step."

"You'd think his wife would be more forthcoming," said Vega. "The guy's dead. What difference does it make?"

"It makes all the difference in the world if you're an Archer," said Greco. "You don't tell the community that your little princess got knocked up or that your paterfamilias is a recovering alcoholic with a pill problem. You don't suggest that you're swimming in debt and hanging on by your fingertips if the Crystal Springs Golf Resort doesn't get built."

"Is that last part true?" asked Vega.

"It is if Mike Carp decides to ditch the deal, now that Archer's dead. Least that's what one of the bankers in town who holds the loans told me." Greco crumpled a piece of cellophane in his pocket. "This whole case is like a set of dominos that just keeps falling. Catherine's murder. Archer's death. Now, Steve's son's in the hospital and the whole town's ready to explode. All because one little high-school girl tutored the wrong guy."

"You don't know that yet."

Greco pulled up the collar on his coat. "Yeah, I think I do. And it's not just because that would ease my conscience and Sanchez's. Benitez was one of the last people to see Catherine alive. He had that key chain with her picture on it in his room. We've got that video that shows him buying beer for her at Hank's Deli." Greco's dark eyes held Vega's. "There's one other thing too. One thing we haven't made public yet."

"What's that?"

"Something we found comparing Catherine's phone records to Benitez's," said Greco. "Two days before Catherine's death, Benitez made four calls to her phone over the span of two hours."

"He *called* her? Why would he call her?"

"My theory? I think this guy was developing a fantasy life around her," said Greco. "First, he swiped that key chain. Then he made those calls. Maybe he was drunk. Maybe the last one was to apologize. It sure explains why she'd follow him to that deli. She *knew* him. Maybe even trusted him a little. And all the while, he was building up some sort of sick scenario in his head."

"But the baby wasn't his," Vega pointed out.

"Who knows if that wasn't the thing that tipped him over the edge? He thought she was a virgin princess. He felt deceived. Or jealous."

One of the officers called over to Greco to ask him something.

"Be right there," said Greco. He turned back to Vega. "We're not releasing this information—you understand? Bad enough that the community thinks this was a crime of opportunity. They don't need to find out Benitez was stalking her."

Chapter 28

Vega felt the cold, wet nose on his bare forearm first, followed by a steamy lungful of dog breath. Daylight had barely crested the horizon.

"*Ay, puñeta,* Diablo! Were you a rooster in a previous life?" If Vega didn't get up soon, he'd have seventy pounds of dog pouncing on his chest, along with whatever chewable goodies Diablo decided to refashion in his honor. Sneakers. Vega's bike helmet. Pillows. The dog had the good sense at least never to touch Vega's guitars or amps. He knew his limits.

Vega swung his legs over the side of the bed and slipped into sweats and a T-shirt. Diablo raced down the stairs and pressed his wet nose against the sliding glass doors to the deck. Clouds as clotted as spoiled milk hovered over a lake the same texture and hue. The world was devoid of color this morning. White hillsides. Gray stalks of trees. Frost on the glass. Heaven and earth were in agreement for once. It was impossible to tell them apart.

Diablo pawed at the glass and barked.

"You want to go for a run?"

At the sound of the word "run," Diablo tore around the living room in circles, his tail in the air, his little flaps jiggling on his upturned ears. Vega laughed.

"Okay, okay. I hear you." That was the thing about Diablo. He knew what Vega needed, even before Vega knew.

The early-morning air tasted of peppermint and wood smoke. The burn felt good in Vega's lungs. Invigorating. He and Diablo ran five miles around the lake, waving to the few other year-rounders who lived up here this time of year. They all knew each other. There was a camaraderie that wasn't there in the summer when owners and renters and extended families crowded the place. Vega liked the off-season better.

When they returned to the house, Vega saw a silver Mercedes idling in his driveway behind his truck. He stopped short when he caught the figure at the wheel. In the six years Vega had lived at the lake, he couldn't recall his ex-wife ever visiting—not even to drop off Joy. Vega usually did all the shuttling.

Wendy turned off her engine and cracked open her car door. Vega grabbed the dog's collar. Wendy was allergic to dogs. Plus, Diablo was an effusive greeter. He could be intimidating if you didn't know what a marshmallow he was.

"It's okay," Vega called out, snapping a leash on Diablo's collar. "I got him!"

She stepped out of her car, but stayed close to the door. "He won't bite?"

"Slobber? Yes. Bite? No." Diablo jumped eagerly as if to prove his point. "Is everything okay with Joy?"

"Yes and no," said Wendy. "I have a breakfast conference in Whitman Falls in about forty-five minutes. I figured I'd stop by on my way up. Do you have a few minutes to talk?"

"Um . . . sure," said Vega. "Come in. I'll put Diablo upstairs so you don't get all watery-eyed for your meeting."

Vega grabbed Diablo's favorite rawhide chew and his water dish and took him upstairs. When he came back down, Wendy was standing by his sliding glass doors, looking out past Vega's deck at the lake.

"I can see why you like it here."

"It has its charms. The commute, unfortunately, isn't one of them." Vega peeled off a sweatshirt and tossed it across a chair in the dining area. He would have liked to have showered before talking to Wendy. But hey, it wasn't like they didn't know every inch of each other already.

"Would you like some coffee? Tea? I have Joy's herbal crap. Looks more like something you'd smoke than drink."

Wendy smiled. "Herbal crap it is." She always got Vega's sense of humor, even when she pretended not to. It was part of their shtick. He was the blue-collar wisecracking urchin from the Bronx and she was the princess—until she discovered it was much more comfortable being married to a king.

Vega walked into the open kitchen area and put the kettle on. Wendy took a seat at the counter. There was an awkward silence between them. It had been years since they'd tried to converse one-on-one without a lawyer or Joy between them. Vega wanted the situation to feel natural. But inside, he still felt like that skinny twenty-three-year-old he'd been when he first met her—

outmatched and outclassed in every way. She was an Ivy League Ph.D. fresh out of a relationship with a Jewish cardiologist. He was a commuter-college grad, five years her junior, dying behind a desk at an insurance agency and itching to go on the road with his band. Their relationship was supposed to be a fling. And then— surprise, surprise—Joy came along and everything changed. For a while, anyway. You can only pretend so long to be something you're not.

Vega searched his cabinets for a mug that wasn't chipped. The only one was Max's *I Love You A Latke*.

"My, uh . . . condolences to the Archer family," said Vega.

"Thank you."

"This must be really hard on you."

"It's hard on everyone."

"Yes. But . . ." He placed the mug on the counter in front of Wendy and held her gaze. "You personally."

"I'm not here about me," said Wendy. "I'm here about . . ." She mouthed the words on the mug. "'I Love You A Latke'? Where did you get this?"

"From Adele's elderly neighbor. It was supposed to be for Joy, but she didn't want it. I'm going to hold it for her until she changes her mind."

"Hmmm." Wendy studied the mug. "It might be a while."

The kettle boiled. Vega poured Wendy's tea. He filled a glass of cold water for himself. It was the only thing he ever wanted after a long run.

Wendy stirred her tea. She seemed to be gathering her thoughts. Vega didn't rush her.

"The other day at Catherine's wake," she began,

"you got me thinking. About Joy and this professor. I think it's more than a schoolgirl crush."

"What's the attraction?" asked Vega. "Have you seen this guy? He's like something out of *Harry Potter*. Professor Dumbledore after one too many bong hits."

Wendy laughed. It felt good to see her laugh. Her face turned soft and girlish. It loosened Vega. This was probably the most relaxed he'd felt in her presence since they were married.

"I think this professor's got a Svengali hold over Joy," said Wendy. "She talks about him like he's a candidate for the Nobel Peace Prize."

"Have you confronted Joy about any of this?"

"Confronted her, how?"

"Asked her if Dr. Huggy's put any moves on her, I don't know. Mother-daughter talk."

"'Moves on her' is not mother-daughter talk, Jimmy. Mother-daughter talk is 'which shoes would you like to borrow?' If I ask Joy if she's sleeping with her professor, she'll only get angry and defensive. She'll tell me I'm the last person who should judge her."

Vega fingered the beads of water on his glass. He didn't want to admit that Joy had a point.

"I know what you're thinking," said Wendy. "I can still read you like you have no skin. You're thinking I lost my creds in that department years ago."

"It's a little difficult to think otherwise with all the rumors flying."

"The rumors are wrong."

"Okaaay."

"Stop saying that like you don't believe me." Wendy

threw up her hands. "Why do we always rehash the same history?"

"Maybe because history repeats itself?"

She pushed her stool back from the table. They'd been together twenty minutes and already they were fighting. "For your information—and *only* your information—John came to me as a psychologist, not as a friend or lover. That's why I'm duty-bound not to reveal anything about our sessions."

"But he's dead," said Vega. "It doesn't matter anymore."

"The rules of confidentiality don't end with death, Jimmy. Unless I'm given permission by his next of kin, I can't discuss anything. Even telling you he was under treatment is technically a breach of confidentiality."

"In your circles? Admitting you're seeing a shrink's like offering up the name of your Pilates instructor."

"You know I hate that word."

"Okay, *ther-a-pist.* But either way, you know I'm right. So level with me, Wendy. It's more than that."

Diablo whimpered from the bedroom upstairs.

"I'm so sorry you have to confine him on my account."

"I'll let him outside," said Vega. "He never goes far. He knows where his meal ticket is."

Vega fetched the dog and let him out the front door. He hoped Diablo would find a stick to gnaw on. Something other than the garden hose, which now had nice big teeth marks in it.

He walked back into the kitchen area. Wendy was staring at her tea.

"Look, Jimmy," she began. "If you knew the stress

John was under, you'd understand why his sessions with me had to remain secret. That's why we held them at odd hours. So people wouldn't know."

"I hear he had big financial troubles on account of that golf resort deal he made with Carp."

Wendy raised an eyebrow. "How did you find *that* out?"

Vega shrugged. "Not everyone is bound by the same stringent confidentiality rules as you. From what I saw at the vigil, Archer also had some drinking and drug issues to boot."

"You're wrong. On both scores."

"So you're telling me he died of a heart attack?"

She slid away from the question. "Why does my relationship to John matter to you so much anyway?"

"Because my . . ." He didn't want to use the word "girlfriend" in front of Wendy. "Adele lost her job on account of Catherine's murder and Benitez's involvement. And now Catherine's father's dead under mysterious circumstances and I'm hearing he had financial troubles and was undergoing secret psychological treatment. All of it makes what happened seem less and less straightforward."

"John's situation has nothing to do with Catherine's murder," said Wendy. "John was just trying to do the best for his family. And now . . ." Her voice drifted off.

"Now what?"

"His family is ruined."

"Because they can't repay his business loans?"

"Because Carp is going to pull out of their deal. The only insurance John had to stop him is gone."

"You mean, like, business insurance?" It had been two decades since Vega, the college accounting major, had had to deal with such things as annuity clauses and term conversions. He broke out in a cold sweat just thinking about them.

"Not that kind of insurance," said Wendy. "John had some sort of . . . video. I don't know what was on it exactly, but I know it was important. It kept Carp from bailing. And it's gone."

"When did it disappear?"

"A couple of weeks ago. I believe he kept it in his safe."

"Can't be more than half-a-dozen suspects who would have access to something like that. Did he call the police?"

"No. That's not the Archer style," said Wendy. "I think John knew who took it. He didn't want to make a fuss. He just wanted it back."

"I can let the Lake Holly PD know—"

"Absolutely not, Jimmy. John is dead. His daughter's dead. I have no idea what the future holds for Robin and Todd. That's why everything I told you has to stay between us." Wendy pushed her mug to one side. "Besides, I didn't come here to discuss John. I came here to talk about Joy."

"You could have called me on the phone for that."

"But then I couldn't have shown you this."

Wendy took out her cell phone and scrolled down to a text message someone had sent her with a video attached. She handed her phone to Vega.

"You don't know this girl. She was in Joy's high-school graduating class. She goes to Valley now—just like Joy. I warn you, the video is disturbing."

Vega pressed play. A naked white teenage girl lay faceup on an unmade queen-size bed in a room lit only by some incandescent bulb off-camera. At first, Vega thought she was asleep. But the position looked too uncomfortable for sleep. Her legs were splayed. Her socks were still on her feet. Her bra was unhooked and pushed up uncomfortably under her chin. Those were the only pieces of clothing she was wearing.

She wasn't asleep. She was passed out.

Whoever was filming didn't touch her, but he captured every part of her, leaving nothing to the imagination. Right down to the butterfly tattoo across her lower hip. Vega recognized her immediately from her short dyed purple hair and the ring through her nose.

"That's Zoe Beck, isn't it?" asked Vega.

"You *know* her?"

"Joy mentioned that Zoe was friends with Catherine. I saw her approach the family at the vigil the other night. Where did you get this?"

"Zoe's mother is a cashier at Safeway. She knows Joy also goes to Valley and that you're a cop. She was very distraught when I saw her at the store last night. She told me Zoe just dropped out of Valley. No explanation. Nothing. This girl was working three jobs to stay in. She had an internship she loved. Her grades were good. Her mother thought that Catherine's murder was the reason. Then she found this video on her daughter's cell. She tried to confront Zoe, but Zoe won't talk about it. She said it was some frat boy who filmed her, but she won't say more. Either she doesn't know the boy's name or she's too embarrassed. She refused to go to the police."

Vega played the video again, this time paying attention to the girl's surroundings. The room was so shadowy that Vega couldn't make out much. The camera picked up plain beige sheets on a four-poster bed and a patterned plaid comforter that could have come from any standard department store. There was no ambient noise, save for a cat meowing off-camera.

"Are fraternities allowed to have pets?"

"The dorms aren't, but the frat houses are, I think," said Wendy.

"You want me to talk to Zoe's mom? I think it might freak Zoe out too much if I confronted her directly."

"Yes, you're probably right," said Wendy. "That would be good. Zoe may not know the boy's name, but she could certainly identify him."

"If she's willing to come forward, she can put this guy in jail."

"I think she's humiliated," said Wendy. "Which got me thinking about Joy. About how she thinks she can take care of herself—just like this girl, Zoe. But things can go horribly wrong—with lifetime consequences."

"We can't tell Joy about Zoe," said Vega. "That would be a breach of the girl's privacy."

"I realize that," said Wendy. "But maybe you can, I don't know, *impress* upon Joy, as a cop more than a dad, how she's got to watch out for herself."

"I'll do that," said Vega. "And if she doesn't listen, maybe my next talk will be with Dr. Huggy."

Wendy finished her tea, Vega went outside to collar Diablo. He expected he'd have to whistle for the dog. But Diablo was in the driveway, pawing at something in the snow beneath the rear bumper of Vega's truck. Vega snapped a leash on Diablo and then nudged him aside to examine the object. It was a GPS tracker. Vega scooped it out of the snow. It was black and rectangular, the size and shape of a pack of cigarettes. A small green light flashed at four-second intervals.

Vega showed the tracker to Wendy when she stepped out of the house.

"Is that Mercedes of yours in hock? Because I just found this in the snow behind my truck." Vega knew that sometimes dealerships installed GPS devices on leased vehicles to guarantee a quick return if the client defaulted.

Wendy looked offended. "We bought our Mercedes outright. In cash. From Alan's bonus last year."

It figured.

"Besides," said Wendy, "why would you think it came from *my* car when it was sitting in back of *your* truck?"

"Because my truck's paid off too." Vega turned the tracker off and walked the perimeter of his black Ford pickup. He'd hit a bad pothole turning onto the lake community's main road last night. Could that have dislodged it from his rear bumper? If so, who put it there? And why? No one would be interested in taking possession of a seven-year-old truck with eighty thousand miles on it. He didn't have a wife looking for proof of infidelity. He didn't owe anyone money. Those were the usual reasons people put a tracking device on a vehicle without the owner's permission.

"Well, you turned it off now." Wendy shrugged. "Problem solved."

Vega wondered if the problem was just beginning.

Chapter 29

Zoe's mother's name was Patsy Walker. She lived above a nail salon at the north end of Lake Holly, in a neighborhood that had largely turned Hispanic. She was home this morning because one of her younger children was sick with a respiratory infection and her mother, who had diabetes and was in a wheelchair, needed Patsy to drive her to the doctor later. When Vega entered the small, well-kept living room, he could smell the acetone from the nail salon radiating through the floorboards. He wondered if that was one of the reasons the child had a respiratory infection.

"Thank you for coming over," said Patsy. "Maybe we can speak in the kitchen. I don't want Travis, my little one, overhearing any of this."

The boy with the croupy cough looked to be about eight. He was sitting in front of a large flat-screen TV that took up most of the living room. A cartoon was playing at top decibel. Patsy's mother, sitting in the wheelchair, was watching too.

"Sure. No problem," said Vega. He tried to gauge Patsy's age. He couldn't. She had girlish eyes and brassy hair, which was growing out pale brown at the roots. And yet her cheeks were gaunt. Two parentheses bracketed her lips. He wondered if she'd lost a tooth or two due to lack of dental care or an accident. She looked like she'd been quite stunning as a teenager—far more than her daughter. But her stomach bulged now and her shoulders sagged. He had a sense she'd had Zoe young. Probably as a teenager. Which meant she was no more than about thirty-five.

"This is my third sick day this month," Patsy explained. "I'm probably going to lose my job at this rate."

"At the Safeway?"

"At Lake Holly Discount Tires. I work at the Safeway in the evenings and at the tire store on weekends and while the kids are in school. I also do nails downstairs when they need me to fill in."

Patsy Walker held three jobs—seven days a week, it seemed—and she still lived here, in these few rented rooms above a nail salon. Vega hadn't seen her car or Zoe's, but he was betting they both were on their last legs, held together with repairs they were still paying off on maxed-out credit cards. Vega thought back to his own single mother and their couple of rooms in the Bronx. He wondered at the grit and determination it had taken for Luisa Rosario-Vega to get him beyond this. It didn't look like Patsy ever would. And now Zoe might not either—all because of some callous and twisted boy.

Patsy gestured for Vega to have a seat on one of the mismatched chairs at a rickety kitchen table. There

were jam stains in one corner where the laminate had
peeled off. She wiped the sticky spot down. On a wall
above the table, Patsy had tacked up a poster of footprints in the sand. The "Jesus carried you" poem.
Vega's mother used to tack up inspirational religious
poems all over their apartment as well. Vega saw more
such poems on the refrigerator, along with a formal
snapshot of a young, fair-skinned black man in a U.S.
Marines uniform. It sat next to a magnet from the Mike
Carp campaign: *Take Back Our County!* Nobody needed
to ask from whom. Everybody who voted for him knew.

Patsy assumed Vega was staring at the photograph.

"My nephew," she said. "He's done three tours in
Afghanistan."

"You must be very proud of him." Vega looked at the
photo and back at the campaign magnet. He couldn't
reconcile the two. Patsy Walker's nephew was biracial.
Her daughter's friend, Lydia Mendez, was the child of
undocumented immigrants. Her daughter's other close
friend, Catherine, volunteered at La Casa. Patsy
Walker lived among Latinos and had more in common
with the poor, deeply religious people here than with
the Mike Carps of the world. And yet she'd obviously
voted for Vega's new boss. Maybe it was the way Carp
promised something to a woman whose life seemed so
desperate for promise. Like a secular version of the
Old Testament God—powerful, vengeful, ready to
smite all enemies. Promising much to the faithful. Delivering little but their faith.

"Would you like some coffee?" Patsy asked him.

"No, ma'am, thank you—"

"Patsy. Please call me Patsy. I feel like I sort of know

you, since I know your ex-wife a little. And Joy, of course."

"Where's Zoe right now?" asked Vega.

"She's at work over at the department store. She hustles between jobs, like me. I guess you saw the video. She'd be mortified that I showed you."

"Did she tell you anything about where it came from?"

Patsy shook her head. "Only that some frat boy took it. I have no idea if she even knows his name. He wasn't a boyfriend. She doesn't have time for a boyfriend and well . . . boys have never been especially kind to Zoe, as you can see."

Patsy's eyes turned glassy. She snuck a glance out to the living room to make sure her son hadn't seen. Vega wished he had a tissue to offer her. He noticed a stack of tiny square napkins by his elbow with a McDonald's emblem in the corner. He held one out to her now.

"Thank you," said Patsy. She dabbed her eyes.

"Why doesn't Zoe want to see this boy punished?"

"Embarrassment, I guess. Humiliation. Zoe doesn't do drugs. She's not a drinker. It was totally out of character for her to get drunk and pass out. Totally out of character to end up in some boy's room."

Every parent says that. Even Vega. They were almost always wrong. He'd misjudged Joy more than once.

"I know what you're thinking," said Patsy. "You see her purple hair and nose ring and tattoos. You look at where she comes from and you figure her for a druggie and a girl who sleeps around—"

Vega started to protest, but Patsy stopped him. "It's

all camouflage—more to keep people away than to at-
tract them. Until Catherine and Lydia came into her
life, Zoe never had a real friend. She spent all her time
holed up reading science fiction and fantasy books. It
breaks my heart what happened to Catherine. She was
a year younger than Zoe, but they just clicked on every
level. Do you know what she did for Zoe's birthday
earlier this month?"

"What?"

"Between tuition and everything, Zoe didn't have
any extra cash at all. I baked her a birthday cake, of
course. But Catherine—she came over while Zoe was
at work and decorated the whole apartment with bal-
loons and butterfly stickers. Zoe loves butterflies. It
was just so Catherine—to figure out what Zoe needed
and then try to make it happen. It really lifted her spirits. She'd been sort of down before that."

"Did she say why she was down?"

"I think it was just the workload. Classes. Her jobs.
She loved her internship, but that was a lot of work
too."

"So Zoe and Catherine were still close after she
went off to Valley?"

"Oh, very. Catherine went to the campus nearly every
Friday night. I think she liked the social life there."

"Really?" Vega thought about the Archers insisting
that Catherine spent her Fridays at La Casa. Their
daughter wouldn't be the first teenager to lie about that
sort of thing.

"What did Zoe and Catherine do together there?"
asked Vega.

"They took in a lot of the art films. They went to
some rallies. Zoe was involved in a lot of environmen-

tal issues on campus. She wanted to go into wildlife conservation. She loves animals. We're not allowed to keep pets here, but if she could, she'd keep a whole menagerie. That's the saddest part about her quitting college," said Patsy. "She had to quit her internship as well. That was going to be a really big opportunity for her. She didn't want to do anything to mess it up."

"Did Catherine's parents know she was spending so much time with Zoe?"

Patsy hesitated. "They have . . ." She stopped herself. "I feel so bad for her mother right now. I don't think it's my place to say anything."

"I'm not asking for the sake of gossip," said Vega. "I'm asking as a cop."

Patsy balled up her napkin and took a deep breath. "Robin Archer didn't want her daughter socializing with my Zoe."

"Was there a specific reason?"

"Well," Patsy gestured to the small kitchen with its mismatched appliances, "we aren't them, clearly. But also, Zoe has always been her own person. Very headstrong. She probably encouraged some rebellion in Catherine toward her mother and her mother's values. She would have been against the Archers going into business with Mike Carp and building on those wetlands. I'm sure she expressed her beliefs to Catherine."

"At the vigil the other night," said Vega, "I saw Zoe go over and try to speak to Robin Archer. Robin rebuffed her."

"I think Robin blames Zoe for Catherine becoming more independent-minded as she got older. She probably thought that once Zoe started Valley, their friendship would fade. But if anything, it grew stronger. I'm

sure they both thought they'd be best friends forever."
Patsy dabbed at her eyes. "Catherine even wrote that
on Zoe's birthday card."

"I'd really like to speak to your daughter," said
Vega. "Can you ask her to call me?"

"I will," said Patsy. "But like I said, Zoe's very stub-
born. I can only hope she follows through."

Vega rose from the table. Then a thought occurred
to him.

"Do you think Catherine knew about this video?"

"Possibly," said Patsy. "The girls shared everything."

Vega wondered if "everything" included Catherine's pregnancy and the identity of the baby's father. If
so, then Zoe knew far more about Catherine than anyone imagined. Including the police.

Chapter 30

Vega left Patsy's apartment unnerved by all she'd told him. At the very least, some frat boy on Joy's campus had filmed a girl he'd likely raped—and scared her enough she was unwilling to come forward. Vega couldn't tell Joy all of this, but he could warn her. He sent her a text: **dinner tonight?**

She didn't answer. She wasn't the only one ignoring him.

Adele.

Vega couldn't take the silence between them any longer. So he swallowed his pride and stopped by Hank's Deli to pick up some bagels and cream cheese—a peace offering. Maybe food could do what his words could not. Lord knew, Oscar needed the business. Daily it seemed, the shrine to Benitez outside his store grew bigger and the number of patrons inside grew smaller.

He expected to find Adele home, but when he got to her house, her car wasn't in the driveway and there was a police cruiser parked outside Max Zimmerman's.

Two uniformed cops were banging loudly on the old man's door.

Vega pulled into Adele's driveway and ran over. He recognized both officers from the vigil the other night, though he'd forgotten their names. The younger one was so fair-skinned that Vega could see the blue of his veins on his wrists. The older one had a name Vega could never remember. Something Italian with a lot of vowels.

"What are you doing, Vega?" asked the Italian cop. His name tag read, *Ianelli*. "Following us around?"

"My girlfriend lives next door. I know Max Zimmerman. What's wrong?"

"We got a report that some old guy was walking around on the sidewalk exposing himself. When we got here, he was already back inside. He won't answer his door. We may have to break it down."

"What? For an eighty-eight-year-old man? He forgets to lock half the time anyway."

Ianelli tried the handle. It was unlocked. That's when Vega remembered the gun on Zimmerman's side table. "He owns a .357 Magnum."

Both cops felt for their holsters. Vega threw himself in front of the door.

"Before you guys get any ideas of pulling a Benitez here," said Vega, "the gun's legal. Zimmerman has no criminal record—not even a driving infraction. The man just got out of the hospital from a fall. He's probably shaky and nervous. Let me talk to him, all right? He knows me."

Vega knocked on the front door. "Mr. Zimmerman? Sir? It's Jimmy Vega. Adele's boyfriend? I helped you when you fell the other day? Please open up, sir. There are police officers here. We're all trained professionals. We just want to make sure you're okay."

"They want to break into my house and take me away!" came a raspy voice on the other side of the door. "Nobody will ever do that to me again! Nobody!"

Vega decided not to point out that Zimmerman had forgotten to lock the door and no break-in was necessary. "Mr. Zimmerman, nobody is going to take you away. I promise. Just open the door and talk to us. I'll be right here."

Zimmerman opened it a crack and stood there in his dead wife's fluffy pink bathrobe, holding on to his three-pronged cane. Vega saw right away what some neighbor—Mrs. Morrison, no doubt—had called about. He wasn't wearing any clothes beneath his robe. Not even boxer shorts. He probably hadn't realized it.

"Mr. Zimmerman? The police just want to talk to you. Can you please open the door and show us both your hands?"

"Why?"

"So we can make sure you're not armed. You're afraid of these men. But believe me, they're just as afraid of you." Vega could feel the two officers behind him shuffling around. No cop likes to admit that he's scared of the people he comes into contact with. And yet, if civilians realized how often simple fear, rather than malice, played a role in police encounters, maybe everyone would calm down a little.

Zimmerman opened the door wider and showed Vega and the two officers his hands. One was wrapped around the handle of the three-pronged cane. The other was empty. It was pretty clear he wasn't carrying a concealed weapon. His open robe left nothing to the imagination.

"Sir? May we come inside?" asked Vega.

"Okay."

Vega stepped into the foyer, followed by the two uniforms. The air was hot and fetid.

"Mr. Zimmerman," said Ianelli, "we received a complaint from a neighbor—"

"What?" asked Zimmerman. "Speak up! I can't hear you."

"I said, we received a complaint from a neighbor that you were walking around on the sidewalk exposing yourself."

"You mean like some queer fairy or something?" Zimmerman was old-school. No PC here. "Who said this terrible thing? Who? Mrs. Morrison?"

"Mrs. Morrison lives right across the fence," said Vega. "She and her kids are always throwing dog feces and garbage in his yard—"

Ianelli put up a hand to silence Vega. He turned to Zimmerman. "Sir, the issue is not who alleged it, but whether it took place."

"I have a cane. I'm wearing a robe that requires two hands to tie. *Two hands*. Please tell me how I'm supposed to keep my robe closed and also get my morning paper. And what sort of meshuggener goes looking at an old man anyway?"

Vega noticed the two cops taking in the house. News-papers all over the floor. The smell of stale food in the garbage or left on a counter. The younger cop wrinkled his nose. *Hart* was his last name. Ianelli got a kind look on his face. Maybe he had older relatives he cared for too. "Sir?" Ianelli asked. "Do you have a nurse's aide? A helper who comes in?"

Zimmerman waved the question away. " I can take care of myself."

"You should probably get someone. A family member or someone from an agency. If we have to come back here again for the same complaint or similar complaints, we may have to notify social services. The matter may be out of your hands and ours."

"You would take an old man from his house? Against his wishes?" Zimmerman's eyes grew wide. Something like fury burned deep within. Vega sensed he'd been a fighter in his youth—if not physically, then certainly in spirit. Vega had an image of Zimmerman taking his cane and swatting the officers in the legs. Assault. They would definitely take him then.

"This is supposed to be a free country. A free country!" Zimmerman shouted. Vega stepped in between him and the officers. He turned to the cops. "How about you let me take it from here, okay?"

Officer Hart went to object, but Ianelli stopped him. He turned to Vega. "He needs care, Vega. I'm happy to step back, but someone's got to get him help. He can get help from an agency. Or go to a home. But something has to change. Otherwise, the next time, we may have to act." The cop looked over Vega's shoulder. "You understand me, Mr. Zimmerman?"

"Nobody takes me out of my house," Zimmerman repeated. "Nobody." Vega wasn't sure if the old man was responding to the officer's threat or restating what he'd said before. Vega just wanted the two cops gone. He ushered them to the door.

"Let me see what I can do."

After the officers left, Zimmerman was still muttering about being taken from his house. Vega tried to make him sit down and get calm. He brought him a glass of water. He sat across from him on a chair in the living room beneath a colorful framed poster of a carousel. He leaned forward, his elbows on his thighs, relaxed and casual. But his voice was stone-cold serious.

"Mr. Zimmerman—you need to listen to what I'm about to tell you," Vega said. "You can't stay alone anymore. You've got to get someone to come in and help you. That, or maybe go to assisted living. Some of those places are very nice."

"They're like having one foot in the grave and one on a banana peel. No thank you! I want to die in my home."

"Who's talking about dying?" asked Vega. "Look, let me call your son—"

"No."

"Why not?"

"He's not my son. He's my ex–son-in-law."

"Okay. We'll call him—"

"No."

"Then how about your daughter?"

"She's dead. Died of cancer right before my wife passed. I don't need anyone's help. I'm okay with dying in my own home."

"Stop talking about dying," said Vega. "Is that what that gun on your dresser's about? I sure hope not."

"That gun is for my protection."

"Then you need to secure it better."

"I did. It's now next to my hospital bed in the den."

"I mean, lock it up," said Vega. "And you need to

stop talking about dying or I'm going to take it away. For your own safety—"

"That gun *is* my safety!" Zimmerman insisted. "As for dying? We're *all* dying, Jimmy. You. Me. The only question is where and when."

Ay, puñeta! Vega was no good at handling heavy subjects like this. "Let me text Adele." He sent her a quick message to explain where he was and what was going on. He thought about Greco's advice last night—about how he and Adele needed to find common ground. Maybe Max Zimmerman was it.

"I'm not suicidal, Jimmy." Zimmerman reached across and put a hand over Vega's cell phone. He peered at Vega over the tops of his black-rimmed glasses. "I'm an old man who wants to spend what's left of my life in the comfort of my own home. Is that such a crime?"

"Then please stop talking about dying."

Zimmerman sat back and laughed. Vega wasn't expecting that. "Ah. You're a Catholic, aren't you? You were raised on all that talk of heaven and hell. Hell is right here, Jimmy. Trust me, I've seen it." Max thumped his left hand with the partially missing finger on his chest. "Nothing on the other side scares me in the least. The only thing that scares me is on this side."

"What are you scared of?"

"Losing my independence." Zimmerman shot a glance at his front door like the cops were still behind it. "Please don't let them take it from me."

"Then let Adele get someone in here to help. She knows a lot of people."

"I can't afford it. I'm living on Social Security and my small pension from Adventureland." *The county amusement park.*

"Maybe Adele can work out an arrangement. Room and board in return for *some* care."

"And what if I don't like the person?"

"She'll find someone else." Vega tried to get inside Zimmerman's head. "Look at this in simple, logical terms. You do nothing, okay?"

"Uh-huh—"

"And then you fall or the police come back here. They may make the choice for you. Why not make it for yourself?"

"I'll think about it."

Vega's phone dinged. It was a text from Adele. The first text they'd exchanged in days. It was a start.

"She's on her way home," said Vega. "Let me talk to her about this, all right?"

"Talk. Of course . . . talk." Zimmerman shrugged. "Talk costs nothing. *Del dicho al hecho hay mucho trecho.*"

Vega froze. *"Between word and deed, there's a great distance."* A Latin-American proverb. Zimmerman delivered it with his trademark Eastern European accent. But there was no mistaking the fluidness in his words. "You speak Spanish?"

Zimmerman smiled. "A little."

He'd never mentioned it to Adele. He'd never tried once to communicate in Spanish with any of the landscapers and handymen she'd sent over. Maybe he wasn't confident in his command. Still, Vega felt like there were layers to Max Zimmerman that he was only barely aware of.

Chapter 31

Vega sat in his truck, checking his cell phone messages, while he waited for Adele to return home. He had one from Mike Carp.

Need you at a press conference at noon in Broad Plains. Meet me at the offices of Americans for Sensible Immigration. Carp included a website link with an address. There were eagles and American flags all over the website, along with immigration articles that carried words like "scourge" and "menace" in their titles. Vega was pretty sure after looking at the website that "sensible immigration" was code for "deport all foreigners."

Vega texted Carp that he would be there. This was his life now. He didn't make the policies—he just drove the policy maker. Everything else was out of his hands.

Then why did he feel so uncomfortable all the time?

Adele pulled her pale green Prius behind Vega's pickup. Vega sprang from the car with his bag of bagels

and held them out to her as a peace offering. He read
something broken in her face.

"*Nena,* what's wrong?"

"No one will take him."

"Take who?"

"Wil Martinez. Rolando Benitez's brother. He's still
in jail."

"So?"

"I'm trying to get him out."

"Why?"

Adele gave Vega an exasperated look. "Because
he's an innocent teenager locked up in a place full of
dangerous felons, that's why!"

"There's nothing you can do about that."

"The judge said he'd spring him if I could find a responsible person for him to live with."

"No responsible person's going to take on the
brother of a suspected murderer."

"And just like that"—she snapped her fingers—
"you toss him over." She breezed past him and his bag
of bagels and walked up the front steps of her porch.
Vega didn't have a clue why she was so angry. But
now, he was angry too.

When they got inside, he tossed the bag of bagels on
her dining-room table. He wasn't hungry anymore.

"For crying out loud, Adele, what is wrong with
you?" Sophia was at school. He could say what he
wanted. "Is this teenager more important than us? I
came all the way over here to talk to you and all you
can do is worry over a young man you met for what?
Twenty minutes?"

She turned to face him. There was something deep
and sad in her eyes. Everything that came out of his

mouth seemed to be the wrong thing and he couldn't understand why.

"I just want to make things right with us. I don't know how." He felt embarrassed by the need in his own voice. It made him want to run away. But for some reason, it had the opposite effect on Adele. She wrapped her arms around him and buried her head in his chest.

"It's not your fault," she whispered. "I'm sorry for taking it out on you."

They stayed like that, their bodies saying what their words couldn't. Then he gently pushed her back.

"You saw my text, right? About Max?"

"Yeah." She frowned. "That Mrs. Morrison—"

"But even if there was no Mrs. Morrison," said Vega, "he can't live alone anymore."

"I know. I can try to find him some help, but he's so proud. He doesn't want it."

"You're going to need to convince him."

She broke away. "How can I convince him of anything when I can't even convince people in this town to talk to one another?" She walked the bag of bagels into the kitchen and pulled down a couple of plates. "I wish you weren't working for Mike Carp. It makes everything so much harder."

"Believe me, *nena*, I wish that too." Vega pulled out a chair at the kitchen table and straddled it, leaning his arms along the seat back. He'd spent the last two sleepless nights trying to come up with an escape route. He couldn't find one. He didn't have enough time in the pension system to retire. He had too much baggage since the shooting to work as a cop someplace else. He was good with his hands, but lacked the licenses to make any real money in the trades. And as far as his accounting degree went, he'd rather put a bullet in his head.

"You can't ask Captain Waring for a transfer?"

"The police department's like the military, Adele. You get an order, you have to obey it."

"You weren't *ordered* to work directly for Carp."

"I was ordered to work for his staff. What he does with me after that is beyond my control. Getting mad at me is like getting mad at the janitor who cleans Carp's office."

She leaned against the counter and studied him. "I don't know, Jimmy. Ever since the Benitez shooting, it's like we're on two different wavelengths. I'm trying to keep this town together. And you're working for a man who wants to tear it apart."

"Mike Carp's not the reason this town is coming apart," said Vega. "The town's eating itself. That fight at the vigil—"

"Was started by a cop's son and two of his friends—who didn't get arrested, I might add."

"Yeah, well, that cop's son got his ass kicked last night. By three Latinos. So I'd say the hate's flowing in both directions."

"Well, you're not helping things!"

"You want me to quit? I'll quit. But that's my only choice right now. The job won't take me back in any other capacity. Not now. Maybe not ever. I'm miserable, *nena*. Miserable because the man I work for has all the sensitivity of a wrecking crane. Miserable because I'm never gonna be a detective again. And miserable most of all because I'm hurting you."

Adele walked over and stroked his hair. He felt her

forgiveness radiating off her like tropical sun. It unclenched the knot in his stomach.

"Do you want me to slice some bagels?" she asked.
"Brew some coffee?"

"No." He grabbed her by the wrist and pulled her
close. "Something else." He buried his head on her ab-
domen and kissed her. He untucked her shirt from her
jeans and snaked a hand around her backside. Her
body turned sweaty and liquid beneath his touch. It
soothed him to know he still had this effect on her.

He rose and kicked the chair aside. Then he unbuttoned
her shirt and tossed off his own. Her bare skin pressed
against his made him feel like a teenager again. They
cleaved to each other, two limbs of the same tree, their
bodies entwined as one.

"Not here," she whispered. It was a weekday morning. They were standing by the windows in her kitchen.
"Upstairs."

Sophia was hours from coming home from school.
Their careers were in ruins. But maybe—just maybe—
there were some small compensations.

He made love to her with an urgency he hadn't
known he'd felt. She was the one good thing that had
happened to him this past year. He could stand to lose a
lot of things. But he could never stand to lose her.

He kissed her shoulder as he rose. "I've got to be at
work by noon today. I'd better take a shower." When
he returned to her bedroom to get into his clothes, he
found Adele dressed and standing at her bedroom window, the one that overlooked Max Zimmerman's
house.

"Jimmy?"

"Yeah?"

"If I don't find someone by the end of the day, Wil is going to sit at the county jail for months—maybe even lose his DACA."

"That's too bad. But what can you do? You can't take him in. You've got Sophia. End of story."

"But . . . Wil is innocent."

"A, no one can say that for sure. And B, whether he is or isn't, he's the brother of an extremely contentious high-profile murderer."

"*Alleged* murderer," said Adele.

"Mobs don't care about words like 'alleged,' Adele. You can't take him in. Peter would forbid it, and for once, I agree with him. You've already had one threatening letter in your mailbox. You'd be buying trouble for yourself and—more importantly—for Sophia."

"There is another alternative."

Vega sat on the edge of the bed and slipped into his socks. "Hey, don't look at me. I work for Carp. Can you imagine the trouble I'd get in?"

"I wasn't thinking about you," said Adele. "I was thinking about Max Zimmerman."

Vega stopped putting on his sock. He'd been warm from the shower and their lovemaking. But now, he felt a chill across his back. "Are you for real?" He whispered the words, as if someone might overhear them. "You want to put the brother of a murderer in the same house as an eighty-eight-year-old infirm man?"

"Wil Martinez is just a scared kid whose life has been upended. He has no one. And Max needs someone to help him."

"Not *this* someone."

"I'm not going to blindside Max," said Adele. "I'll

tell him everything. Absolutely everything. If he says no—as I think he will—at least I'll know I tried."

"He's an old man."

"He's a tough old man," said Adele.

Vega's phone dinged with a text message. He squinted at the screen and cursed. "Carp wants me there fifteen minutes earlier. I gotta run."

"Where are you going?"

"Carp's giving a press conference about 'Catherine's Law' at Americans for Sensible Immigration."

"Jimmy! That's a rabidly xenophobic group!"

"I don't make the itinerary."

"But you don't seem too bothered by it either!" He went to kiss her. She pushed him away. "Sometimes I think I don't know you."

Vega strapped on his duty belt and maneuvered the holster for his gun. "I haven't changed, *nena*."

"Yeah? Well, maybe that's part of the problem."

Chapter 32

Mike Carp made sure Vega stood next to him at the press conference while he expressed outrage at the beating of a "police officer's son" by "violent illegals" in Lake Holly. Flashbulbs clicked. Spotlights danced across Vega's field of vision. He didn't like being used as window dressing for any cause, much less one he felt so conflicted about.

A couple of the reporters tried to play cute with him while he was standing around at the event. They must have taken his name and Googled it, because by the time the event was over, they all seemed to know exactly who he was.

"Officer Vega, didn't you shoot and kill an unarmed civilian in December?"

"As a Hispanic, how do you feel about your boss's proposed legislation?"

"Isn't it true that the man you gunned down was an undocumented immigrant?"

Vega felt blindsided. He was trying hard to retreat

into the shadows and this new position had dragged him front and center again. He was thankful when Doug Prescott ushered him away and Hugh Vanderlinden blocked the reporters.

"Detective Vega has no comment," said Vanderlinden. "He is here in an official capacity on assignment by the county police. Please direct your questions to Mr. Carp."

Outside, Vega thanked Prescott and Vanderlinden for rescuing him. He stayed in the Suburban after that, waiting for Carp to finish glad-handing supporters. His phone rang. He picked it up. *Greco*. The man wasn't even supposed to be working today.

"Listen . . . Vega. Lake Holly's got enough problems without your boss adding gasoline to the fire."

"You saw the press conference? Already? It just finished."

"I didn't need to see it. He was all over the talk shows this morning, shooting his mouth off about illegals beating up a cop's son."

"I can't control what he says."

"You can correct his facts, can't you? The story's changing on our end."

"You found the three guys who beat up Brad Jankowski?"

"They're down at the station now, being interviewed. Two are Hispanic. One is white. All of 'em were born and raised right over in Granville and as American as you and me."

"So it wasn't retaliation for what happened at the vigil?"

"More town-related than anything else. It had to do with some grudge match over a girl. We're gonna charge 'em with assault, of course. But we're trying to dance away from escalating things. It'd help us if Carp keeps to the same script."

"It's too late as far as his press conference at Americans for Sensible Immigration. He just finished speaking."

"What's done is done," said Greco. "But at least let him know that he's got to stop spreading that story. It's not only going to rile people up, it's gonna put our department in an embarrassing position when the facts come out."

"Will do."

When Carp got back in the Suburban, he had a huge grin on his face. "We've hit the big time, Jimmy. Just got the word—CNN's doing a profile on me. Got a reporter meeting me at my real-estate offices in an hour to discuss 'Catherine's Law' and that terrible situation up in Lake Holly—the way things are escalating and all."

"Uh, sir?"

"Yes?" Carp looked up from his paperwork.

"I just got a call from a friend at the Lake Holly PD. You might want to leave out any mention of that incident involving the beating of a police officer's son." Vega explained the call and circumstances.

Carp's eyes never left the document he was reading. "Thank you, Jimmy. I will certainly take your concerns under consideration."

Vega wondered if he hadn't made himself clear. "Uh, Mr. Carp? These aren't *concerns* exactly. They're facts. From one of the detectives who interviewed the suspects. American-*born* suspects, one of whom is white."

"Yes, well. I'm sure Lake Holly has many reasons at this point to sugarcoat the situation." Carp grabbed his phone and began tapping out a text.

"Mr. Carp," Vega interrupted. "The situation in Lake Holly is pretty tense right now. If you go on CNN and start telling people—"

"Do we need to change seats here or something, Jimmy? Because the last I looked, the voters of this county elected *me* to county executive. They entrusted *me* to decide what's in the best interests of the people of this county. You, on the other hand, are a screwup with the current policing powers of a meter maid. You caught a break here, Jimmy. I took a little pity on you. Don't let it go to your head."

Pity? The word burned. Vega wanted to pull over to the curb, dump Carp on his fat ass, and drive away. He'd have two glorious seconds of satisfaction—followed by a lifetime of regret. He'd been debating whether to tell Carp about Sarah Kenner's connection to Jeffrey Langstrom. But now, he couldn't see the point. Why help a man who thought so little of him? So he bottled all the words he longed to say inside him and drove.

Mike Carp's real-estate headquarters was in a lush office park that bore no resemblance to the drab building that housed the county government. The rolling fields surrounding it looked perfectly manicured, even in winter. Huge metal sculptures and weeping willows dotted the grounds. The lobby was all glass and bright chrome. A fountain burbled in the middle. All the secretaries appeared to be natural blondes under thirty.

The reporter from CNN was there. A woman in red with a hypercaffeinated attention span and a sharklike smile that only worked when the cameras were rolling. Her name was Lucy Park. Her ethnicity looked to be everything: Asian eyes, caramel skin, dark kinky hair with highlights. She and the news crew seemed to really like that Vega was one of Carp's "aides." Carp's word. Vega wanted to correct the impression. But he couldn't very well do it in front of a reporter.

Vega followed Carp's entourage and the camera crew as Carp walked Lucy Park around his headquarters and showed off shelves of awards he'd won and an entire wall of framed photographs of various buildings he owned. Office complexes. Hotels. Sports clubs. Resorts. In the middle of the wall was a full-color rendering of an eighteen-hole golf course with a stone clubhouse, a dozen cottages, indoor and outdoor pools, and tennis courts. Two hundred and fifty acres on the shores of Lake Holly.

"When this project is done, it will be the premier golf destination in the country!" Carp told the reporter.

Vega stared at the color rendering. It took up a huge center section of the wall. Vega had no idea Crystal Springs was so big.

"You've had quite a bit of opposition to this project," Lucy Park said. "Almost as much as you've had with your stance on immigration."

"And just like my immigration stance," said Carp, "people come around. You've just got to know the right buttons to push. The environmentalists dropped their suit a few days ago. The judge lifted the injunction this morning. Ground breaking's in April. See? That's how you get things done!"

Vega was taken aback. Joy was so passionate about stopping Crystal Springs. About how the project was going to carve up the wetlands and destroy Lake Holly's drinking water. She made it seem as if Langstrom was determined to stop the project at all costs. What happened?

Vega thought about that package he'd delivered to Sarah Kenner's office. Sarah *Langstrom* Kenner's office. All this time, he'd assumed that Carp had no idea of their connection. But what if he was wrong? What if there was some kind of deal?

Compromise is good, Vega told himself. Then again, nothing about Carp suggested restraint. He seemed to be the sort of man who did what he had to do to get his way.

If that was the case here, what had he done?

The rest of the day felt like one long infomercial. Lucy Park and her camera crew trailed Carp to meetings. They filmed him in his county office and at his estate in Wickford. They took footage of him before two large blowup portraits—one of Catherine Archer and the other, that mug shot of Rolando Benitez. Carp got teary-eyed when he spoke of the brave Archer family, how close he was to them, and how fond he was of their Inn, which had been in the family for generations.

"Catherine was like my own daughter," he told Lucy Park. "And John—let me tell you—a stand-up guy! The best! He died of a broken heart, plain and simple."

In the Suburban, while Vega was driving Carp to his next photo op with CNN, Vega overheard Carp on his cell phone setting up a meeting with someone for ten the next morning.

"Uh, sir?" said Vega when Carp hung up. "Ten a.m. is Catherine and John Archer's funeral. Don't you want to be there?"

"Why? You think CNN will film it?"

"I don't know," said Vega. "But seeing as you're so close to the family . . ."

Carp made a sound, halfway between a throat clearing and a laugh. "Yeah, right? The son of a bitch thought he could hang on until the ink was dry."

Vega couldn't hide his surprise.

"Oh, come on, Jimmy. You saw it yourself at the vigil. The guy was a walking pharmacy."

"I'd probably be doped up like that if my daughter was murdered," said Vega.

"He wasn't *doped up*," said Carp. "He was hiding his illness. Taking it straight to the grave. Whole family's nothing but smoke and mirrors."

"John Archer was sick?"

"John Archer had ALS," said Carp. "Lou Gehrig's disease. You know the one? Your mind stays sharp, but your body goes into revolt? You die in, like, two years, gasping for breath. Hell of an end. It's probably better the drugs got him."

"Does the family know he had ALS?" asked Vega.

"Of course they know!" said Carp. "Just like they knew their daughter was this little tramp, sleeping around." Carp saw Vega's shocked expression in the visor mirror. "Don't look so surprised, Jimmy. I go into business with someone, I make it my business to know them. Archer didn't want me or anyone else to know he had ALS because he figured I'd pull out of our deal to connect the Magnolia Inn to my new golf resort."

"But you wouldn't do that."

"And that's why you're driving me." He smiled. "Not the other way around. Archer got it. He knew his illness was a deal breaker. Doctors won't tell you shit these days, HIPAA regs and all that. But you pull some little chippy aside who's working for minimum wage at a pharmacy, slip her a couple of bucks, and ask her what's behind her drug shelf? You can find out anybody's medical history. Riluzole is a medicine used for only one thing—ALS." Carp shrugged. "As for his tramp daughter—I didn't know until the police gave me an update on the case. But looking at her—jeez. She was a *Playboy* centerfold—am I right? Girl like that's not going to stay a virgin for long."

Vega drove in silence after that. Carp seemed to sense his coolness. "Aw, for chrissakes, Jimmy. Don't get all priggish and PC on me. Everything I'm saying—you know it's the truth."

Carp leaned over the front seat. "Look. If you're going to drive me, you need a crash course in business and politics. The Archers understood it. It goes like this. Not every fact is a truth. And not every truth is a fact. That's what you didn't seem to get earlier today when you tried to lecture me on what the raccoon patrol up in Lake Holly considers important and not important about that beating of a cop's son."

Vega said nothing. There were so many different things he wanted to fight back on, he didn't know where to begin. But he didn't want to get into a pissing match. It served no purpose. Not with this man. Carp would always win.

"So . . . you still think truth and fact are the same," said Carp.

"To me, they are," Vega said.

"Someone told me you're a musician, am I right?"

Vega nodded. He was uncomfortable with Carp knowing anything about his personal life.

"Okay," said Carp. "Notes and beats—those are facts. But how you play them? That's truth. Two musicians have the same facts. They don't have the same truth. *Now* do you get what I'm saying?"

"Sort of," said Vega.

"People invent their own realities, Jimmy. You can give them all the notes and beats you want. But when the music starts, they're going to play what they hear in their heads. And that's what I do. That's my talent. I hear what they're singing and then I turn it into a tune and hum right along with them."

Chapter 33

Adele had a couple of hours before Sophia got home from school. The deadline for Wil's release weighed heavy on her. If she couldn't provide Judge Keppel with a plan by the end of today, Wil would remain in jail.

Max Zimmerman was her last hope.

She opened her refrigerator and unearthed a container of chicken and rice soup, which she'd made the other night. She'd been meaning to drop some by for him anyway. She heated it up on the stove and then trekked the container over to Zimmerman's front door.

She knocked. She waited in the cold. It always took the old man a while to answer. He opened the door a crack. Adele held out the soup.

"Jimmy told me what happened this morning."

Zimmerman leaned on his cane and studied the big, covered aluminum pot Adele held out to him between two oven mitts.

"What is this?"

"Chicken soup with rice. I made it myself."

"You don't have to feed me. I keep telling everyone, I can take care of myself."

"Of course you can," said Adele. "But it's customary to bring a gift when you want to ask someone for a favor."

"A favor?"

"May I come in?"

He opened the door wider. "Why not? Everyone else has."

Adele stepped inside. She carried the pot into the kitchen and set it on the stove. Zimmerman followed behind her. His kitchen was straight out of the 1980s. Adele had a sense that was the last time he and his wife redid it. Beige appliances. Dark brown cabinets. Avocado-colored wallpaper, with some sort of fern design across it. It was old enough to be vintage at this point.

"I don't know what you heard from Jimmy or the police," Zimmerman began. "But I'm not a pervert. Those officers—they listened to that crazy Mrs. Morrison. She's got nothing better to do all day than spy on me and throw her dog's business on my lawn."

"I know that," said Adele. "She and those kids are a terror. Jimmy or I can speak to them for you."

"That's not necessary."

"But they'll just keep throwing dog doo on your lawn if you don't say something."

"Let them." He shrugged. "You get to my age, you learn what matters and what doesn't. A little fertilizer doesn't."

Adele turned a light on under the pot. She unearthed

a spoon from a drawer and stirred. The kitchen filled with the warm scent of chicken soup. Zimmerman eased himself into a chair. "I know why you're *really* here," Zimmerman said. "Jimmy thinks I'm depressed. Maybe even suicidal. He's a good man. But he's wrong. There's a Yiddish expression—a man should stay alive, if only out of curiosity. I'm not going to do anything to change that. You don't have to worry."

"Mr. Zimmerman?" Adele turned from the stove. "I really am here to ask a favor."

"Huh." He studied her. "For you, anything."

"You may change your mind when you hear my request."

"I have no money," said Zimmerman. "I'm too old to marry. Eliminate those two and there's not much left to worry about."

Adele grinned. He had a way of putting things into perspective. She pulled two bowls from a cabinet and filled them with soup. She set them on the table, along with two spoons from a drawer. Zimmerman ate as soon as the food was in front of him. Adele had a sense that even with the Meals on Wheels van coming by, he wasn't eating enough.

"There's this boy," she began.

"Boy?"

"Well, not boy. Teenager. He's nineteen."

"Your family?"

"No," said Adele. "He's originally from Guatemala, but he grew up here. I met him through a legal matter."

"He commit a crime?"

"His brother did. Or was alleged to have anyway. A very bad crime." Adele took Zimmerman through the basics.

"I saw," he said, "on TV. That politician, Mike Carp, is always talking about it. You know? The one who looks like his name?" Zimmerman puffed out his cheeks and stuck his hands at his side like fins. Adele had never really thought about it, but it was true. "I look at him," said Zimmerman, "I see gefilte fish that's sat around in a jar too long."

Adele laughed. "Yes. That's our county executive. And this teenager I'm telling you about? He was the one who arranged his brother's surrender. But instead of arresting him, the police ended up killing him. Right in front of this boy. And now he's in jail."

"Why would they put him in jail for that?" asked Zimmerman.

"Technically, they put him in jail for lying to the police about his brother's whereabouts. That's a crime, of course. But if he were an American citizen with family ties in the area, they would've just released him on his own recognizance while they investigated the murder. The problem is, Wil only has temporary legal status. Something known as DACA. He has no family in the area. His mother was deported back to Guatemala three years ago and is dying of cancer. His father is dead. His brother was all the family he had left and now he's gone."

"Huh." Zimmerman put down his spoon. "Your soup is delicious. Thank you."

"You're welcome."

"His name is Will? Like William?"

"Wilfredo Martinez," said Adele. "But everyone calls him Wil."

"So . . . you're saying that the police put Wil in jail to make sure he doesn't run away?"

"Pretty much," said Adele. "Wil had a bail hearing the other day. I went to it and asked the judge to release him. I offered to take legal responsibility to ensure he stays in the area. The judge agreed, but only if he is under my direct supervision, either living with me or living near me with someone the court considers to be an upstanding member of the community."

"I see," said Zimmerman.

"Before this, Wil was working as a busboy at the Lake Holly Grill and going to college."

"College?" The old man's eyes brightened.

"He wants to be a doctor. An oncologist—a cancer specialist—to help people like his mother. His legal status is so complicated, no one knows if that can ever be. But he's a bright young man with no criminal record. No misdemeanors. Nothing. If he stays in jail over the months it will take to clear up this case, he'll lose everything. His legal status. His college prospects. Any hope of carving out a real life in this country."

"And you are telling me this . . . ?"

"Because I can't let him live with me," Adele explained. "Peter, my ex-husband, would have my head if I let a stranger live under the same roof as Sophia."

"So you're here to ask if he can live with me."

Adele took a deep breath. "I totally understand if you say no, Mr. Zimmerman. Jimmy already told me I was crazy. He said it was a terrible idea to ask you to take the teenager in. It was too dangerous, given how upset many people in Lake Holly are over Catherine's murder. I don't think Wil had any part in that. I don't even know if his brother did. But people are angry. You don't know him. You don't owe him."

"And why do you think that *you* do?" Zimmerman

peered at her over the tops of his black frames. He was a perceptive man.

"Because his brother . . . If I hadn't . . ." Her words trailed off. She couldn't get herself to admit what was in her heart. *His brother died because of me. All the hate and heartbreak that's happening in Lake Holly is because of me.*

Adele felt like she was walking around with a set of scales on her shoulders. On the one side were all the people she'd tried to help in her ten years at La Casa. On the other sat a man's life. Nothing could ever—*ever*—balance out those scales. The only thing that could begin to mitigate the burden would be helping his brother.

She took a deep breath and tried to gather her thoughts. "Have you ever wished you could do something over in your life?"

"Many times," said Zimmerman. "If only life were that simple. We would all sleep more soundly, wouldn't we?"

She pushed her soup to one side and met his gaze. "Trying to help Wil Martinez is the one thing keeping me sane right now, Mr. Zimmerman. I realize that to you, he's just some teenager from another culture with no family or roots in this country. But he's important to me. He needs a place to live where I can keep an eye on him. And it might be good for you to have a pair of strong, young hands around the house."

Zimmerman sat very still. Adele could hear the second hand of his big rooster clock as it rotated from the bird's feathers to its comb and back again.

"There is a story a rabbi once told me about Abraham," he began. "I would like to share it with you. May I?"

"Of course," said Adele. "You mean, the biblical Abraham?"

"Yes," said Zimmerman. "Abraham was a great man. A generous and faithful man who showed his love of God in many ways. One was welcoming strangers into his home. A practice we call *hachnasat orchim*."

Zimmerman tented his arthritic fingers in front of him. His face was flushed with the thrill of telling a good story.

"One day," he continued, "an old man came to Abraham and Sarah's tent. Abraham gave him food and drink, a place to bathe and rest. The old man was so grateful that he took out his collection of idols and began to pray to them. Abraham saw this and became enraged."

Zimmerman's voice dropped an octave. He pointed an index finger at the ceiling.

"Abraham said, 'My God—the one true God—fed you. He is the only one you should offer your prayers to.' The old man disagreed. He told Abraham, 'I prayed to my gods to send someone like you and they did. So I'm thanking them.' Abraham couldn't believe that this man had accepted his generosity and then uttered such blasphemy. So"—Zimmerman clapped his hands together—"Abraham kicked the old man out of his tent!"

Zimmerman leaned in close and smiled. "Do you know what God did?"

"No," said Adele. She was caught up in the story now too. Zimmerman sat back in his chair.

"He berated Abraham," said Zimmerman. "God said, 'For all these years, I have taken care of that old man. I made sure he had food and drink, a place to bathe and rest. And now? I send him to you? And you throw him out? If his idol worship hasn't offended me all these years, why should it offend you?' So Abraham rushed down the road and found the old man and apologized."

"That's a great story," said Adele.

"Do you know why I'm telling it to you?"

"To tell me it doesn't matter where Wil comes from. He is a stranger and should be welcomed."

"That's right," said Zimmerman. "But not because I am a great man like Abraham. But because I have known men and women like Abraham and Sarah. *I* was the stranger. And they welcomed me." Zimmerman gestured to a cabinet above the refrigerator. "There's a box in there. Can you bring it down for me?"

"Of course."

The only box Adele could see was a cardboard shoe-box. It was so old, the cardboard had turned spongy and the corners had gone white with wear. She brought it to him. He opened it. She expected him to show her pictures of his long-dead wife and daughter. Instead, he put a black-and-white picture in her hands of a gaunt young man dressed in a threadbare shirt and jacket that seemed two sizes too big for him.

"That's me," said Zimmerman. " When I was nineteen. The same age as your Wil. That was two years before I came to the United States."

"Oh." He looked sallow and skinny, nothing like the jaunty picture Vega had found of him as a toddler in the drawer upstairs. "Where was this taken?"

"In Cuba." He said it the way Cubans do—*Cooba*.

"You lived in Cuba?"

"For almost five years. After the war. They were the only country at the time willing to take me in."

"So . . . you speak Spanish?"

Zimmerman smiled. *"Por supuesto hablo español. Cómo podría vivir allí durante cinco años y que no?"* ("Of course I speak Spanish. How could I live there for five years and not?")

Adele couldn't hide her astonishment. His accent carried a heavy lilt of his native inflections, but the fluency was undeniable.

"I was young." Zimmerman added. "The world was different. I had to learn to communicate to survive."

"You never said. All this time—"

Zimmerman shrugged. "Some things are too painful to explain." He gave her a knowing look. "You have some of those yourself, I think."

Adele swallowed. It was like sitting next to someone with X-ray vision. Did you have to reach a certain age to see the world so clearly? Or did you have to lead a certain kind of life?

"I went to Cuba because I had no country anymore," Zimmerman explained. "The Poland of my early childhood was gone. My whole family was exterminated in the camps. My father. My mother. My two sisters." Zimmerman's voice caught. "My older brother. I don't even have pictures of them anymore. Everything was destroyed. All except for a picture of my older brother when he was three. Taken by a friend of my mother's who visited us from Chicago before the war. I keep it in a drawer upstairs."

Adele felt the weight of what he was telling her. "You were in a concentration camp?"

"And many other terrible places besides." Zimmerman's glasses fogged up. He took them off and wiped them on his shirt. "I know what it feels like to be nineteen and alone. To have no country and no family. I was that stranger. That old man in the story of Abraham. Some Cubans—Christians and Jews—took me in. And later, some Jewish Americans. To them, I owe everything."

"I had no idea," said Adele.

"I don't speak about it usually. For most Americans—even Jewish Americans—it's a page in a history book. For me, it's my life." He put the picture back in the box and handed it to Adele to return to the cabinet. "Wil and his brother—were they close?"

"Yes. I think so," said Adele. "I get the impression Wil felt a great responsibility for him. Rolando didn't get to grow up in the United States like Wil. I don't know the backstory, but I think it's probably rather sad. Not in the way of what you experienced, of course. But any time two siblings are separated—"

"It's done then," said Zimmerman. "I can't pay him, mind you. But he can live here and have a roof over his head."

"Are you sure about this?" asked Adele. "There are people in this community who might shun you—maybe even threaten you—for opening your doors to him. Not that I'm going to tell anybody. But still."

"Adele, the *world* refused my family—my people—shelter. I don't care about the opinions of a few neighbors. It'll serve that crazy Mrs. Morrison right." Zimmerman laughed. "Give her something to really get mad about."

"Oh, Mr. Zimmerman!" Adele wrapped her arms around him. "Thank you so much, sir. You don't know how much this means to me."

Chapter 34

Joy texted, **Can't catch dinner tonight, Dad.** Vega was getting off work, parking the Suburban and exchanging it for his own set of wheels in the county garage. **I've got to stay late on campus. Dr. Jeff offered me an internship with POW. I'm so psyched!**

Vega stared at the text. Everything having to do with Jeffrey Langstrom filled him with unease.

We need to talk, Vega typed back. **It can't wait. Heading over to campus from work now.**

The last time Vega stepped on the Valley Community College campus, he'd taken a smashed beer bottle to the head. But he was in civilian clothes now. And he wasn't anyone's paid security.

Protect Our Water had a small office in the Neumann Sciences Building, a three-story brown-brick building with all the charm of an upended UPS carton. Vega walked up the front steps and through doors papered over with flyers for chemistry tutors and roommates. He saw more posters announcing a campus concert from that hip-hop group, 5'N'10. Joy liked them. She'd probably bought tickets.

Vega texted Joy when he was in the building and told her that he was either coming up or she was coming down.

I'm by myself right now, she texted back. **If you want to talk, it will have to be while I work.**

Good. No Dr. Huggy there. Though Vega would have preferred a couple more interns around. He didn't like the idea of Joy working late on her own.

POW's office had one desk, a computer, a filing cabinet, a couple of chairs, and the ubiquitous microwave and fridge for hungry college students. It wasn't exactly a high-tech operation. Joy was on a laptop computer, inputting columns of figures on a form. Vega knocked on the side of the door so she didn't jump when she saw him.

"Hey," he said. "Aren't you going to take a break for dinner?"

"Dr. Jeff is going to bring me a salad later."

Vega pulled up a chair and sat down. "Listen, Joy." He drummed his fingers on the edge of her desk. "Maybe you want to rethink this internship with Dr. Langstrom. You seem a little too . . . close to him."

Joy kept her eyes on the numbers she was copying into the computer. "I admire him. And besides, he's in a bind. His last intern walked out right in the middle of the semester. He needs the help."

"His last . . . Do you mean Zoe Beck?"

"Yeah. Dr. Jeff said she was real messed up about Catherine's murder."

And other things, besides. But he wasn't going there

right now. "Are you aware that Langstrom has called off his suit against Crystal Springs? The judge lifted the injunction."

"I'm aware."

"And that doesn't bother you? I thought that's what you were fighting for."

"Dr. Jeff put pressure on Carp to change the plan. Crystal Springs is no longer building a road on the wetlands that connect the resort to the Magnolia Inn."

"How's that going to affect the Magnolia Inn?"

"I would imagine it's not good," said Joy. "I'm sorry for the family. But the safety of the town's drinking water comes first."

Was safety the paramount concern? Vega wondered. Listening to Carp in the car today, he didn't think so. Was it even Langstrom's?

"I don't get what POW gets out of this," said Vega.

"Carp is giving the organization a really big grant from the county to monitor water use and conservation."

"In other words, a payoff," said Vega. Maybe the package he delivered to Sarah Kenner's office had something to do with that.

"You're so cynical, Dad."

"No, I'm not. I'm a realist," said Vega. "From my vantage point, it looks like Carp is stiffing the Archers on a deal he made with them because John Archer is dead, then buying off Langstrom with county funds so he can do business as usual."

Joy stopped typing and frowned. "Well, you're wrong," she said. "You don't know what a brilliant, clever man Dr. Jeff is. That's why this internship is such a big deal. He's expanding POW and he wants me to be a part of it. Now if you'll excuse me, I have work to do."

Vega got up from his chair. "What if it's more than that?"

"More than what?"

"What if Langstrom's playing everyone? Taking a buyoff from Carp? Buttering you up so he can take you to bed."

"*Dad!* That's crude! And untrue."

"Sorry. But you need to hear it, Joy."

She swiveled her chair to face him. "Hear what? That I'm a young woman? That you don't think a man like that could actually appreciate me for my intellect and drive?"

"You know that's not what I meant—"

"Oh, yes it is!"

"*Chispita,* you're reading this all wrong."

"What I'm reading is that you think far less of my abilities than my professor seems to. Now tell me—which one of you I should listen to?"

"I don't want to see anything bad happen to you."

"Then you're going to have to trust me, Dad. I'm not a little girl anymore. I know what I'm doing."

"But"—he played with a paper clip on her desk—"you're *my* little girl."

She leaned across the desk and kissed him. "And I always will be. But maybe it's time to stop squeezing me so tight—okay?"

Vega left the campus, disappointed that everything he'd tried to say to Joy had only managed to alienate and insult her. Maybe Wendy would have better luck. He didn't want to think about it anymore tonight. He was tired and hungry—too hungry to wait until he got home to cook. Hank's Deli was on the way. Oscar needed the business. He could get something and eat half. Diablo would gladly finish the rest later. Both man and dog would be happy.

The shrine in front of Hank's had grown again. There were nearly two dozen votive candles with cheesy images of Jesus and saints emblazoned on their sides. They flickered at the entrance to the deli like some giant birthday cake topping that somebody forgot to blow out.

"Hola, Oscar. Qué onda?" asked Vega as he walked into the store.

Oscar swept a hand across the vacant aisles. "See for yourself how it's going. People see that shrine, they think I support a rapist and a murderer."

"You can't sort of *discourage* it?"

"You don't discourage a religious shrine. The community would never forgive me. I just have to hope I can ride this thing out. What would you like?"

Vega ordered an Italian hero.

"You want hot peppers?"

"Sounds good."

Vega grabbed a Coke from the refrigerated case and paid for it and the sandwich. Then he walked both back to his truck. He'd eat some now to take the edge off his hunger—and the rest with Diablo. He kept his engine running and the heater cranked up to stay warm while he scanned the stations for music he liked. He was an eclectic listener. Reggaeton, salsa, rap, R&B. He ate and listened as he watched people getting pizza, buying alcohol at the liquor store, and walking in and out of the laundromat with bundles of clothes. It was cold, of course. People didn't hang around. But there was a new furtiveness that Vega couldn't ascribe to the weather. Latinos were scared. Everything in town felt different since Catherine's murder.

Vega wrapped up the rest of his sandwich and searched the bag for a clean napkin. When he looked up again, he saw a female in a black puffy hooded coat walk up to Benitez's shrine with yet another religious candle. Vega almost felt like getting out of his truck and telling her to take it someplace else. But it was like Oscar said. Any interference could backfire. So he stayed put and watched her place the candle next to all the others. The mourner was young—just a teenager—and fair-skinned for a Latina. She had her hood cinched tightly around her face. All Vega could see were her nose, her lips, and her almond-shaped eyes encircled by charcoal liner and mascara. On her legs were skinny jeans shoved into black ankle-length boots.

She bent down before the collection of candles and made the sign of the cross. Vega wondered if she was a neighbor or just someone like his grandmother, who found comfort in the process of grieving. She looked younger than his own daughter. Fifteen, if he had to guess. The heavy makeup made her look older.

She unzipped her jacket to her collarbone and pulled something out from around her neck. A medallion—probably religious. It was about the size, shape, and thickness of a nickel. It dangled from a gold chain. She went to pull it over her head.

Was this teenage girl leaving a religious medal behind? At a shrine for a dead man? Vega sat up straighter.

He felt a charge of electricity zip through him. He watched the girl more closely now. Benitez didn't have a sister. The teenager didn't seem old enough to be a girlfriend. Then again, with girls, you could never be sure.

The teenager tried to slip the medallion over her hood. But the hood was too puffy. She unzipped her jacket a little more and uncinched the hood. She pushed it down onto her shoulders. For the first time, Vega saw her hair. Dyed *blond* hair. Blond like a wheat field. Blond like poured honey.

Blond like Catherine Archer.

The girl yanked a shoulder-length mass of it to one side and slipped the gold chain over her head. She placed the necklace on top of the wilting carnations and roses. Then she tucked her hair back into her black jacket and recinched the hood. Vega was out of his pickup in seconds.

"Miss?" He came up behind her on the pavement. "Can I speak to you a moment?" Vega took out his badge and showed it to her.

"I didn't do anything!" The teenager's face scrunched up like she was about to cry.

"I just want to ask you some questions, miss. That's all. Starting with your name."

"But I didn't do anything. I swear!"

"No one is saying you did."

She looked like she might bolt. He knew he had to act fast.

"If you prefer, we can do this down at the police station." A bluff. Vega had no authority to haul this girl into the Lake Holly PD. On what charge? But the teenager wouldn't know that.

"Your choice." Vega shrugged.

"Jocelyn," she answered in a tight, panicked voice.

"Jocelyn? You go to Lake Holly High, Jocelyn?"

"Yes."

"Got any school ID?" Whether she was here legally or not she'd have reliable school ID.

Jocelyn fumbled inside a shiny black purse and handed Vega a card with her picture on it: *Jocelyn Suarez-Blanco*. She was fifteen, a sophomore at Lake Holly High. Her school picture showed a girl with long black hair swept up in a ponytail and no makeup. She looked five years younger—and reams more beautiful.

Vega opened his truck door and sat on the seat. He copied Jocelyn's information onto a notepad in the glove compartment, then handed her ID back to her.

"Where do you live, Jocelyn?"

She hesitated. Vega lifted an eyebrow. "Like I said, we can do this here. Or at your school. Or perhaps your house—"

"No! Please! Not my parents. They'll kill me." She looked around, as if she half expected one of them to shoot out of a door and grab her by the arm. Or perhaps that dyed hair. "I didn't do anything wrong."

Vega tapped his pen on his notebook. He knew she'd tell him her address. She'd tell him anything he wanted, so long as he didn't call her parents. She reeled off an address that Vega copied onto the pad. She lived around the corner, above the plumbing-supply store. He knew the building.

Vega got out of his pickup and walked over to Benitez's shrine on the sidewalk. He reached down and picked up the gold necklace Jocelyn had left there. It was a woman's necklace. The links were delicate and draped easily between Vega's fingers. The medallion, too, was gold. On the front was a raised outline of the Virgin Mary with her robed arms outstretched and golden rays shooting off her halo. On the back were the words from the Hail Mary that Vega had known so well as a boy: *Ruega por nosotros pecadores, ahora y en la hora de nuestra muerte.* (Pray for us sinners, now and in the hour of our death.)

Vega held the medallion out to Jocelyn in his outstretched palm. "Who does this belong to?"

"I didn't steal it."

"But it's not yours."

"I was trying to give it back."

"Give it back to whom?"

"He gave it to me. To hold on to. Until he could pay me back."

"He? Who's *he*?"

"I gave him a twenty to buy me some beer. He asked if he could borrow the difference to buy some vodka at the liquor store. For himself." The words poured out breathlessly, delivered with a teenager's fever-pitched logic. "He promised to pay me back."

"*Who* promised to pay you back, Jocelyn?"

"I should have just given him the money," she continued, as if she'd never heard Vega's question. "I mean, he knows my boyfriend and all. But I thought he'd forget and stiff me. So he gave me his religious medal. As collateral. He promised he'd bring me my money this week. And now he can't. Not ever. And . . . that medal. It's not right for me to keep. It belonged to his mother."

"Whose mother, Jocelyn? Who are we talking about?"

"Darwin," she said.

"Dar . . . You mean, Rolando Benitez?"

"He used to work with Carlos."

"And Carlos is . . . ?"

"My boyfriend. He used to work at Burger and Brew until he got fired."

"Carlos got fired?"

"No! Carlos would never get fired!" She wrinkled her nose. She reminded Vega of Joy—that same petulance when anyone failed to understand the ramblings of a teenage mind. "*Darwin* got fired. He was a dishwasher at Burger and Brew. He got in a fistfight with one of the other busboys. But he was always real nice to Carlos. He used to fix his bike. Even fixed my little sister's bike once. He was nice when he wasn't drinking."

"So you gave Darwin money to buy you beer. Am I right?" asked Vega.

The girl played with the zipper on her coat. "Yeah."

"When?"

"*When?*" She rolled her eyes. Just like Joy. Everything seemed so obvious to her. But it was only slowly becoming obvious to Vega. "Last Friday night."

Vega looked up at the security camera outside the building. "So it was *you*? You were the blonde on the security video?"

"I don't know anything about a video."

"Jocelyn, listen to me. I need to know. What time were you here with Dar—Rolando Benitez?"

"Around ten-thirty, I guess. He was walking into Hank's to buy a lottery ticket. I asked him to buy me some beer. I let him keep the change."

"And then what?"

"I took the beer and split," said Jocelyn. "And then like, I heard about the Archer girl and then the cops shot Darwin."

"Why didn't you come forward and tell the police you were with him?" But Vega already knew the answer to that. Jocelyn Suarez was fifteen years old. She was begging beer off a grown man. Probably to share with this boyfriend, Carlos, who may or may not still be in his teens. Her parents would kill her if they found out any of this. So she kept quiet.

Her concerns weren't all that different from Catherine Archer's.

"Did you see Catherine Archer with Darwin at any time?"

Jocelyn made a face. "She wouldn't hang with him."

"You knew Catherine?"

"Well enough," she said. "She used to hang with Lydia Mendez, whose family goes to my church. And Zoe Beck, that weird girl with the purple hair who was, like, obsessed with her or something. Followed her everywhere. Not that we were friends or anything. Catherine got my boyfriend's cousin fired from the Magnolia Inn."

"When was this?" asked Vega.

"A couple of weeks ago," said Jocelyn. "Alex was a waiter there."

"Alex Romero?"

"Um . . . Yeah." It suddenly dawned on Jocelyn that she was throwing out names to a cop.

"Relax," Vega told her. "I already know about Alex Romero. Todd Archer fired him for coming on to Catherine, am I right?"

"More like, she came on to him. Not that he got past first base with her. She wasn't interested in him for *that*."

"What, then?"

The teenager glanced over her shoulder. "I need to go. Can I go, please?"

"As soon as you tell me why Alex got fired."

Jocelyn fumbled with the clutch on her pocketbook. Vega had managed to calm her down before this last round of questions. But now she seemed more scared than when they'd started. Vega decided to hazard a guess. Maybe he'd get lucky.

"Was Alex keeping drugs in his locker?"

"No!"

"Well, he couldn't have stolen anything," said Vega. "The Archers would have filed a police report for that."

Car doors slammed. Voices drifted over from the pizzeria. Jocelyn said nothing.

"Jocelyn?" Vega waited until the girl met his gaze. "Did Alex get fired for stealing?"

"No!" She bit her lip. "Well, not exactly."

"What do you mean, 'not exactly'?"

"He didn't take anything. But, like, he sort of covered for someone who did. I think he thought it was a prank."

Vega wasn't following. "Are you saying that someone at the Magnolia Inn committed a theft and Alex covered for them? What did they steal?"

"Some, like, computer drive or something."

"You mean a flash drive?"

"Maybe. I'm not sure." Jocelyn twirled a strand of

blond hair around her finger. "Alex didn't even know what was on it."

"And the person who stole this? Why didn't Alex tell on him?"

"Because it wasn't a *him*. It was Catherine."

Chapter 35

They never tell you anything in jail.

Wil had no idea he was being released. He was marched to dinner. Lukewarm overcooked spaghetti with tomato sauce, white bread, a cling peach half, and colored water for coffee. He was marched back for head count. He stood in a line of men with tattoos on their knuckles and hate in their eyes. It took all his energy to stay alert. He had nothing left over to sort through what he'd lost. College. His job at the Grill. The attic room he used to live in. And, most of all, his brother.

Forgive me, Lando. Never in his life had Wil felt more alone. He tried to fight the rubber-band tautness in his chest. Every time he closed his eyes, he replayed those last moments of his brother's life. The sloppy kisses and sweaty hug. The way Lando teetered in his arms. It was Wil's fault things had gone the way they did. And now he could never make it right.

A female guard came to his cell after dinner. She asked Wil to repeat his inmate number, then opened the cell door. "Move."

Wil thought perhaps they needed another piece of paperwork from him. They were always doing paperwork here. The entire jail felt like one large metal filing cabinet. The people in it were incidental to the forms they generated.

The guard marched Wil into a room and handed him a bin that contained the clothes he'd been arrested in.

"Get dressed."

Wil changed in front of the female officer. A few days ago, he'd have blushed and tried to be modest about it. Now he didn't blink an eye. He tried to finger comb his hair.

"Hurry up!" the guard shouted. Then she marched Wil down another hall and buzzed open a door. A lone figure waited on a bench. *Señora Adele.*

He stepped forward. She rose and embraced him like a mother. He felt bad that he only belatedly returned her hug. He was confused. "Am I . . . free?"

"I wish it were that simple, Wil." She turned up the collar of her coat. "Come. I'll explain in the car. My daughter's at a friend's house, so I don't have much time."

It was dark outside. In the jail, Wil had little sense of night or day or even weather. Above, the bright security lights of the prison bleached the sky free of stars. But the moon remained, a hazy pearl dancing between fingers of gauzy cotton. He took a deep breath and felt the cold pinch his nasal passages and travel through his lungs like he'd just inhaled a jar of Vicks VapoRub.

Never had the simple act of standing outside on a frigid night looking at the sky felt more beautiful to him.

The señora led him to her car in visitors' parking. As the guard at the booth lifted the gate and they drove north, she explained the arrangement. He was free, but he wasn't. It felt to Wil like he'd exchanged one prison for another.

"Why can't I just check in with you every day?" he asked. "That would be easier on everyone."

"This isn't about what's easier," she said. "It's the judge's ruling. The agreement stipulates that you live with Mr. Zimmerman and that I am responsible for you and make sure you don't leave the area."

"So . . . I can't try to get my room back?"

"Actually, your room's still your room," she said. "Someone paid your rent for the month so your things wouldn't be put out on the street."

"Really?" Wil felt grateful. And uncomfortable. He didn't like taking handouts. "I will repay the person as soon as I can. Please tell me who they are."

"I promised I wouldn't. He asked that the arrangement be just between us."

"But then . . . how can I pay it back?"

"He's not asking for you to pay it back. So stop worrying. When I get a chance, I'll help you pack everything up and drive it over to Mr. Zimmerman's. In the meantime, we need to get you settled."

With an eighty-eight-year-old stranger? Wil was such a bundle of trauma and anger right now, he'd be terrible company. And besides, he didn't know the first thing about caring for such an old person. Everyone in his family seemed to die before they had a chance to turn gray.

"Is this Mr. Zimmerman able to feed and dress himself?"

The señora laughed. "Oh my, yes. Mr. Zimmerman doesn't want anyone taking care of him. You're just there for company and to help him get around and look after himself a little better. He can't pay you, but I think the arrangement will work for both of you. You can still work at the Grill and go to school. And this way, neither of you will be alone."

"Why would he care what happens to me?"

"Well . . . first, because he's a good man and I asked this of him. But also because he came to this country when he was around your age. He's a Holocaust survivor. From Poland originally."

"Do I have to do anything special? Like, I don't know, keep kosher?" Wil wasn't even sure what keeping kosher meant, other than you couldn't mix milk and meat, and things like ham were forbidden.

"I don't think Mr. Zimmerman keeps kosher. But I'm sure he'll tell you if there's something he needs you to do. He's a very sweet old man. He knows you've been through a lot."

Wil wished he were just going back to his room.

"One of the things we'll need to talk about," the señora said softly, "is your brother. His body's still at the morgue."

Wil pulled out his cell phone and tried to turn it on, but it was dead. The battery had run out while he was in jail. It was on its last legs anyway. Sometimes it worked. Sometimes it didn't. He and Lando always borrowed each other's phones. He wondered if his mother had been trying to reach him these past few days.

"Wil?" The señora tried to catch his attention. "Does your mother know? About Rolando?"

"No." Wil felt the jab of a feather leaching from his faded green goose-down jacket. He pulled it out, running his fingers against the soft curve of the feather. It soothed him. He needed soothing.

"You need to tell her," said the señora. "I can tell her if you prefer. But either way, she deserves to know."

Wil turned his gaze to the side window and watched the golden glow of houses on the streets they passed. Televisions flickered. People sat down to meals. A boy held a video game console as he sat on a couch. A girl held up a cell phone and took a photo of herself as she twirled in front of her bedroom mirror. Wil wanted any life but his own.

"I know this is hard for you," the señora tried again. "But your brother deserves to be buried properly back in Guatemala. We need to work with the Guatemalan consulate to repatriate his remains. We can't do that if you don't tell her."

"Mmm." He couldn't handle a discussion of that right now. The señora didn't press. They were both silent after that.

Max Zimmerman's house was brick with a red front door and a sharply angled roof. In the driveway was a light gray Cadillac that looked as if it rarely left the street. Lights glowed behind heavy drapes.

"What if Mr. Zimmerman doesn't like me?" asked

Wil as the señora pulled into his driveway. "Do I have to go back to jail?"

"That's not going to happen."

"But . . . if it does?"

"We'll think of something."

Wil got out of the señora's car and followed her up the front steps. It took a few minutes after they rang the bell for Zimmerman to answer. Wil expected a very frail and unkempt man, but the man before him was dressed in pressed gray slacks and a wool sweater. He was shaved and scrubbed. His thick white hair was held in place with so much styling gel Wil could see where the tines of a comb had gone through it.

The teenager felt like a mess by comparison.

Zimmerman extended a hand. His shake was warm and firm. "Wil? Is that what you like to be called? Or Wilfredo?"

"Wil is fine, sir. Thank you for taking me into your home."

"You're welcome. Adele has told me good things about you."

Wil could smell something delicious in the air. The old man's dinner. Wil's stomach growled. He was supposed to have eaten dinner at the jail, but the meals were always small and starchy. They never satisfied.

"Are you hungry?" asked the señora. "Please say you are, because I made a plate of lasagna for me and Sophia and put half of it in Mr. Zimmerman's oven for the two of you to share."

"But Mr. Zimmerman probably had dinner already."

The old man smiled. "I waited for you. How else do you get to know someone except over a meal?"

Wil thought the señora would join them. He felt

panicked when he noticed that she hadn't removed her coat. "I have to fetch my daughter," she explained. "I'll check in on you both later."

And then she was gone. He was alone with the old man. Zimmerman shuffled in the direction of the kitchen. "Come," he said. "You can get the plates. You need to learn where things are. This is your home now too. I can't get up and down the stairs until my hip heals a little more, but you will see that there is a guest bedroom upstairs where you can sleep."

"Thank you, sir."

Wil walked into the kitchen. The old man directed him to the cabinets with plates and glasses and the drawer with silverware. Wil set the table and dished out the food. He filled their glasses with water. Wil felt clenched, waiting for questions that he didn't know how to answer. But they never came. The old man seemed comfortable with silence. Wil noticed when Zimmerman reached for the peppershaker that the top digit of his left middle finger was missing. Wil averted his gaze.

"You are wondering how I lost part of my finger," said the old man.

"I didn't mean to—"

"It's okay, Wil. Our scars tell our life stories. You see the wound. I see all the healing people around it. Would you like to hear the story?"

"Only if you want to tell it," said Wil.

"I will tell you because then you will know me a little better." The old man put down his fork and wiped his lips on a napkin. "My older brother, Samuel, and I were hiding in the woods in Poland when we were rounded up and sent to Treblinka, a concentration camp. You know about the Holocaust?"

"I studied it in school," said Wil. "I know millions of Jewish people were killed."

"More than six million," said Zimmerman. "And others besides. When one of the commanders in the camp asked if anyone had construction experience, Samuel volunteered us. It was the only way to survive. We had no experience, mind you, but Samuel was very strong and a fast learner. Me? Not so much. One day, I'm so exhausted, I accidentally feed a board onto a circular saw and end up cutting off the top of my finger. I had to hide this from the guards. They would have shot me if they'd found out."

Wil couldn't believe what he was hearing. "You lost part of your finger? And you hid the injury?"

"One of the inmates was a doctor. He helped my brother staunch the bleeding. There were no drugs for pain or infection. We just wrapped it up and hoped for the best."

Wil put down his knife and fork. He couldn't imagine the strength it must have taken to endure something like that. "How old were you?"

"Fourteen." Zimmerman nodded to Wil's plate. "I've ruined your appetite. My apologies."

"No. It's not the story. It's . . . Where were your parents?"

"Dead. Along with our two sisters and baby brother. All shot the day Samuel and I ran into the woods. We were all that was left."

Wil stared at his plate. "My mother was deported

back to Guatemala three years ago. She is all I have left now and she has cancer."

Zimmerman reached across the table with his good hand and squeezed Wil's arm. "I'm so sorry."

"It's not like your story," said Wil. "But it . . . hurts."

"Yes." Zimmerman nodded. "The wounds others can't see are often the ones that hurt the most."

They talked more freely after that. About baseball (Zimmerman was a die-hard Yankees fan). About Wil's plans for college. Wil cleared the table when they were finished and washed the dishes. He tied up all the garbage and walked it out the back door to a small wooden shed that contained an aluminum trash bin. The shed was near a chain-link fence on the opposite side of the house from the señora's. Mr. Zimmerman had planted big evergreen shrubs up along the fence, but even so, Wil could hear a dog barking and leaping on the other side. He didn't sound friendly.

Wil tried to ignore the dog. He opened the trash bin and tamped down the garbage. He threw in the new bag and secured the lid. He turned to go back into Zimmerman's house. That's when a figure caught his eye. About twenty feet down the fence line. Someone threw something over the fence into Zimmerman's yard. Wil ran over to investigate. Even in the pale light of the moon, he could see what it was: dog feces.

"Hey!" Wil called out. He saw the figure stepping away from the fence. A teenage white boy. Maybe fourteen or fifteen. "You just threw your dog's business on Mr. Zimmerman's lawn."

"I don't know what you're talking about," said the boy. The dog jumped up at his side. A big black dog.

Some mix of pit bull and retriever perhaps. Or pit bull and shepherd.

"I saw you do it!" Wil shouted. "You need to pick it up."

The boy peered at Wil through the bushes. "Who are you? The live-in help?"

Wil wanted to reach through the fence, grab this kid by the collar, and force him to pick it up. But no—he didn't want to draw attention to his being here. So he backed away. "Just . . . stop it. You hear me? Just stop."

"Or what?"

Wil hesitated. The teenager laughed. "Yeah, I thought so. You're the hired asswipe for that old fart. Do what he's paying you to do, beaner. Or maybe my family will call La Migra and get you deported back to where you came from."

The teenager and dog walked back inside. Wil was shaking with anger, his breath clouding in the night air, when he heard the neighbor's back door slam. He fished a piece of newspaper out of Mr. Zimmerman's trash and picked up the feces. He flung it back over the fence into the neighbor's yard. He heard it smack against something. *Good.* Wherever it landed, these people deserved it.

Nobody was going to take advantage of Max Zimmerman that way. Not while Wil Martinez was around to help it.

Chapter 36

Vega drove down to the Lake Holly station house as soon as he finished talking to Jocelyn. He parked on the street and raced up to the desk sergeant. "Is Greco still here?"

"You might catch him if you run. He just checked out."

Vega caught up with Greco as he opened the door of his white Buick LeSabre. Vega opened the passenger side and stepped into the pearl-gray crushed velour interior that Greco kept showroom clean. The Lake Holly detective gave Vega the same warm reception he might accord a carjacker.

"I'm hungry, cranky, and armed, Vega. So if you want to see the sunrise tomorrow, you'll get out of my car."

"Not until you see this." Vega reached into the front pocket of his pants and pulled out the religious medal Jocelyn Suarez had placed at Benitez's shrine. He dropped it into Greco's lap. "This town is coming apart over a lie, Grec. A lie that needs to stop. Right here. Right now."

Greco draped the chain between his fat fingers and held it up to the light. "It's a necklace." Greco wasn't enthused.

"It's a necklace that belonged to Rolando Benitez's mother. Benitez gave it to a fifteen-year-old bleached-blond Latina the night Catherine Archer disappeared. A Latina who asked Benitez to buy beer for her at Hank's Deli. While she waited for him. *Outside*." Vega walked Greco through Jocelyn Suarez's statement, including the part about Alex Romero taking the heat for a theft Catherine committed.

"Convenient that this Lolita should come forward now," muttered Greco.

"She didn't 'come forward,'" said Vega. "She came to bring a candle to the shrine outside the deli. I just happened to see her. Take another look at the surveillance footage if you don't believe me. Show Benitez's brother the necklace. He should be able to tell you if it's his mother's. I know Adele's in the process of springing him from jail."

Greco grunted. Vega wasn't sure which was ticking him off more: Vega showing him the necklace or Adele springing Wil from jail.

"C'mon, Grec," said Vega. "Don't you see? Catherine's presence at Hank's Deli was the only real piece of evidence that tied Benitez to her killing."

"Are you forgetting about that key chain of hers found in Benitez's room?" asked Greco. "About those phone calls a few days before her murder?"

"You don't know that she didn't give that key chain to Benitez. She *was* tutoring him," Vega pointed out.

"As for those calls, they could have been about anything. Without that surveillance video, you've got no real case. Nothing that would have stood up in a court of law."

Greco drummed his fingers on the steering wheel and stared out the windshield. A Lake Holly cruiser sped by, lights flashing.

"If you're right, this is going to cost Lake Holly a bundle," he said. "Everybody's already got their pound of flesh. The Archers. Our department. Mike Carp. This is gonna kill the town."

"This is gonna *heal* the town," said Vega. "Lake Holly's set for self-destruct. Every day, there are more fights. More tensions. More shrines to Benitez. If it's all a lie, it's bound to come out. The longer you delay, the worse the situation is going to get."

"I'm not just talking about Lake Holly taking a hit, you know," said Greco. "This is going to go down badly with your boss. Carp's getting a lot of mileage out of portraying Benitez as the bogeyman of every white American's nightmares. This case may single-handedly vault him into the Governor's Mansion. We come out with, 'Well, maybe we were wrong,' it's going to get ugly, especially since we don't have a replacement perp. Our only theoretical suspect is the baby daddy, and we don't have a DNA match to anyone."

"I realize that," said Vega. "That's why you need to go back to this waiter, Alex. There's stuff he's not telling you about Catherine that may go to the heart of this case."

Greco tucked the medal in his pants pocket. Vega waited for him to lay out a plan. He didn't.

"You're not going to bury that evidence, I hope," said Vega.

Greco's eyes flashed. "I do my job, Vega. Did it when you were still having wet dreams and ogling center-folds. And I'll be doing it while you're pumping gas for that egomaniac in a suit. Know why? Because I don't try and light a candle with a blowtorch."

"Yeah? What was pulling your gun on Benitez then?"

Greco opened his mouth to argue. But both their attentions were drawn to the wail of sirens. Two volunteer fire trucks sped past. Four officers dashed out of the station house and jumped into two cruisers. Greco powered down a window and called across to the nearest officer.

"What just came in?"

"A fire," one of the cops answered. "Over on Industrial Drive. First due engine thought it might be an arson."

Vega pictured the cul-de-sac now. The propane company, with its stacks of white tanks. The auto salvage yard full of smashed cars behind razor wire and chain link. The small janitorial service, with a couple of barely functioning minivans in its lot. And one other building. The largest building there. The former seafood wholesaler that was now La Casa. Vega knew which building the fire was in before the cop confirmed it.

Things had just gotten a whole lot worse.

Chapter 37

By the time Vega turned onto Industrial Drive, two fire rigs were lined up by the hydrant in front of La Casa's parking lot. Their red lights flashed in staccato bursts across the bare trees and cement walls of the warehouse. Smoke the color of cigarette ash poured out the shattered front window. Men in helmets, black rubber boots, and fluorescent-striped turnout coats muscled hose lines through the smashed-in front doors. The sad little sign on the doors that had read CLOSED UNTIL FURTHER NOTICE in English and Spanish had been torn aside and was lying in a soggy heap on the asphalt, its carefully Magic-Markered letters now a blur of unreadable smudge marks.

Vega stood freezing near the curb and watched a hose line snake like a slick python across the empty front lot. Water pulsed through it like some undigested last meal. Still, more water spilled across the pavement, reflecting the flashing red lights on the rigs. Greco wagged a finger at Vega.

"Stay out of the way, keep your yap shut, and I'll try to give you some updates. Anything else, and I'll get you forcibly removed—*capisce?*"

Vega thought about the medallion in Greco's pants pocket. It hadn't been officially tendered as evidence yet. It would be so easy to lose. He knew what Carp would say in a situation like this: There are facts and there are truths. The medallion might be a fact. But the truth was in those soot-stained windows. In the wreckage of what had once been La Casa. No medallion was likely to change that. Not in the short run anyway. Vega just had to trust that his friend would do the right thing.

He walked back to his pickup and texted Adele about the fire. She didn't text back, so he got out of his truck and stood by the curb of La Casa's parking lot, watching firefighters pour into the building and black water and debris pour out. A couple of firefighters took a circular saw to the roof and cut a hole to vent the smoke. No flames popped out—a good sign. The fire hadn't gotten into the enclosed portions of the ceiling.

Greco trudged over. He looked shaken. The uniformed cops were running yellow crime-scene tape around the parking lot and building. *Again.* Spectators were gathering. This was definitely going to make the news.

"How bad is it?" asked Vega.

"As far as the fire goes? It was small," said Greco. "Mainly limited to the area by the front window. The smoke and water damage, however, is pretty extensive."

"Any indications it was arson?"

"It was definitely arson," said Greco. "Your classic

Molotov cocktail. The chief and his men found a broken beer bottle and burnt rags near the front window. You can smell the kerosene."

"Do you think La Casa can rebuild?"

Greco stared at the broken glass and soaked debris. "Structurally, the building's still sound. A lot of the contents are salvageable. Psychologically? I don't know. I don't think anyone does." For all his dark jokes and bluster, Louis Greco had always possessed great affection for his community. He pretended not to care. But he did. And right now, he looked like he'd just been socked in the belly by his best friend.

"Grec?" said Vega. "Lake Holly can't go on like this."

Greco reached into his pants pocket and pulled out the medallion. He held it in his palm as if the Virgin Mary emblazoned on it could grant some of the grace she'd failed to offer in the parking lot of Hank's Deli that Friday night. They needed that grace now. The whole town did.

"I'm driving back to the station to enter this into the evidence log," said Greco. "In the meantime, talk to Adele. Ask her if she can broker a meeting between the police and the Latino community. There are things we can tell them—like this new evidence. And there are things we still can't—like Catherine's pregnancy. But we need everybody on the same page." Greco looked over at the firefighters packing up their hoses. "This shit stops, and it stops now."

"What about Carp?" asked Vega. "You want him to come?"

"What I want"—Greco held Vega's gaze—"is for him to stay the hell out of Lake Holly."

* * *

Vega drove to Adele's. As he turned down her street, he noticed a small crowd gathered on Max Zimmerman's front step. Even with his truck windows closed, Vega could hear the anger in their voices. He double-parked across the street and dashed over.

"Hey! What's going on?" Vega used his command voice. Lots of Bronx in the accent. If he was walking into something, he always took control.

He recognized the figures at once. The large white woman in a heavy shapeless coat was Mrs. Morrison. The three lanky youths in NFL and NHL team jackets were her sons. Adele was in the middle of the melee, standing in front of Zimmerman as he leaned on his cane, trying to speak over the commotion. Benitez's brother stood next to Zimmerman, tugging on the old man's sleeve as if to coax him back inside.

Mrs. Morrison saw Vega approach and pointed a gloved hand at Martinez. "You're a cop. Arrest this criminal. He vandalized my minivan."

"It was an accident—" Adele sputtered. "Greg Morrison threw dog doo over the fence onto Mr. Zimmerman's property and Wil threw it back. It accidentally landed on the hood of Mrs. Morrison's minivan—"

"My son did nothing of the sort," the woman interjected. "That doo could have come from any dog on this street. It was a malicious act of vandalism. And don't tell me that illegal's not capable. I know who he is. I saw his picture in the newspapers. He's the brother of that rapist and murderer. A person like that doesn't belong in a neighborhood like ours. My family isn't safe!"

"Whoa!" Vega held up his hands. "Hold on, will ya?

Calm down." *Puñeta!* He knew that taking this kid in would only bring trouble. For Adele. For Max Zimmerman. But he had to de-escalate the situation.

Vega turned to Adele. "You and Mr. Martinez," he said formally, using his best cop voice, "take Mr. Zimmerman inside."

"But—" Adele went to argue, then caught his sharp look and obeyed.

Vega turned back to Mrs. Morrison and her sons. "Send your boys home, ma'am. No sense them standing out here in the cold. You and me can talk about this across the street. By my truck." Vega wanted to get the woman off Zimmerman's property. Divide and conquer. That's what he always did when he worked with a partner. He was alone here, but that was good. He didn't want the Lake Holly Police involved if he could help it. It would only escalate the confrontation.

Mrs. Morrison didn't move. She frowned at Vega. He tried to soften his tone.

"Mrs. Morrison—please?"

He could see her debating whether or not to trust him. Beneath the pudgy face, there still lurked the soft outlines of a once-guileless young girl. Something had turned her hard and brittle with age. A deep disappointment. An illness. An unfair twist of fate. Life had made her wary. Vega had found as a cop that it was best to try to see the good in everyone—or at least the potential for good. He gave her a point for following him across the street to his truck. And another for sending her two older boys—one of them, likely, the poop slinger— back home. The youngest one—all of eleven—stayed behind, looking as surly and mistrustful as his mother.

"The, uh, dog excrement," Vega began. "Is it still on the hood of your minivan?"

"Yep. Took pictures and everything. For my lawsuit."

"What if I asked Mr. Martinez to clean it off for you?" Vega offered. "Would that put an end to this argument?"

"I don't want that felon on my property!"

"He's not a felon, Mrs. Morrison. He's a college student. With a clean record."

"I want him out of that house! And I'll do what I have to, to make sure that happens!"

Vega held her gaze like a school principal whose star student had just disappointed him. "You *do* realize that you just made a threat in the presence of a police officer? That if anything after this happens to Mr. Martinez, Mr. Zimmerman, or their property, that I'm going to have to alert the local police about your comments. At the very least, a judge is likely to issue a restraining order against you. Depending on the circumstances, he could throw you in jail."

"*He's* the criminal? And *I'd* go to jail?"

"Again, he's not a criminal, Mrs. Morrison. He is a legal resident of the United States. He's entitled to all the protections under our laws. Now, we can end this matter, right here and now, with Mr. Martinez cleaning off the dog poop, and you and your boys promising to stop throwing it into Mr. Zimmerman's yard—"

"We never—"

"Uh." Vega held up his hand. "We both know the truth to that."

Mrs. Morrison's lips tightened and her eyes scrunched

up. "Your girlfriend thinks because she called her boyfriend cop on me that I'm going to shut up about this outrage on our street?"

"She didn't *call* me," said Vega. "I just happened by."

"Sure. Right. Well, you can throw all the threats you want at me, *Officer.* But what are you going to do? Threaten the whole neighborhood? The whole town? People are going to find out how that murderer's brother is living on our street in that old man's house. You can't stop me. One way or another, I'm going to war over this!"

Coño! Vega didn't want to get ahead of himself, but he had to do something. "Look, Mrs. Morrison, you're wrong about this kid. Wrong about his dead brother. All the assumptions the police made about Catherine Archer's murder? They were wrong. You think you're protecting Lake Holly. But what you're really doing is letting your fear get the better of you. It's what's destroying this town and driving everyone apart. *Please.* Listen to me. Not as a cop but as a man who loves this town, like you do. I spent part of my childhood here. Things don't have to be this way. We can make a decision to stop this, here and now. While we still have a chance."

Vega had his back to Adele's house. He didn't notice the small figure in a bright lavender bathrobe as she padded across her front porch, down the stairs, and out to the sidewalk in bear slippers. He and Mrs. Morrison were locked in such a heated conversation that neither of them heard the small, sleepy voice call out to them from across the street.

"Jimmy? Where's Mommy?"

Vega had grown past the stage of listening for small children's voices and watching their every move. He caught the motion belatedly as Sophia stepped off the curb and crossed the street to his truck. He saw it all unfold before his muscles could react. Her lavender bathrobe and long tousled brown hair backlit by the glare of oncoming headlights. Her sleepy eyes growing wide and astonished as the beams grew larger, sucking the color from her skin.

It took Vega only a second or two to process what was happening and leap into the road. He leapt out too late.

Too late.

"Billy! Billy!" Mrs. Morrison screamed.

Another figure—smaller and faster than Vega— broke from his mother's side and raced in front of the oncoming SUV. Tires screeched. Grit exploded off the pavement. Vega braced himself for the thud of little bodies striking several tons of rubber and steel.

A shaken woman got out of her vehicle and ran around to the front bumper.

"Oh, my God! Please, God!"

"Ow!" said a petulant voice in a snowbank by the curb. *Sophia.* Vega ran over just as Billy Morrison was pulling her to her feet. Both children dusted clumps of dirty snow from their clothes. Neither of them had a scratch. Vega's entire body turned into a bowl of jelly. He couldn't stand. He knelt down and threw his arms tightly around Sophia. She seemed more annoyed than shaken.

"Billy!" she fumed. "You didn't have to push so hard!"

The eleven-year-old wiggled out of his mother's embrace. "Next time, look both ways, Soph. I'm not your crossing guard anymore, you know?"

Of course, thought Vega. *The children knew each other—maybe even liked each other, even if the adults didn't.* They were only about two years apart in age. Billy didn't seem to comprehend the enormity of what he'd done. Neither did Sophia. But Vega did. And Mrs. Morrison too. She looked at her son with tears in her eyes. Vega saw a softness return to her face. Her voice was small and tired when she spoke.

"Let's go home, champ," she said to him. "Let's forget this ever happened and go home."

Chapter 38

Catherine Archer and her father were buried at Holy Cross Cemetery one day before a snowstorm stopped the county in its tracks. By the time the snow had receded, the world seemed to have moved on. The turquoise ribbons in town grew limp and faded, until one by one they all disappeared. The candles for Benitez soon went the same way. The wounds in the town became less visible. But the scars remained.

Meetings were held between community leaders and the police. Everyone agreed that things needed to improve. No one agreed quite how.

"When we find Catherine's killer, the town will begin to heal," Greco promised Adele.

"When the police apologize for their grossly negligent behavior toward the Latino community," Adele replied, "the town will begin to heal."

Around and around, it went—one giant stalemate. Everyone was suffering. Latinos, because La Casa remained closed and boarded up. Anglos, because a lot of the downtown businesses depended on immigrant patrons, who no longer felt comfortable walking the streets of their own town.

The Lake Holly Police worked Catherine's murder. But at every turn, they were stymied. Alex Romero, the former Magnolia Inn waiter, had left the area. His cousin Carlos said Alex came into some money—no one knew from where—and had moved to Florida. Either Carlos didn't know or, more likely, wasn't telling where in Florida Alex had gone, or what name he was using—which slowed efforts to find him.

"I don't like the sound of 'came into some money,'" said Vega as he helped himself to a seat in Greco's cubicle. Greco had invited him for once. Vega wasn't sure why. "What's that mean? That he won the lottery? I'd like to have that kind of luck."

"You and me both." From the look of Greco's cubicle, he was pulling a lot of overtime and taking all his meals at his desk. His trash was filled with empty coffee cups from Starbucks. His stapler was balanced on top of a stack of napkins from Dunkin' Donuts. Assorted packets of ketchup, mustard, and soy sauce were fanned out like playing cards next to his computer. Beside his phone was a plastic bottle of Tums—the economy size—to wash everything down.

"How about the arson at La Casa?" asked Vega. "Have you made any progress there?"

"That's why I called you in," said Greco. "We're about to make an arrest."

"Shouldn't you be telling Adele?"

"My chief asked me not to make a public statement. What you do with the information is up to you."

"An arrest is a public act," Vega pointed out. "Whether or not you make a statement about it."

"Yeah, but this 'public act' is being handled with as little fanfare as possible. One, because the arsonist is fifteen years old. And two, more importantly, because he's the son of a major Carp supporter."

Vega cursed. "So you're going to charge him with the equivalent of littering, and the judge will give him a slap on the wrists."

"Not if I can help it," said Greco. "But then again, I'm just a pair of eyes and legs, cataracted and arthritic—"

"Yeah, yeah. Save it for your retirement speech." Vega rose. The law looked pretty one-sided to him right now. "Looks like this kid won the lottery too."

The following morning, Vega picked up Carp from a racquetball game at his sports club. On the drive over to county headquarters, Carp was all smiles and good humor.

"You see the latest approval ratings, Jimmy?"

"No, sir."

"Well, you should. My future's your future—never forget that. I'm up twenty points since that CNN profile aired. Not to mention that my 'Carp for Governor' campaign chest is fifty percent ahead of goal. Hell, at this rate, I may skip the governorship and go for even bigger game. I'm the guy who could do it too. You gotta give the people what they want. That's the secret. That's why I'm the best. I understand that."

Carp was on a roll. Vega had driven him enough now to recognize the signs. He was audience, speaker, and biographer wrapped up in one. A full-service wall of words. Most of the time, Vega tuned it out. He lived for his off-hours these days. His music. Jogs with Diablo. Dinners with Joy. Time with Adele. When they were together, Vega shut off everything in his life that had to do with Carp.

"So . . . Jimmy." Carp leaned forward between the two front seats. "You're good friends with the Lake Holly PD, right?"

"I know some people on the force," Vega said. He was always circumspect around his boss.

"That, uh . . . fire at that community center. You know the one I'm talking about?"

"You mean La Casa?"

"Yeah. I hear the local cops drummed up an arson case against some feckless kid just to appease the illegals. Sort of a tit for tat."

"That doesn't sound like something the police in Lake Holly would do," said Vega.

"From what I hear," said Carp, "the whole thing was an accident. Seems a shame the police are caving in to community pressure, trying to ruin a promising young man's future over a prank."

"You just said it was an accident."

"*Accident. Prank.* It's piddling shit either way—you hear what I'm saying?"

Vega said nothing. He kept his gaze on the windshield as he snaked the Suburban in and out of stop-and-go traffic.

"You know, Jimmy, I like you. I really do," said Carp. "What I like about you is that you understand me. Understand my problems. Like this problem I have here. I mean, I feel bad for this kid. The police mishandled the case. They manufactured some flimsy evidence to make a few professional troublemakers happy. I can understand the pressure the department is under. But hell—I wouldn't blame them in the least if that evidence just . . . I don't know . . ." Carp threw up his hands. "Got lost. Or maybe ended up in the wrong file. It happens, right? Cases don't pan out for any number of reasons. If that happened here, you tell your friends, I'd totally understand. No officer would ever be questioned in the matter."

Vega nearly crashed into the car bumper in front of him. He couldn't believe what the most powerful man in the county was asking him to do. He caught his boss's eye in the visor mirror.

"Mr. Carp, sir—do you understand what you're suggesting? You're suggesting that I—as a police officer—ask other police officers to tamper with evidence in a criminal case. That's a serious crime. For a cop? It's an automatic felony. I could get fired—maybe even go to jail—for asking such a thing."

"Did I say that?" Carp touched his chest like Vega had just shoved it with the heel of his hand. "Did I order you to do *anything*? All I did was *suggest* you inquire about the evidence against this kid. He's fifteen. Don't tell me you didn't have lapses in judgment when you were fifteen. You really want to destroy this kid's whole future?"

"I don't want to do anything, Mr. Carp. And neither does the Lake Holly Police. The matter's up to a judge."

"Keppel," Carp grunted. "Liberal asswipe who released Benitez's brother on his own recognizance. Who let that illegal who interrupted Catherine's vigil get off with a fine."

"Whatever Judge Keppel does or doesn't do," said Vega, "I can't ask fellow cops to destroy evidence."

"Did I ask anyone to destroy evidence?" Carp gave every syllable his full indignation. *"I resent your tone and insinuations, Jimmy. How dare you even suggest that?"*

Vega forced himself to concentrate on the traffic in front of him. The grip of the wheel. The friction of rubber on asphalt. Inside, he felt stripped of bearings. Had he misheard? Misinterpreted? Or was Carp just good at manipulating any situation to his advantage?

"I'm sorry if I misunderstood you, Mr. Carp."

"I think we both suffered a big lapse in judgment here. Because you see, Jimmy, I'm a very simple guy. I'm all about loyalty. You do for me? I do for you. You screw me over. I make sure it's the last thing you *ever* do. I think we can be pretty clear on that message, yes?"

So that was it. Vega was being fired. In truth, he felt like a burden was being lifted from his shoulders. He didn't care what he did after this—pistol permits, directing traffic, evidence storage. Anything was better. "I take it that I'm being relieved of my duties as your driver."

Carp laughed. "You think you can just walk away? Like this is some job flipping burgers—which, by the way, after this, you won't even be able to do in this county."

"Clearly, we don't share—"

"You think I give a shit about what we *share*? This isn't a partnership, Jimmy. You work for me. You do what I tell you to do. I told you I check out the people I do business with. You think you're any different? I know about your little girlfriend who used to run La

Casa and is now spending her days looking after that old Jew and the brother of that murderer. I know about your daughter who's all excited to work an internship with that con artist, Langstrom. I know the names of all the cops in your band—where they work, who they report to. You want to mess with me? There are a thousand and one ways I can mess back. And not just with you—with everyone connected to you."

Vega felt he'd swallowed a fistful of needles and they were piercing the lining of his gut. There was only one way Carp could know all these things.

"You put that GPS tracker on my truck. You've got it bugged. And maybe other things as well."

"I wouldn't know anything about that," said Carp. He smiled because, of course, he didn't. He had others who did those things for him. "But I'll tell you this," he added. "I make it my business to know other people's business. So go ahead, Jimmy. Be noble. Make your stand. It's not like anyone gives a damn one way or the other. You're a throwaway cop."

Carp leaned forward and caught Vega's eyes in the visor. "Just remember, I got a long memory. So the payback will come. Maybe your daughter will get pulled over one day for speeding and the police will find drugs in her car. Maybe that girlfriend of yours will get implicated in some ring that's smuggling in prostitute immigrants. You can check their vehicles every day of your life. Spend your off-time looking over your shoulder. But I'll find a way, Jimmy. Bank on it. And when your daughter's crying from some holding cell, ask yourself then if her freedom wasn't worth a little misplaced evidence against some snotnosed kid."

Chapter 39

Wil had to do this. Alone. Without the señora. Without Mr. Zimmerman. He'd been putting it off for a week. But he couldn't any longer.

He was carrying too many ghosts. He had to lay them to rest. Or try to, in any case.

It was a sunny weekday morning when he took a taxi to his old street. Icicles dripped from the bent gutters of the narrow clapboard houses. The wind rattled the chain-link fences. A train barreled past on the tracks out back, sucking all the ambient noise from the landscape and sending a shiver of air in its wake.

Wil hefted his flattened cardboard cartons up the porch steps of an old yellow row frame. He still had his key, so he unlocked the front door and climbed to the attic. The hallway was dark and smelled of mildew and fried food.

At the top of the second set of stairs, he braced himself for the sight of his room. He hadn't been inside since the police tore through it with a search warrant.

On the center of the door were several big black scuff-marks. The hinges were partially torn from the frame. Remnants of yellow crime-scene tape were still twisted around the handle. The cops hadn't been bashful about making an entrance.

Wil dropped his folded cartons and fished out his room key. The Lake Holly Police had already provided him with an itemized list of what they'd taken. His laptop computer. His brother's cell phone. Textbooks, personal papers, and photographs. They'd returned his computer and personal effects, but not his brother's cell phone. Or his mother's religious necklace, which some girl turned in. Or Catherine's key chain. He figured he'd get the phone and necklace back eventually. But not the key chain.

Not that he could ask for it.

Wil unlocked the door and pushed it open. He expected the room to stink of food that had rotted in the mini fridge. He expected to find everything in his drawers and shelves dumped on the floor and then walked on and broken by the police. He propped his cartons against the open door and pulled back the bed-sheet from the window. Dust motes danced on a shaft of light across the wood plank floor.

There was no mess. No chaos. The floor was bare. The fridge was empty. Were the cops this neat and courteous? He didn't think so. He wondered if his anonymous benefactor, who'd picked up his rent, had also picked up his room. If so, Wil wished he or she hadn't. Everything was here. His clothes. His shelf full of science-fiction paperback books. His box full of old mementos—menus from restaurants he used to work in. A game token from an arcade where he and Lando once spent an afternoon. A postcard of the whitewashed church in Santiago where his mother went to pray.

Still, something about the neatness made Wil uncomfortable. He couldn't put his finger on why, but he felt more invaded by the order imposed than he ever would have felt if it had just been left in a shambles.

Someone knocked on his open door. Wil jumped. He turned to see a tiny Mayan woman, with a long, shiny black braid down her back.

"Señora Calderon." His neighbor. She was standing in the hallway, struggling to zip a toddler into a snowsuit. The child was so bundled, his arms stuck out like the ends of a coat hanger.

"Wil!" She straightened and gave him a hug. "Are you back?" she asked in Spanish.

"Just to pack up." He pointed to the cardboard propping open the door. "I'm taking care of a man in town. I'm living there now."

"That's good—yes? Your life is okay?"

Wil wasn't sure how to answer that. He went to classes. He had his job back at the Lake Holly Grill. He'd settled in with Mr. Zimmerman. The old man and the señora were both kind to him and gave him plenty of space. The Morrisons had stopped throwing their dog's doo over the fence. There had been no more incidents with the neighbors.

And yet Wil felt a great weight inside him. He still hadn't called his mother and told her about Rolando. She deserved the truth. He wasn't sure he could give it.

"I'm doing okay."

"I pray for your family," Señora Calderon told him.

"Thank you," said Wil. "Do you know if the landlord let himself into my room since the police raid?"

Landlords were always poking around, even under the best of circumstances. Still, Wil had never met one who picked up after his tenants.

"He's let a bunch of people in after the police took the crime scene tape down," said the señora. "I wanted to say something but some of us," she hesitated, "we weren't sure you'd ever be back."

"Who did he let in?"

"Some neighbors on the street who were curious—curious enough to slip him some cash, I think. I wasn't always here to know. There was one . . . a blond man. With a beard. He cornered me in the hallway. He asked a lot of questions. I was afraid not to answer."

"What did he ask?"

"About the girl who was murdered. He wanted to know if I'd ever seen her here. I told him no. Why would she come here?"

"Did he spend any time in my room?"

"He was in there a while, yes." Señora Calderon hefted the toddler into her arms. "I thought maybe he was your lawyer or something. Maybe he was helping with your case—no?"

Wil felt like a wet towel had just been snapped across his face. Someone—maybe more than one someone—had been in his room, carefully sorting through his and Rolando's things. Not a cop. Definitely not a friend. What was he looking for? Wil wondered.

And more worrisome—had he found it?

Chapter 40

Vega waited until Carp had gone into a meeting to dial his old boss, Captain Waring. He didn't do it inside the Suburban. He couldn't be sure whether the whole vehicle was bugged. Instead, he paced the far end of the parking lot, shivering, while he waited for the call to go through. He was relieved when Waring picked up.

"Captain. It's Detective Vega. It's very important that I speak with you."

"We're not reconsidering the assignment, Detective."

"This concerns a criminal matter."

"Can you be more specific?"

"Mike Carp wants me to engage in evidence tampering."

That got his attention. "Continue, please."

"Lake Holly just arrested a juvenile for the La Casa arson. His father's a major Carp supporter. Mike Carp wants me to ask them to lose the evidence."

"You're sure about this? You didn't misinterpret?"

"He made himself crystal clear," said Vega. "And that's not all." Vega told Waring about Carp's threats against Vega's daughter and girlfriend if he didn't co-operate. He mentioned, too, about the GPS device placed on his truck and the suspicious packages Carp regularly asked him to hand deliver, but he didn't dwell on those. He didn't have the same level of proof and he didn't want Waring to think he was paranoid.

"I'm already in enough trouble with the shooting," Vega explained. "I don't want to get swept into a cor-ruption scandal."

"I see." Waring's voice was flat and unreadable. Vega scanned the parking lot for signs of Carp or any of his en-tourage. He ducked out of the line of the building's sur-veillance cameras. Everything spooked him. Maybe he really was paranoid.

"So you'll pull me off this detail?"

"I fail to see how that addresses the problem," said Waring. "All it does is expose some other officer to the same alleged situation." Vega heard the word "al-leged" like a knife between the shoulder blades. Didn't his boss believe him?

"What we need," said Waring, "is documented evi-dence of criminal activities."

Vega's insides shrank. He had a sense what was coming.

"If what you're saying is true, Detective, then we'll need recordings from your phone. Notes from conver-sations. A thorough and detailed log of dates, times, and places of suspected illegal activities, along with the names of anyone who appears to be engaging in them along with Carp. Meanwhile, I will take your concerns through channels. If the evidence is strong enough, we'll hand you over to the FBI."

Then they will force me to wear a wire and entrap people who may only be tangentially involved. Local police officers, like the cops in Lake Holly. Maybe even Greco. The feds would have no allegiance to Vega or his career. By the time they were through with him, he could kiss off any future in the county police. Every cop in the area would remember him as the guy who wore a wire against fellow officers.

"I'll inform you of any updates," said Waring. "In the meantime, keep thorough records and don't divulge your situation or our discussions to anyone inside or outside of this department."

Vega stared at the phone after Captain Waring hung up. He was in this alone.

Vega had band practice that evening—one of the few things these days that made him happy. That, and the fact that tomorrow was Saturday. He had the day off. He drove home after work and changed into jeans, then walked and fed Diablo. He ate a plate of fried eggs and grilled cheese as he checked in with Adele. Then he texted Joy to remind her that her next tuition payment was due and he hadn't yet seen the bill.

I'll give it to you next time I see you, she texted back. **Guess what? Dr. Langstrom's going to pay me a stipend. $200 a semester! I'm the first undergrad he's awarded a stipend to!**

Vega stared at the text. He wanted to be happy for

his daughter. Despite what she'd said the other day, he really did value her intellect and ambitions. He just wished she'd found this passion with some other professor. Still, he didn't want to become a parent who greeted every high point in his child's life with negativity. So he typed back: **Congratulations, chispita. I'm so proud of you. Hope you get a chance to celebrate.**

Thanks, Dad. I will, she texted back. **Going to see 5'N'10 tonight on campus.** At the bottom, she added a smiley face emoji. She was happy. She was doing work she loved. She was going to a concert with friends. Maybe he just needed to cut her a little slack.

He threw his dishes into the dishwasher and then loaded his guitar, amps, and pedals into his truck for the drive down to Danny Molina's house in Port Carroll. He was on the road before he realized it was his turn to bring drinks and snacks to practice. He remembered right near the turnoff for the Safeway, just north of Lake Holly. He pulled off the exit, parked, and ran inside, scouring the aisles for stuff Danny's wife wouldn't ban (no doughnuts, no sugary sodas). Danny was trying to lose weight, but it was always a losing battle.

Vega settled on beer (they practiced so long, it always washed out of their systems), baked potato chips, and air-popped popcorn. He stood in the express checkout aisle, which had seven people on it, so it didn't look very express.

"I can help someone over here," said a cashier in the next aisle. Vega dashed over. He was so busy putting his stuff on the conveyor belt that it took him a minute before he looked up and saw the young woman ringing up his purchase. Short purple hair, razor-cut on one side, flipped on the other. A gold ring through her nose.

"Zoe."

She blinked at him. "It's me, Jimmy Vega. Joy Vega's dad?" *The cop,* he wanted to say, but didn't.

"Sure." She offered a shy smile and rang up his order.

"I, uh, spoke to your mom the other day."

"I know," she said. She kept her head down. "I got your message."

Vega pulled a plastic bag from the rack and bagged the beer and chips. "Listen, Zoe. I'm here if you want to talk. I know you've been through a lot, what with Catherine and everything."

She kept her gaze on the register and punched in a code. It seemed to be taking all of her effort.

"I need to see ID," she said.

"Huh?"

"For the beer. I need to see your driver's license."

"Oh. Sure. Sorry." He pulled out his wallet and held his license up to her. She keyed in his date of birth.

Vega tried again. "So, like . . . if you ever want to discuss things with me. It doesn't have to go anywhere . . ." His words hung in the air, mixed with the sound of clerks bagging groceries and someone asking for a price check. The line was long. Vega couldn't hold the girl up at her job.

"Thank you," said Zoe. "I appreciate your concern. Maybe some other time."

"Okay." Vega fished out his credit card and ran it through the machine. "I'm sure Joy would like to speak to you anyway." He caught her shocked expression. "Not about that. Don't worry—I'd never divulge a confidence. I'm talking about your internship. With that professor? Langstrom? Joy's got it now. Maybe you can—I don't know—give her some pointers?"

Vega picked up the electronic pen to sign his receipt. He forgot he was holding it when he saw Zoe Beck's face. All the color had drained from it, until her skin looked like some washed-out version of her hair.

"I say something wrong?"

"That's him," said Zoe.

"Him, who?"

"The one who took the video of me."

"Wait." Vega reared back. "Your mom told me it was a college student. At a fraternity."

"I lied to her. I had to." Her voice turned high and choked. "No one would have believed me if I'd said it was Dr. Jeff."

Zoe couldn't talk in the Safeway, not even in the break room. Vega waited in his truck until she could meet him outside. In the meantime, he called Joy. Her phone went to voice mail. He left her a message: "Call me, chispita. It's important." He did the same on a text. No answer. He tried to calm down and remind himself that his daughter was going to that 5'N'10 concert on campus tonight. She wouldn't hear the phone or the ding of a text over the music. There was no imminent threat to her well-being.

He couldn't get his gut to agree with him.

No way could he go to band practice now. He called Molina and apologized for having to "work late" this evening. The guys would have to go on without him—raid Danny's refrigerator and let their bassist, Brandon Cruz, fill in the gaps as best he could.

By the time Zoe stepped into Vega's truck, they were both a bundle of nerves. Zoe, for all that had happened. And Vega, for all he feared might.

"Please, Mr. Vega. I'll tell you what you need to know for Joy's sake. But I don't want to press charges. I don't want that video all over the Internet. It will ruin my life. I'll never break free of it."

"I won't do anything you don't want me to," Vega promised. "But I need answers. As a father, if not a cop. Did Jeffrey Langstrom sexually assault you?"

Zoe let out a long, rattled sigh. "I don't know. That sounds crazy, doesn't it? You probably think I'm such a skank."

"I don't think anything of the sort," said Vega. He always tried to keep his judgment neutral when it came to sexual assaults. It was so easy to get caught up in stereotypes and miss the truth completely. So he waited, keeping his mind blank, while their breath fogged up the windows of his truck.

"It wasn't . . . I never intended . . ." Zoe settled her gaze on her hands. She had pretty, delicate hands, but her nails were bitten to the quick. Vega wondered if she'd always been a nail biter or whether that started after the assault. "We were working on a research paper together," she began. "Dr. Jeff promised me a publishing credit. That's a big deal—especially for an underclassman. I was so excited. It seemed like my big break."

"Where were you working on this paper?" asked Vega.

"Mostly in POW's campus office," said Zoe. "On the third floor of the Neumann Sciences Building. I worked late a lot for him. He said he felt bad that he always made me miss dinner."

Vega thought about Joy missing dinner the other night when Vega visited her. Something curdled in his gut.

"One night," Zoe continued, "Dr. Jeff suggested I come over to his house for dinner. He said he wanted to make it up to me for all the dinners he'd made me miss." Zoe ran two hands down her square face. "I'm not beautiful, Mr. Vega. Boys don't fall at my feet—not the nice ones anyway. So it's not like I had any reason to doubt Dr. Jeff's sincerity. It just seemed like a really thoughtful gesture."

"When did this happen?"

"Over the December break. Classes weren't in session. Dr. Jeff made pasta with some sort of cream sauce. He opened a bottle of red wine. At first, I begged off the wine. I know you probably think I'm lying, but I'm not much of a drinker. I don't use drugs. My mom was sort of wild when she was young. I never wanted to go the same route."

"So . . . he insisted you drink the wine?"

"Not *insisted,* exactly. Just—I don't know. We were having these deep, important discussions about greenhouse gases and the rate of attrition of the polar cap. No one had ever treated me this way before—made me feel like I was smart. Like I was going places. He was drinking the wine. It felt sophisticated to join him."

"So you had three glasses? Four? More?"

"Just one."

"Just *one*?" Vega raised an eyebrow.

"I don't think I even finished it. And then, like ten hours later, I woke up naked on his bed."

Either Zoe was lying—which didn't seem likely, given the smoothness of her narrative—or Langstrom had spiked her wine. Vega was betting he'd used Rohypnol—a powerful sedative and easy to obtain on the Internet. It was a common date-rape drug.

"Did you leave your wine unattended?" Vega asked her.

"I probably used the bathroom at some point. I don't remember. I know that when I woke up the next morning, Dr. Jeff made it seem as if I'd gotten drunk and come on to him. I was humiliated. I took my clothes. I didn't tell anyone."

"Not your friend Lydia? Or maybe Catherine?"

"No." At the mention of Catherine, Zoe turned away. Vega noticed her bring a bitten nail to her lips. "Not then anyway."

"But later you mentioned it?"

"Yeah."

"Did you know at the time that he'd made that video of you?"

"No. I kind of thought Dr. Jeff and I could put it all behind us. But after that, he started pressuring me for sex. Violent, kinky stuff. I refused, but he started groping me. He was very insistent. I told him I was going to report him to the school. And that's when he showed me the video."

"So in other words, he blackmailed you," said Vega.

"He said if I didn't do everything he asked of me, he'd make sure that video circulated all over campus and the Internet." Vega heard the quake in her voice. She was fighting hard not to break down. "He pointed out that since he's not on it, he wouldn't be implicated."

"Did you file a complaint with the police?"

"I'm the Goth-looking, tattooed daughter of a single mom who lives above a nail salon and drives a car held together with duct tape. Do you really think anyone's going to believe my word against a man like Dr. Jeff?"

Vega didn't try to contradict her. Rape cases were hard enough to investigate and prosecute. One that pitted a victim like Zoe Beck against an assailant like Langstrom would have been an uphill battle.

"So you quit the internship and dropped out of school," said Vega. "But he still sent you that video?"

"Yes. But he didn't spread it around. He didn't post it on the Internet."

"Why did he send it at all? Was it some kind of warning to keep your mouth shut? You're gone from the college now, I don't see the point."

Zoe toyed with a grimy-looking rope bracelet on her wrist. "Catherine made this for me."

"Your mom said you two were very close."

"Best friends forever. That's what she always said." Her breath came out choked. "When this wears out, I'm going to get a tattoo just like this in her honor."

Vega felt like the conversation had veered off on a tangent. But maybe not. If he'd learned anything from being the father of a teenage daughter, it was this: What a girl *doesn't* say is far more important than what she *does*.

"Zoe." Vega turned to face her. "Did Catherine's murder have anything to do with why Dr. Langstrom didn't post that video to the Internet?"

"I can't . . . He'll kill me if I say anything."

Vega couldn't believe what he was hearing. "Do you mean to tell me that Jeffrey Langstrom sent you that video as a warning not to talk to the police about Catherine's murder? Why?"

"It's complicated, Mr. Vega."

"Uncomplicate it for me."

Zoe stared out the side window. A cold and antiseptic light emanated from the Safeway across the parking lot, reflecting back in the puddles of melted snow. People passed the truck with their shopping carts, checking their cell phones and grocery lists. Vega wanted to be in their shoes at the moment, worrying about what to cook for dinner or whether they'd bought enough milk. Anywhere but in this cab, dragging out a seedy story to spare his daughter the same fate.

"Catherine was trying to help me," said Zoe.

"Help you how?"

"Get Dr. Jeff to leave me alone."

"She was a high-school girl," said Vega. "What power would she have to compel that?"

"She had something of her dad's Dr. Jeff wanted. Some sort of video." Zoe exhaled. "I don't even know what was on it or why Dr. Jeff wanted it so much. Not that it matters now. She got cold feet and backed out."

"Where's the video?"

"I don't know."

"Why didn't you come forward and tell all of this to the police?"

"I got scared. And besides, it has nothing to do with Catherine's murder. That illegal from La Casa killed her. Mike Carp said so himself."

Vega winced at the girl's words. At his own mistakes. At the town's rush to judgment. People always wanted the police to solve crimes quickly. And here was the result. A dead man who was likely innocent. A guilty one still walking the streets. And a witness who assumed the case was over, when, in truth, it had never really begun.

Vega had so many questions. But as he sat in the cab of his truck, his pulse quickening like he'd run wind sprints, he knew the biggest question of all was the one he was afraid to ask.

"Zoe, is there any chance that Catherine met with Dr. Langstrom on the night of her murder?"

"I don't know," said Zoe. "It's possible. I mean, she wanted to help me and all . . ." Zoe looked ready to cry. It seemed to be dawning on the girl what Vega was asking.

All this time, Vega's chief worry had been that Jeffrey Langstrom might take advantage of his daughter. But now a whole new level of fear invaded his being. Maybe Zoe Beck's life was no longer in this man's hands.

But Joy's was.

Chapter 41

Vega escorted Zoe back into the grocery store. His mind was racing. He wanted Langstrom picked up and questioned as soon as possible. But even more, he wanted to get ahold of Joy. He dialed her cell again and texted her, but she still didn't respond. He called his ex-wife and forced himself to sound relaxed.

"She went to see 5'N'10," said Wendy. "Do you really think she's going to respond from a hip-hop concert?"

"But if she does? Can you have her call me right away?"

"Is something wrong?"

Vega wanted to pour out his fears to the one person who'd understand and share them. But he couldn't. It was a breach of Zoe's confidentiality. And besides, it would worry Wendy for no reason.

"Everything's fine," Vega lied. "I just need to ask her a question about her tuition bill."

"You're calling all over creation on a Friday night

for that?" She laughed. "You really are too controlling with her sometimes."

Vega's next call was to the Lake Holly Police. If he couldn't get to Joy, at the very least, he could get the cops to pick up Langstrom. Vega asked the desk sergeant if Greco was around.

"He's out on a call with Jankowski."

"How about Detective Sanchez?" He was on desk duty since the shooting. He probably never went anywhere.

"Hold on. I'll get him."

Vega waited on the line for what seemed like hours, but was probably only two minutes.

"Everybody's in a meeting here," Sanchez grumbled when he picked up. "What do you need?"

Vega told him as succinctly as possible why Jeffrey Langstrom needed to be questioned in the murder of Catherine Archer.

"You're talking about that water activist?" asked Sanchez. "The 'Pied Pisser' of the county?"

Vega smiled. Sanchez had been spending too much time around Greco.

"That's the one." Vega walked him through the connections between Catherine, Langstrom, Zoe, and the missing video that belonged to John Archer—a video that seemed to be cropping up in a host of different witness statements, including Jocelyn's story about Alex Romero.

Vega didn't mention Zoe by name, a fact Sanchez picked up on right away.

"So this witness—is she planning to come forward?"

"Not yet," said Vega. "But I'm working on it."

"Can she place Langstrom with Catherine the Friday night of her disappearance?"

"No. But there's no reason your department can't question him right away and check his alibi."

"Did you just get promoted to chief here, Vega? Because last I heard from Greco, you were pumping gas for our county exec—who happens to be with us this evening."

"Mike Carp is at the station?"

"With a couple of his associates," said Sanchez. "That's what the meeting's about. They're putting pressure on our department to close the Archer case. So I'll tell you right now, your boss and mine aren't going to share your enthusiasm for interviewing a respected county professor on the say-so of a witness who won't come forward."

"It's more than that," said Vega. He knew he had to. "The witness Langstrom allegedly assaulted? The one who won't come forward? She was the professor's intern. And now? That intern's my daughter."

Vega could hear a slow breath of air leave Sanchez's lungs. He had daughters too.

"All right," he said. "I'll do a little digging and let Greco and Jankowski know when they get back. Maybe they can visit the guy tomorrow. He's a tenured professor, so he's not going anywhere. And your daughter's not in any immediate danger, I'm assuming."

"She's out at that 5'N'10 concert on the Valley campus tonight," said Vega.

"That concert was canceled."

"What?"

"My niece goes to Valley," said Sanchez. "She just called my sister and told her. She's driving home now."

"But I've been calling my daughter all evening. She's not picking up her voice mails or texts."

"She's probably just bummed about the concert being canceled," Sanchez assured him. "Bet if you take a ride over to the campus, you can track her down. In the meantime, I'll go back in the meeting and let my chief and Carp's people know about Langstrom."

Vega heard a clicking on his phone. Another message was coming in. *Joy?* He raced to get Sanchez off the line. The call had gone to voice mail by the time he picked up.

Hi, Dad. 5'N'10 cancelled. I can't believe it! Dr. Jeff felt so bad for me, he invited me to dinner. Catch you later.

"Invited me to dinner." Does that mean out *to dinner? To a restaurant? Or to his house?*

Vega hit the reply button. His call went to voice mail. He left a terse message: "Call me right away. Whatever you do, don't go to Langstrom's house." He sent the same message on a text. No reply. He jumped on the highway and drove over the speed limit the whole way to Valley. He'd feel foolish if it turned out that all Langstrom had done was take Joy for a pizza at the local student dive.

Then again, nothing felt foolish when he thought about that video of Zoe Beck.

He was almost at the campus when a set of flashing red-and-blue lights lit up the interior of his truck. He saw a Mayfair Police Department cruiser in his rearview mirror. *Puñeta!* Mayfair was two stoplights bookended by the county hospital on one side and the community college on the other. The cops here likely never saw anything bigger than a fender bender or a drunken frat boy who'd wandered too far off campus. They didn't know Vega. They weren't going to be in a hurry with him.

Even so, he was surprised when they spoke to him over the loudspeaker.

"Get out of the car. On the ground. Hands behind your head."

What? For going ten miles over the speed limit? In a pickup with a PBA sticker on the back windshield?

Vega opened his truck door and stepped out, his hands over his head. "I'm a county police detective!" he shouted. "I'm on my way to an emergency."

"On the ground! Now!" shouted a male voice.

The ground was wet, covered in the remnants of melting snow and grit. It was the last place Vega wanted to be. But he knew that once the guns come out, the only thing cops understand is absolute, abject obedience. This was how civilians got shot. They assumed their explanations meant something.

Vega lowered himself to his knees, then his stomach. The asphalt felt icy and wet against the front of his jacket. He shivered as he laced his gloved hands over his head.

Vega heard two voices approaching him—one male, one female.

"I've got a nine-millimeter Glock in my holster," said Vega. "My badge and ID are in my wallet in my right back pocket."

The male patted him down and removed his gun. The female cuffed him.

"Hey!" Vega protested. "What's going on?"

The two cops pulled him to his feet. The man was black with a shaved head. His name tag read, *Tripp.*

The woman was white with a narrow face and an over-bite. *DiStefano.*

"Got a nine-one-one call of shots fired from a sus-pect matching your description in a truck with your plates," said Tripp.

"*What?* I didn't fire any shots." *Who would report such a thing?*

But Vega had a sick sense he already knew. Carp was in Lake Holly tonight. Carp was doing business with Langstrom. He'd have a vested interest in tipping Langstrom off that the police were onto him. And an even greater interest in slowing Vega down if he found out that Vega's daughter was with Langstrom this evening. Vega was betting the "associates" Carp had with him tonight were Prescott or Vanderlinden. Either of them could have put in a 911 call easily. From any-where. Maybe even one of the station house phones.

"This is a crank call," Vega protested.

Tripp removed Vega's wallet from his pants pocket and fished out his police ID. He shined a flashlight on it and frowned at his face. "Hey, aren't you that cop who shot that guy—?"

Coño. Now they really wouldn't believe him. "Yes. That's me. But I didn't discharge my weapon. Check it out for yourself if you don't believe me."

"We'll check *everything* out," said Tripp.

Vega had a feeling they would. Very, very slowly. "Can this wait?" he asked. "My daughter's in danger."

"What sort of danger?" asked DiStefano.

"She went to dinner with a professor who's a sus-pect in a rape, maybe even a murder."

"A professor from Valley?" asked DiStefano.

"Yes. A guy named Jeffrey Langstrom."

The two cops traded looks. They both seemed to recognize Langstrom's name—which made Vega's story sound even more dubious.

"The professor's been charged?" asked Tripp.

"Not . . . yet," Vega admitted.

"The police have a sworn statement from a witness? Some evidence?"

"No. But I spoke to someone who claims Langstrom abused her."

"You're the investigating officer?"

"No—"

"Is your daughter underage?"

"She's eighteen," said Vega. "And this guy's, like, fifty."

"So in other words," said Tripp, "a grown woman is splitting a pizza with her professor. I think you can cool your heels while we run your ID."

"You're assuming they went out to eat," said Vega. "What if she's at his house?"

DiStefano shot a glance at her partner. They weren't worried like Vega. But they believed in covering their asses. It was every cop's default mode.

"What's the address?" asked Tripp. "We can send a car to check on her."

"I don't know," said Vega. "I was going to campus security to see if they had it. He's supposed to live near here."

"All right," said Tripp. "Let me see if I can find anything in our database."

Vega sat in the back of their cruiser while DiStefano examined his truck for shell casings, evidence of drugs, or other contraband.

Tripp leaned in the cruiser and looked at Vega. "Jeffrey Langstrom lives at 12 Boucher Road," he said. "I asked one of our patrols to check the place out now."

"Thank you."

"You have your daughter's cell number? I can text her for you."

Vega reeled it off. "I tried already. She's not answering."

Tripp tried. She didn't get an answer either. Also no answer. Every second in the cruiser filled Vega with more dread.

They detained him all of six or seven minutes while they ran his ID, verified that he wasn't under the influence, and had no suspicious items in his truck—just his guitars and amps, which he clearly played. Tripp, it turned out, was a guitarist too, so they both knew the lingo. They were just about to let him go, when Tripp got a radio reply from the two cops who'd checked out Langstrom's house.

"The professor was home, but your daughter's not there," he told Vega.

"Are they sure? Did they check?" Vega caught the smolder of irritation in Tripp's eyes. No cop likes to be second-guessed.

"Her car wasn't there, Vega," he said more emphatically. "Langstrom said she came over, had a quick bite, and left."

"Did they try to gain entrance to the premises?"

"They made inquiries. He declined. You know the rules, Detective. We can't do more."

Maybe *they* couldn't. But he could.

Chapter 42

Wil couldn't put the call off any longer. He walked into his bedroom upstairs—the room across from the pink flouncy one that looked unchanged for twenty years. Wil sensed that space was occupied, even if the inhabitant was unseen.

The old man carried a heavy burden of grief himself. That much was clear.

Wil pulled out his cell phone and dialed the number. He heard the catch in her voice as she picked up, the way she forced a brightness he knew she didn't feel. The deportation had taken the first part of her. The cancer had taken the rest. Two pieces of official paper separated them forever: his DACA permit, which wouldn't allow him to leave the U.S.; her order of removal, which wouldn't allow her to return.

"Mami?"

"Mi rey," she breathed into the phone. Her nickname for him, "My king," ever since he was small. Wil could hear the way the words filled up her chest. Made

her sound almost well again. Made the two-thousand-mile distance between them disappear. "It's been a long time since you called. I've been so worried." Her words felt stilted, even in Spanish. Wil had to remind himself that in the Guatemalan Highlands, she spoke her native Mayan tongue—one she dropped with him once they moved to the States. He knew only a few words of Tz'utujil—another reason he could never make it back in Guatemala. He was a complete stranger to his own culture.

"I'm sorry I didn't call sooner, *Mami*," he replied in Spanish. "I've been . . . busy." The words burned at the back of his throat. Was the sin of omission as great as a lie? If so, he was a very guilty man. "How are you feeling?"

"Well enough, thanks to God."

"You're going to the doctor in Santiago? Getting your chemo? Doing the radiation treatments?" The only doctors in the region were a thirty-five-minute bus ride from his mother's house. That was, when the buses were running. Not broken. Or trapped in a muddy ditch. Or waiting on parts that might take months to arrive.

"Yes. But I feel bad taking money from you and Lando."

Wil felt like his heart was encased in barbed wire. Every breath dug in a little deeper. "Don't worry. I have enough."

"But I don't want you to drop out of school because of me. You are our future, *mi rey*. Your success—that's what matters. I know Lando feels the same way. All we want is for you to graduate."

Oh God, oh God! Do all immigrant kids feel such

pressure? It was like a vise grip pinching the nerves at the back of his neck. For as long as Wil could remember, his family's hopes and dreams had all been planted on his shoulders. His success was their success. It didn't matter if *Mami* got deported. Or if Lando got jailed or drank too much. What mattered was that Wil graduated. That Wil became a doctor. An American. If he made it, they could all die fulfilled.

"Keep making me proud. Keep making Mami *proud."* Weren't those Lando's last instructions to him?

He'd failed them both.

"How is Lando?" asked his mother. "Is he behaving himself?" She spoke as if Lando were a small, errant child. Wil had the sense his mother had long ago reconciled herself to her oldest child's limitations. "I called his cell phone, but it's out of service. Did he forget to pay his bill?"

"Maybe."

"I went to the church in Santiago yesterday," said *Mami.* "Do you remember it?"

"I remember." Wil thought of those thick, white-washed stucco walls that kept the interior cool and damp—even on the hottest days. The air itself felt like God's breath against his cheeks.

"I said a prayer to Ixchel," she continued. *Ixchel.* A Mayan goddess.

"I pray you get better too," said Wil.

His mother laughed. "Oh, *mi rey.* I don't care about me. I said the prayer for you. You and Lando."

So much for Ixchel's powers. Wil suspected the prayers of a pagan female goddess were no match for walls and faith built by men.

His mother tried for lighter topics. She told him how

she'd wandered the markets after church and bought a lemon ice next to a narrow, cobblestoned road flanked by colorful houses with wrought-iron balconies and long, shuttered windows. She re-created the streets of his early childhood, omitting the crumbling walls, leaning roofs, and feral dogs.

Wil closed his eyes and hung on to the soothing lilt of her words. He felt like a little boy again, nestled in bed beside her. When he was growing up, it was the only chance they ever got to be close. She often worked three jobs and came home so tired that all she had the strength to do was feed him and fall into bed with the TV blaring. It was her body Wil came to know far better than the woman who inhabited it. He loved her for the arms that would hold him against her pillow-soft contours. For her humid breath on his skin. Other little boys had memories of their mothers playing games with them or teaching them to ride a bike. Wil remembered those nights watching her sleep. He learned to take comfort in her presence. In the simple act of her being. She was like gravity—a force you felt only in its absence.

He'd felt weightless since she was taken away. And every month, more of her seemed gone. Her breasts. Her hair. The doctors were carving her up, piece by piece.

"You're so quiet tonight, *mi rey*. What's wrong?"
Tell her.
"See, *Mami,* it's Lando. He's . . ."
"He's not drinking again, is he? You tell him to reconnect his phone. He has to look after you and help you. You tell him I said that."
Wil's heart beat so fast, it felt like it could leap out

of his chest. *She's dying,* said a voice inside him. *In a land she cannot leave. A land you cannot enter. Let her die a happy woman. Why destroy her with such devastating news?*

"The thing is . . . Lando is . . ." Wil held back the choke in his voice.

"What?"

Maybe he could let her down gently. Do this over time. *Lando isn't well. He's getting worse. He's very sick.* Anything but telling his dying mother that her firstborn was shot and killed by the police for a crime he didn't commit.

"Lando hasn't been around lately."

"He's . . . not living with you?"

"He's just . . . gone. A lot."

Silence. "You have him call me."

"No! *Mami,* please. He's . . . He's staying with a friend. A friend who's helping him get sober."

"Really?"

"Yes." The words came out before Wil could stop himself. "A woman. A good woman. She's helping him. *Mami*—you should see how well he's doing. How happy he is!"

"Well, that's good, I guess." Wil heard the fatigue in her voice. "You tell him I love him and I'm praying for him. I know you have to go. I know you're studying hard. Thanks to God, one day you will graduate. I love you, *mi rey.*"

"I love you too, *Mami.*"

Wil hung up. He didn't expect the wave of grief to wash over him like it did. It started somewhere deep in his gut. A wrenching, spasmodic pain that seized his chest and constricted his lungs. He felt like he'd been sucked down by a strong undertow. Every time he tried to take a breath, he was pulled back under. He shoved a pillow into his face, but he couldn't entirely stop the anguished sobs that came unbidden from inside him.

A loud knock on Mr. Zimmerman's front door forced Wil's head from the pillow. He looked out the window to see two hulking figures in identical dark blue jackets. One had a buzz cut of silver-tipped hair. He vaguely remembered the man questioning him in the aftermath of his brother's shooting. The other was the bald cop Wil had first met at the Lake Holly Grill.

Wil's first thought was that Mrs. Morrison had complained again. But no—the neighbor hadn't bothered them since that first night. And besides, these guys were detectives, not patrol officers. They wouldn't show up about something as petty as dog doo. If they were here—at this hour—they meant business.

Wil felt like he'd swallowed a sponge that was slowly expanding inside his gut.

He wiped his tears and walked down the stairs. The two cops thumped the door again. Couldn't they see the doorbell? Then again, maybe the brute noise was intended. It woke up Mr. Zimmerman in any case. He came out of his room with his wife's pink bathrobe wrapped around his pajamas.

"What is this racket?" he shouted, slipping his heavy black glasses onto his face.

"I think it's the police," said Wil. He ran ahead and opened the door. The cop with the buzz cut gave him a sharklike smile.

"Hey there, Wil. Remember me? Detective Jankowski? And my partner, Detective Greco? May we come in?"

Wil looked at Mr. Zimmerman. It wasn't his place to invite anyone into the house.

Max Zimmerman hobbled forward with his cane to the door. "What is this about? And why are you coming here at this late hour?"

"We're very sorry to bother you, sir," said Jankowski. "Please feel free to go back to bed. It's Wil we need to see." Jankowski kept his smile plastered to his face. "In fact, Wil, you can just come to the station house with us if you want, so we don't disturb your host."

"Uh, okay—"

"What? No way!" said Zimmerman. "Are you arresting him?"

"Well, no," said Jankowski.

"We just want to ask the kid some questions," Greco added.

"Then you ask them here," said Zimmerman. "In front of me."

The two cops exchanged glances. "Where would you like to talk?" Jankowski asked him. "The kitchen?"

"Okay," said Wil.

The four of them sat down at Zimmerman's kitchen table. Normally, the old man offered visitors something to drink. But not this time. He seemed to feel as threatened by their presence as Wil did.

Greco took out a small vial that looked like a toothbrush holder. He twisted it open and handed the wand to Wil. "We just need you to touch the swab to the inside of your cheek." A guard at the jail had made Wil do the same thing after Wil was locked up. He didn't have a choice then, and he suspected he didn't have a choice now. He reached for the wand to comply.

"Why?" asked Zimmerman.

"Relax, sir," said Jankowski. "Mr. Martinez did this at the jail already. He knows the procedure."

"If he did it already, why does he have to do it again?"

Wil could see that the old man's interference was annoying the cops. Something flashed in Greco's eyes, but his voice stayed calm and patient. "Because we need one too."

"So? Get it from the jail." Zimmerman turned to Wil. "Maybe I should call Adele. Or that lawyer of yours."

"Seems to me," Greco grunted, "you're doing a pretty good job of obstructing all by yourself." He turned to Wil and shut Zimmerman out.

"Look, kid, me and Jankowski just want to get our job done here and punch out. You want to turn this into a big deal? We're going to have to take you down to the station, lock you up overnight, and let someone else handle this in the morning. Either way, it's going to happen. So which is it going to be? The easy way? Or the hard?"

Wil stared at the wand in Greco's outstretched palm. He knew what the cops wanted. They wanted his DNA. Wil had assumed they'd gotten it from the mandatory cheek swab every inmate gets at the jail. But maybe the sample was corrupted. Or got thrown out. Either way, they were determined to get it. Wil could delay giving it to them. But ultimately, he'd have to. People lie. Science? Never.

Wil grabbed the wand, touched it to the inside of his cheek, and handed it back to Greco. "There."

Greco shoved the swab into the cylinder and sealed it in a clear plastic bag. He and Jankowski rose. Jankowski smiled at Wil like he was prey. "Don't leave town." The detective laughed to make it sound like a joke.

It wasn't.

Wil leaned his head against the door after they left. He thought Zimmerman had gone back to bed. But the old man was standing there, watching him.

"I'm sorry about all this," said Wil.

"There's nothing to be sorry about," said Zimmerman. "Come into the kitchen. I'll make tea."

"You don't have to do that, sir. Really."

Zimmerman fixed Wil in his gaze. "You haven't told her, have you?"

Wil felt his blood turn to ice water in his veins. "Pardon?"

"Your mother. You haven't told her your brother is dead. I overheard your conversation upstairs when I got up to use the bathroom." The old man switched to Spanish. "*Mijo,* in your shoes, I would have made the same decision."

Wil wasn't sure if he was more shocked at the old man's perfect command of Spanish or the fact that he'd called Wil, *mijo*—"my son." Max Zimmerman was full of surprises.

Then again, so was Wil.

"I didn't know you spoke Spanish," said Wil.

"I spent five years in Cuba after the war. Come"— he gestured—"it's time for another story."

In the kitchen, Wil poured hot water into two mugs. They sat in companionable silence, listening to the hands of the rooster clock on the wall.

"Your brother," Zimmerman asked finally, "were you close to him?"

"It's complicated," said Wil. "We didn't grow up together."

"But you loved him, yes?"

Wil played with the tab on his tea bag. "It's my fault he died."

"Ah." Wil expected the old man to grill him on the details or launch into some lame reason why Wil shouldn't feel he was to blame. Instead, he stared into his mug.

"I believe I told you the other day about my older brother, Samuel?" Zimmerman fluttered his left hand with its partial missing finger for emphasis.

"Yes," said Wil. "I remember."

Zimmerman's lips moved without sound, as if he were trying to coax his words from hiding. "Samuel was the fastest boy I've ever known," he said slowly. "Before the war, he had stacks of racing medals in his drawers. Me? I was the slow one. When we were in the camps, Samuel told me that if I ever got the chance to run, I must run and not look back."

Zimmerman took a sip of tea. Wil noticed his hand was shaking.

"One day," he continued, "we had a work detail outside the fence. Deep in the forest. Chopping wood for fuel. The guards turned their backs to urinate. Samuel told me to run. I thought we were both running. I thought he was running with me. And then I heard a shot. The sound? Wil—the sound stays in my head forever. I did not understand at the time. I thought Samuel ran and the guards shot him and missed me. But that wasn't it."

"He didn't run?"

"Oh, he ran," said Zimmerman. "He ran straight at the guards as they raised their guns. He blocked their fire. He paid for my life with his own. He—the faster one. The smarter one. He died so I could live. And every day of my eighty-eight years, I feel the burden of his choices. His expectations. You could say God spared me, *mijo*. But I know, it was my brother who spared me. My *brother*."

Zimmerman leaned in closer. "Your brother spared you for a reason, Wil. He believed in you. He deserves your honor now. That means a proper burial. In Guatemala. Where your mother can pray over him."

"I know."

"What if I made the call for you?"

"Then I'd have to . . ." Wil's voice trailed off.

"Have to what? Tell your mother how he died?"

"Yeah." And other things. Stuff bottled up in a human heart—and now a test tube as well.

Chapter 43

Vega found Joy's car—her mother's old white Volvo—still parked in the student parking lot closest to the Neumann Sciences Building. If her car was still there, there were only two possibilities. Either she'd gone back to POW after dinner with Langstrom to finish some project, or someone had driven her elsewhere. Vega walked into the Neumann Building and up to the third floor. The offices of POW were closed. He tried Joy's cell again. No answer.

He knew in his gut: Langstrom had lied to the Mayfair Police.

Boucher Road was a modest street of small, funky houses that appeared to have sprung up in the 1970s and hadn't been updated since. Lots of dark, discolored cedar siding. Lots of right-angled roofs with bubble skylights that popped up from their siding like boils.

Langstrom's house was the third on the cul-de-sac. A faint light radiated from his picture window, casting a bluish glow over the snow-smeared front lawn. In the driveway, Vega saw one car: a dark green Volkswagen minibus covered in bumper stickers for Greenpeace, POW, and the Sierra Club. Vega parked his truck on the street. He had to be careful. Langstrom wasn't yet a suspect in anything. If Vega tried the direct approach, he could end up with a harassment charge or restraining order—both of which could get him fired. Not to mention that it would cost Joy her internship and erase any daughterly goodwill toward Vega for the next decade.

He wished there were a way to know if Joy was still here. All the windows were too high to see in or had their blinds drawn. He needed a way inside. One that was legal *and* plausible. When he was a boy, all the cops in his Bronx neighborhood used to gain access to dealers' apartments by "dropping a dime"—calling 911 from a pay phone to report a robbery or domestic dispute at the address they wanted to raid, then responding to their own call. Cops couldn't do that stuff anymore.

Then again, no one would question a cop who mistakenly called in the fire department.

Vega took out his phone and dialed 911.

"This is Detective Vega of the county police," he told the dispatcher. "I'm at 12 Boucher Road in Mayfair. I think I see smoke coming out of the residence."

"Copy that, Detective. Please remain at the scene. An engine will respond in ETA four minutes."

Good. He'd validated his reason for being here. It would now make perfect sense for him to try to vacate the premises. He walked up to Langstrom's door and rang the bell. Twice. No answer. He pounded on the door. A lock released from the inside. The professor opened the door a crack.

"Yes?" Jeffrey Langstrom looked glassy-eyed. His long gray hair hung loose at his shoulders. His John Lennon glasses were crooked. The buttons on his denim shirt were mismatched, the mistake largely covered by his ZZ Top beard. Vega wondered if he'd woken the man. Then he smelled the sweet perfume stench of marijuana emanating off his clothes. Was that all this was about? Had Langstrom kept the cops out simply because he was smoking a doobie?

"Sir?" said Vega. "I was driving by your house and noticed smoke."

"There's no smoke here." Langstrom didn't seem to recognize Vega from the protest at the campus. Vega was glad. It would have blown his cover.

A siren cut the night. Vega heard the rumble of a diesel engine as the rig turned onto Boucher Road. It underscored Vega's claim better than his words ever could.

"I'm a police officer, sir." Vega flashed his badge. "I don't want you to be unsafe. Mind if I come in and take a look?"

"There's no fire."

"Is anyone else home besides you?"

Langstrom hesitated. "No." Beads of sweat broke out on his bald head, glistening under the dusty yellow glow of a foyer light. The professor swept a gaze at the street behind Vega where a shiny red, rarely used Mayfair Volunteer fire company engine was pulling up to a hydrant by the curb. A bunch of young, too-eager kids, barely out of their teens, hopped off the rig. They all looked excited for action. Vega was sorry to disappoint them.

"This is a bad time," said Langstrom.

Shit. It was still within the man's legal rights to refuse them all entry. Vega was going to have to force the situation. He pretended to lean a hand on Langstrom's front door. What he was really doing was pushing it open. Trying to see inside. He could only see a corner of the living room beyond the foyer. A black-and-white cat jumped off the armrest of a chair and sauntered over to a coat tree in the foyer; there was a tumble of jackets and hats piled on it. That's when Vega saw it. A suede jacket. Tan in color with a corduroy collar. Some designer brand that you don't see on every third person walking down the street. Wendy's jacket. But Wendy wasn't the one wearing it. Not tonight.

Langstrom had no idea Vega was looking at the jacket. He seemed more agitated at the firefighters pouring from the rig and fanning out across his driveway. Two men in turnout coats and rubber boots climbed the steps to Langstrom's door. One of them was carrying a portable extinguisher. Langstrom stepped out.

"There's no fire!" he said sharply. "Go away!"

The firefighter in the white helmet, likely the volunteer chief, started explaining to Langstrom why it was a good idea to check the property. More firefighters were walking the perimeter. If they didn't see smoke and Langstrom refused them entrance, Vega's whole ruse would collapse. Vega had just seconds to take advantage of Langstrom's distraction. He slipped inside.

"Joy?"

Vega raced through the living room. It was decorated in Third World kitsch and reeked of marijuana. Beanbag chairs were scattered across the woven rug. Statues of Buddha and Hindu gods sat on shelves crammed with books. Latin-American folk art adorned the walls. Langstrom's Baggie of weed and rolling papers were sitting on a low wooden table.

Normally, Vega would be fixated on the weed, furious that Joy might have been smoking it with him. But now Vega found himself praying for that to be the worst of their problems. He stepped through an archway into a kitchen and dining area. Two dinner plates sat across from one another at the table. One had only an oily residue of tomato sauce on it. The other had a full plate of pasta under a lump of sauce. It looked cold and congealed. A wineglass sat beside each. Both held only a tint of red at the bottom.

Red wine—just like Zoe had said. Vega's heart beat wildly in his chest. Where was Joy?

The black-and-white cat pawed and meowed at a closed door off the kitchen. Vega put his hand on the knob.

"You there!" shouted Langstrom. "What are you doing walking through my house? Get out of here. Get out!"

Vega kept his back to Langstrom and threw open the door. The room was dark, lit only by a slash of light from the dining area. It took Vega's eyes a moment to adjust. The images that assaulted his vision felt imagined, not real. Something he'd conjured off a screen. Because until this moment, that was the only place he'd ever seen them.

The four-poster bed. The patterned plaid comforter. A girl lying naked and passed out across the sheets.

His worst nightmare.

"You son of a bitch!" Vega wailed. "What have you done to her?"

Vega threw open the door and ran over. He listened to her chest. She was breathing, thank God. Deep, rattling breaths. But at least she was breathing.

Langstrom stood in the doorway. He tossed off a nervous laugh. His voice was as thin and tepid as a whiny child's. "She's my niece. She's just a heavy sleeper. She's—"

Vega grabbed Langstrom and slammed him hard against the wall. The professor's eyes grew wide with fear.

"She's my daughter, you sick, twisted bastard!"

Vega let Langstrom go. He didn't have time to deal with him right now. Joy needed all his attention. He wrapped a blanket around her and scooped her in his arms. He cradled her head on his shoulder and raced to the front door, where the firefighters were packing up to leave.

"I need an ambulance and police response!" he shouted to the men. "Unconscious female, eighteen years old. Suspected poisoning." No way was he going to have anyone think she was just some junkie or drunk who did this to herself. "That man is Professor Jeffrey Langstrom," Vega told the firefighters. "He did this. Don't let him leave."

Joy mumbled. She tossed in her father's arms. Vega sat on a beanbag chair in the living room and tried to get her to wake up, while the firefighters surrounded Langstrom and assured Vega that EMS was on its way.

"It's Dad," Vega whispered into Joy's ear. "I'm here. You're safe now." He rubbed her arms to try to stimulate her into responding. He patted her chin, traced his knuckles across her back. Anything to keep her aroused. He was conscious of his grief being played out among strangers, but he couldn't worry about that right now. All his focus had to be on Joy. "Wake up, *chispita*. Mom and I love you so much. No matter what's happened. You're going to be okay."

Joy opened her eyes at one point and stared at her father. But Vega could see she had no control over her body. *He drugged her. That son of a bitch drugged her.* And then more terrible thoughts started coming.

He raped her. He filmed her.

Vega had seen the room. It was the same room Zoe Beck had been filmed in.

The police arrived first. Tripp and DiStefano—the same two officers who'd detained Vega earlier. They looked guilt-ridden as they stepped through the doorway and avoided Vega's gaze. It wasn't their fault. Not really. But still—he couldn't shake the anger that he could have stopped it if he'd been here sooner. When EMS arrived, they bundled Joy onto a gurney. In the back of the ambulance, they started a saline drip.

"He used some sort of date-rape drug on her," Vega told the EMTs. "I'm thinking Rohypnol, but I can't be sure."

"Do you know if she was sexually assaulted?" asked one of the EMTs. Vega kept his gaze on his unconscious daughter and shook his head. He'd handled dozens of sexual assaults in his career. He knew what to check for. But he couldn't bring himself to look at his own daughter's body that way.

DiStefano, the female cop, walked over just as Vega was about to hop in the ambulance.

"I just want to say I'm sorry," she told him. "I wish we could have stopped it sooner."

"Me too," said Vega. "Did he say if he'd . . ." Vega couldn't get the words out. DiStefano knew what he was asking.

"He denied everything. But we've got his phone. We'll check it to see if he filmed anything. The doctors at the hospital will take a urine sample to test for the presence of sedatives. They'll perform a . . . kit." She omitted the word "rape" for Vega's sake. "You know the procedure."

On the way to the hospital, Vega called Wendy and broke the news. Wendy sobbed into the phone. "Will she be all right?"

Yes. No. The drug itself was likely to wear off after a few hours. But it could take a couple of days before the nausea, vomiting, and headaches abated. And that was assuming that's *all* that happened to their daughter.

In the emergency room, Vega waited outside a curtain while a female doctor and a nurse performed a rape kit and took a urine sample. He called Adele and told her what was happening. She offered to come over, but Vega declined. Wendy would be here soon. It didn't feel right to have his ex-wife's grief on display. Adele agreed.

By the time Wendy arrived, Joy started to regain consciousness. She was dizzy and nauseous. She couldn't recall anything about the evening. The doctor took both parents aside.

"Your daughter doesn't appear to have been sexually assaulted, although there's no way to tell with absolute certainty. We'll know within an hour or two what drugs she has in her system and how long it will take for them to wear off. We can probably treat and release her tonight."

"Thanks," said Vega. The news should have lifted his spirits a little. But Vega couldn't shake the feeling at how close this guy had come. It wasn't the first time. It wasn't necessarily even the worst time.

Catherine.

An orderly wheeled a cart down the hallway. The rumble felt like it was coming from inside Vega's chest. He was glad his daughter couldn't remember much about tonight. He was pretty sure he'd never forget.

Chapter 44

Vega called the Mayfair Police Department first thing Saturday morning for an update on Joy's case. The detective in charge, Garrison, was an amiable guy who told Vega the cops had already obtained a search warrant and seized Langstrom's phone and computer. They'd found plenty of coeds' videos on them—thankfully, none of them Joy's.

"So it's a strong case," said Vega.

"I would have said so—if the DA hadn't informed us this morning that Langstrom wants to cut some kind of a deal."

"For assaulting my daughter and all these girls?" asked Vega. "No way! Besides, Lake Holly needs to talk to him about the Archer murder. For all we know, he's involved in that too."

"That's why you need to bring your daughter in this afternoon so we can get a statement."

"She'll be there," Vega promised. "And another girl too." *Zoe.* He had to convince Zoe.

But first, Vega wanted to spend a calm and quiet morning with his daughter. Breakfast at the Lake Holly Grill. A walk in the park. Maybe one of those stupid art films she liked seeing. Anything to restore normalcy to her life and help her start to heal.

"I'll take you down to Mayfair for your interview this afternoon," he told Joy when he called to lay out his plans for their day together.

"Um . . . I think Mom's going to take me down there this afternoon."

"But I'm the one who knows my way around a criminal investigation," said Vega. "I already spoke to the detective—"

"Which is why I don't want you there, Dad. It's embarrassing enough without having your father listening in. Plus, you talk cop stuff when you're with other cops. I just want Mom."

"Oh. Okay." He felt slighted. He tried to brush it off. "How about lunch afterward?"

"Mom's taking me to lunch at the mall," Joy told him. "Retail therapy."

"Your favorite kind," joked Vega. "So when do I get a chance to talk to you about everything?"

"That's just it, Dad," said Joy. "I'm going to be talking about this to the police. To lawyers. To a therapist. I don't want to talk about it with you too."

"Because you think I'll judge?"

"Because I don't want our relationship to be defined by what happened last night. I'm really, *really* grateful to you for rescuing me, Daddy." *Daddy.* She hadn't called him that since she was maybe six. "You were right about Dr. Jeff. But . . . I want to have fun with you. Like we always did. I don't want that to change."

"It won't," he promised.

"Good."

"So can you think of something you *would* like to do with me this morning before you're off with Mom?"

"You'll laugh."

"No, I won't."

"You remember when I was little? You used to take me to that place in the mall? Build-A-Bear?"

"You want to . . . make a stuffed animal?"

"Yeah. But . . . can we pretend we're building it for someone else? Some five-year-old cousin?"

Vega laughed. "Your secret's safe with me, *chispita*." Every one of them. Always.

They made a pink rabbit with long floppy ears. Joy picked out a sparkly white dress, ballet slippers, and a straw bonnet to dress her in. Vega called the slippers "shoes" and the bonnet a "hat." He fumbled with all the zippers and bows. Joy loved every minute of his ineptness. She was happier than if Vega had gotten her new tickets to see 5'N'10.

On the way home, they stopped at Joy's favorite candy store in Lake Holly and bought lollipops shaped like diamond rings that turned their tongues blue. They tossed around names for Joy's new rabbit: "Princess." "Bella." "Pinkie."

"The Mayfair Police aren't going to believe anything I say with blue-stained lips," said Joy.

Vega grinned. "Just don't take the bunny. They'll think you're smuggling heroin."

Vega drove her back to her mother's and wished her

luck with Detective Garrison. She opened the door and closed it again. "Dad?"

"What is it?"

"How did you know Dr. Jeff was going to assault me? I mean, all you saw was him putting his hand around me at a rally."

Vega tapped the steering wheel. "There's another girl who was also his victim. I'm trying to get her to come forward and testify."

"Zoe Beck?"

Vega stared at his daughter.

"It doesn't take a rocket scientist to figure that out, Dad. She worked as Dr. Jeff's intern before me. She dropped out of school. Was that why?"

"I can't comment."

"I feel so bad for her." Joy fingered the ears of her rabbit. "Zoe never had anyone in her corner—except maybe Catherine, and now she's dead. I'm a lot more fortunate." Joy kissed Vega on the cheek. "Pinkie Girl."

"Huh?"

"That's what I'm naming the bunny. Pinkie Girl. Because she's pink and she's . . . well . . ." Joy flushed. "She's her daddy's girl."

Vega hugged her. "Never forget that."

Joy was right. Zoe didn't have anyone in her corner. It was time he put someone there. As soon as Vega left Joy's house, he drove over to Zoe's mother's place. He wanted to find the girl and give her the good news that Langstrom was in jail. She didn't have to be scared anymore. She could step forward and testify—the same as Joy. He would help her every step of the way. But when he got to Zoe's apartment, the girl's mother, Patsy Walker, greeted him at the door.

"Detective? You heard already? That animal! I hope they put him away forever!"

Vega was surprised Zoe's mother knew—and even more surprised that she had no idea Joy was also a victim.

"That's why I'm here," said Vega. "To see if Zoe might come down to the police station with me and give a statement."

"She did already. Early this morning." A television blared from the living room. A commercial for Pop-Tarts. Two little boys sat on a shag rug smashing toy trucks into one another. Patsy shouted at them over her shoulder.

"Hush up! I can't hear myself think!" Then she turned back to Vega and finger combed stray wisps of her brassy blond hair. "It's very nice of you to stop by like this."

"Not at all," said Vega. "I'm so glad Zoe came forward. Can I ask if she showed the police that video? It's crucial evidence."

"Video?" Patsy gave him a blank look. "You mean the one . . . ?"

"That Langstrom took."

"Langstrom never took a video."

Vega felt like he'd walked in on someone undressing. He wanted to back out without being seen. He didn't know how. "I'm confused," said Vega. "Who did Zoe go to the police about?"

"That monster," said Patsy. "The brother of Rolando Benitez. I thought you knew."

"You mean Wil Martinez?"

One of the boys was whining that the other one hit him. Patsy yelled at them from the doorway. "If I have to come over . . ." She turned back to Vega. "Zoe found a letter Catherine wrote to that creep. So she confronted him. And he confessed."

"To . . . ?"

"To killing Catherine," said Patsy. "Wil Martinez murdered Catherine Archer!"

Chapter 45

Vega tried calling Adele, but she didn't pick up her phone. He left her a message, then raced down to the police station to find Greco and Jankowski. The desk sergeant told Vega they were busy, but Vega happened to see Greco coming out of the men's room. He cornered him before he could cross to the detectives' bull pen, a room partitioned like a rat's maze into cubicles with computers, phones, desks, and not much else. The place had all the ambience of a cut-rate telemarketer's office.

"I just came from speaking to Zoe Beck's mother," said Vega. "She told me that Wil Martinez confessed to Zoe that he killed Catherine Archer?"

"Yep. The arrest warrant just got approved. My guys are at the Lake Holly Grill now, putting the cuffs on Martinez." Greco's eyes softened. "I, uh . . . heard about what went down in Mayfair last night. With your daughter. I'm real sorry, Vega."

"Thanks. But it's not over, Grec. I'm convinced

Langstrom had the motive and means to kill Catherine. Are you sure this stuff about Martinez is correct?"

"Jankowski just got off the phone from a detective down in Mayfair," said Greco. "Garrison, I believe? His guys confirmed that Langstrom was at an academic social the night of Catherine's murder. Twenty different faculty members saw him there. He's a bastard of the first order. No argument there. But he didn't kill Catherine. Martinez did. We ran the DNA last night. Martinez is the father of her unborn child."

"Didn't you run his DNA when he first got locked up? I figured you would have cleared him by now."

"The jail gave us DNA from the wrong Martinez," said Greco. "We discovered the error when we were revisiting the evidence. We took another sample last night and there was no doubt." Greco turned to the bull pen. "Again, my condolences to Joy and your family."

Vega blocked his path. Down the hall, he could hear cops debating, with the same intensity as a stakeout, New England's chances in the Super Bowl. Alpha males on caffeine. The job was loaded with them.

"So . . . Zoe just walked in here and told you all this?" asked Vega. "And you're not a little bit curious why she waited this long? Because I sure as hell am."

"Teenage girls are secretive," said Greco. "You, of all people, should know that. She probably thought she was protecting Catherine by not mentioning her pregnancy to anyone. Then she opened a paperback that Martinez loaned her and found a letter inside that Catherine had written to him. She confronted him. He confessed." Greco raised his eyebrows in mock resignation. "It's the usual story. Girl meets boy. Girl leaves boy. Boy gets angry and bashes her brains in."

Greco was such a hopeless romantic.

"This letter," said Vega. "Do you have it?"

Greco let out a slow breath of air. "Look, Vega, if I show it to you, will you be a good boy and go home after that?"

"Your odds are greatly improved."

Lake Holly's evidence storage room was only slightly larger than a walk-in closet. It had no windows, only a ventilation fan. Even with the fan, it still smelled like coffee and Lysol.

Greco unlocked the room, signed the evidence log, then retrieved a tray from a gray metal locker. He set the tray on a standing-height table—designed, Vega supposed, so that you didn't get too comfortable hanging around the evidence.

There were two items on the tray, both sealed in plastic bags with the case number, item description, and date typed on a label on top. One bag contained an old, dog-eared science fiction paperback by Philip K. Dick. The novel was opened to the inside cover, where Wil Martinez had carefully scrawled his name in black Magic Marker. The other bag contained a single sheet of lined loose-leaf notebook paper with five sentences in loopy, girlish scrawl:

I care about you, Biffle. It's not that I don't. But I have to think of my family. They'd kill me if I went through with this.
Love, Catherine

"'Biffle'?" asked Vega. "Who the hell is 'Biffle'?"

"Text speak," said Greco. "You know—'best friends for life'?"

"If Martinez knocked her up, I'd say they were more than 'biffles.'"

"I think 'biffle' used to be someone of the opposite sex you didn't sleep with," said Greco. "Then it turned into someone you did. Friends with benefits—that sort of thing. There are probably thirty other uses for the word. Who knows?"

"You got a night job as a Starbucks barista or something?" asked Vega. "'Cause even I don't know all this millennial crap."

"My niece," said Greco. "She's crashing with us for a couple of weeks while my sister's on vacation. I swear, we don't need a nuclear bomb to destroy our country. All we need is an Apple virus and everyone under thirty's a goner."

"Where did Zoe find this letter?"

"She said she found it tucked inside that paperback. Apparently, Martinez loaned it to her shortly before Catherine's murder."

"So Zoe knew Martinez well enough to borrow books from him. Yet not well enough to tell the police he was screwing around with her friend?"

"She was holding back, clearly," said Greco. "Maybe out of loyalty to Catherine."

Vega smoothed the evidence bag to study the note more clearly. It was written in blue ballpoint pen. The wording felt formal and impersonal for a teenager. Then again, teenagers rarely write real notes anymore, so maybe she intended it to be formal.

"How do you know Catherine actually wrote this?" asked Vega.

"Her mom and brother came in this morning and confirmed that it was Catherine's handwriting. They provided a couple of samples. As far as I could see, it looked like a match."

"Did they know Martinez was involved with her?"

"Judging from their reactions? No," said Greco. "Catherine's mother was livid, and you don't see Robin Archer lose her cool too often. As for the brother? He seemed more—*disappointed*. I think he really wanted to believe that Martinez was an innocent in all of this. He's been trying to heal the ill will in the community. This was a complete blow to his faith."

Vega knew he should have felt relief that Catherine's family would get justice. And yet something about the letter bothered him. He read the last line again. "Grec? What do you make of the words, 'They'd kill me if I went through with this'?"

"Sounds to me like Martinez was putting pressure on Catherine. Was the pressure to have his baby? Or to abort it? I don't know. But either way, she was clearly having second thoughts." Greco removed the tray and locked it back in the cabinet. "C'mon. I'll walk you out."

The desk sergeant found them in the hallway. "Detective? You've got a call on line two."

"Okay. Thanks." He turned to Vega. "I've gotta take this."

"Listen, Grec . . ." Vega didn't like betraying a confidence, even to a fellow cop. But if Zoe was going to come forward like this—out of the blue—then Greco deserved to know about all the other stuff she'd been holding back.

"Did Zoe tell you anything else?" asked Vega. "Anything about Jeffrey Langstrom?"

"What about Jeffrey Langstrom?"

"Did she tell you that he'd sexually assaulted her as well? That he'd filmed the assault? That Catherine tried to engineer a horse trade to get the film back?"

"Where did you get this information?" asked Greco.

"From Zoe," said Vega. "You can follow the bread crumb trail yourself from here. Langstrom filmed Zoe, then blackmailed her with the film for more sex. Zoe told Catherine. Catherine knew about some video her father had that Langstrom would be interested in. So she offered to make a trade. Don't you see, Grec? This was probably the flash drive that Jocelyn Suarez claimed Catherine stole and Alex Romero got fired over."

"Where's this flash drive?"

"Zoe doesn't know. She said Catherine got cold feet and never turned it over."

"What was on the video?"

"She doesn't know that either."

"So at the center of this convoluted story is a video of unknown content that's now missing, though no one but Zoe and that fifteen-year-old Mexican chick have ever mentioned it—both to you, I might add. Meanwhile, I've got a flesh-and-blood murderer to arrest. Now, if you'll excuse me."

Greco walked into the bull pen and disappeared behind his partition to take the call. Vega turned to leave. He had only taken a couple of steps, when he heard Greco cursing loudly. A stream of invectives so colorful, it could almost double as poetry. In the middle of it, Vega heard "Martinez." He spun around, walked straight into the bull pen, and leaned over Greco's partition.

"What's up with Martinez?" asked Vega. "I thought you were arresting him."

"Yeah? We thought so too. He's split."

"He won't get far on a bicycle."

"He's not on a bicycle anymore," said Greco. "O'Reilly just talked to your girlfriend. Martinez and Zimmerman left in his Cadillac a half hour ago. And I'll tell you right now—I have no doubt Zimmerman's gun left right along with them."

"Martinez wouldn't hurt the old man," said Vega.

"Martinez just confessed to murdering the seventeen-year-old mother of his unborn child. After that, pretty much anything is possible."

Vega drove straight to Adele's. A police cruiser was parked out front, halfway between Adele's and Zimmerman's driveways. The old man's pearl-gray Cadillac Seville was missing, the only telltale sign that it had been there, the square on the driveway that was free of snow and ice.

Vega parked behind Adele's Prius, then bounded up the front-porch stairs. He rang Adele's doorbell. "*Nena.* It's me. Open up."

Adele opened the door a crack. Vega pushed in and closed it behind him. She fell into his arms.

"Oh God, Jimmy. Have you heard? I was so blind! You were right all along. I should never have trusted Wil."

"You, me, and the Lake Holly PD," said Vega. "Greco just told me, so I came right over."

"You should be with Joy today." She gave him a searching look. "How is she?"

"Honestly? I don't know," said Vega. "She's down in Mayfair with Wendy, giving a statement. I feel like I should have been able to keep her safe. Then again, I'm sure the Archers feel the same way about Catherine."

"Did you know? That Catherine was pregnant?"

Vega didn't answer. Adele gave him a shocked expression.

"C'mon, *nena*. I'm a cop. Just because I know something doesn't mean I can tell you. Right now, we need to concentrate on getting Max back safely. Have you tried calling his or Wil's cell numbers?"

"Calling and texting," said Adele. "I haven't gotten a reply. Both phones are probably turned off." She paced the floor. "I feel so helpless. Sophia's at a birthday party and I've got to take her to gymnastics later. What do I do, Jimmy? I'm going crazy here, worrying."

"I'm off today. I can do some checking around."

"But you need to be with Joy—"

"I was. All morning. She's spending the afternoon with Wendy. I can't interfere with a police investigation. But I can canvass some of the area bus terminals and train stations and alert the PD if I see them."

"After everything Max has survived in his life, I can't believe he might come to harm over this."

"He'll be okay. You'll see." Vega pulled her into his arms and chucked a hand beneath her chin. "Max has survived worse than this. He can take care of himself. Believe me. He's a tough old guy."

Chapter 46

It had been months since Max Zimmerman last got behind the wheel of his Cadillac Seville. Even so, he kept it waxed and cleaned and always had a full tank of gas.

He drove just under the speed limit. It was a bright Saturday afternoon, but he put his headlights on and signaled at every turn. He took no highways or major roads, where speed patrols might be lurking. He could see Wil was panicked. He didn't want to make him more so.

Wil hunkered down in the crushed velour front passenger seat. He tilted the brim of his Yankees baseball cap low across his forehead and stared at the screen of his cell phone. His fingers dashed across the keys. He was having an intense conversation with someone.

"Can you drive me down to the bus terminal in Warburton?" the teenager asked him.

"I don't know where that is."

"I'll find out." He typed another text into his cell and waited for a response.

Zimmerman licked his lips and chose his words carefully. "Wil—listen to me. You need to think this through. The police aren't idiots. They'll check the bus terminals. They'll be waiting for you. You run like this, they're going to think the worst. Now, I know a lawyer—"

"The cops aren't going to wait for a lawyer," said the boy. "Did they wait for a lawyer for my brother?"

"You're not your brother, *mijo*. You need to calm down . . . and stop texting whoever you're texting. It's only making you more agitated."

Wil looked down at his screen and cursed under his breath. "I can't go to the bus terminals. The cops are already there!"

"See? What did I tell you?" asked Zimmerman. They came to a traffic light near a one-story shopping center. A cop car shot out of nowhere, sirens blaring. Zimmerman slowed down and pulled to the side of the road. His pulse was racing. His fingers trembled as they gripped the steering wheel. He heard Wil mumbling prayers in Spanish and he mumbled a few in Hebrew as well.

The cop car zoomed past. The sirens weren't for them.

It was a second or two before Zimmerman was able to catch his breath enough to put the Cadillac in drive and nose back on the road. He looked across the seat to the glove compartment. His .357 Magnum rattled about inside.

"Maybe it wasn't such a good idea to take my gun after all."

Wil pressed the heels of his palms to his eyes. "I'm sunk." At the next stretch of open road, he powered down his window and tossed his phone to the curb.

"Why did you do that?" asked Zimmerman.

"The cops will follow the signal. It may buy me some time."

"To do what?"

Wil didn't answer.

"You know," said Zimmerman, "sometimes, our first impulses aren't always our best ones. You need to talk to someone."

"I was. Before I tossed my phone."

"Who? That wasn't Adele."

Wil didn't answer.

"You don't need someone's advice," said Zimmerman. "Just tell the police what you told me."

"They won't listen."

"*I* listened. What am I? Chopped liver? You just have to explain yourself."

"Could you explain yourself when they accused you of flashing the neighbors?"

Zimmerman shrugged. "Some explanations are harder than others." They were coming to a T-intersection. "Right or left, *mijo*?"

"I don't know. I don't care anymore."

"But you *must* care. You must *always* care. If not for yourself, then for those who love you. What about your mother? She doesn't even know about your brother, and you're going to hand her this?"

"I just don't know what else to do."

"Then I'll keep driving. And you'll think."

* * *

Wil turned his head and gazed out the side window. They'd been heading south to Warburton before this. But the old man had turned east on a two-lane that moved from cookie-cutter developments to pizzerias and chain stores. It had been sunny before, but a veil of clouds drifted in, papering over the sun, turning the symmetrical asphalt roofs and concrete buildings into an endless sea of gray. Wil closed his eyes, searching for a memory that might lift his despair. And she came to him, as always.

Catherine.

Her name felt like a tropical sun—warm and delicious at first blush, blistering in its aftermath. She was beautiful, of course. And for some, that might have been the allure. But to Wil, it was that smile. The way it unwrapped itself like a Christmas present, always full of surprises.

Never in his life had Wil felt handsome or sexy. When girls liked him in high school, it was always because he could help them with their homework— sometimes even *do* their homework. But Catherine wanted nothing from him—accepted that he had nothing to give. She seemed to take pleasure merely in his being. He didn't know that was possible.

He remembered the night they met. He was coming out of the Valley Community College library. Dreading the long bus ride home. That was his whole life. Bike to work. Bus to class. Sleep—with occasional excursions to hunt down Rolando and sober him up in between. He never had time to be a teenager. No parties. No movies or pizza with friends. No girls. How could he expect to meet girls? He had no money. No car. No permanent legal status. Hell, he wasn't even good-looking.

A rally was taking place outside the campus library. Some environmental group. Lots of peace signs and posters. A girl with purple hair and a pronounced hunch was leading the crowd with chants and fist pumps. *Zoe,* though Wil didn't know her back then. Didn't know how inseparable she and Catherine were. "Beauty and the Beast," some of the frat boys on campus used to jeer when they walked past. Wil couldn't tell who took those words harder: Zoe or Catherine.

That night, there were no frat boys. There was only the chanting. Catherine was there, but not there. It was the way Wil always felt in any group situation. And yet, unlike him, she stood out, as striking and ephemeral as a shaft of light on polished chrome. He couldn't look straight at her. He couldn't look away.

He assumed she was a student at Valley—a freshman like him. He supposed he was staring at her. He supposed any other girl would find it creepy and walk away. But she just walked up to him and pressed a flyer into his hand. Whatever was on it, sign him up. He didn't care. So long as he could hang out with her.

He searched for conversation and instead pointed out the constellations of Pegasus and Cassiopeia in the sky. *What a geek! What a nerd!*

She smiled and told him that when she was a little girl, she thought a Pegasus was real.

He fell in love with her then and there.

They left the rally together. She must have told Zoe where she was going, but Wil had no memory of it. They walked over to a frat house party, where the beer flowed like water. They both got a little drunk. He wasn't used to it. He stayed away from alcohol for the most part, especially because of Lando. But she held hers surprisingly well. It was still early fall back then. Indian summer. They found an alcove by the theater. They didn't make love that night—just explored each other's bodies. But the tension, the anticipation, was greater than any sensation he'd ever known.

They met after that, on and off for several months. Always in secret. Sometimes on campus. Sometimes at the Magnolia Inn, where there was a little former maid's room that only Catherine knew about. She gave Wil a key—and that key chain with her picture. At the end when he was angry, he threw the key back at her. But not the key chain. That he held onto.

Their time together wasn't just about sex. Often, they had no sex at all. Just kissed and held hands and talked. About Catherine's frustrations with her uptight parents. About Rolando's drinking and how much Wil missed his mother. Sometimes they talked about nerdy stuff too. Quarks and atoms and brain circuitry for Wil. Politics and social issues for her.

They kept their affair secret from everyone. But Lando guessed something was up.

"You've got *chocha* on the brain," he teased. "Pussy" in English. Wil hated hearing Catherine spoken of that way. He wanted to tell Lando what she meant to him. He didn't know how.

In seventh grade, Wil's biology teacher told the class that for a plant to bear fruit, it must first grow leaves. To grow leaves, it must first develop strong roots. He knew the moment his teacher said those words that he was doomed. His life would never bear fruit. How could it, in a land where he could never put down roots?

Then Catherine came along. And in her desire, Wil found the belonging he'd been yearning for. She was the rich, nurturing soil that made him flourish.

He thought they'd go on like that forever.

But they couldn't. Of course they couldn't. Anyone over the age of fourteen should have known that. She was from one world. He from another. Neither of their own making, but that didn't change things. She figured it out before he did. She stopped returning his instant messages. She was warm and kind when he phoned her at the Inn. She told him he was "a great guy" and she wanted to "stay friends."

"But I love you," he'd blurted. A mistake. He could tell right away by the silence that followed.

"I've got to go."

She didn't message him again until those last few days before she died to tell him she might be carrying his child. His phone was dying. His reception was unreliable. Frantically, he borrowed his brother's cell. He called her and told her he loved her. He'd marry her. He'd care for the baby. Anything she wanted.

What she wanted was to move on. Without him.

Mr. Zimmerman's Cadillac crested a hill and began its descent. In the front windshield, Wil could see a distant swath of lint-colored water. The old man cleared his throat.

"When the police were looking for your brother, you called Adele, didn't you?"

"Yeah. But I'm way beyond her help now."

"Not beyond her boyfriend's."

"He's a cop."

"Better one than a hundred—don't you think?" asked Zimmerman.

"The police are gunning for me."

"Says who?" Zimmerman thrust his chin at Wil's empty lap. "Says your text buddy? The one who told you to go to the Warburton bus terminal? Then told you not to?"

Wil didn't answer.

"What if I took you someplace the police won't think to find you?" asked Zimmerman.

"I don't know anyplace like that," said Wil.

"I do. I keep the keys in the glove compartment. We could ask Adele to find Jimmy and have him call you back. It beats driving in circles, waiting for the police to surround the car."

"I'm sorry," said Wil. "I know you're tired."

"Tired? No. But an old man like me? My bladder can only hold out for so long."

Chapter 47

Vega drove south to Warburton, the biggest city in the county. There was a large bus terminal there—a dull, Band-Aid–colored building, where assorted charter companies did a brisk business in cheap transportation. Everything from ferrying seniors to the casinos, and students to college, to providing an easy, passport-free way for the undocumented to travel. It was America's last great melting pot. An unvarnished amalgam of people all scurrying about in a haze of diesel fumes and the promise of a destination that was, at least temporarily, better than their own.

The cops weren't being subtle about their presence. Vega saw a Warburton cruiser at the main entrance and another at the side. There were uniforms everywhere. He double-parked across from the terminal and asked the first officer he saw, a big black sergeant, if there had been any word.

"We thought we got him about ten minutes ago,"

said the sergeant. "Just north of here. But it was just his cell phone. He must have ditched it to throw us off. There was also a reported sighting over by Port Carroll. But the police couldn't confirm it. That's so far east of here, I'd put more stock in the cell phone lead."

"Okay. Thanks." Vega got back in his truck and asked himself where a nineteen-year-old Guatemalan murder suspect might travel unnoticed with an eighty-eight-year-old Jewish Holocaust survivor.

He didn't have a clue.

Vega's phone rang. *Adele.* She'd heard from Max.

"He won't tell me where he is," she sputtered. "But he's okay. Or at least I think he is. He convinced Wil to turn himself in."

A truck gave Vega the horn. He wasn't going to be able to stay double-parked much longer. "Have you contacted the Lake Holly PD? They'll need to make the arrangements."

"I did," said Adele. "But Wil will only surrender to you."

"I can't be involved in this, *nena.* I got kicked out of the squad the last time I did something without clearance. I could get fired this time."

"But there's no time to get clearance," said Adele. "I gave him your number. He's going to call. For God's sake, Jimmy, Max is with him! Do you really think a man his age can survive that?"

"All right," said Vega. "Give me the number. Maybe I can convince him to turn himself in."

"If something happens to that old man," said Adele, "I'll never be able to live with myself."

* * *

Max's cell phone went to voice mail when Vega dialed. He left a message. He couldn't believe the patrols hadn't picked up a sighting of Max's Cadillac by now. Except for that unconfirmed report from Port Carroll, there had been nothing.

Vega nosed his truck back on the road and headed for Port Carroll. If the report was wrong, at least his friend Danny Molina was a cop there. He might be able to offer some help. Vega made it to the outskirts of Port Carroll before his phone rang. He pulled into a shopping plaza and picked up. Never had he been so glad to hear that Eastern European inflection.

"Mr. Zimmerman. Are you all right?"

"Meh. My hip could be better. I didn't bring along my blood pressure pills. But who knows if they work anyway? I'm not the one who's got troubles, though." Vega heard mumbled conversation. A handing off of the phone. And then the uncertain voice of Wil Martinez.

"Hello?"

"Wil? Where are you?"

"I don't want Mr. Zimmerman to get hurt."

"I don't want that either," said Vega. "Tell me where you are. I'll make sure you can give yourself up safely."

"No police."

"I'll help you," said Vega. "Every step of the way. But I can't promise there won't be police."

"I was told you'd say that."

"By Adele? Wil, I have to follow—"

"Mr. Zimmerman said I should trust you, not my

friend. But my friend said you're going to lie. No matter what I say at this point, the police will shoot me on sight."

"Who said this? Who?" Vega demanded. "No cop is going to shoot you on sight, Wil. Not unless you aim Mr. Zimmerman's gun at them. Or at him. You're not going to do that, are you?"

Vega heard Max mumbling to Wil in the background. He couldn't catch the conversation, but it sounded like Max was getting frustrated with the teenager.

"Wil," said Vega. "Mr. Zimmerman doesn't deserve to be in the middle of this."

"I didn't force him to come."

"Wait. You mean . . . ?" Vega straightened. The whole interior of the truck seemed to vibrate with the teenager's words. "You didn't take him at gunpoint?"

"I was going to run away on my own. Mr. Zimmerman *asked* to drive me. *He* brought the gun. He always carries it for protection."

So Max figured he could talk Wil into surrendering. That would be his style. The old man wasn't afraid of the boy. Not just because he had his gun, but because . . .

"Wil, can you put Mr. Zimmerman on the phone for me?"

"You talked to him already. You know he's safe. He knows this park better than I do."

"Park? You're outdoors?"

"Not that kind of park." Wil took a deep breath, like he was coming to terms with his predicament. "My friend is driving down here now to take Mr. Zimmerman home. Don't worry, he won't get hurt."

"And how about you?"

Silence. The teenager didn't have a plan. Or maybe he did. The plan of last resort. Vega massaged his eyelids. This wasn't the ending he was hoping for.

"Please, Wil. Just tell me where you are."

The boy disconnected the call.

Chapter 48

Wil and Max were at a park. In the dead of winter. In a place remote enough that no one would notice the old man's light gray Cadillac. A place this friend could drive to and take Max home.

That narrowed the list down to only about a hundred parks in the county.

"Not that kind of park," Wil had said.

What other kind was there? *An office park?* Only developers ever called office complexes, "parks." *A car park?* Americans didn't generally refer to garages that way.

Vega would have felt better if he knew who this friend was. A friend who'd convince Wil that the cops would shoot him on sight didn't seem like much of a friend at all.

Adele knew Wil and Max much better than Vega did. She'd know who Wil's friends were. She'd know if Max had a favorite park. Vega called her from his truck and told her about his conversation.

"You've got to let Lake Holly know that Max isn't a hostage," Vega explained. "He's there to convince Wil to surrender. Wil isn't even in possession of the gun. Max is." Vega would have called the police himself, but he wanted to keep his line free in case Wil called back.

"I'll let them know as soon as I hang up with you," Adele promised.

"So who's this friend Wil keeps referring to?" asked Vega.

"I don't know," said Adele. "Between work and school, he doesn't have much time to socialize. Plus, I can't see anyone getting involved this deeply, especially now that Wil's been charged with . . ." She couldn't bring herself to say it. "Did he . . . admit to it?"

"I didn't ask him." As a cop, Vega knew that confessions were best obtained in an interrogation room with a video camera running. Besides, everyone on the run says they're innocent.

"I can't believe Max put himself in the center of this," said Adele.

"I can," said Vega. "He's got a soft spot for the boy. He thinks he's innocent."

"He told you that?"

"He didn't have to."

"Do you?"

"I've been at this too long to think anyone's innocent," said Vega.

"Max should have been spending his retirement going to Yankees games and collecting his pension," said Adele. "Not this."

His . . . pension. From Adventureland.

Not that kind of park . . .

Vega felt like he'd just touched a live wire. His whole body tingled with nervous energy. Adventure-land was here in Port Carroll. Vega was less than ten minutes away.

"Jimmy? Is everything all right?"

Maybe. Until Vega dialed 911 and the cops discovered that an armed, accused rapist and murderer was hiding out at a shuttered amusement park with his eighty-eight-year-old alleged hostage. The police wouldn't hear, "Zimmerman's not a hostage." They wouldn't hear, "Martinez isn't brandishing the gun." They'd trust protocol and instinct before they trusted a disgraced, off-duty detective.

The odds of something bad happening would multiply exponentially.

"I gotta go, Adele. I'll call you later."

He didn't tell her what he had to do. He didn't want the ghost of another Rolando Benitez riding on her shoulders.

In summer, the traffic heading to Adventureland could be backed up for miles. In January, Vega made the journey from the Port Carroll turnoff to the visitors' parking lot in less than four minutes. The park was county-owned and abutted the silver-gray waters of the Long Island Sound. There were no houses, stores, or gas stations anywhere near it. Just windswept trees, heavy brush, and sandy soil that held neither snow nor dirt particularly well.

If Max wanted remote, this was it.

Vega pulled his truck into the empty lot and scanned

the property. The half-moon beach was pockmarked with snow and a necklace of trash at the shoreline. The boardwalk arcade booths were shuttered, their hundred-year-old Art Deco trims faded from too much sun and salt. The roller coaster's towering latticework was streaked with rust. Seagulls nested in the joints and cawed overhead.

Vega did not see Max's Cadillac.

The only car Vega saw on the lot was parked at the far end, next to a Quonset hut for maintenance equipment. Vega drove over and parked next to the vehicle. It was a dark red Toyota sedan. A subcompact. It looked to be about ten years old. The paint had faded to the color of dried blood. The wheel wells were rimmed with rust. The rear bumper was dented. Vega assumed the car was used by the maintenance staff. Maybe it sat here all season. He got out of his truck, walked over, and put his bare hand on the Toyota's hood.

It was warm. In January. Someone just drove it here. Someone was on the property.

Vega cupped a hand over the driver's-side window and peered into the interior. The upholstery was faded and frayed. A Valley Community College parking permit sat on the front dashboard. On the rearview mirror, the car's owner had strung a religious cross and a key chain with three little charms. An elephant. A butterfly. And a heart, with the letters *BFF.*

Was this Zoe Beck's car? Was she the "friend" who was taking Max Zimmerman home? If so, she was either the bravest girl Vega had ever known. Or the most foolish, given that she was the one person who could testify that Wil Martinez had admitted to the murder of Catherine Archer.

And then he heard it. Sirens. Lots of them, heading this way. Had Adele figured out where he was going and told them?

Two Port Carroll cruisers sped over the bridge and into the lot. Their tires screeched as they pulled up short in front of Vega. Doors swung open. Cops in uniform crouched behind them, drawing their weapons from their holsters.

Vega raised his hands. "I'm a county cop! Don't shoot!"

"Hold your fire! Hold your fire! I know him!" screamed one of the uniforms, a baby-faced man with a shaved head. Never in his life had Vega been more relieved to see his keyboardist, Danny Molina. The cops holstered their guns. Molina stepped forward.

"Jimmy? What the hell? This place is going to be crawling with cops any minute. What are you doing? Getting an early start on season tickets?"

"I know you're here about Martinez," said Vega. "Who called you about it?"

Molina raised an eyebrow. "Who called *you* might be more the question here."

Vega told Molina about his calls to Wil and Adele. He pointed to the red Toyota. "I think if you run the registration, you'll see it belongs to a girl named Zoe Beck. Catherine Archer's best friend. I have no idea what she's doing here, especially since she was the person Martinez confessed the murder to."

Molina went back to his cruiser to run the plates. More police cars arrived, along with the county SWAT van full of cops whose physiques, even without the heavy armor, reminded Vega of comic-book characters. A helicopter thundered overhead, its blades low enough to pulse the air.

"The Toyota's Zoe Beck's," Molina said as he emerged from his vehicle. "And I also just got confirmation—she's with Martinez and Zimmerman in the carousel building on the northern edge of the park. SWAT's setting up a staging area over there." Molina put a hand on Vega's shoulder. "If it was up to me, Jimmy, I'd let you stay. But your SWAT captain, Speers, is calling the shots on this one. You want to be here, you're going to have to go through him."

"I understand," said Vega. "Thanks." Vega was as likely to be welcome here as a video camera at an arrest. Molina turned away.

"Hey, Danny? Do you recall when the nine-one-one came in?"

"It's on the system." Molina leaned into his cruiser and keyed a code into the computer console. "We got word from dispatch at two-twelve p.m. A female called it in." *Zoe.* It had to be.

"Okay, thanks."

Vega got back in his truck, opened his cell phone, and checked his recent calls. Max had initiated Wil's phone conversation with Vega at one forty-five p.m. Vega had called Adele at one fifty-five—right after he got off from Wil. Zoe's call to 911 came in seventeen minutes later. Could Wil have had a change of heart in seventeen minutes? It was possible. If the time span had really been seventeen minutes.

But it wasn't.

Vega's pickup was still parked next to Zoe's Toyota. He walked over and put his hand on the hood. He checked his watch. It was two-twenty p.m. The hood was cold. As it would be in January after sitting outdoors for a spell. It had been warm when Vega first arrived around two-fifteen.

In five minutes, Zoe's car had gone from warm to cold. Which meant that in all likelihood, Zoe had arrived at the park just a few minutes before Vega. At or just before two-twelve p.m.

The exact same time that she called 911 to report that Martinez had taken her hostage. Vega saw Captain Speers and his men suiting up in helmets and Kevlar vests and going over maps to set up sniper positions. Something niggled in his gut like a splinter.

Wil had already confessed to Zoe. She'd given the police a statement. Killing her now wouldn't help him. Her being here wouldn't help her either. Nothing could be gained by this encounter. She'd already lost her best friend.

Her best friend.

Vega shot a glance at the Toyota's rearview mirror, at the butterfly and elephant charms grouped around a heart with the acronym BFF.

Best Friends Forever. Best Friends for Life.
Biffle.

Vega thought about those words Catherine had penned in that note: *I have to think of my family. They'd kill me if I went through with this.* Those words weren't to Wil, about the pregnancy. They were to Zoe, about the flash drive Zoe wanted Catherine to turn over to Langstrom in exchange for his video.

Zoe had every reason in the world to be here, Vega realized. The only way the truth wouldn't come out was if Wil weren't alive to speak it.

Vega caught up to Molina as he headed to the staging area.

"Danny, you gotta get me to Captain Speers."

"I told you, man. It's not my call."

"But the whole thing's a setup. Martinez didn't kill Catherine Archer. Zoe Beck did. If Martinez dies, her guilt dies with him. You gotta get me in before it's too late."

Molina cursed under his breath. "I'll radio SWAT. See what I can do."

Behind them, the whole park got so quiet that the only sounds Vega could hear were the static from the radios and the caw of the seagulls overhead.

Vega knew that quiet. It was the sound before an assault.

Chapter 49

"This isn't a courtroom, Detective," said Captain Speers as he paced the staging area, his big jaw pulled tight, his eyes buttoned up like they were about to take incoming fire. "You want to make a case that Martinez is innocent, fine. Do it when the threat's been neutralized. Right now, he's refused to engage, despite our repeated attempts to make contact with him. He hasn't sent the hostages out."

"Can you see what's going on inside?" asked Vega.

"The building's a sniper's nightmare," said Speers. "Eight sides of windows. Three-sixty visibility. All those carved figures. My guys are worried about mistaking a horse for a hostage and vice versa."

Vega looked past Speers's hyperdefined shoulders at the carousel building. It was styled like a wedding cake. The top was domed with filigree trim. The windows and doors had lacy flourishes. The walls were covered with small individual panes of glass that obscured the interior rather than clarified it.

"Sir—all three of the people in that building know and trust me. I respectfully request department clearance to enter the premises."

"You're not trained SWAT, Vega."

"I'm not planning to shoot."

Speers' massive jaw set to one side while he considered it. "I'll give you ten minutes to make it work. But don't talk to me about your peaceful plans, Vega. That's how cops get shot."

Two SWAT officers outfitted Vega with a Kevlar breastplate, groin padding, and a helmet. They gave him a radio and handcuffs and confirmed that he had a full magazine of ammunition in his Glock, and that it was clean and in working order. Then Captain Speers spoke over his bullhorn to inform Martinez that Vega was entering the building to convince him to surrender.

No one replied.

The front-door hinges squeaked as Vega pushed open the panel and slipped in. The air smelled of varnish, wood shavings, and motor oil. A pale gray light filtered in through the panes of glass and threw shadows on the horses. Their faces looked fierce and startled in the half-light. Their intricately carved flanks were set in hyperalert poses, four abreast. The whole place felt less like a fairy-tale stable and more like a slaughterhouse. Vega's heart thumped in his chest. He kept a grip on the handle of his Glock. He kept his back to the wall.

"It's me, Jimmy Vega," he called out. "Nobody's going to hurt you if you come out now and surrender." He didn't address his plea to Wil or Zoe. The longer he could feign ignorance, the better. He swept his gaze across the carousel. It had the gaudy exuberance of a Russian heirloom. Horse bridles glittered with jewels. Brass crank handles gleamed. Colors mixed together with preschool abandon.

Nothing moved.

"I know about what happened to Catherine." Vega's words floated up through the double-height ceiling. "I know it was an accident. A moment of panic. You were scared. You deserve to tell your story."

He took a step, keeping his back to the wall as he navigated the railing at the carousel's perimeter. Grit on the bare plank floor scraped the soles of his boots. His muscles felt like twisted rubber bands.

To the left of the doorway was a small ticket shed, closed this time of year. Vega caught the shadow of something behind it, crouched on the floor, beneath a panel of buttons. He pulled his gun from his holster and inched forward.

"Don't shoot, Jimmy. It's me."

Max was on his knees, trying to claw his way to a standing position, using the sides of the ticket booth. His cane was nowhere in sight. Vega holstered his weapon and ran over.

"Mr. Zimmerman! Are you hurt, sir?"

"It's Wil I'm worried about! She's got Wil! She said she'd shoot him if we said a word."

"Where are they?"

"Right here," came a voice from the carousel. Vega grabbed his gun from his holster and spun around.

She was standing three deep in the horses, with Wil in front of her. His faded army-green jacket hung from his skinny frame the way it did that day at the preschool when Vega first laid eyes on him. From the pained expression on the boy's face, it was clear Max's gun was aimed at his back.

"Put the gun down, Mr. Vega," she said in a husky voice. "Or I'll shoot him." The flip to her purple hair had gone limp and greasy. Her face was blotchy. The hunch to her shoulders looked more pronounced. Between all the horses and Wil's body, there was no way Vega could get to her.

He spread his arms with the gun still in them in a gesture of mock compliance. And he did what he did with any suspect: He gave their crime the most sympathetic spin he could.

"Zoe, please. Think this through. What happened is understandable. You loved Catherine. You didn't intend to kill her. You were counting on her, and she let you down—"

"My life is ruined!" she sobbed. "First that bastard, Langstrom. And now, this!"

"Langstrom is going to prison," said Vega. "For a long, long time. Your video will never be public. It's over. Put the gun down. Now!"

"No!" She moved the barrel from Wil's back to his head. *Coño!* She was going to shoot.

A loud buzzer reverberated through the building. Lights flashed and a second later, the carousel began spinning, the horses bobbing to the amphetamine-charged gaiety of a Wurlitzer organ.

"What the . . . ?" *Who started the carousel?*

But Vega knew. He shot a glance at the ticket shed. Max Zimmerman had managed to claw himself to his feet, unlock the control panel, and power up the motor.

Of course he could, thought Vega. If he'd kept the

key to unlock the carousel building's doors all this time, surely he'd kept the one to start the carousel.

"Vega?" Captain Speers shouted over the radio. "What's going on?"

SWAT was itching to take control. But there was too much noise and commotion. Too many moving parts. It would be like shooting fish in a barrel. They'd all die.

"Hold your position!" Vega shouted into his radio over the organ. Then he leapt onto the spinning platform. It was moving faster now, the windows flying by in a dizzying loop, the officers behind police cars and riot shields forming one continuous menacing blur.

Zoe was two horse lengths ahead of him, her back braced against a jeweled chariot. Unlike the horses, it was anchored to the platform. It didn't move. She still had Wil in front of her. There was no way Vega could rush her without the teenager getting shot.

"She was supposed to care about me!" Zoe cried.

"She did."

"But not more than that horrible family of hers. Not more than Wil!"

She aimed her gun at the base of the teenager's neck.

"No!" Vega leapt forward.

The music stopped midmeasure.

The carousel did too.

Vega felt the full force of physics as his body hurled forward and slammed into Wil's and Zoe's. Zoe had been braced against a stationary object. The forces had nowhere to go but through her body, compressing her chest and knocking the breath from her with sharp and sudden fury. The gun tumbled from her hands as she labored to gulp in air. Vega kicked it to the side, then pushed her facedown on the platform and cuffed her hands behind her back.

"Let me hold on to your gun for the moment," Vega told Max. "We don't want any misunderstandings." Then he radioed Captain Speers that SWAT wasn't going to be necessary. The Port Carroll Police and regular county officers could take it from here.

Vega returned Max's gun to him just as Wil and Danny Molina were helping the old man back into his Cadillac.

"You must have been hell on wheels as a carousel operator," Vega teased. "I owe you my thanks. Wil owes you his life."

"Eh." Max shrugged. "I pushed a few buttons. What else can you do?" The old man turned to Wil and held his gaze an extra beat. "Sometimes, if you push enough buttons, something's bound to work."

Chapter 50

Zoe Beck was charged with involuntary manslaughter in the death of Catherine Archer. Under police questioning, she quickly confessed to picking Catherine up a short distance from La Casa and driving her to the post office parking lot where she begged Catherine to hand over the flash drive Langstrom wanted. Catherine refused, let herself out of the car, and ran into the woods. Zoe followed, assuming Catherine was throwing the drive away.

When Catherine insisted she didn't have it, Zoe slapped her across the chin. The blow sent Catherine reeling. She lost her footing and fell backward, hitting her head on a tree stump that caused massive bleeding in the brain. The rest—staging her death as a rape, discarding her cell phone and wallet—were the poor choices of a panicked teenager.

There was a brief flurry of media coverage about Zoe's confession and then the story disappeared. Mike Carp never mentioned it. He wiped the Archer family and the Magnolia Inn from his memory banks, as if none of it had ever existed.

Not Adele. She'd grown fond of Todd Archer since the death of his sister. She wanted to work with him to restore trust in the town, keep the Magnolia Inn afloat, and rebuild La Casa. In February, they formed a committee and began a series of fund-raisers at the Inn. The money they raised allowed La Casa to rebuild.

The board, impressed by her commitment, offered Adele her old job back. She accepted. The next day, the plyboard came off the doors and windows. Volunteers and former clients arrived with buckets and brooms to scrub the interior.

A female volunteer discovered an open box of tampons in the bathroom that had been sitting on a shelf since La Casa closed its doors. She showed it to Adele. Inside, next to all the wrapped tampons, was a thumb-size flash drive.

Adele mentioned it to Vega, who immediately called Greco. An hour after the Lake Holly Police took possession of the item, Vega got a call.

"Get some popcorn," Greco growled. "You're gonna want to see this."

"What is it? Porn?"

"Much better, my friend. Think of it as winning the lottery."

There were four videos in all. Mike Carp had a starring role in every one. Not that he knew he was mugging for the cameras, of course.

In one, he discussed with John Archer how much to

bribe a zoning official. In another, he paid off a state senator. In a third, he got Langstrom to agree to drop POW's lawsuit in return for $30,000 in cash and a promise of county funds. In the fourth, he laid out a way to funnel campaign contributions through his soon-to-be-built Crystal Springs Golf Resort.

John Archer's "insurance" had been sitting in a tampon box at La Casa all this time—stuck there, presumably, on the night Catherine Archer decided not to turn it over to Zoe Beck. From the settings, Vega and Greco guessed that Archer had secretly recorded them in a private dining room at the Magnolia Inn. Archer knew he was dying. He knew he wouldn't go to jail for what was on them.

But Carp could. And so, too, could Langstrom—which was what had made them so valuable.

"Oh, we are going to have so much fun with this," said Greco. "Carp wants his big Hollywood moment? I think we just might be able to hand it to him."

Two weeks later, as Vega was picking up Carp in Wickford, Greco called him on his cell.

"It's all set. The warrants are in place. The U.S. Attorney's Office is salivating like I just promised them a week in Vegas on the state's dime. Powder your nose, Vega. It's showtime."

"Can I make one request?" asked Vega.

"You name it."

"I have a special location in Lake Holly I'd like this little party to take place in."

"We send cops to La Casa we're going to make clients nervous."

"Not La Casa," said Vega. "Someplace else that could use a little good publicity for a change."

Carp had his head buried in paperwork that morning on the drive out of Wickford. He didn't pay attention to where they were headed until Vega nosed the Suburban into a small strip shopping center and parked in front of Hank's Deli.

"What the hell are we stopping here for?"

"Oscar Gutierrez is the owner of Hank's," said Vega. "You hurt his business. Now you can help it."

"I don't have time to press the flesh with some taco maker."

A black-and-white Lake Holly patrol car pulled up behind Vega's Suburban. The red flashing lights reflected in the rearview mirror. Vega turned off his engine, got out of the driver's seat, and opened Carp's rear door.

"Get out," Vega ordered.

"What the *hell* did you just say?"

"I said—*sir*—get your fat ass out of the car. You are under arrest for extortion, bribery, racketeering, official misconduct, and—" Vega scrunched up his face in mock concentration. "Oh yeah—threatening an officer of the law. Namely me."

Carp blinked at Vega like he'd gone crazy. But the boldness was gone. He unfolded himself from the seat of his car. Three news vans came out of nowhere. Greco had obviously tipped them off. One of the reporters was Lucy Park. Her smile had the same number of teeth in it when Carp was getting arrested as it had touring his real-estate headquarters.

Oscar came out of his store, wiping his hands on his white apron. He suddenly understood what was happening. His storefront would be the background shot on tonight's news. His business would be on coast-to-coast TV. It was the least Vega could do for the man.

"You do the honors." Greco handed Vega the handcuffs.

"You sure?"

Greco grinned. "I'm just another set of eyes and legs, cataracted and arthritic as they are."

Vega patted Carp down, snapped the cuffs on his wrists, and walked him over to Greco's patrol car. Carp began to stammer.

"Jimmy . . . I never . . . I did right by you. Always. That's the truth."

Vega put a hand on Carp's fish scale hair and pushed him down into the back of the patrol car. Then he leaned in and looked him in those bulging blue eyes.

"I think you need a crash course in the law, Mr. Carp. See, there's facts. And there's truth. The facts are that you're a lying, corrupt snake of a man who hurt this community and everyone in it. And the truth? The truth is the same damn thing. You know why? Because it's *always* the same damn thing."

Vega had done as Captain Waring had instructed. He'd kept records of all the packages he'd delivered for Mike Carp. He took notes on conversations he'd overheard. He snapped cell phone shots of some of Carp's personal notes when Carp left them behind in the Suburban.

As a result of the videos on the flash drive, Langstrom's statements, and Vega's records, the U.S. Attorney's Office was able to build a massive corruption case. It was not only against Carp, but against several other local officials: a state regulator for the Department of Environmental Conservation, Lake Holly's building inspector, a couple of assemblymen, some legislators in other towns. Each was eager to lessen his legal troubles by testifying against Carp.

Three days after his indictment, Carp resigned from office. He put the land that was supposed to be the Crystal Springs Golf Resort up for sale. Vega drove over to the campus to tell Joy the news. He was watching her closely these days, worried that after what happened with Langstrom, she might drop out of school. But when he met her, she seemed excited about her classes this semester. She thrust a flyer in his hand. It was an announcement for a protest march against the firm that was slated to purchase the Crystal Springs property. The developer was planning to build luxury housing on it.

"So . . . now you're protesting the houses?" Vega asked Joy.

"We're protesting the lack of *affordable* housing," said Joy.

"No kidding," said Vega. "*I* can't afford to live in the county."

"Which is why you should sign Dr. Fenter's petition. She's on your side."

She. Joy's new professor was a *she.* Vega breathed a sigh of relief. His daughter had survived her ordeal. So had Adele. So had Vega.

* * *

The next day, Captain Waring, impressed with Vega's work in bringing down Carp, offered him his old job back in the squad. Never had three ratty, stained fabric partitions looked so good.

One evening after work a few weeks later, Vega pulled into Adele's driveway and found Zimmerman and Wil in her dining room, raising a toast with a bottle of wine that Zimmerman claimed he'd been saving for "a special occasion."

Wil had been cleared of all charges. He didn't have to live with Max Zimmerman anymore. Vega had expected each to go his separate way after that. But the experience had forged a bond between them. Adele told Vega that it was Zimmerman who broke the news—in Spanish—to Wil's mother that Rolando was dead. It was Wil who contacted Zimmerman's ex–son-in-law in California and tried to rekindle some sort of connection. After Wil's DACA got renewed, the old man helped Wil get a driver's permit. The last few times Vega had seen them, Wil was behind the wheel of Zimmerman's Cadillac, while the old man coached and kvetched about his driving in equal measure.

"So what's the occasion?" Vega asked as he stepped into the dining room. He could smell the delicious scent of chicken and rice wafting through the house.

"Wil's paperwork—it came through," said Adele.

"I thought he already got his DACA renewed."

"He did," said Adele. "I'm talking about his other paperwork. The visa."

One of Adele's last projects before she returned full-time to La Casa was to put in a special request with U.S. Citizenship and Immigration for a humanitarian visa for Wil—so he could visit his cancer-stricken mother in Guatemala without jeopardizing his tenuous legal status.

"So he's going to Guatemala?"

"Just over the spring break," said Adele. "For two weeks."

"That's . . . great." *That's expensive,* thought Vega. The kid could barely afford classes. Where was the cost of airfare coming from? Not Adele, Vega hoped.

Adele set a plate of food in front of Vega and poured him a glass of wine. Zimmerman raised a toast. "To good people, where you find them." Then he turned to Wil. "God bless your mother, Wil. Comfort her and then come back to us. You will always have a home with me."

Vega shot Adele a questioning gaze. She caught his meaning and nodded. Max Zimmerman had paid for the teenager's trip. As unlikely as it seemed, he'd become a sort of substitute family in the young man's life. And the young man, in his.

"Thank you," said Wil. "I'm very grateful. To all of you. For everything you've done. I don't know if I can ever repay—"

Zimmerman patted the teenager's arm. "All these years, I couldn't either. And now, like Abraham, I can."

Acknowledgments

One of the things I love most about being an author is that I get to take a tour of another person's life. None of this would be possible without the many generous people who have patiently opened up their worlds to me.

My special thanks to Geovanny Lopez, an amazing young man, originally from Ecuador, who has lived in this country since the age of five and yet still remains on temporary legal (DACA) status. Without loans or financial aid, Geovanny managed to graduate a four-year state college with a science degree while holding down two and sometimes three jobs. His life story is entirely different from Wil Martinez's in the book. But his heart and determination are the same. Thank you, Geo, for sharing your story with me. And thanks, too, to Graciela Heymann, executive director of the Westchester Hispanic Coalition, and Giuliana Urrelo, program director, for bringing Geovanny and his story to me. It's my hope that our country can find a way to permanently embrace all those with DACA status and make use of their rich potential to our nation.

I've also been fortunate to get to know several amazing police officers in the Ossining (NY) Police Department, who have gone above and beyond to help me understand the daily stresses of being a cop. Last year, I got to take their six-week civilian police academy course (complete with flash/bang grenades, video shooting simulations, and cool T-shirts). Many thanks to Sergeant Drew Maiorana for a great course. And an extra special thank-you to Sergeant Paul Schemmer, who patiently indulged my questions over many hours and months. You really helped me find my way around the story.

Thanks, too, to the usual team of incredibly talented people who do so much to make these books happen. To private investigator Gene West, who is as adept at understanding characters and plot as he is at sizing up an investigation. To Rosemary Ahern, who is always my first set of eyes on a draft. To my agent, Stephany Evans, who helps navigate the journey from beginning to end. Also, thank you to Jenn Fitzpatrick, who won the Girl Scouts Heart of the Hudson auction to have her name in this book.

A special thank-you to the crew at Kensington. There are so many wonderful people, from editorial to sales. Please know that I am grateful to you all. A special thank-you to my editor, Michaela Hamilton, and assistant editor, Norma Perez-Hernandez, for championing the series so passionately. And also to the publicity and marketing departments, including Morgan Elwell, Alexandra Nicolajsen, and Lauren Jernigan, who work tirelessly to get the books into new hands. Thanks, too, to Kensington's CEO Steve Zacharius and publisher Lynn Cully for their support of the series.

Thank you most of all to my family and friends, who have to live with me through all of this: my husband, Thomas Dunne, my children, Kevin and Erica, and also Bill Hayes, Janis Pomerantz, Elizabeth Feigelson, Jennifer Greenwald, Phyllis Garito, and Elizabeth Kasulka. Thanks for keeping me grounded.

In case you missed the first book in the Jimmy Vega mystery series, here's a sample excerpt for your reading pleasure.

Turn the page to enjoy the first chapter of
Land of Careful Shadows!

Chapter 1

It was the Day-Glo orange basketball sneakers that nearly got him killed. Adidas adizeroes with EVA midsoles. A hundred dollars on sale. You could have picked him up on a satellite transmitter as he swung his legs out of the open door of his black Escalade to untie the laces.

"Stop right there, sir." The voice, full of sinew and muscle, didn't fit the freckle-faced altar boy in the police raincoat before him. "Step out of the car slowly and put your hands on the roof of your vehicle."

Jimmy Vega stopped untying the laces and pushed back his Yankees baseball cap. "Hey man, chill. I only pulled over because—"

"Sir? Get out of the car and put your hands on the roof of your vehicle."

It was the "sir" that got to him. The knife-thrust of the word. All that coiled aggression tricked out as politeness. And okay, maybe he looked suspicious in his dark hoodie, pulling up on the gravel shoulder of this wooded two-lane a few hundred yards from where the Lake Holly cops had just found a body. But did this rookie really think he'd put it there?

"Just give me a minute to change out of my sneakers." Vega slid a hand toward his back pocket. "Hey, if it makes you feel any better—"

That's when he heard the familiar rattle of plastic. A cheesy claptrap sound, totally out of sync with the smooth piece of hardware that produced it or the fresh-from-the-academy holster that cocooned it. Vega's hand shot out of his pocket like his jeans were on fire. The cop had his Glock nine millimeter pointed inches from Vega's chest.

"Out of the car! Now! Hands on your head!"

All the blood drained from Vega's extremities. His throat constricted. His bladder muscles developed amnesia. He was almost more embarrassed at the prospect of pissing his pants than at the prospect of getting shot. How odd that this little man-made contraption could so completely unmake a man.

He laced his fingers behind his head and willed his voice to stay calm by pretending he was still undercover, still behaving like somebody he wasn't.

"Okay, officer. Relax. I'm getting out of the car. My hands are locked behind my head." He stated the obvious because he felt he needed to, felt this guy needed all his senses relaying the same information if Vega was going to walk out of this in one piece. Stupid what runs through your head at a time like this. He hadn't finished his paperwork on last night's job. He had a lottery ticket in his wallet worth twenty dollars that he hadn't collected on yet. He was no more than half a mile from his daughter's house and she had no idea he was in Lake Holly, though maybe under these circumstances, it was best she didn't know.

He tried to sidestep a puddle but it ran the length of the driver's-side door. Cold, gritty water sloshed between his toes the moment his feet hit the ground. Rain slipped under the sleeves of his hoodie when he locked his hands behind his head. A few hundred feet east, a circus of emergency vehicles beat out a blood-red rhythm against the bare trees that stood in mute witness on either side of the road.

"So you don't panic, I've got a nine millimeter in the waistband of my jeans. My badge and ID are in my back right pocket." He supposed the rookie had already surmised the first part and never considered the possibility of the second or he wouldn't be in this mess. Something burned slow and deep. He thought he was past the stage where people judged him by the color of his skin or the cast of his features. He thought his line of work insulated him from that. But now, spread-eagled across the Escalade, he wondered if all he'd really done was get better at navigating people's prejudices. When he steered himself within the bounds of their assumptions, he managed to avoid the shoals and reefs that used to cut him so unexpectedly. When he didn't—well, here was the result.

A vacuum cleaner of a voice suddenly boomed over his shoulder. "He isn't that detective the county was supposed to send by any chance? Vega? James Vega?"

The young cop's voice faltered, the testosterone wavering as it sank in. "I thought—he looked—he didn't show me any ID—"

"You wouldn't give me five freakin' minutes to change out of my sneakers," hissed Vega. He felt safe enough to turn around and face the kid now. The cop's eyes, so full of suspicion a minute ago, now looked wild with panic and bewilderment. Vega studied the wavy brown lines that ran along the sides of his orange high-tops and shook his head. Water squished out of the fabric when he shifted his feet.

"I'll take my stuff back."

The cop held out his gun, keys, and ID without meeting his gaze. Vega waited for an apology. It didn't come. Not that it would have changed anything. But still.

"I'll take it from here, Fitz." The man with the vacuum cleaner voice casually stepped into view. He was a head taller than Vega, broad as a side of beef, with the put-upon look of a cop near retirement who felt he was not near enough. He was dressed head-to-toe in white Tyvek coveralls that made him look like a giant marshmallow. He held out a fleshy hand.

"Detective Lou Greco, Lake Holly PD." The detective dropped his chin and peered at Vega over the black rims of his glasses, beaded with rain. "I see you came dressed for the occasion."

"I didn't get the part that said 'black tie.'" Vega shoved his badge and keys into his pockets and returned his gun to his waistband. "I was up all night doing a meet-and-greet between a couple of heroin dealers and a rookie undercover. I didn't have time to change." His skin still felt coated in sweat and nicotine.

Greco nodded to Vega's sneakers. "You got another pair of shoes?"

"I was trying to switch into them when your local representative from the Aryan Brotherhood stopped me."

"You should have been clearer that you were a cop. Fitzgerald sees a gun under your hoodie at a crime scene, he's going to think the worst."

"Not that he was profiling or anything."

Greco ignored the dig. In his mind at least, the situation was already behind them when in fact Vega was just feeling the recoil. His fingers were only beginning to get back sensation. His bowels and bladder still felt temperamental. The back of his head throbbed as if he'd been cold-cocked. It would be hours before the flutter in his chest died away, weeks before the memory lost its primal hold on his senses. Still, what choice did he have except to move on? He had to work with these guys. He'd had to work with guys like Fitzgerald and Greco his whole career.

It might have been easier if being a cop had been a lifelong ambition. But the truth was, it just happened. One minute, he was the reluctant holder of an accounting degree (his mother's idea), planning for the day when he'd chuck it all for the wide-open road and his steel-string guitar. The next, he was out of work and in debt with a baby on the way. The county was recruiting Spanish-speaking officers. Vega needed a steady job with medical benefits. So he traded in his six-string for a nine millimeter and told himself he was doing for his kid what his old man had never done for him. There were worse reasons to give up on your dreams.

He sat in the Escalade and peeled off his high-tops and socks, tossing them onto the floor of the passenger side where they immediately formed their own ecosystem. He shoved his bare feet into black leather work boots.

"You don't have another pair of socks?"

"Nope." He had a pair of white crime-scene coveralls and booties that would keep him dry enough, and a button-down shirt and pants for later. But he hadn't anticipated his run-in with Fitzgerald.

"Gonna have blisters tomorrow," said Greco.

"Better than bullet holes."

"True."

Vega suited up and followed Greco down a path slick with mossy rocks and acorns. Through the bare branches, Vega could see the tin-colored reservoir for which this town fifty miles north of New York City was named. Back when he was a boy, the only things you could find in Lake Holly were the fan-tailed sun perch you could catch with a cheap rod and a loaf of Wonder Bread, the snapping turtles that sunned themselves on the broad, weather-beaten rocks, and the flakes of shale that if you threw just right, you could skim halfway to Bud Point.

Now unfortunately, you could find much, much more.

She was lying in a soupy mix of dead leaves and branches that had gathered in a pocket along the shoreline. If not for the reams of yellow police tape strung like parade garland or the dozen or so officers milling about in white coveralls, Vega might have assumed he was staring at an old picnic blanket. Its pattern, once distinct, was now brackish and covered in algae.

"Dog-walker called it in around o-seven-hundred this morning," said Greco. "Female. Been in the water for at least a few weeks is my guess. No obvious trauma to the body."

"You've ruled out drowning?"

"Duh. Give us townie cops *some* credit." Greco

snapped on a pair of blue latex gloves and squatted before the victim. He edged up one sleeve of her jacket. The underside of the material showed some sort of black-and-silver snowflake pattern. Beneath the sleeve, a frayed, algae-covered rope encircled her skeletal wrist.

"She's got three more just like it—one on each limb. Don't think it's a fashion statement."

"Any indications whether she was dead going into the water?"

"The medical examiner will have to rule on that. The ropes are pretty thick. Three-strand nylon. She was tied down to something. Whoever tied her wanted her to stay a spell."

"Find any ID?"

"On her? Negative," said Greco. "But we found a handbag about thirty feet up the hill with a photograph in a zippered pocket. Forensics is gonna have to figure out if it's related, but I've got a feeling it's her. She's Hispanic, in case you're wondering."

"How can you tell?" A bumpy, gray-white film covered the victim's face. Both eye sockets were empty. Only a long, thin tuft of black hair remained on the back of her head like some ancient Chinese scribe.

"We played Ricky Martin and she danced."

"Better Ricky than Dean. I'd have tied the ropes myself."

Greco grinned. Puerto Ricans versus Italians. Cops never tired of ethnic jokes.

Vega pulled on a pair of gloves and bent down to examine the victim. She was lying on her side; her body bloated to perhaps twice its normal size, yet her jaw had receded, exposing an overbite. Her clothes had begun to fall apart but the zipper on her jacket still worked. Vega opened it to reveal the remains of what appeared to be a pink buttoned-down polyester blouse over blue jeans. No jewelry, though that may have been stripped. Her ankles had decayed much faster than her sneakers. The contoured soles sported the brand name Reebok. Vega could still make out the red racing stripes along the sides.

"The sneakers made me think jogger when I first saw her," said Greco. "We had that freak warm spell early last month. But the clothes are all wrong for it."

Vega had to agree. He exercised in whatever old T-shirts and gym shorts happened to be lying around. But his ex-wife and teenage daughter seemed to have whole wardrobes devoted to getting sweaty and none of it looked like this.

Vega shielded his eyes from the rain and searched out a thirty-foot overhang on the far side of the lake. The steady April drizzle had turned the rock face black.

"Guess it's safe to say, given the time of year and the ropes on her limbs, she didn't Bud out, either."

"You know about Bud Point?" asked Greco.

"Jumped off it, actually. At seventeen." After a few cold ones, if you hit the water just right, you became a legend. If not, you became a statistic.

Greco's jaw set to one side. "So were you suicidal, shit-faced—or just plain stupid?"

"I did it to impress a girl. Though I think I inspired more pity than awe that night."

Vega could still see himself at the edge of that cliff, his hair in an embarrassing mullet, dressed in discount-store jeans his mother—the only parent at his school with an accent—bought in one of her many excursions back to their old neighborhood in the Bronx. He didn't fit in at Lake Holly High. Not with all those fair-haired kids in Top-Siders and polo shirts. So he decided to stand out in some way he'd chosen, some way that wasn't thrust on him without his consent. When that girl batted her blond lashes and told him she didn't think he was brave enough to jump, he proved her wrong. If adolescence were a permanent state, the species would die out.

Greco wiped the rain off his glasses slowly and deliberately. Vega felt the grind of gears as he did the math. "I thought the closest this town got to Hispanic culture back then was watching reruns of *I Love Lucy.*"

"I guess we were what you'd call, 'the tokens.'"

"Different place now, that's for sure. Whole town's crawling with 'em."

"Them?"

"I'm talking illegals, Vega. Not *your* people."

He said it the way Anglos often did—like there was a chasm of difference between the two groups when to Vega, the distinctions sometimes felt as porous as the paper that divided them. Maybe that's why the words stung so much. The acid couldn't help but leak through.

"Come on, Vega. Don't get all PC on me. You drove through town this morning. You had to have seen them."

He saw them. Of course he saw them. They were huddled in groups in front of the Laundromat and under the deli awning where Vega went to fetch his coffee. Their eyes were wary beneath the soaked brims of their baseball caps. Their shoulders were hunched, whether from rain or cold or fear, he didn't know. He felt their collective intake of breath when he walked by, the way their adrenaline seemed to hitch up a notch and their voices turned soft as prayers. They were like soldiers in a war zone, bracing for everything and nothing, all in the same instant.

"Are we discussing the latest census figures? Or does this conversation have a point?"

"Got something you should take a look at on the hill."

Greco led Vega up an embankment slick with mud. On the other side of a downed tree, two county crime-scene techs Vega knew were on their hands and knees, poking around a thicket of thorny barberry bushes. Greco picked up an evidence pouch beside one of them and handed it to Vega. It contained a red shoulder bag with two buckles across identical outer pockets. The vinyl had flaked off in places, exposing a whitish backing beneath.

"You haven't found a wallet, I take it?"

"No wallet, driver's license, cash, or ID," said Greco.

"Sounds like a robbery."

"Could be. The photograph was zipped into a small pocket. I don't think the person who tossed the bag even knew it was there."

Greco handed Vega another evidence bag containing the snapshot. A square-shouldered young woman with almond-shaped eyes was sitting on a sagging beige couch with an infant girl on her lap. Both the woman and child appeared to be Hispanic. The resolution was fuzzier than Vega would have liked, as if the woman had been bouncing the child on her knee when the photographer snapped the picture. Still, Vega could make out enough details that he would have been able to identify the woman if he'd known her. Her smile revealed two prominent front teeth that were slightly bucked. Around her neck, she wore a silver-colored crucifix with tiny bird wings dangling beneath each of Christ's bound arms.

"Never saw a crucifix with wings on it before," said Greco.

Vega thought about his own much simpler crucifix that his mother had given him when he got confirmed at Our Lady of Sorrows. He'd stopped wearing it after he married Wendy. Not that she'd asked him to. It just seemed hypocritical to pretend to a faith he had no connection to anymore. Looking at this photograph, however, he felt a sudden urge to dig that crucifix out of his dresser drawer and wear it, if only for the joy it would bring his mother.

But it wouldn't. Not anymore. Funny what you remember and what you can make yourself forget.

"If the crucifix doesn't turn up in the lake, we should check the state pawn registry," said Vega. "It's distinctive enough that we might get a hit if someone tries to hock it."

"We'll have better luck tracing the crucifix than we will tracing the kid," said Greco. "Even if the photograph's only a few months old, she'll be tough to identify."

The little girl in the photo had to be no more than about five or six months old. From the tender, possessive way the young woman held the child and the comfortable ease of the baby, Vega felt certain he was staring at a mother and daughter. The little girl was wearing a bright red velvet dress with silk white bows across the front. Her crown of shiny black hair was carefully combed and held back from her face by a headband with an enormous red bow. Gold posts glimmered from her earlobes. She gave the photographer an unfocused smile that could have been the result of familiarity, or the bouncing gyrations of her mother. The red velvet dress made Vega think the picture was taken around Christmas. He flipped the bag over to look for any markings on the photo.

"No date? No names? Nothing? This could have been taken anywhere."

"You got it," said Greco.

"At any time."

"Yep."

The baby could be a year old by now. Or she could be twenty. In the lake, two scuba divers bobbed and dove like overfed seals, looking for something no one wanted to find. If the woman in the photograph was the corpse on the shore, where was the baby?

"That's not the worst," said Greco. "There's one thing more." He picked up a third evidence bag and handed it to Vega. Inside was a single sheet of loose-leaf notebook paper that was beginning to disintegrate.

"This was found inside the main zippered compartment."

Vega brushed the rain off the bag and looked down at the handwriting. The words were printed in capital letters using black ballpoint ink that had blurred slightly from dampness and exposure to the elements. But the words—in English—were still easy enough to read:

> *GO BACK TO YOUR COUNTRY. YOU DON'T*
> *BELONG HERE.*

"Shit," said Vega.

"Shit is right. Walk with me," said Greco, handing

the bagged envelope back to the techs. "We need to talk."

They walked in silence, their boots kicking up the slick leaves underfoot. Vega tugged the drawstring tighter around the hood of his coveralls to seal out the rain and fought the limp that was coming on from the blisters that were blooming, large and watery, at the back of each ankle. Voices and sounds came at him from every direction. He could hear the whoosh of water as divers broke the surface. He heard the rustle of a body bag being loaded and zipped by the lake. He listened to the static of walkie-talkies from different police agencies drowning each other out until even the occasional moment of radio silence seemed punctuated with feedback.

Greco removed his latex gloves, one inside the other, and shoved them into a bag. From a pants pocket beneath his coveralls, he produced a package of red licorice Twizzlers and held them out to Vega. Vega declined. Greco took one and shrugged.

"Used to smoke." The detective looked down at his gut. "Sometimes I think smoking was better for my health."

He yanked a piece of red licorice off with his teeth and stared out at the lake. The edges were indistinct this time of year. Runoff from the winter snows swelled the shore, drowning small saplings and birches that would normally rest on solid ground. Mud compressed around their heels, tugging at them like an insistent beggar. Above, a canopy of bare branches laced a lint-colored sky.

"Both our agencies need to sit on that letter," Greco said finally. "Far as I'm concerned, we're best off not calling this a homicide until we get a suspect. It'd be like putting a torch to gasoline, if you know what I'm saying."

"Because of Dawn and Katie Shipley," said Vega. It wasn't even a question. Everyone in the county knew about the mother and her four-year-old daughter who were struck and killed in Lake Holly on Valentine's Day by an illegal alien driving drunk without a license. For weeks now, there had been rallies and angry editorials in the local newspaper calling for more stringent laws against illegal aliens—though not, Vega noted curiously, for stricter penalties against drunk drivers, as if the man's immigration status was what killed the mother and child rather than his intoxication.

"They just set a court date for Lopez this week," said Greco. "It'll be months before he's tried—on the taxpayers' dime, no less. Who knows if they'll even deport him after he's served his sentence? Probably depends on who's hanging curtains in the White House."

"So I guess we'll blanket the media with that photo and hold back the rest."

"Yeah. If the press asks what happened to this chick, we'll just tell 'em it's under investigation."

"She's a mother," said Vega softly.

"Huh?"

"The woman. In the photograph. She's a mother. Same as Dawn Shipley." *Same as my mother,* Vega wanted to say. But he refused to offer up any more of his grief to police indifference.

"Yeah, okay, she's a mother. Whatever. I'm just saying we're best off doing this slowly and quietly, without all the ruckus you know will take place if we make this public."

"What about the baby?"

Greco surveyed the lake where the divers continued their grim search mission. One of them suddenly broke the surface, holding something over his head. It was a Velcro-strapped sneaker. Toddler-sized. The white leather had turned dark green from the water but Vega thought he could make out the round cartoon face and punchbowl haircut of Dora the Explorer on the side. Suddenly, everyone got a little quieter.

Greco cursed so softly, it sounded like a prayer. He swallowed the rest of his Twizzler and wiped a sticky hand down the side of his coveralls. Even the radios went silent. Vega saw one of the officers near the shore make the sign of the cross. Greco did the same. Vega kept his hands at his sides.

And he tried, as always, not to think about Desiree.

Connect with

Us

Visit us online at
KensingtonBooks.com
to read more from your favorite authors, see books
by series, view reading group guides, and more.

Join us on social media

for sneak peeks, chances to win books and prize packs,
and to share your thoughts with other readers.

facebook.com/kensingtonpublishing
twitter.com/kensingtonbooks

Tell us what you think!

To share your thoughts, submit a review,
or sign up for our eNewsletters, please visit:
KensingtonBooks.com/TellUs.